OURS IS THE STORM

OURS IS THE STORM

D. THOURSON PALMER

Boyle
— & —
Dalton

Book Design & Production
Columbus Publishing Lab
www.ColumbusPublishingLab.com

Print ISBN 978-1-63337-020-3
E-book ISBN 978-1-63337-021-0

Printed in the United States of America
1 3 5 7 9 10 8 6 4 2

"There is such a thing as the feeling of a rainstorm. Along the way, you meet with a rain shower and hurry down the road so as not to get wet. But even though you make your way beneath the eaves, awnings, and what have you, there is no escaping the damp. If, from the beginning, you were certain of getting wet, there would be no pain in your heart, for it would be all the same to be soaked. This is a way of understanding that extends to many things."

— Yamamoto Tsunetomo, *Hagakure*
Translated by Nicholas Theisen

For Mephit. Dear friend, your storms have passed.

—One—

Teh'rahin did not come back from the hunt, and he was the first warrior Ahi'rea had known well who did not return. Father said they had been hunting evil spirits, but Mother, when she returned bearing news of Teh'rahin, was more forthright. She said they were hunting men.

"You should not speak of these things before Ahi'rea," Father said to Mother. "She is too young for such evil thoughts."

"She must think on them soon enough. Halkoriv knew we were coming, and his soldiers were ready."

"Halkoriv," Father said. Then, they shooed Ahi'rea from the tent, telling her to go wait by the fire.

She stepped into the cold night and shivered, pulling her doeskins tighter. The winds were swift and harsh over the plains, and the dry grasses whispered around the camp. She heard her parents' voices from within, muffled and low. Ahi'rea could see the glow of the fire ring from around the Huumphar tents, and the shadows of the returned warriors and their kin. She smelled steppe yams and red squash cooking, and the stinging-yet-sweet vapors of bonebark tea. There would be no meat for days, not until after the Sendings, and her stomach was already growling at the thought. She heard Naph'oin beginning the Sending songs for Teh'rahin and the others. She heard Rahi'sta, trying to sing with him, but crying instead, for her father would never return.

Ahi'rea did not go to the fire. She circled the tent, stepping soft, placing each foot with care, as Mother had taught her. Then, she focused her mind, as Father had taught her, and felt the Sight come to her. She shut her eyes, so as to cast no light, and Saw.

Inside the tent, her parents whispered in anxious tones. Mother was angry; she jabbed her finger out, toward the tent flap and the world beyond. "He may never come this close to our lands again. We should go back. We should call the tribes and kill him now."

Father's eyes were downcast. "Lasivar's son will come to us when it is time. Until then, we cannot beat Halkoriv. We will go deeper into the plains, and await Lasivar's son."

"And what if he does not come?"

"He will." Father looked up; though he was smaller than Mother, he always seemed taller in the Dreaming. He took Mother in his arms and kissed her. "You must trust me. I cannot lose you now, and that is what will happen if you attack Halkoriv. All the warriors in the plains and the skies could not defeat him—but we can hold him where the grasses end. I need you. Ahi'rea needs you."

Mother returned his kiss, and embraced him. They held each other for a long time, and just as Ahi'rea was about to cease her Sight and go to the fire, Mother spoke again. "He butchered them. Halkoriv. He butchered Teh'rahin and the others. I've never seen anything like it. The dark came from inside him, and it ate them." Father brushed her hair and held her, but she went on. "The dark came from him and ate them, and when it lifted there was nothing left but blood and bone."

—Two—

The boy knew there was no point in calling for help, because it never came. He'd shouted and cried for days, until his voice ran hoarse. He was unsure how long ago that was, or how long he'd been confined inside the dark cell. He could no longer remember; not because he had been there for so long a time, but because someone was inside the cell with him, stealing his memories.

He could feel them slipping away, one by one. When he slept he awoke unable to recall a friend's name or a forest path. If he concentrated on a face, it would vanish. If he thought of an event, the details would blur, and then fade entirely. The boy was conscious of the loss, but of nothing else. He was afraid; afraid of the darkness and silence, but most afraid of losing the few memories he still had. He was afraid of whoever was taking them from him.

He wasn't sure how he knew there was someone in his cell with him. He heard no one. Seeing his companion was out of the question—there was no light. He felt around in the dark, but his fingertips met only rough stone walls, a thin blanket, and the privy hole in the corner. He couldn't even feel a door. Despite all that, he could feel the presence, as if he were being watched. The sensation gnawed at him. He found himself shouting into the darkness when it grew too strong.

Every day, he discovered a bit of food on a small trencher and a cup of water when he awoke. He wondered if his cellmate brought them. He tried to stay awake to see who brought the food, and how, but the food and water never came until his exhaustion overcame him and he slept. Soon, he stopped trying.

At times he would wake, screaming for his mother and father, but no one ever answered. He wept until his chest ached and his throat rasped, curled in the filthy blanket, sick to his stomach. In time, the crushing darkness and utter silence wore on him and he could no longer tell if he was awake or dreaming—his dreams became of the dark and of his cell. Thoughts of his parents, his home and friends, all faded. He lost names first, then faces. One by one, they were stolen away. He forgot about the presence with him in the cell, as if it stole the memory of itself. Last of all, he forgot his own name. He was alone, and could remember only flashes of the time before his imprisonment.

—

The boy awoke in shock at the sound of the first voices he could remember hearing in all his time in the dark. He listened, overjoyed at the mere sound, forgetting in his rapture to call out. One voice stood out, angry; he realized he could understand it, though it bore an accent that sounded strange to him.

"He is my vassal. This may be his home, but Cunabrel still owes allegiance to me. Now leave, while I speak to the boy." This was followed by an answer in the strange tongue he had heard…

where? Fragments of memory, broken and meaningless, fluttered through his mind. He'd heard the same tongue before the cell. There had been fire. He'd been lifted and carried, and he had cried for his mother. He thought he'd seen a man die. He struggled to recall, but could think of nothing to connect the images and feelings.

Light streaked down from above, piercing his eyes like hot needles. He cowered, covering his face with his hands. There was a sharp intake of breath, then the voice he had heard spoke again, this time soft and kind. "By the Ancestor. My dear child... how could he do this to one so young?" The boy dared to look up, seeing only a blurry silhouette against a circle of light overhead. There was an opening in the cell, several feet higher than he could reach. "Here, Revik. Take my cloak. You must be freezing." The silhouette let a dark robe fall down to him. The boy—*Revik*, he thought, recognition stirring in him—wrapped himself in the cloak. It was warm and thick, soft as silk and more comforting than he could have imagined. It smelled of wood smoke and incense, glorious smells which might have overwhelmed him had he not been so intent on the voice of the kindly man above him. "I have little time—your jailer, a man called Cunabrel, does not approve of my presence here. Though I command his allegiance, he is both willful and powerful. I will return—do not fear. I will see you free of this foul prison soon."

Revik, the child thought again, turning the name over in his mind. Yes, it was familiar; he remembered a voice calling that name—or was he imagining it? Then, overhead, the silhouette vanished and he panicked, trying to shout and producing only a hoarse gasp. As his strangled voice reached his own ears, he wondered how long it had been since he had even tried to speak.

The silhouette reappeared. "I am sorry, Revik, but I cannot help you. Not yet. Take care, child, and be strong." It vanished again, the opening was covered, and the light disappeared. Revik was once again alone.

He wept in the dark. He felt at his hair with filthy hands; it was long, longer than it had ever been. Why could he remember that, but not his family? His home and friends? The gentle voice echoed in his mind—*be strong*. Revik breathed deep, willing his tears to cease. He sat for a long time, focusing on those words. He almost began to cry again when he realized he could no longer remember hearing any others, but stopped himself, holding back the tears. He tried to think of his father and mother but could not. He thought of the man who had spoken to him instead. *I have to be like him.* He wondered when the man would return. He wondered if that man were like his father.

He sat in the dark, waiting. Several meals passed, and through those empty hours, the voice echoed in his mind; *be strong*. He felt strange as the time stretched on. The terror of his mind-numbing imprisonment was starting to fade, as if some of it had escaped through the opening above his cell.

An idea, like a candle light, flickered to life in his mind. Why was he imprisoned? He wondered if he had ever known. Revik remembered only fire, blood, and fear. More than anything, he remembered being afraid. *Be strong,* the voice said. *Weakness,* Revik told himself. He did not know why he had been locked away, but weakness had kept him afraid and imprisoned. *No more,* he thought. *I will never be weak again.* He had not tried to stay awake to see who brought his food for weeks, or perhaps months. He resolved to try again; to push past his exhaustion; to overcome his weakness.

He sought about the cell until he found the small, ceramic cup his captors filled with water each day. He clutched it, drew the cloak up over himself, and lay on the floor as if to sleep. He closed his eyes, lay still, and breathed slow and steady. Time passed—he had long since stopped wondering how much, or even noticing. He kept himself awake by repeating the kindly man's words: *be strong.*

There was silence for a long time. Then, a near-imperceptible grate of metal on stone reached him from the dark; a near-imperceptible glow of red shone through his eyelids. He opened them ever so slightly. There was a doorway into his cell, disguised behind the stone wall. He saw a hulking figure, outlined by the meager light from beyond the door. To Revik's eyes, so used to blackness, it was like looking into the sun. The figure was dressed in dark leather and poor cloth; a griffon in fading black dye was on his armored jerkin. The guardsman reached into the cell and leaned down, and as he felt around at the floor, Revik's hand tensed around the cup. All his terror, his pain, his rage at his imprisonment came rushing to the fore of his mind. *I will show them strength.*

He lashed out with all the force he could muster. The guard was almost blind in the dark, but Revik could see everything. He could make out the man's jaw, his pale eyes, the stubble on his scalp. He saw a scar under the guard's eye and put all his strength, thin and starved though he was, behind the hard piece of ceramic in his hand, driving it toward the scar. Desperation and rage lent him speed, and hate bolstered his frail muscles.

The hard ceramic struck the guard's face just below his eye

socket, shattering. Revik felt hot blood on his hand and saw crimson drops fly from the man's face. He screamed and Revik felt power surge in him. Emboldened, he leapt at the guard, using the dark to his advantage. Overwhelmed by pain and surprise, the guard reeled under Revik's assault, holding his arms up against his smaller attacker.

Regaining his senses, the guard rallied and seized Revik by the hair, holding the youth aloft at arm's length. Squinting from one eye, the other streaming blood, he spat words Revik could not understand. The sound of them brought images of fear and flame to Revik's mind, but he struggled and fought rather than give in to them. The guard pulled back a meaty fist, and still holding Revik by the hair, struck him full in the face. Revik felt the blow, felt a knot of hair torn from his skull, and then felt only blinding pain.

When he awoke, he was on his back in the dark once again. His scalp burned and he felt as if his face had been beaten with a hammer. His nose ached, and it cracked and clicked when he touched it. He tasted blood and could feel that one of his teeth had been knocked loose. Revik groaned, clenching his eyes shut and trying to shut out the pain. He prepared for tears, but was surprised to find he did not want to cry. Despite his injuries, despite still being in the cell, in the dark, alone—Revik smiled.

—

More time passed: numbing, featureless hours that slipped from memory before they even took root. Revik's thoughts came slowly, filling the vast expanses of darkness, slow and great as glaciers. They sheared away all concerns except freedom and pushed aside his need to remember. His old life seemed to be nothing but one of the many hallucinations he had suffered in the dark, fleeting and ephemeral, lacking form and meaning. A full day went by again before they brought him more food or water, and Revik did not try to stay awake or lash out again. Patience, he felt, would be strength, and he would do himself no favors to invite punishment by further starvation.

Days later, his food came unexpectedly while he was awake. Light cascaded from above once again, and the blurry silhouette stood against the blinding rays. "Revik," said the voice from above, "do you remember me?"

His throat ached at the mere thought of speaking, but Revik forced his disused vocal cords to action. "I remember. Have you come to free me this time?"

"Not yet child—I am so sorry. What days in which we live, when a man like Cunabrel will do this wickedness to a child." The man's voice was sorrowful, but then brightened. "I have brought you food, however." A small bundle dropped into the cell. Revik caught it, surprising himself, and felt a wash of joy at the package's weight. "There is good bread there, and some dried venison and an apple—some rations from my long journey from the south. Do not worry, young Revik. I will not leave until you are free."

Revik listened as he tore open the bundle and began wolfing down the food. It was the best he had ever tasted and he almost wept when he bit into the apple. It was sweet and a little dry, but not mealy.

"You have been here quite some time, my boy," the man above said as Revik ate. "Do you remember the last time you had proper food?"

"I don't know." Revik shook his head, chewing a mouthful of salted venison. "It feels like I've always been in here."

"Indeed?" the man asked. "You remember nothing from before you came here?"

Tears came to Revik's eyes, but he squeezed them shut and clenched his jaw. "No." The feeling passed. "I remember nothing."

The man seemed to consider this. "Your captor, Lord Cunabrel, is wicked and untrustworthy. Disobedient. However, he commands great wealth and many soldiers—for anyone, even me, to challenge him, would cause much unrest. Thus, it will take time for me to win your freedom. I know something of your past, child. Your father was a great man, but Cunabrel was his enemy and he will not let you go easily."

"My father?" Revik said, looking up from what remained of his food. His eyes had adjusted to the light, and he could now see his benefactor better than he had before. He was tall and muscular; his pale eyes shone from beneath thick dark hair and brows. He was dressed in a fine, dark robe, sash, and furs, and he sported a trimmed beard the same color as his hair. Lines were beginning to show the man's age, or perhaps his great cares. A crest adorned his thick robes—a great eagle in golden thread. He wore a gold amulet around his neck and many rings shone from his thick fingers.

The man's eyes flickered strangely at Revik, as if all color had vanished from them for a moment. "Yes, your father. I met him, once. He was called Konik Naghan, at least in Gharven."

"No…" Revik's voice trembled. "Wait—yes… it was… I don't remember."

"But that was not his true name. He was Koren Lasivar, and though you are young and untrained, I see you will one day be a man of great power, as he was." The man's eyes unfocused as if he were looking into the distance. They turned dark and featureless in what Revik thought must be a trick of the light. "I see that there is nothing that you will not be able to accomplish."

The food had tired Revik, and the man's words and manner confused him. He didn't trust his own eyes or ears. "I don't understand. Please… get me out of here. I don't want to be alone anymore. Get me out and tell me what you're talking about. I want to see my mother and father." His voice cracked.

The man's eyes were pale and ordinary again. He smiled. "Do not despair, Revik. Soon you will never be alone again." His expression hardened. "But you must be strong if I am to help you. I heard of your attack on your guard. That was good. That was very good. But," he lowered his voice to a whisper, "you must do more. Cunabrel will not kill you, but he will keep you here as long as you are not a nuisance. Become a nuisance to him, and I will convince him to let me take you—to remove the source of his irritation." He reached into his sleeve. "I have another gift for you." He looked over his shoulder at persons unseen to Revik and spoke in another tongue, keeping his hand inside his sleeve. Revik heard several sets of footsteps, growing softer as they receded.

Satisfied that they were alone, he turned back to Revik. "That is Cheduna, the southern tongue. Most men of this land, including my guards and Cunabrel's soldiers, do not understand your Gharven; few of them have ever been so far north as to have heard it." Meanwhile, the man withdrew his hand from his sleeve. He was holding a small knife, which he passed down to Revik. The hilt was decorated with an eagle, and the blade was dark. "Next time your guard comes here—you must kill him."

Revik dropped the weapon.

"Cunabrel will see you as an annoyance and I will be able to take you."

Revik gaped. He picked up the knife and felt the weight of it in his hand as he closed his fingers around it. He looked back up at the man standing high above him.

"It is the only way. Do you not want revenge for what has been done to you?" the man asked.

"But… I'm just…" Revik protested, but the man cut him off.

"No. You are much, much more than you believe."

Revik studied the blade, imagining it stained, shining wet and red with blood; he imagined sinking it into the guard's chest; stabbing him; killing him. He thought about how the guard had struck him. He wondered again how long he had been confined, and clenched the knife in his fist.

"Yes," the man said, as if seeing his thoughts. "It is your chance to show Cunabrel his error. Remember, young Revik, you will only go on if you seize all opportunity, if you seek to overcome all those who oppose you." His form grew darker as he leaned closer to the pit. "Throw down your foe, Revik, and crush him if you are to survive. Become great. You can accomplish anything you desire—show no mercy or weakness. Take what is your due."

Revik knew he was right. No one would give him his freedom; he would have to take it. He looked up again at the shadowy figure above. "Who are you?"

The man smiled again, pale eyes glittering. "You will find out soon enough. Who I am is not important now."

"No, it is!" Revik fought to control the volume of his voice. "You are the only friend I can remember anymore. I want to be like you. I want to go with you. Please, tell me what I should call you."

The man licked his lips. "I am Halkoriv. My people call me king, but you, Revik, may call me Halkoriv."

———

After Halkoriv left, Revik thought only of his imminent freedom and the short, sharp blade in his hand. Doubt gnawed at him—he was young and small, emaciated and weakened by his time in the cell. He had forgotten even how many summers he had seen, but he felt it could not be more than twelve. When his fear threatened to overtake him, he tried to think of his parents as he had in the past. Like the rest of his life, however, they had faded into the shadows of the cell, apparitions cloaked in the consuming darkness of solitude and deprivation. He thought of home but saw only fire and visages of pain and cruelty. Then, he thought of Halkoriv—his friend. Halkoriv was strong, though he seemed old. *King.* He thought he could remember tales of a southern king, one who made war and conquered distant lands. Halkoriv seemed kindly and brave. Revik could not doubt his words, and imagined that his wars must be for good and just causes. He was comforted thinking about his friend. He waited, laying as if asleep once again.

The quiet grate of metal on stone, slow and cautious, reached his ears. *They fear me.* The idea made him smile. The weak light filtered in, once more aiding his sight more than anyone could know. Once again, he clenched his hand—but this time on a real weapon; a deadly weapon. He waited until he knew the time was right, until he could hear the creak of leather and rustle of cloth nearby, as if his visitor were kneeling down. Then, he rolled, bringing his arm and the blade around in a wide arc, striking with all his might and more, bolstered by echoes of Halkoriv's urgings. He could hear them as if the king were beside him, speaking again, whispering to him. Throw down your foe. Crush him. Take what is yours. No mercy. No weakness. Crush him. Crush him. Crush him.

Before he realized what had happened, Revik's eyes widened and he saw the same guard that he had attacked before, his good eye staring, his mouth opening and closing like a fish's. His other eye was hidden behind a bandage. He was on one knee, shaking. The knife protruded from the base of his throat, driven in up to the hilt. Thick, dark blood ran in a slow trickle down his chest. The keys he held clattered to the stone floor of the cell.

The sound startled Revik, who had been staring in awe at what he had done. He, a starved, naked child in a pit, had killed a man.

No, he thought, hot blood on his hand, rage welling inside him. *He isn't dead yet.* Wrath clouded his vision; he could hear nothing but his heart hammering in his chest, see nothing but the dying man in front of him. Revik grasped the bloody hilt and pulled. Weakened, surprised, and mortally wounded, the guard had no strength to resist. He dropped to both knees and Revik stood, feeling tall and powerful. His rage overflowed within him and his hands shook with righteous anger. Grasping the knife hilt, he took hold of the man's chin and forced him to meet his eyes. Revik said nothing as he stared into the guard's face. He reveled in the power he felt over the gasping, choking thing before him. Then Revik screamed, wordlessly giving voice to the cold rage inside him, the pain, the endless hours of darkness and loneliness and despair, and twisted the knife as hard as he could. Blood gushed from the wound and the guard's mouth. He gurgled and gasped, then fell back, twitching. Revik stared at the corpse, the knife still clenched in his bloody fist.

He heard running footsteps and the clank of weapons—others had been alerted by his scream. Smiling, Revik awaited them. He watched as a lantern appeared in the dark, illuminating two men rushing toward him. Revik forced himself not to squint or blink, though the sudden light pained him. They were like their fallen compatriot, hulking and brutish, their pale skin contrasting against the dark uniforms. Shirts of leather were all they wore in the way of armor, emblazoned with a black griffon. They came to a halt in a hallway of stone, damp and in disrepair, and gaped at their dead comrade. They moved toward Revik, mouths clenching in anger. He drew himself up to as great a height as he could and they stopped when he lifted the knife. "No." Revik bared his teeth. They did not move, and he saw doubt and fear in their eyes. He backed into the cell, holding the knife before him, and let the dark of his prison shroud and conceal him. One of the men crept forward, his hands out and empty, and pushed the door of the cell shut behind him. Revik waited.

—THREE—

Within hours, Halkoriv returned. This time, he came to the door rather than the hatch above, flanked by muscular soldiers with gleaming, dark coats of mail and deep red tabards. Revik stepped out of his cell, clutching his knife, weak with relief and happiness. A child once again, he threw himself at the king, embracing him as he might have his father. He didn't dare speak, lest his voice belie the emotion welling in him. He was soon clothed in warm robes the same color as the king's and the group withdrew from the dungeons. Revik was overwhelmed and frightened by the onslaught on his senses—after so long with so little to smell, to see, to hear, he had forgotten how chaotic the world could be.

The dim torchlight and damp, rotten smell of the dungeon gave way to the jail. He was led through the upper cells and into a hall where there stood several guards, better attired than their fellows below had been. *Cunabrel's men.* Revik noted the different colors and heraldry. He had little time to consider them as they passed through the hall and out into the cold night air.

They were now in a great courtyard surrounded on all sides by a high, crenellated wall. The moon shone above and snowflakes drifted down, catching its light and that of two great torches on stone plinths to either side of the jail door. The plinths were inlaid with the same griffon he had seen on the guards' jerkins. The courtyard was abuzz with activity, and directly ahead of the jail sat a huge carriage, made of dark-stained wood, hung with lanterns and decorated with gold. Six horses stood harnessed to the carriage—huge, powerful beasts, nothing like the clumsy animals Revik remembered from... *where?* He tried to recall and his mind met only the dark.

All around the carriage stood dozens more horses and the rest of Halkoriv's guards and attendants. The king's red and gold banners fluttered alongside the tall plumed helms of the soldiers. All were outfitted with long swords and spears—a grim company of deadly men. In the moonlight, Revik could see another group of soldiers to his right. They stood about a great stair before the entrance to a high and imposing castle. Looking back, he saw that the building they had just left was but a small part of a complex of enormous stone structures. The tallest part of the castle swept up higher and higher, disappearing in the night sky but for torchlight dancing in its windows. The heavy, imposing edifice was bedecked with gargoyles and black banners hanging from small stone windows or soaring high above even the lofty towers. Revik almost lost sight of them against the starry sky as the snowflakes floated down around them.

Looking back to the entryway, Revik saw a man standing among the soldiers. His arms were crossed before him and his deep gaze caught Revik's attention. The man's blue eyes were set and hard, and his dark hair hung about his shoulders. A thick beard, black as his hair, was on his jaw. He looked similar to

Halkoriv but for the unveiled malice in his eyes as he looked at Revik. Revik realized the man must be Cunabrel, his captor and tormentor. He returned the glare and felt cold hatred rising up in him even as gloved hands took hold of him and lifted him into the carriage. Halkoriv spoke to his guards in Cheduna, then entered the carriage as well. In seconds, they started moving and Revik was borne away.

Sitting in the warm, plush interior of the carriage, he was silent, trying to understand all that had happened. Halkoriv sat across from him, seemingly content to wait for Revik to speak. The carriage was lit by a small oil lamp encased in yellowed glass. It swung back and forth from the ceiling, casting warm, welcome light about the otherwise dim interior. Cushions sat upon ornate carved benches of dark wood, one facing forward and the other back. A thick woolen rug covered the floor and embroidered padding made up the walls, depicting battles long passed. Revik saw a man sitting astride a great horse in the embroidery. Light seemed to emanate from him; he was in the midst of thrusting a great spear through the chest of a huge creature, like a man but with a vile, brutish look. Curiosity overcame Revik's silence and he pointed. "What is that? An ogre?"

Glancing over his shoulder at the image, Halkoriv chuckled. "It may as well be. It is a plainsfolk warrior; they are a savage people who roam Feriven, threatening simple folk. I personally fought them for many years, and now I fight them still, but only through Feriven's valiant armies. Beasts like the plainsfolk, and worse, still threaten my people. I think, with your arrival, that we may finally have found a way to bring peace. You have much to learn, young Revik, if you will one day fight those creatures as I did."

"I just want to go home!" Revik surprised himself with his outburst. A knot rose in his throat and he choked. He tried to force down the feelings threatening to overwhelm him. When he regained control, he continued. "I want to go back to…" He searched his mind, looking for something to return to, but he found only the darkness of his cell. Revik nearly wept again, grinding his teeth and squeezing his eyes shut against the tears.

Halkoriv stared, then sighed. "Revik, you must understand—you cannot go back. There is nothing now in the Gharven forests, not for you. Cunabrel hunted your family. You were taken." He looked into Revik's eyes. "And your parents were killed."

Dumbstruck, Revik stared in silence. He had known. In his heart, he had known that they were gone, in life as they were from his memory. But he had hoped, all that time in the dark, that he was wrong. He thought he would surely cry now, but no tears came. He could not cry for something that he could not remember. His feelings of loss were for his memories themselves.

Halkoriv spoke, choosing his words as a master mason chooses and lays stones. *The foundation*, he thought, *is the most important*. His voice became earnest, sympathetic, as he laid his stones. "Within your village dwelt two men, both great in their own ways. One was great and wicked, a saboteur and a traitor. He lived there secretly, often traveling south to these lands to sow dissension amongst my people. This man believed that I command armies and war because I am cruel and vicious. Revik, do you feel that he was right?"

Revik shook his head. "You freed me from that place. You gave me food and your cloak."

Halkoriv smiled. "I did. And that is what I seek to do for

all in my kingdom. I wish them to be safe and fed and warm and happy. Your father knew that, Revik. He was the second great man I spoke of. His name was Koren Lasivar. He told us where to find the wicked man. His dream was for Feriven to be united and safe.

"I sent my most powerful vassal, Lord Cunabrel, to capture the traitor, who sought to discredit me and bring chaos and war to all lands, South and North. Cunabrel, however, appears to have his own designs. Instead of just capturing the traitor, he ordered him slain along with all they found with him." Halkoriv's voice grew sorrowful. "Even your poor, honorable father."

With those words, Halkoriv saw his hopes take root. Revik's young eyes became as steel and the king saw only hatred in them. Halkoriv went on. "But even Cunabrel could not kill a child, so you were taken, imprisoned, left to be forgotten. He hoped I would not find you in that pit. Revik, I know of the valor of your father. That is why I came for you. You have been wronged, child, along with many others. Cunabrel stole something very precious from all of us—the peace your father sought. Someday, I believe you will see it; the North joined with the South in peace and unity."

Revik heard Halkoriv as if from afar. He was beginning to understand. He remembered flashes of fire and blood. His imprisonment was evidence of Cunabrel's wrongdoing. Cunabrel must have known that Revik's father was the better man, a man in Halkoriv's favor, and killed him out of jealousy or to protect his wealth and power.

"Yes." It was as if Halkoriv heard Revik's thoughts. "Cunabrel is to blame. I wish you could return to your home, Revik, but it is gone. If you wish, I can see to it that you go north once again and are well cared for. You could go back, and I will see that your life is as comfortable, as much like your old one, as possible." His voice grew in depth, then, and took on the quality it had shown when he had first spoken to Revik in the cell. "I will do whatever you wish to make things right."

The words bored into Revik's mind. *Whatever you wish.* Revik realized what he wanted even as the words reached his ears. He answered, the words flowing unbidden, with more grace and weight than any he had ever uttered. His voice came out low and steady, no longer the voice of a child. "I wish to stay with you. I wish to see my father's hope for a united Feriven made true. I also wish..." He paused, summoning up the thought and relishing it. Blood had run over his hand; he had felt powerful as he watched life end in the guard's eye.

He yearned to feel that power again.

"I wish to bring justice to Cunabrel, to kill him, for my father and mother, for my village, and for myself."

"So be it." Halkoriv's eyes glittered in the lamplight. "He took much from you and betrayed me. I will give you the power to see justice done: to destroy Cunabrel and bring peace to this land; our land." Halkoriv smiled. *The foundation,* he thought. *And you, Revik Lasivar, son of my greatest foe, will be its cornerstone.*

—

Revik embraced his new life with Halkoriv; it was one of privilege, luxury, and learning. Revik soon found that no expense was spared on his account and that there was little that was not provided for him.

He was taken to Halkoriv's palace in the great capital of

Ferihold. The city was perched at the zenith of the highlands which arose from the center of Feriven. A verdant forest lay to its west, and in the summer vast emerald fields spread below it. Five rivers, wide and deep, provided swift alternatives to the well-kept roads for travel and trade. Boats bearing passengers, crops, and other goods trawled the waters, and trading caravans kicked up the road dust from sunup until sundown each day. Troupes of soldiers came and went from the capital at all hours, led by majestic armored knights.

Even near the end of winter when Revik arrived, Ferihold and the land around it was beautiful. Perhaps it was only due to his newly-gained freedom, but he reveled in the open spaces and the clean, glaring light of the sun on the snow. His new studies, however, kept him from spending too much time outside the city.

The walled capital was also a place of wonder to him. Revik had never imagined such structures or such a press of people. Moreover, his status as the king's charge gave him unparalleled access to the city. Not a day went by that he was not carried by coach or horse through Ferihold's gardens and avenues.

The buildings reared up like cliffs capped with shining steel-gray tiles, disappearing amidst the plumes of gray smoke from fires heating homes and shops below. The winding streets were canyons, twisting among the pale stone of the structures while banners of maroon and gold hung across them from the upper balconies. Laid with great stone blocks, the streets played host to markets, festivals, parades, and the daily bustle of the capital. Surrounding the hill was a high wall interspersed with towers and turrets. Twelve feet thick, the wall had been completed in Halko-riv's youth as the greatest protection the city could offer its citizens. Fierce guards patrolled it at all times, armed with long spears and strong bows. The gates, facing north, east, south, and west, were closed from dusk till dawn to all except those traveling on the king's business. During the day, however, they flowed with carts and drivers, oxen and horses, tradesmen and farmers. Some brought grain, fruit, and livestock; others' carts were laden with cloth and spices, coal and iron, wood for building and clay for tiles. Outside the wall were the poorer homes and neighborhoods, and outside those great farmlands spread across the fields.

Upon his arrival, Revik was immediately taken to Halkoriv's palace, a walled, towering place of beauty, strength, and grandeur. He was dressed in fine, soft clothes and his hair was cut short, like a soldier's, as was the style for a noble's son. Within weeks he was in fine health and physically recovered from his imprisonment. Halkoriv saw him frequently at first, personally ministering to his ills and pains. It was then that Revik first learned of sorcery. Halkoriv told Revik that his touch could heal wounds; Revik had laughed until the king put his hand to one of Revik's scars and it vanished. His muscles, weak from disuse, were healed and strengthened overnight.

Halkoriv spent a great deal of time arranging and even administering Revik's instruction. Revik, driven by a desire to avenge himself on Cunabrel as well as the belief in the right of his strength, sought to become better in every way. He was taught language and swordplay, politics and art. He learned battlefield tactics, history, and all he would need to one day become Halkoriv's heir.

As the years passed, Revik grew stronger and faster. He never was as tall or muscular as some of his sparring partners, knights in training and career soldiers, but he came to outmatch them all with the sword. His gray eyes never missed a detail and his lithe frame suggested a speed and precision he was more than happy to demonstrate.

He was an ardent pupil, though he asked few questions of his tutors. He preferred study to play, more so as he grew older. He formed few strong friendships, using his free time to read or practice his swordsmanship.

Through it all, however, dreams of revenge upon Cunabrel remained in the forefront of his mind. He imagined having Halko-riv's powers of sorcery, powers which he saw displayed more and more often. He heard the king's voice become a razor blade, forcing obedience from its listeners. He saw his movements become lightning when he demonstrated his swordsmanship. He heard stories from other nobles' sons, stories of more terrible powers, of weather commanded with words, of wounds opened with a thought. He craved all of it.

—

Revik felt the wind knocked out of him and his head strike the ground; he was thankful for the sawdust covering the large, square flagstones of the practice circle. When his vision stopped swimming, he focused first on a hand hovering above his face, then the concerned face beyond it. He reached up and clasped the hand, and Draden pulled him to his feet as if he weighed nothing at all.

"You all right?" The older boy's dark eyes looked out with genuine concern from under sable hair lank with sweat.

Revik nodded, angry with himself. He had seen the blow coming, but had moved too slowly to stop it. He picked up the weighted wooden sword from the ground and cursed, wiping sweat and sawdust from his face.

"You were close," Draden said. "I saw you getting ready to parry. Your arms are too stiff—push from the floor, and move fast and fluid." He demonstrated, holding his own practice sword to one side and whipping it first one way, then the other. Revik watched and indeed, the movement built from Draden's feet and stance and traveled all through his body but came in a final burst from his wrist.

The practice circle was at the center of a courtyard; other young knights and noblemen's sons shouted and fought in the sun, learning drills and sparring. It was a fine summer day, but Revik would have been outside even if it had been sleeting; he could not stand to be indoors any more than he had to, and rooms without windows still made him shudder.

"I did just that." Revik mimicked Draden's movements almost perfectly.

Draden looked up, and immediately fell to one knee as a shadow fell over the two boys, "You did not," a voice said. Revik looked up at the towering figure of Halkoriv standing over them. He ignored Draden and addressed Revik again. "Employ your entire focus, child. You must capture each aspect of the movement, without thinking of any one aspect individually."

Revik nodded. He did not protest again; he knew better. Halkoriv was good and generous, but he gave his displeasure as freely as his kindness. Revik had only spoken against him once, a few months after he had arrived in Ferihold, and his mind had ached for days afterwards.

"Again." Halkoriv gestured for Draden to stand. "Focus, Revik."

Draden stood and took his stance, wooden sword held high. Revik faced him, and at Halkoriv's word, they struck. Draden was older than Revik by several years and much larger. Revik struggled to parry and dodge his heavy, powerful blows, his arms shuddering each time their swords met. He focused, as Halkoriv had said, and felt the movements building all through him. When Draden spun and lunged, Revik was ready; he let the parry build from his feet, pushing against the ground and whipping his sword across his torso.

His arms shook as he knocked aside Draden's strike. Draden smiled and paused, ready to stop. Revik, however, caught sight of Halkoriv's face and lunged, driving the hilt of his practice sword into Draden's stomach. The older boy fell, coughing.

Halkoriv nodded his approval. "Good. Never hesitate if you see an opportunity for a killing blow. That is enough for today. Come." He turned, striding toward the palace. The courtyard was silent now but for Draden's coughing as the other boys and their trainers remained on their knees, waiting until the king had left to stand.

Revik started to follow, then paused and looked once at Draden, then after Halkoriv. He put out a hand to Draden's shoulder and the older boy looked up with a pained smile. "I'm fine," he whispered. "Go on."

Revik smiled back and nodded, then hurried off after the king.

—

Halkoriv's visits grew rarer; he told Revik that he was watching over the kingdom and meditating on his powers. Revik knew that the king had several palaces, but he spent most of his time far to the south of Ferihold, in his fortress in the Stonewood forest. "It is ancient," the king told him. "My ancestors built it long ago, and, but for one other place, it is there that my connection to our power is strongest."

Revik had said that he would like to see it, and Halkoriv had agreed after some thought. They had travelled there in the winter, heading south from Ferihold with a caravan of Halkoriv's servants, soldiers, and attendants. Revik rode outside the carriage, sitting astride a proud black horse. Gray clouds made the sky as slate, and tiny, hard snowflakes blew up around them as they rode. The soldiers left him to himself, and the attendants spoke only when spoken to. The strangest of their traveling companions, and most frightening, were Halkoriv's servants.

He had heard of them, but never seen one. Here there were three; now they rode at the head of the group, occasionally spurring their mounts and vanishing in the blowing snow ahead, other times falling back and riding amongst them. No one talked to them, or even looked at them if it could be helped. They spoke with Halkoriv in soft, wet voices; they were cold, lifeless beings with dead eyes and pale skin, wearing fearsome armor. They emanated dread and their presence chilled even the icy winter air. They were the first things Revik had feared since being set free.

His eyes were torn from them, however, as they drew close to Halkoriv's fortress; ahead, the shapes of mountains rose like ghosts, pale and insubstantial in the snowy skies. Below them a great smear of dark resolved itself into bare, high trees. Revik could see no undergrowth, and the forest looked dead. As they passed the outermost trunks, he saw why—each tree was petrified, a rough branching column that looked as if it had been hewn from rock. He touched one as his mount passed; a flinty piece of bark broke off in his hand.

He looked up as a shadow fell across them; ahead, hidden amongst the stone trees, was the fortress. It was black and terrible, and it twisted up like a cancer from the ground, as if it had not been built there, but grown. Revik saw no village or guards, and no sound but the hoofbeats of their horses could be heard echoing from the stony skeleton of the forest. He shuddered to look at the fortress and fell back to Halkoriv's carriage.

Halkoriv peered at him from the carriage window. "What do you think, Revik? It was constructed by my ancestor Sitis—the first to truly master sorcery."

"It is very imposing," Revik said after some thought. *It reminds me of Cunabrel's cell.*

"Indeed." Halkoriv's voice had taken on an odd quality that Revik could not identify. He looked at the king, and his eyes seemed darker than usual. "I must go to my sanctum once we arrive; we have much to consider." Revik nodded; he had hoped to spend more time with Halkoriv if he accompanied him to the fortress. Throughout the stay, however, he felt more alone than ever, and soon longed to return to the capital.

—

Revik did not return to the fortress after that visit; he remained at Ferihold and continued his studies while Halkoriv spent more and more time in the Stonewood. Revik was impatient to confront Cunabrel, and year after year Halkoriv told him that the time was not right, that Revik was not ready. He learned quickly, effortlessly, and year after year he thought of little but going back to Cunabrel's realm. The thought drove him, and whenever he tired of practicing and learning and laboring, he thought about what he would do to the man who had stolen his life from him.

—

When Halkoriv, in one of his increasingly rare visits, told him that there was trouble brewing on the north march, Revik knew before the words were spoken that Cunabrel was at the heart of it. He had revolted and declared himself and his lands independent of the rest of Feriven. His treachery was now undisguised, his disloyalty clear for all to see. Revik had thought of little else for over a decade.

Revik and Halkoriv sat, alone in the midst of dozens of courtiers, fawning servitors, nobles, and others at a great banquet commemorating the fall of the garrison at Norishe fifteen years past. It had been the last bastion of rebels south of the plains, and its conquest had been an important symbol of a united Feriven.

"This is your time, Revik," Halkoriv said. "All of your training has been for this—finally, you shall avenge yourself and your family on Cunabrel, who has shown his true allegiances at last. I am appointing you to ride at the head of the army that I will send to crush him. I am also issuing orders that his head is to be yours alone."

"Thank you, Lord Halkoriv." Revik had desired little else for the last dozen years than to feel that sense of power once again, as he had when he had killed Cunabrel's guard back in the dungeon.

"My purpose in this is twofold. Until now, you have trained under my finest scholars and warriors. This campaign will test your abilities, for true skill comes only through experience." Halkoriv had changed little, if at all, in the years since he had rescued Revik. He was still tall and broad-shouldered, and his beard was still only flecked with gray. "You have become a fine young man, Revik. Your father would have been proud," Halkoriv said. "There is one last thing you must learn if you are to take up his mantle."

"What is that?" Revik thought about what he had seen Halkoriv do, how he bent others to his words and moved like lightning.

He and Halkoriv were at the head of the banquet hall, their seats raised to look down over the court. Halkoriv's throne had been bereft of neighbors until Revik had joined his household. Revik savored the envious glances of the nobility as Halkoriv continued to whisper his plans to him.

"My second purpose in sending you is, quite plainly, to test you," Halkoriv said.

Revik nodded. "Then I shall surpass your expectations."

"I do not share the secrets of sorcery with just anyone. I have servants, warriors and spies to whom I have granted power…"

Revik nodded, thinking of the cold, dead creatures riding through the snow. He shivered.

"…but you are different. You have the gift," Halkoriv continued. "You will not be a servant of my power, but master it yourself. Your parents had it—your father and mother were both sorcerers." His eyes narrowed. "I sense you have not displayed your power yet only because you have not been shown how."

Revik was aware that those others sitting closest had ceased their own conversations and were listening. He did not care.

"Sorcery is the greatest power of my family, Revik, and I will teach its secrets to you. I told you that my ancestor Sitis was the first to master it. My knowledge exceeds his. Few others can even grasp it. You will, in time, and you will gain unfathomable power. None will best you. The minds of the weak will lay open before you. We will conquer all its secrets. Sitis and others sought immortality." His eyes glittered beneath his black and gray brows. "And finally, it will be ours."

Revik heard Halkoriv's voice change and saw his eyes become like black pits. His skin grew cold. Halkoriv's empty eyes locked on his. He felt something, cold and light as gossamer, brush against his arms, his forehead; he could not take his eyes from Halkoriv's. The touch moved to his neck, then the base of his skull. It intensified in cold and pressure until the touch became a knife's point. Revik could not cry out, or move, or avert his eyes. Then, as quickly as it began, the feeling was gone.

Revik felt there had been a pause in the conversation, but could not recall why.

Revik shrugged off the feeling. "Lord Halkoriv, I would not presume to think I am capable of something like that. I thought all other sorcerers had been stamped out." He swallowed, desire for the power plain on his features. "Surely this is beyond me."

"No, Revik," Halkoriv said. "I have told you before of your parents; patriots, heroes, powerful warriors, and sorcerers. They wanted to aid me in my duty to unite Feriven, and they were killed by Cunabrel who now profits from dissent and chaos."

Revik's fists clenched at the mention of the name. "I wish I could remember them. His dungeons even robbed me of that. I have nothing of them but what you've taught me."

"It is true, but Cunabrel's one mistake will be his last. He should have killed you along with them. Instead, you will destroy him." Halkoriv stood to leave. The assembled nobility quieted their conversations and arose. Revik stood beside Halkoriv while he addressed them:

"Many of you have journeyed far to be here, and many of you already know why it is I have called you. One of our own, Count Cunabrel of the Northmarch, has rebelled against our great nation." He paused, gazing around the room. Candles flickered, their light reflecting from silver platters and gilded cups. "This will not stand," he continued. "In one week's time, Feriven marches North. We will remind Cunabrel who it is he serves. We will remind him where his loyalties lie." The king raised his cup, and those listening followed suit. "Death to the traitor!"

The assembled knights and nobles cheered, raising goblets and fists. Revik smirked, watching them. He could almost see them straining to appear the most eager, the most loyal. All hoped to be given the honor of leading the armies, but all would be disappointed.

"In one week's time, Feriven marches North, with Revik Lasivar at its head!" They cheered again, some more convincingly than others, before drinking. The king placed his goblet, still full, back on the table.

Halkoriv took his leave and the banquet was ended. The nobles broke into groups, discussing what Halkoriv had said and what it meant for their counties and estates. Revik walked amongst them, clasping hands and accepting congratulations from some and receiving dark looks from others.

"Do you think you're ready for this?" a grinning dark-haired man said, clapping Revik on the shoulder with a hand like a bear's paw. "You've only been training for what, ten years? You're finally going to be allowed out of this place."

"Thank you, Draden." Revik gripped his friend's shoulder in return. "It is an honor I do not deserve, but I am pleased to finally have a chance to put our sparring days to the test."

"An honor you don't deserve?" a voice cut in. "A grand understatement, Lord Lasivar." Revik turned to see the glowering face of Undarten, another of the younger lords.

"You are displeased, Baron?" Revik said. He smiled, without humor. "Perhaps you should take it up with our king? I am sure he will see reason if you should present your case."

"Go home, Undarten. This is not the place." Draden stepped between Revik and the baron.

"You're right." Undarten's clear blue eyes were fixed on Revik's. "We may discuss it further during the march. My knights and I will meet Cunabrel, led by a spoiled child or not." He ignored Draden, stepping closer to Revik. "You may be King Halkoriv's pet, but you know as well as the rest of us that you are nothing."

Revik stepped back, immediately cursing himself for doing so. Undarten smiled. "In fact, I have heard rumor that your father was really a traitor, a rebel leader in the North. We'll see what you really are in a week's time." He turned and swept from the room.

The warning shook Revik. Baron Undarten was a distinguished warrior, one instrumental in winning at Norishe. His actions there had, in the minds of the nobility, earned him his hereditary title. His father had only recently died, leaving Undarten at the head of a powerful estate in the eastern hills.

"Don't let him bother you," Draden said. "He's just grandstanding, trying to force a reaction from you. You know," he turned back to Revik, "if you're going to be King Halkoriv's heir, you can't show fear in front of someone like him."

"I'm not afraid of him," Revik said. He sounded petulant and weak even to himself.

"Good." Draden hesitated. "You have a lot to think about, and I have knights to prepare. I'll see you in a week's time, Lord." He bowed, and Revik nodded as his friend took his leave.

—Four—

It was bright and cool the morning Revik mounted his horse and, escorted by an honor guard of white-robed knights, rode out of the palace grounds and into Ferihold. Passing beneath the high arched gate and over the bridge, he could not help but to swell with pride at his glorious departure. Members of the nobility, separated from the crowds of commoners arrayed behind them, stood to the sides of the road to wish the king's heir well as he began his quest to pacify the rebellious Cunabrel. The knights, twenty strong, rode before and behind him and the people bowed and cheered as Revik passed. It was all he could do to avoid acting like a thunderstruck child. He reminded himself of what he was doing, what was at stake, and with that the crowds and pomp receded from his mind.

Caught up in his thoughts, Revik little noticed the rest of the procession. They passed through the wide, clean-swept streets of the palace district and reached the road to the north gate. They descended, passing the common market and the residential areas, the road turning from stone to earth as they approached the city gates. Staring down from the highlands on which Ferihold rested, Revik looked over the farms and villages outside the walls and onward, over the spring fields, just planted, and the wide river to the lightly wooded land beyond. He spied a dark form just past the farms and the thin wisps of smoke from their chimneys floating up through the still morning air. There stood the rest of the army, prepared to march upon his arrival. The company descended the hill, leaving Ferihold behind. Revik allowed himself a small smile; all those warriors, knights, generals—all awaiting him. He knew he would not be the center of strategy or command, but it would be him that the soldiers looked to, at first to see what he was made of, and later for courage, purpose, and faith that they would win the day.

He looked to the north again, anger washing over him at the thought of the rebels and plainsfolk lurking there, trying to do his people harm; but even more so at the thought of Cunabrel, skulking in his stronghold. Cunabrel—murderer, jailer, and soon, prey.

—

The way north passed through fertile fields in the first stages of planting, along straight and well-maintained roads. The army moved quickly, supplied along the way by the people of the towns and villages. Workers were sent ahead, preparing the food, drink, and other necessities for the army.

Cunabrel's lands were the farthest north of all Halkoriv's vassals. For a week the army marched northwest, eventually reaching and passing into the hills of Dheravay. There, the scouts began to go more heavily armed and in greater numbers, on the lookout for the plainsfolk. The hills were low and round, swept bare of heavy growth by high winds blowing out of the North. Small evergreens grew gnarled and angular atop them, little higher than a man's waist. Dry blades of grass rattled in the wind, new shoots only beginning to appear at their feet as spring took hold of the land.

Each day the army broke camp at dawn. Revik was waiting while stewards saw to his tent and belongings when a rough voice called his name. He recognized the bearded, grizzled face of Hranel, a celebrated strategist and Count of the East March.

"Good morning to you, Count," Revik greeted the older man. "You are ready to go early."

"I thought you might accompany me to observe some of our scouts," Hranel said, indicating a group of lightly-armored horsemen nearby. Revik agreed.

The dawn was cool and gray. Cresting a hill, the scouts halted at a word from Hranel, who pointed north with his heavy riding spear. As he did so, the sun rose over the eastern horizon with a flash and light flooded the hilltops. Then it fell like a wave, sweeping from the east to the west. Drops of dew glittered and sparked on the golden blades of grass. Hranel smiled as Revik gaped at the sudden beauty.

"That is our road, Lord Revik. I do not imagine you have seen a horizon like that before."

The plains seemed limitless, warm gray and gold, like sandstone, undulating and rippling in the headwinds. Hearing the amusement in Hranel's voice, Revik tried to appear stoic once more but the sheer size of the sky and clouds above still left him in awe. The sun's swift ascent came to his aid, however, and the sudden wash of first light ended. The rays grew less intense, and the moment passed.

"Very nice, Count Hranel." Revik turned his eyes back to the lord. He hoped he appeared regal and controlled.

"It is only matched by the sunrise over the Eastmarch, along the coast. Many mornings my wife and I arise and ride out early just to see it." He paused, then met Revik's gaze. "I have heard rumors of your purpose in this campaign. If they are true, then a worthy purpose it is, and I will be the first to say that there is a certain satisfaction to be had in ending the life of your enemy—especially one with which you have personal business." He turned his horse back toward the army, "However, remember that when you go to war, it must not be for yourself, or even for your lord. War is destruction, and there is much that should be saved." He spurred his horse forward, neither waiting for nor needing a response.

Revik sat for a moment longer as the scouting patrol followed Hranel. In silence, he looked north once again, and the wind stung his eyes. Then he, too, turned and rode back.

—

They passed through the plains at full speed. Fearful of ambushes by the plainsfolk, the scout patrols were in a constant rotation of shifts and the army was skirted on all sides by keen-eyed sentinels. There was no sign of them, and word began to circulate that the savages had finally accepted their place.

The first losses almost went unnoticed. Soldiers were thought to have deserted or gotten lost. Scouts and patrols were sent to seek them out. It was when those patrols did not return that the commanders and their generals grew concerned. They met in Revik's tent and Revik listened while the others discussed how to approach the problem. He rested against one of the cushions scattered around the carpets laid out on the ground. About a dozen knights and lords sat with him in a rough circle.

"We must tighten our patrols." Hranel's bald head almost reached the height of the tent as he addressed the group. "We cannot waste time dealing with the plainsfolk while we have our own mission. Every delay only benefits Cunabrel." He sat, leaning back against one of the cushions and opening the matter to other speakers.

"The savages have to be crushed," Undarten said, taking the opportunity. He arose, setting down a cup of wine and casting his gaze about the gathered leaders. He did not bother to address Revik, leaving his back to him. Revik glowered. "Two dozen men dead, if not more? And you think we should just keep going? If we simply move on, we tell them that there are no consequences for their attacks. We should take this chance to teach them a lesson. Place bait, isolate a group of soldiers or some such, then cut the bastards down with arrows when they appear. Our men say they cannot be killed, that they are demons. We must show them the truth." He remained on his feet, creating an awkward moment for anyone who wished to speak. The nobles waited. Hranel was about to say something when Draden interjected from his seat.

"Count Hranel is right, Baron. If we delay, Cunabrel will be more prepared and we will be weakened." He did not move from where he sat, back straight and head high. Undarten opened his mouth, an expression of disdain and a word of consternation on his lips. Draden cut him off. "And don't act as if I'm interrupting, Undarten. If you had more to say, you'd still be talking. I would add that I agree. The plainsfolk should be dealt with. We can't let them think they can attack us without retaliation."

Undarten, scowling, nodded to Draden and took his seat. Hranel hid a smile. Revik was amused; *Draden is more than a simple soldier. Few others could have quieted Undarten without a fight.* He already knew Draden to be a fantastic fighter. His shrewdness, too, was an asset Revik promised himself to remember.

Hranel stood again. "Then how should we proceed? I feel we cannot waste time fighting the plainsfolk on their own terms, and even if they are not ghosts or demons, our losses would be heavy and our men shaken. Who here has even seen a dead plainsfolk?" He waited, and the other lords muttered and shrugged. None answered. "Draden and Undarten have convinced me, however—the plainsfolk must be punished." He returned to his seat.

A thought struck Revik, and he stood. "So we can waste no time, but we must make a statement." He was determined to show himself to be more than a figurehead. "I propose we continue north. The winds blow south, and our foes attack our rearguard. They take cover in the grasses, hide in darkness, and this is their home."

"Your point?" Undarten asked. "If you have such experience on the battlefield, please, share it with us."

Revik looked around, making sure he had all of their attention.

"Burn it," he said.

Hranel grimaced. Undarten smiled broadly despite himself. Draden nodded. "A strong warning, and maybe deadly."

"I agree with Lord Revik," Undarten said. Revik blinked. "These lands are nothing. The savages understand little, but they will not be able to ignore a message of fire and ash."

One by one, the remaining lords agreed. Hranel sighed. He caught Revik's eye but addressed Draden. "You are in command of our scouts tomorrow morning?"

"I am," Draden answered.

"Very well," Hranel said. "Prepare tonight, and do it at dawn, if the winds are with us. I want the men ready to move when the fires start."

"As long as the winds still blow from the north, we should be in no danger." Draden stood, followed by the other lords, and called for one of his lieutenants and waited at the entrance to the tent. While the rest of them said their good evenings and left, Revik watched as a soldier entered and spoke with Draden. The soldier's salute was exaggerated, almost mocking, and Draden spoke low and sharply to him. The soldier grinned with a mouth full of small, crooked teeth as Draden explained his task. He gave only the slightest bow before leaving. Draden turned back to Revik, brow furrowed.

"Why do you not punish him?" Revik asked. "He was mocking you."

Draden shook his head. "Malskein is good at what he does, even if he is an ass. Well done tonight, my friend. They'll respect you yet." He clasped Revik's shoulder, bowed, and exited the tent.

"Well done indeed." Hranel was now alone with Revik in the tent. "Do you think it will be worth it?"

Revik grinned at the older man. "A view lasts a moment, Count. Halkoriv envisions a kingdom that will last forever, and a power that cannot be denied. That is worth anything."

Hranel set his jaw. He said nothing before leaving the tent.

—

The sun had just begun to rise over the eastern horizon. Bor, still exhausted from the previous day's march, hustled along, looking over his shoulder as often as he dared.

"Keep your eyes on your path. Don't spill those coals," Hendeff grunted between breaths beside him.

Bor tried to concentrate on the bucket of smoldering coals. He was only glad that running disguised his shaking. "Commander says the plainsfolk are probably watching us right now. I'd feel better with a shield in my hand and you carrying the damned coals." He pushed through the grasses. The last five minutes had felt like a lifetime. *Just a little farther,* he told himself. *Just a little farther.*

—

Revik watched the flames spread and grow, like something alive. Smoke began to sting his eyes as the brushfire flared. The golden grasses quickly turned black and the fires consumed one hilltop, then another. He and Draden, atop their mounts, waited while the last of the rearguard passed by before turning their horses north once again. "Do you think they were out there?" Revik asked. "Are they really so deadly?"

Even in the sunlight, the fires behind them cast a reddish light on Draden's face. "They move quickly, and they're cleverer than Undarten gives them credit for. The men say they are not human, and that fear is their greatest asset. The best thing about this plan is that the plainsfolk can't hide in cinders."

—

The plains came to an end after another week's travel, giving way to a deep forest, the border of Cunabrel's realm. When they reached it, the army halted for a day as the officers met once again to discuss their plans. Revik found that he was consulted more often than he had been at the outset of the journey. Some of the lords and officers began to display a heartfelt respect for the young heir.

They moved on, prepared for the worst but meeting no resistance at or near the borders. Cunabrel was no doubt aware of the army's approach. The consensus was that he had saved his strength to fight from a well-defended position inside his stronghold. The next few days saw few of the realm's commoners, let alone any soldiers. On the final day of the march, the reason for this became apparent; the vacant homes and emptied villages had been abandoned by the people as they moved, by Cunabrel's orders, to surround his castle. The forward scouts reported that thousands of people, along with carts and livestock, were camped in a dense crowd encircling the castle walls.

Revik remembered little of the castle from ten years ago, his mind at the time more occupied with other matters. As it was described and mapped for the benefit of the other officers, fleeting images returned to him. The great outer wall was two dozen feet high and wide enough for two men to pass each other while walking along the top. The main gateway was four times as thick and flanked by towers and platforms riddled with arrow slits. There were two sets of reinforced oaken gates and a third of iron. Within the walls lay a flagstone courtyard surrounded by utility buildings and stables, and across from the gate was Cunabrel's fortress. Once the gate was breached, the courtyard would be hard to win as well, especially if Cunabrel's men maintained control of the walls.

It was likely then that they would concentrate in the main fortress and could hold up for days unless surrender was somehow forced.

The officers and nobles were most concerned with the mass of people surrounding the walls. The presence of the crowd was an unexpected problem.

"Cunabrel has made another wall of them," one of the lords said. "He's trying to prevent us from using our forces to full effect by putting those people in the path of our archers."

"We should just ride them down if they will not move themselves," Undarten suggested, his voice belying only cold efficiency.

Hranel spoke, the veteran of many campaigns throughout the kingdom. "We are trying to take this country, not kill everything in it. Slaughter them, and we will only stir further rebellion in the North." His eyes met Revik's, and the message was clear. *You will be the one held accountable.* "King Halkoriv's hold this far north is tenuous as it is," he continued. "Indeed, if they see us turn on them, it will only lead more of them to join Cunabrel in the fight. There are thousands of people camped there. They will do half of the work for him, and this campaign will become far more dangerous and bloody than it has to be." Most of the others grumbled agreement, but some among them only became more vehement. The officers' tent was soon filled with shouting.

The meeting was breaking down. Revik saw a chance to show leadership and asked for order. No one seemed to hear or pay attention, so he spoke louder, then shouted, only adding to the growing din. Anger rose in him, his face flushing hot—but there was something else; a growing cold at the base of his skull, icy and light as gossamer. He felt as if Halkoriv stood beside him, almost heard his words in his ear, in his mind. Command them.

"Silence." Revik's voice cut like a blade. The assembled lords started at the sound, staring at the quiet, slight young man they had come to know, now seemingly grown large and dangerous before their eyes. Revik settled into his seat, drawing out the moment, knowing that none would speak until he allowed it. *I do have the gift.* He struggled to contain his excitement. *I am a sorcerer!* He had never felt such power.

"We, the king's army, did not come here to ask permission or offer appeasement. These peasants have no choice. Cunabrel no longer commands them. The king has sent us as his emissaries and his blade. If it were me, I would ride out and command that they move. Those that leave as commanded shall be offered our protection, just like all others in the king's care. Those that do not are aiding Cunabrel, and so forfeiting their lands, goods, and lives. They will be cut down by our archers, executed as traitors." Revik smiled. "Thus, our mercy and fairness will be known, and an example made of the treasonous." Hranel opened his mouth to speak but Revik went on. "I may be inexperienced in the field, but I know best of all gathered here our king's mind, and I am here in his stead. If there are no arguments—" he paused, "—then have our archers readied within the hour, and a few squads of pikemen as well. I will deliver this message."

One by one, the noblemen nodded their assent. Even Undarten said nothing. More than one of them remembered that this campaign was Halkoriv's test for Revik. His failure would be his alone, not a reflection on the rest of them. Halkoriv, in this case, cared how success was achieved; there were always more soldiers to send, and even with mistakes their forces would be more than enough to defeat Cunabrel's.

Revik noted Draden's cautious smile and Hranel's impassive gaze. For his part, Revik tried to maintain an emotionless expression. Looking around at the men, however, he was struck with another idea and pressed his advantage. "If you will entertain a novice in battle and strategy for a few moments more," he said, "I have something to say about gaining entry through the gate as well."

—

While the soldiers were organized and their orders relayed, Revik prepared himself in his tent. Servants polished his lightweight, black and gold armor and sword as he mentally readied himself. He knew he had to appear to be the personification of the king's strength and will if his plan was to work.

A page informed him that the soldiers were prepared. Donning his cloak, Revik strode out to the muster, mounted his horse, and took his place at the front of the column of fearsome warriors. He was joined by Draden and a contingent of knights. Draden ordered the column forward, and Revik spurred his mount. Before them lay Cunabrel's castle. It was late evening, and bright fires flickered about the base of the walls. The peasant camp was like a moat ringing the stone face, a moat of glittering flames and shifting, black shadows, two hundred yards across. Atop the walls, the torches of sentries and soldiers moved back and forth, winking out and reappearing as they passed the high crenellations. The massive gate was illuminated by a quartet of great flames rising from iron sconces, as tall as a man, flanking the gate on the wall and at ground level. The towers of the fortress were black columns against the sky, starless and dark with clouds.

As they drew nearer, Revik could see the edges of the peasant camp; the people were packed close together, one family's cart or camp pressed up against the space of the next. They did not stop until they were mere yards from the edges of the camp.

The nearest commoners looked on, fearful and timid; the entire mass of them could in no way be gathered to hear Revik, but if he could do what he thought he could, it would not matter. All of them would hear him. He sought the chill in his mind, the gossamer touch at the base of his skull. He was surprised how easily he found it this time and wondered why he had never felt it before. The power flowed in him; Revik felt as if he had been holding his breath all his life, and now he could let himself breathe.

He found the power pushing against him; he released his restraint, feeling the mass of people, seeing their minds. It was as if he could see all of them, each one a point of weak, pale light in the darkness. Hundreds, thousands of minds, arrayed all around him and around the fortress. Some were nearly a mile away. He did not feel he could control them—but he knew he could make them all hear.

People of the Northmarch, he said. His voice was a knife, a spike that he drove into their consciousness. Those that he could see, flinched. Some gasped, some cried out. He felt fear flood the rest. Revik was giddy, overwhelmed. *I am the heir of your king. I am Revik Lasivar. Cunabrel's reign is over. You are no longer his subjects. Leave this place, and you will know your king's mercy. Stay, and you will know his wrath. Go.*

Some of the peasants began to break camp. Others argued

and shouted. Some just ran away. He felt their confusion, their terror. He knew some would stay, unsure of what else to do. They had been warned.

Revik left the column of archers and pikemen. Their commanders knew their orders. He and Draden, accompanied by Draden's knights, approached the gate. As they drew nearer, one of the men on the wall shouted for them to halt. Draden raised his hand and the group of knights stopped. Revik rode a step farther and looked up at the top of the wall.

"What is your purpose here, Halkoriv's slave?" a soldier called down. In the torchlight, Revik could discern the clean-shaven features of a young warrior. He was flanked by a pair of archers, their bows stretched, their arrows trained on Revik. Other soldiers watched from their places along the wall.

"Address your king's heir with respect, cur," Draden shouted. Revik said nothing, watching the archers and the soldier.

"Ah, excuse my insolence," the soldier replied to the amusement of his men. "Welcome, great pet of Halkoriv! Have you come to willingly return to Lord Cunabrel's shackles? Have the old king's appetites driven you away?" The men cackled, but the archers did not so much as smile.

Revik heard grumbles and threats behind him but raised his hand for silence. He smiled and replied, "Tell your snake of a master to come out from his hole. I would speak for the king, who does not deign to converse with vermin, so I must do so in his stead."

There were cries from above and the soldier who had first spoken called for silence. Cunabrel's men were incensed. "Enough!" roared one of the archers. "Die, you scum!" He loosed his arrow.

Revik registered only his own surprise and sudden terror as the bowstring twanged. He later recalled only two things; the surety that he was about to die, and the touch of ice and gossamer in his mind.

There was a ring of steel and a snap. Years of training came to the fore, propelled by the icy tide in Revik's mind. The next moment, Revik realized that the arrow was gone, shattered, his sword was in his hand, and the previous moment's panic had been replaced with a terrible silence from Cunabrel's men as well as his own.

Tendrils of utter blackness, like ribbons of starless night, writhed around Revik. The fires flanking the gates diminished and guttered as if under a heavy wind. The arrow lay on the ground in rotten splinters.

Revik seized his unexpected advantage. He pointed up at the wall with his blade. "I tire of this, but I will overlook this slight. Open the gate, or I will tear it asunder!"

They gaped as the black tendrils faded and the fires rose again; some of the soldiers above backed away from the edge of the wall. The young soldier stared in fear. Regaining his senses, he turned away and disappeared from the wall without a word. Revik heard whispers from above, but nothing else over the crackling fires flanking the gate.

Draden moved closer. "So Halkoriv gifted you with power already," he hissed. "Your plan may work after all. You could kill them all yourself."

"This is... something else," Revik whispered. "Not Halkoriv's power, but my gift. He told me my parents were sorcerers. I must have awakened it."

"Of course," Draden said. "I'd heard stories of the elder La-
sivars. They must've passed it to you."

Minutes passed before the gate opened and Revik saw Cunabrel, mounted and arrayed in fine armor, wearing a long sword
with a garnet set in the pommel on his back. At least eighty men
at arms stood around him. All were hard-eyed and scarred from
battles past. Revik saw amongst them the soldier from the gate.

Before the gates finished grinding open, Cunabrel spoke. "If
you would speak, boy, it will be behind my walls and on foot.
Leave your mounts if you would enter." Revik's anger surged
upon seeing him, but he restrained his emotions. Cunabrel looked
almost as Revik remembered him, tall and broad, his black beard
now shot through with silver. A shining helm, inlaid with bronze
and garnet, crowned his head but no visor obscured his hateful,
piercing eyes.

"We will enter," Revik said, "but my men will remain beside
your gate. I have come to talk, not to fight just yet." His voice was
bolstered by confidence from his newfound gift. With a gesture,
he and the men with him dismounted and entered the gate. Draden
and the rest stopped once inside, the knight and his men silent
as they took stock of their surroundings. Revik advanced, halting
before Cunabrel.

"Back to your posts," Cunabrel commanded, looking over
his warriors. "But guard these scum from the South carefully. In-
form me of any movement from outside."

"My Lord," a soldier called from the wall. "The peasants are
breaking camp; they're leaving!"

Cunabrel did not answer. He turned his wrathful gaze to Revik, who smiled. "Let them go," Cunabrel answered. "Keep watch

on the Southerners."

Cunabrel turned to a group of warriors on foot close by, armored and bearing shields and axes. "You four, come with me. Stay close to the whelp." He spurred his mount across the courtyard, toward the great fortress. The four men approached Revik, who did his best to ignore them and followed Cunabrel. *He means to insult me, to anger me,* Revik thought. *He still thinks of me as that weak, helpless child.* His smile remained even as the guards surrounded him and herded him across the courtyard.

A few moments later Revik stood in Cunabrel's audience hall, a room fifteen paces wide and twice as long. Stone fireplaces flanked a lushly carpeted walkway and torches burned in sconces. Their light could not banish the deep shadows in the corners of the hall. At one end of the room stood Cunabrel's throne. Rich tapestries, decorated with the flowing script of the High Tongue, described legends and heroes of Cunabrel's ancestry. The ceiling nearly vanished in darkness overhead, thick beams and rafters barely visible in the glow of the fires and torches.

Revik waited with his guards; they did not speak to him, nor he to them. In the firelight, their helms cast shadows across their eyes. They looked to Revik almost inhuman. He waited, calculating; *A few minutes more.*

Cunabrel entered alone, coming through a set of carved oaken doors behind the throne. He was still wearing his armor, but no longer wore his helm or riding cloak. He strode up to Revik, dispensing with the traditional greetings and customs observed during wartime.

"So your surrogate father has sent you to oversee my destruction? He has become even more overconfident and arrogant than before."

"You have no chance in your little rebellion; you must see that," Revik said. "King Halkoriv has sent thousands of troops, a fraction of the army, against your few hundred, and—"

"And he has sent you to mock me," Cunabrel interrupted, stepping close to Revik. "Ever since I captured you, on his orders, I have been maligned and mistreated by Halkoriv. This may surprise you, boy, but I had no interest in you or your family. It was only when I began to hear the rumors that it occurred to me that something about you was strange, and only after Halkoriv 'liberated' you that I realized that I was being deceived and used!"

"What are you talking about?" Revik asked, snorting.

"Halkoriv used me," Cunabrel said. "He used me to I know not what end. To create you, that much is clear, but in the intervening time I became expendable to him. I suppose you think I started this conflict with Halkoriv. I did not. This is merely a reaction to years of mistreatment at his hands, ever since he took you away from my dungeons. I do not take persecution lightly."

"That is ridiculous," Revik said. He pointed a finger at Cunabrel. "You think me a fool. You will not turn my head with lies and stories. Save that for the children and simpletons you used to wall your fortress. You are a traitor, and you will die here unless you declare allegiance to your rightful king once again."

Cunabrel's face twisted into a snarl. "If I must die here, then go tell your king that others will follow me, that his lust for power and his pursuit of the dreams of his mad ancestor will lead to his own fall." He turned to go, dismissing Revik with a gesture. "There will be no terms. I am resolved to fight as long as I live. Go, lead your fighters, and pray you do not meet me on the field.

Take him away."

The guards turned to lead Revik out. The nearest two reached for his arms. Revik breathed deeply once; to them it may have sounded like a sigh. He felt pressure in his mind; his power, waiting, straining to be released. *This is it. Move.*

Revik drew his sword and a chill flooded through him, starting in the base of his skull and rushing over his body. The guards started at the sound of the steel leaving its scabbard, but Revik struck before they knew what was happening. His sword pierced the nearest guard's chest and the man clutched ineffectively at the blade before he fell. Revik spun, ripping the blade from him and arcing it into the next guard. He was still unprepared and it crashed into his neck, shearing through his armor and splintering his spine.

Revik had time to wonder why they were not fighting back, and it occurred to him then just how effective his training had been. Power pulsed through him, only increasing the speed with which he moved. His mind moved even faster than his body, recounting many hours of combat training each day for years—a routine of study and practice that would have broken him had he not been anticipating this moment the entire time.

Revik did not see, but felt, the remaining guards swing their axes. He heard Cunabrel's footsteps approaching and heard his sword. He spun again, whirling out of the reach of one of the guards and ducking beneath the other's axe blow. *Too hard,* he thought. The guard's swing had put him off balance. Revik lashed out with a kick, sending the guard reeling and stumbling into his compatriot, bowling him over. Revik lunged, his thrust catching the guard in the chest and punching through the chain armor covering it. He kicked again, pushing the man off of his blade. The last remaining guard regained his feet and rushed forward, swinging wildly. Revik dipped back, avoiding the blow, then swung. The guard raised his shield, protecting his neck and face—but obscuring his vision. Revik pivoted, spinning to the man's side, his movements a blur. He encircled the guard's throat with his arm and wrenched, a chill wave of power rushing through him. There was a crack and the soldier's head lolled grotesquely. He went limp, dropping to the floor.

Cunabrel hesitated, aghast. Then he rushed forward, swinging his own blade. He had seen many battles, won several duels, but he appeared shaken, frightened. Even having witnessed it himself, he seemed unprepared for Revik's speed. He swung once, twice, cutting only air; he parried and dodged, then Revik unleashed a cloud of shadow to obscure his vision, then spun his sword with speed he had not known until now that he possessed. Revik watched as Cunabrel swung again, unaware he had been struck—until his legs crumpled with their tendons cut.

Revik stood over his fallen foe and grinned as Cunabrel screamed in agony, his useless legs gushing blood. He wanted to savor the moment, to gloat, to humiliate him, but he sprang back into action. There was little time, with Cunabrel's racket.

He ran to the doors and shoved his sword through the elaborate handles as a makeshift bar, hoping it would be enough to hinder any pursuit. He heard voices already on the other side, but still some distance from the door. He ran back and kicked Cunabrel sharply in the jaw, cutting his screams down to agonized groans as his mouth snapped shut and he spat out a shattered tooth. Cunabrel growled something incomprehensible through his ruined mouth, but Revik paid him no heed. He grabbed the lord by his armor and began to drag him toward the rear doors of the room, stopping only to pick up Cunabrel's forgotten sword.

He made his way to a rooftop doorway over a balcony. It was odd, Revik reflected, straining under Cunabrel's weight, how easy he had been to dispatch but how difficult to drag around.

He kicked open the door to the balcony and pulled Cunabrel, now weakly but comprehensibly cursing, out into the damp spring night. While Revik had been inside, it had begun to drizzle. "I'll see you dead yet, you worm," Cunabrel rasped, blood running from his mouth as he spoke. "I should have killed you when I had the chance, but now I'll see you torn apart first!" He spat on Revik's armor.

"Unlikely," Revik said, taking stock of the scene below. He allowed himself the brief satisfaction of kneeing Cunabrel in the jaw, breaking it this time and reducing him again to painful gurgles.

He looked around the courtyard beneath them—it appeared he had not been noticed yet. He caught sight of Draden, standing with the others by the gate, surrounded by a group of Cunabrel's soldiers.

There was a sudden cry from outside the walls, followed by the sharp whistling of arrows in flight. Cunabrel's men began to shout and point. "Archers! They're firing on the peasants!" one yelled. "You, go get Lord Cunabrel immediately!" another said. A third bolted for the fortress door.

Revik lunged to the edge of the balcony, hauling Cunabrel to his feet. "Cunabrel is here!" Revik roared. He positioned Cunabrel in front of himself. More shouting from below followed, and all heads turned and peered up through the rain. Draden smiled grimly at Revik, nodded, and edged away from the other knights. "Behold your mighty lord, broken before the fighting even began." His voice dropped to a whisper. "Look, lord," he hissed, "watch your people, watching you die."

He continued, addressing the soldiers below. "This is what awaits those who oppose me, King Halkoriv, or the Kingdom of Feriven. Traitors will be killed; they will be broken; they will be destroyed, and all they hold dear will be ripped from under them. You now have a choice." Revik paused as Cunabrel struggled, trying once again to speak. Revik raised the sword in his hand and brought it down, striking the garnet-studded pommel against Cunabrel's face. The battered lord let out a strangled yelp. Revik nearly laughed with joy, his power over his enemy almost tangible. He let Cunabrel drop to his knees, holding him upright by a clump of bloody hair.

"Your choice," he said, "is to pledge yourselves once again to your true king, or die in the mud here tonight. To die secure in the knowledge that your families will share your fate, your lands will be forfeit, your names forgotten. This one," he yanked back Cunabrel's head and exposed his pale throat, "has made his decision!"

Draden looked on from below, and the moment seemed frozen. He saw Cunabrel, kneeling with his head wrenched back; Revik, standing over him, droplets of blood and water running down his black armor; Cunabrel's own sword, bathed red and orange in the firelight, poised to strike, then racing down, down, the arc of its blade plummeting toward Cunabrel's throat. Steel met flesh, and Cunabrel lurched; Revik's eyes shone with triumph. Draden pulled his eyes away, wrenched open the gate, and drew his sword.

His men followed suit, cutting into the nearest soldiers without warning.

Before Cunabrel's men could react, a hail of arrows whistled into the top of the wall, cutting down most of those upon it. Horsemen charged through the gate. Chaos and panic overtook the castle. Revik saw none of it, his attention focused instead on Cunabrel's lifeless form.

Many of the defenders surrendered. Against the force from Ferihold, the few soldiers who attempted to fight were overwhelmed and killed.

The drizzle became a downpour. Hranel and the others handled the remainder of the assault. Revik did not join in the battle. He stood on the balcony, oblivious to the rain. It had all been so easy; he had toyed with the guards, even with Cunabrel—a vaunted and renowned swordsman. They had been like children, like he had been years ago in the practice circle. They moved without grace, and Cunabrel's powerful but clumsy technique could have been outthought by a novice. Revik gloried in his destruction—and his enemy's death left a chasm inside of him. He had lived to see Cunabrel die, and now it was over. Something had to fill it. *More enemies. More power. More foes to crush, more lives to take.*

And the sorcery—the power that had coursed through him—Revik tried not to think that his victory was only through magic, but then he wondered if that were such a bad thing. He wanted to feel that power again, the dark, cold touch like a blade's edge. And he would feel it again, having passed the king's test. He would grow even stronger, as Halkoriv had bid him do all those years ago, in this very place.

Revik stood in the storm, watching Cunabrel's blood thin

and disperse, then finally wash away with the rain. The air chilled around him; light faded and the touch of water felt far away. Revik then felt the king's presence, heard his voice as if he were close. *You have crushed your enemy, and your power has been revealed,* Halkoriv's voice said, a razor in his mind. *Your purpose, your destiny, has become clear. You will lead our forces to exterminate the plainsfolk and their northern allies. You will oversee Feriven's unification. And our enemies in the Northlands shall know, Revik Lasivar has come to end them.*

—Five—

She slammed into the ruin wall hard and felt something pop low in her back. The wall, stone though it was, was ancient and brittle and gave way under the force of the impact. She collapsed among the grass and falling stones, barely able to move. Her vision blurry, Ahi'rea grunted as she pushed herself up on her forearms. The Cheduna soldier standing over her was thrown into sharp relief by the moonlight bathing the plains. As he loomed over her, a feminine figure twice Ahi'rea's size leapt in front of her to block her hulking attacker. Still recovering from his wild shield blow, the soldier's stance was wide open.

Ahi'rea's eyes shut involuntarily as the pain set in, so she only heard a sickening sound, like a rotted tree branch splitting, as her mother's machete struck down the soldier. His sharp cry was cut off; *she must have cut through his throat.* Ahi'rea paid little heed, forcing herself to concentrate through the pain rapidly spreading up her back. She felt it then—the power of Self, like a cool rush of wind traveling down her neck and spine, washing the pain away. She opened her eyes wide and gasped.

Her mother rushed to Ahi'rea and knelt at her side. Ha-ruu'na's eyes still glowed faintly green in the darkness. The long, animal-hide skirt she wore was splattered with blood, as were the yellowed bones lashed together in a loose, tabard-like arrangement of armor over her torso. The natural landscape around them was mimicked by the grass cape and hood falling about her. Her lined and scarred face, darkened by the sun to the color of aged leather, registered first terror and then relief as she saw her daughter's eyes pulse and glow.

"That was careless!" Haruu'na stood and scanned the darkness around them. "If I hadn't been here…"

"It won't… happen again," Ahi'rea gasped, hands reflexively clawing at the ground. Soon she relaxed as the pain ebbed, and after a moment she stood and stretched her aching back. "I let my guard down, and underestimated him. The Cheduna soldiers have been getting stronger." Retrieving her spear, she looked up at the towering older woman. "Thank you."

"Never mind," her mother said. "You're all right." The glow in Haruu'na's eyes dimmed and she seemed to diminish, sighing. "I think this area is clear. The others seem to be handling the rest of them." A cry in the southern tongue rose and fell nearby. "How does it look to you?"

Ahi'rea inclined her head, her sun-bleached hair blowing across her face as the wind picked up. Her eyes shone, casting their eerie, green light on the moonlit grasses and the stones of the ruin beside them. "Three, running… south and east of here." Her eyes cleared and she looked up again. "They have not gone far yet; I know where they will run."

"Your father's Sight." The old woman's voice rasped with exertion. With that, she smiled and her eyes lit again. Her breathing eased, and she hefted the machete as if it were a feather. "We'll head them off before they even know where they're going."

—

"Did you hear that?" the soldier whispered, gripping his axe and looking over one shoulder, then the other.

"Quiet!" The second speaker could barely make out his nervous companion ahead—the grass was too tall and thick. "You keep jumping at every sound, and we'll be noticed for sure."

"It sounded like someone speaking plainsfolk! They're stalking us!"

"Shut it!"

"We'll never get away at this pace—they'll track us down!"

"I said quiet!"

"I can't see anything!" the first man said, his voice growing shrill. "We need to find the road—hurry!" He broke into a run, rushing off into the dark grassland.

"Idiot! Stop!" the other soldier nearly shouted. He gestured to a third man behind him. "Cendro's run off! Let's go, he'll alert the whole damned lot of them." With that, he gave chase, followed by the third soldier.

The moon was high before them. Cendro, his dark-stained armor clattering as he dashed ahead, turned to the left, looking for the road. He was unaware of the smaller figure running alongside him to the right and growing closer by the second. The two running behind him were similarly oblivious until the shaking and waving grass ahead, indicating Cendro's direction, grew still.

They halted and silence met their ears. The sound of the battle behind them was gone; they could only assume the worst for the rest of the squad. They strained to hear, hoping for any sound at all, but none came.

"Maybe the idiot fell and knocked himself out…" the first soldier whispered. He took a few slow, wary steps, axe at the ready.

"We're dead men… by the king, we're dead… they're demons!" The other soldier knelt, stifling sobs and muttering desperate prayers.

"Get up!" hissed his companion, looking over his shoulder. "They're men, like anyone else. We'll get out of this. I'm going to—"

There was a rustle of grass. The kneeling soldier looked up, but there was no sign of his companion save a dark spatter of blood on the grass and earth, reflecting the moonlight above.

He stood, his axe high, and whirled about, swinging and lunging at the grasses around him. "Where are you?" he shrieked. "Damn you! Come out and fight!"

A faint green light illuminated the waving grasses before him, glimmering against the blades as if it were shining through water. He moved without hesitation, as he had been taught, spinning and swinging the axe from high to low with all the force and desperation he could muster. The stalker would be hobbled or incapacitated at least.

He felt no impact, just tall blades of grass falling before the axe. As he spun, he looked up; a green-eyed devil was leaping high and driving a spear point down, down, meeting his wrist at the exact moment it crossed the spear's path.

The apparition slammed into him. The collision drove him back and he fell with a lurch. He felt something restraining his axe-hand. The pain that followed, ripping along his hand and arm, confirmed what he had seen but still had not had time to process: he was pinned to the ground, the spear through his wrist, running with blood. Shock overwhelmed him as he lay, gazing up at the creature that had attacked him. The green light faded from her eyes and he realized it was a girl; one of the plainsfolk. Blood stained her dark skin and the moon shone on the bronze machete in her fist; pale hair roiled behind her and her woven-grass cape blew high in the wind. Her deep brown eyes stared back at his. She was small and slight, probably not a year over twenty.

Perhaps it was shock, or the revelation that she was just as human as he, but his bluster returned. "Your kind are dying! It's only a matter of time; give up quietly and I'll make certain that you're... well treated." The soldier looked her up and down, grinning madly, and winced as he tried to tug the spear from his arm.

Ahi'rea smiled back, a smile that chilled his blood.

"You are a demon." Terror flooded back into him, and he opened his mouth to scream.

Ahi'rea raised her machete, then brought it down with a hard swipe. She pulled free her spear, then turned and disappeared into the grassland.

—

Ahi'rea rejoined Haruu'na not far away, where she had made short work of the one called Cendro. Together they made their way, swiftly and silently, back to the spot on the road where they had first ambushed the patrol. There they saw the tall form of Ruun'daruun, his long hair hanging heavy with sweat, his bare chest splashed with blood. None of it appeared to be his. He was supporting his brother Ruun'gaphuu, who limped along beside him, his many characteristic braids hanging in disarray before his face. Ahi'rea sighed with relief at the sight of them even as she worried at Ruun'gaphuu's injury.

They were like dark shades in the night—no torch or lamp lit the world around them and the only light came from the moon overhead. Ruun'daruun waved but did not call out. Haruu'na waved back, her silhouette now seeming smaller and a little bent. She labored for air but brushed off Ahi'rea's whispered concern. Fear clung to Ahi'rea still; what she had Seen before the fight could still come to pass.

The four of them headed to the nearby ruins—an ancient structure, little more than foundations, long forgotten in the grasslands and now used only by the Huumphar as a landmark and shelter.

Fifteen. Ahi'rea tallied the dead in her mind as she slipped amongst the tall grasses. *We counted twenty before the attack. I hope Naph'oin is all right.* She tried not to think about what she had Seen, what her dreams had told her. *Be wrong,* she thought. *Be wrong again.*

She reassured herself that he was fine. Naph'oin was their most accomplished warrior. Despite his age, there was no chance he would fall to a small group of soldiers, especially here in the plains. *He is probably smoking, making us worry just to tease us about the looks on our faces.* Dread grew in her by the second.

The four approached the ruin, stepping over the body of the soldier who had nearly killed Ahi'rea. The scent of blood hung in the night air despite the breeze. Circling the structure, they spotted a form reclining against the wall's remains not far ahead. Vaulting over a toppled column, Ahi'rea could see that it was Naph'oin. His decorated spear lay beside him and his long gray hair was unmistakable.

Something is wrong. Ahi'rea's heart began to pound. Naph'oin's hair was tangled and no smoke drifted from his nostrils. "He is hurt!" she hissed, dashing forward. She knelt by his side, whispering. "Naph'oin! Naph'oin!" Haruu'na and Ruun'daruun caught up and knelt as well while Ruun'gaphuu held himself up against the wall. Terror swept through Ahi'rea. *It is all happening. No, we can change this. Nothing is set.*

Naph'oin made a gurgling sound, blood running from his mouth. His hands clenched tight across his stomach and dark liquid seeped from between his gnarled fingers. His eyes, eyes Ahi'rea, Ruun'daruun, and Ruun'gaphuu had known since they were children, implored them to help him. Haruu'na opened a pouch at her side and began to pull out leather cords and herbs. She called for water. Ruun'daruun's waterskin was already in his hands. He passed it to Haruu'na and whispered to his grandfather, telling Naph'oin that he would be fine despite the fear in his voice. He put his own hands over the old man's, keeping pressure on the wound. Ahi'rea stood, unsure what more she could do to help and fearing that it would not matter even if she knew.

Naph'oin lurched forward, gripping Ruun'daruun's shoulders. Blood gushed from his stomach and ran from his mouth. His speech was mostly unintelligible, but he struggled to be understood. "South... they ran... ba-, back to the road..."

"Naph'oin—did they see you like this? Did you get away after you were wounded?" Haruu'na asked, dread in her voice.

He slumped back, eyes staring, and his blood-soaked hand

fumbled at the hem of Ahi'rea's skirt. "Stood right here... they saw. Don't give up..." he choked, and with a final gurgle, he ceased to breathe.

Ruun'daruun and Haruu'na worked feverishly, then stopped as it became clear that he was gone. Ahi'rea wept—he had been strength for their entire tribe. His words had guided their struggle for nearly three generations. Ruun'gaphuu sobbed beside her, fear and fatigue finally overcoming him. Haruu'na stood and stumbled a few steps away; Ruun'daruun remained where he had knelt, his grandfather's head now resting in his lap.

Little time passed before Haruu'na returned looking frailer than any of them could remember seeing her. Her voice, however, was strong. "We can't waste much time. Naph'oin's killers can't escape or we will lose our greatest ally—fear. To this day, none of them have seen any of us die and lived to tell it. They have to be stopped before they return. Their king grows stronger while our numbers dwindle. Some say Lasivar's son leads the fight against us, instead of for us. The western plains burn. If we are to have any hope of keeping our lands and our lives, they can't escape. If we wait for the rest of the warband to arrive, they'll get away."

"I'll go," Ruun'daruun said, standing. "They won't make it out of the plains."

Ahi'rea, dulling her sorrow with resolve, dried her eyes. "I am going too."

Ruun'daruun nodded and looked at Haruu'na. "My brother is hurt. Elder, can you stay with him here? The warband will be along in a day or so, and you can direct them after us."

Ruun'gaphuu jumped up, his face contorted with pain and anger. "No, Daruun! I'm going."

Haruu'na opened her mouth to speak, but Ruun'daruun cut her off. "You're in no condition! You will slow us down, and you will only get yourself hurt or killed."

"I'm going. Would you deny me vengeance for Grandfather?"

"No, Gaphuu, I wouldn't, but you can barely walk. I won't risk you going like this," Ruun'daruun said.

"Don't talk to me like I'm a child, Daruun. You'll have to bind me or kill me. I will go regardless of what you say, older brother or not."

Ruun'daruun saw the hard look in his brother's eyes and knew there would be no swaying him. He turned away, embarrassed and angry.

"Ruun'gaphuu," Haruu'na said, "you can't—" but the pain in his gaze stopped her from going on. Ahi'rea made no attempt to dissuade him. Ruun'gaphuu was resolved to go, and though she feared the worst for him, she said nothing. Even if he believed her visions, and he would, it would make no difference.

They were each silent for a moment. Ruun'gaphuu remained on his feet, ignoring his wounds. "We should see to Naph'oin," Haruu'na said. "I regret that we cannot see him on the Journey in the proper fashion, but we can at least start him on his way."

They set to work. Ahi'rea cleaned the old man's face and hair, chanting a blessing for his spirit and reciting what of his many deeds she could recall. The others worked in silence, letting Ahi'rea's voice surround them. They selected a spot high amidst the ruins and cleared away the grasses around it with their machetes. Ahi'rea's chant was wordless now, an ancient supplication in haunting tones to the spirits of their people. It echoed of wolves on the plains and the wind's whisper in the grasses, rising and falling like the breeze before a storm. Ruun'gaphuu and Ruun'daruun sought out small trees and scrub nearby, using their machetes to take them down. All the while, Ahi'rea's chant drew on, punctuated by the harsh chop of metal biting into dry wood. They laid brush and wood atop the wall and soon they lifted Naph'oin's body and laid him upon the humble pyre they had made.

The sun rose as they set flame to the pyre. Silent now, they watched the surrounding grasses, but Haruu'na and the brothers had been diligent in their brush-clearing. No fire caught in the plains. They watched the horizon, too, scanning for anyone coming to investigate the smoke. They saw no one, however, and each was alone with his or her thoughts as the smoke carried Naph'oin's spirit to the wind.

—

The summer sun beat down on the figures of the Huumphar as they loped across the plains. Ahi'rea and Ruun'daruun were ahead of the elderly Haruu'na and injured Ruun'gaphuu, scouting for enemies and searching for their foes' trail as they went.

They spoke little, conserving their breath to keep up their pace; their enemies had too great of a head start. The road was hard and packed, so there were few obvious signs of their passage. However, the trackers were certain that their prey would not stray far from the road.

Near the end of the day, they stopped to rest and consider their next move. Haruu'na and Ruun'gaphuu breathed heavily and from Ruun'gaphuu's face it was clear that he was in great pain.

He favored his left leg and his skin was drawn and pale, despite the exertion and heat. Ahi'rea put her hand on Ruun'gaphuu's shoulder. She concentrated, projecting feelings of relief, guiding his mind away from thoughts of pain—but there was little else to guide it to instead. She suggested they find a place to rest for a few hours. Neither Ruun'gaphuu nor Haruu'na argued and Ruun'daruun assented, though it was clear that he would rather move on.

Leaving the road, they found a thick stand of grasses to hide them from any southern scouts. Ruun'daruun searched out a spring and replenished their waterskins. The sun grew low and red. It was still hot. They sat cross-legged, drawing their grass capes over their heads as shade and shelter. Thin, short poles that they carried served as makeshift tent poles and held up the capes.

"We should move again soon," Ruun'daruun said. "Run at night and rest in the day." There came no reply; they all preferred that schedule as a matter of habit. Ahi'rea responded by shifting a little closer to Ruun'daruun, so that one of her knees touched his. She could almost sense his smile without seeing him—he never smiled broadly, but she knew him too well to think him dour, as many others did.

"I will tell Father what has happened," she said. Her cloak blocked her view, so if anyone had moved she didn't notice, but no sound met her ears save the south wind snaking through the yellowed blades around them. A comfortable warmth settled around her as the day's exertions made themselves felt, and she closed her eyes.

An old man turned to face her. His hair was gray and sprang, rough-chopped, like a dingy halo around his head. His eyes were a vibrant green, contrasting with the dark circles around them. A cautious smile hung on his lips as he spoke.

"Ahi'rea. You seem well enough. I sense you are not coming home as soon as we had hoped."

"Father. I am unhurt, but we are not well. Naph'oin... he was killed. We had to perform his Sending here, after the raid."

The smile faded from his face. He sighed and said nothing.

"Some of them escaped. If we do not track them down—"

"Yes, you must. They will lose their fear of us. You must go." His face grew stony. "Is anyone else hurt?"

Ahi'rea could see that he expected something in particular; it was difficult to read faces in the Dreaming, especially his. *What is it you know?* she wondered. *What are you afraid of?* "Ruun'ga-phuu," she answered. "I am worried about him, Father."

"He will not go home will he? Not after Naph'oin's death."

"No, he will not," she said. Her father said nothing. "He will not come back at all, will he?"

"The future is not set." There was defeat in her father's voice. "Rea," he continued, using her informal name, "things are in motion. A difficult time is ahead and you must meet it as it comes. But you can See what others cannot. Guide them. Your mother... cannot fight forever. Ruun'daruun is strong, but he is only one man. I See... our only choice is to go forward together, and someday..."

"No, Father. I have told you, Revik Lasivar is with them, not us. I have Seen him, heard the stories. Our allies in Cunabrel's realm saw him there not three months ago. He has been leading their armies, doing more to wipe us out than any other commander save Halkoriv's greatest ancestors. He is burning the land, Father."

Her father shook his head. His voice was a whisper. "Lasivar will come to aid us. I knew his mother and father, who led the fight against Halkoriv for many years, as his father did before him. Even if he is with Halkoriv, Lasivar will come to us when the time is right."

Ahi'rea broke in. "No, he will not. You depend too much on your Sight, Father, and not enough on the world. He has been fighting against us! Why would he turn against his master?"

Her father's eyes flared and she was silent. "You say I depend on the Sight too much, and daily, you spit on your gifts!" he snapped. "Without faith, where would we be?"

Ahi'rea could not contain herself. "Without faith, more of us might see reason!" Her voice thundered through the Dreaming.

He stared at her and began to fade. She tried to hold his gaze, but he turned away. "He will come to us. Soon," her father said. "Goodbye, Ahi'rea. May the winds guide your thoughts."

"Goodbye, Father," she answered, embarrassed at her own lack of respect. Her face was burning. He faded, and was gone.

She Saw a vision: she was in the plains at night. She saw Ruun'daruun, Ruun'gaphuu, and Haruu'na. All were bathed in glowing moonlight, so she could see clearly when her breath became visible as the temperature dropped. A black form rose up, blotting out the moon, absorbing its light. Ruun'gaphuu ran toward it, spear held high, and the others ran quickly after. Ahi'rea herself charged, but too late—Ruun'gaphuu fell stricken. Something stung her eyes and she realized a fine dust of ash was drifting down from the sky. Blinded, she heard her mother's cry of pain. She ran toward the sound, flailing, but struck nothing. Biting cold enveloped her, too cold to bear. She was overwhelmed, suffocating, unable to breathe but for the cold. All breath left her lungs and she gasped.

"Rea," came a quiet voice in her ear. She opened her eyes, a last shimmer of glowing green fading from them. Ruun'daruun was beside her, his black eyes searching her face. A nearly invisible smile crossed his face when she looked at him. Night had come while they rested.

Ruun'daruun stood, hefting his spear. She looked at him, admiring not for the first time his solid build and strong jaw, even his crooked nose and the scars on his arms and chest. Ruun'daruun had outlived many of those his age throughout their long struggle against Halkoriv and the South.

"You were dreaming. Dreaming and Seeing. I can always tell."

She stood, wrapping her woven cape around herself. "I was. How long were you watching me?"

"Not long," he said. "I couldn't sleep. Mostly I kept an eye to the road. Not a soul to be seen, although I did manage to get us a rabbit to cook later." He surveyed the horizon. "What did you See?"

She had hoped that he would see that she did not want to talk about it. Maybe he had not noticed, but it was more likely that he had, and had asked anyway. She sighed. "My father. I spoke to him, but…"

"You fought again."

"Yes. And I Saw… we have to be careful. This may be something more important than we thought."

"Southmen managing to kill one of our best and wisest is important. We're not turning back." His eyes were fire, a slow burn of anger and mourning that Ahi'rea knew he was holding back.

"I know, and I am not suggesting that we do. But we all must be careful. There is a danger ahead that we are not prepared for, and we may meet it very soon."

His face twisted. "Lasivar." Ahi'rea said nothing, but Ruun'daruun continued. "That hellspawn, Halkoriv, corrupted him. He's supposed to be with us. It's him, isn't it? Revik Lasivar was in your dream?"

She was silent. Many thought their dreams held hidden meaning—and most were wrong. Dreams from the Sight, however, were not really dreams. They were about instinct, and she was sure it was Lasivar. At the same time, instincts could be wrong, and visions of the future could be second-guessed. Allowing those who could not See to act on the dreams could lead to even greater danger and tragedy. She did not even want to try to verbalize the dream with something so sensitive. The words would not be hers, but the vision's. She hated the feeling of it, the loss of control, the dream-words filling her mouth and twisting her meaning. Even thinking about it, she could feel strange phrases forming on her tongue.

"I do not know." She tried to shake off the feeling. "Maybe it is. All I can tell you is that danger is ahead and none of us are safe. In the dream I was blinded. My Sight, perhaps, cannot be trusted for now—nor anyone's for that matter."

Ruun'daruun nodded, his jaw set. He could never understand Ahi'rea's secrecy regarding the dreams, but he always trusted what she said. She felt awful for not being more truthful. The Sight was a boon for short bursts of insight in the present, but Sight of the future was a curse.

"We should go," Ruun'daruun said. "The moon is high and

the light is good. These southmen have a head start, but we can close the gap tonight. I'll wake the others."

Ahi'rea readied herself and waited nearby. When all were prepared they started out, dashing along the road. Haruu'na and Ruun'gaphuu looked weary still—Ahi'rea tried not to dwell on it, knowing that only they could decide not to go on, and trusting them to say so. She choked on a single sob before she recovered herself. The others did not seem to notice.

—

"Keep moving!"

Bor looked up, sweat dripping from his face in the sun and his breath coming in gasps. His armor weighed on him as if it were lead and only made the heat more intolerable. Malskein and the others had stopped about fifty feet farther along the road and were now looking back at him. The commander, red-faced and dripping sweat, was staring back angrily. Even from that distance, Bor imagined he could see Malskein's little crooked rotten teeth, like an old dog's, bared in anger.

"Get going, pretty boy," Malskein shouted. "You're dead out here if the plainsfolk catch you, and we aren't waiting any longer." His shoulders heaved with his labored breathing.

How do they do it? Bor wondered. He stood up straight, legs burning, and checked his axe and shield. He would have tossed them away to lose the weight, but Commander Malskein would probably beat him senseless and leave him for dead if he did.

Bor put one foot in front of the other, already feeling ready to vomit. By the time he reached the others he had attained a labored jog. The four soldiers fell in around him.

And so they ran, stopping only when the sun was highest, with Bor and Hendeff setting the pace. They were thankful the other three bothered to slow down for them. Malskein seemed tireless, ignoring his own ragged breathing and sweat. Felsen and Harstet never even spoke, conserving their breath for the run.

Bor could not have imagined back in the spring that he would find himself in such dire straits. After setting the fires, he thought the plains would burn up in days; instead the fires lingered, spreading slowly. He had thought he would be sent home after the army took back Cunabrel's realm. Instead, he had been stationed there. After a month, Lord Lasivar and the newly-anointed Count Draden had taken direct command of their unit. It was then that they had been told they were going into the plains; not to pass through, but to conquer and hold them—for good. For the last two months they had traveled, seeing no plainsfolk, losing soldiers one by one in the night or during long marches. The heat had grown along with the army's frustrations until finally the Cheduna forces broke up into smaller squads. Even then, they had seen nothing of their enemies—until that night.

Over a full day had passed. They had run all night after Malskein had struck down the old plainsfolk by the ruin. Hendeff and Bor, elated to find that they were not ghosts or beasts, but men like any others, wanted to stay and fight the rest. "Idiots," Malskein had said. "There are four more of them, and we're on their turf, at night, without support. Run if you want to live a little longer, and follow me if you want to make it out of these plains alive."

Malskein had led them to his companions, and the five soldiers had fled. "They travel at night," Malskein had told them, "and so should we. We'll have to go half the day too, to keep our lead." And so they had, all night, half the next day, the following night, and this morning. Midday approached and finally Commander Malskein called a halt to rest. Bor collapsed just off the road. He thought he saw Hendeff fall nearby before he passed into unconsciousness.

They moved on starting at dusk. Bor felt as if he had barely closed his eyes. Hendeff was sick when they first woke. He vomited, then dry heaved. When Malskein threatened to beat him for wasting water, he forced himself to move on. As they ran, Malskein and his comrades discussed their chances, doing nothing to comfort Bor or Hendeff. *These must be some of the ones we heard about,* Bor thought. *They're lifers, men who won't leave the army till they die; the king's best soldiers, veterans of dozens of battles.* Bor prodded Hendeff as they ran. "Don't worry—they'll get us through this." He gulped air.

"I'd rather stand and fight than all this running. Those plainsfolk animals don't deserve anything but a quick death," Hendeff sputtered through gasping breaths. Bor nodded. Five of the plainsfolk had killed fifteen soldiers in a matter of minutes and lost only one of their own. Yes, they deserved death—for the king, for Feriven, and for their fallen comrades.

"Animals," Bor spat as he ran. He regretted the show of bravado when he thought about his empty waterskin.

Malskein reckoned they had another day's run ahead of them before they reached the nearest outpost. It was only a small village, little more than a garrison, but it had a good water supply and was close to the edge of the plains. The villagers put up with the demands of the soldiers stationed there as long as the plainsfolk were kept at bay. Even still, the plainsfolk occasionally tried to burn the settlement or run off with livestock.

Within minutes, however, the soldiers spotted a cart ahead, coming their way along the road. Four stout horses of the kind favored by farmers pulled the open cart, laden with sacks and crates. A small man with a wide hat sat at the reins. The soldiers continued toward the cart and Malskein ran ahead to stop the driver. The others watched as they spoke, the driver's voice rising in protest then falling off suddenly as Malskein interrupted. He then waved the others forward. As Bor watched, Felsen and Harstet started dumping the man's goods on the side of the road, clearing room in the cart. The driver would have protested again had Malskein not moved unnoticed behind the man, wrapped an arm around his throat, and squeezed until his eyes bulged and his frantic flailing stopped.

"What are you doing?" Bor cried as the driver choked.

"We can't carry him," Malskein answered, looking up from the driver. His voice was casual, as if he were talking about one of the sacks of flour being tossed out of the cart. "The plainsfolk did this, soldier. If we had left him here or let him continue, he'd have died much more slowly and painfully at their hands. We need this cart, and word of his death will galvanize the soldiers and villagers at the outpost." Malskein dropped the limp body beside the road and gestured to the cart. "Get in."

Bor seethed, clenching his teeth. He knew Malskein was right, knew that there was a reason that he had survived for so long. There was little else that could be done. Bor clambered into the small cart. *That was an act of kindness*, he told himself.

—

Rushing at top speed, the Huumphar spotted a cluster of unusual silhouettes down the road, picked out in the rising moonlight. Without a word, the four of them left the road and approached them through the grasses, keeping low and quiet. They found a pile of discarded sacks and crates, some broken open or spilled, and an elderly man, dead, face down in the road dust. "Only a few hours ago," Ruun'daruun said after inspecting the body. "And these tracks—I think our prey have found transport." Ruun'gaphuu swore, casting his eyes over the ground. Ruun'daruun was silent, staring down the road. Ahi'rea studied the injured brother; his breathing was poor and the wound on his leg was growing worse with each step. The bindings they had changed only hours before were black with blood and dirt. She could say nothing. Knowledge of his impending death would never convince him to turn back. He looked up and caught her eye as she studied him.

"What?" Ruun'gaphuu asked.

His question shook her from her thoughts. "Nothing," she answered. "Just thinking."

Still worried, Ruun'gaphuu glanced around at the rest of the group. "Well, let's go. We're wasting time while they widen their lead." Ruun'daruun nodded, and the four started running again, following the cart tracks south.

—

The cart drew through the outpost's border as dawn crept over the grasslands. Low earthen buildings lined the rutted street.

The outpost's single shop was opening, displaying sundries and trade goods. The garrison, the only walled wooden structure in the village, stood directly ahead, towering among the smaller structures, partially veiled by the thin streams of smoke issuing from their sod rooftops. Maroon and gold flags fluttered in the smoke. The garrison's wooden walls were topped with jagged timber sharpened to points and the gate stood closed. Its blocky shape made it even starker against the slumped earthen houses of the village. Soldiers standing atop the garrison pointed and called orders as the cart approached. The villagers, already about their day's chores in the streets, ignored them.

Creaking and rumbling, the cart pulled up to the garrison. They were soon inside and Malskein met with the commander while Bor, Hendeff, and the others found food and water. They were bombarded with questions by the few dozen men stationed there. Bor and Hendeff told them about the fight and the long run from danger, but Harstet and Felsen remained taciturn.

Within an hour orders had been issued. The village was to be guarded and barriers erected around its borders. The north road was to be watched. No strangers were to enter and no travelers to pass unchallenged. Word amongst the men was that the plainsfolk were the advance scouts of a large warparty and that they would come for the survivors of the raid. The men were anxious. They'd seldom, if ever, fought plainsfolk before—none among them save the new arrivals had stood face to face with one and gone unscathed, and they had never seen any of them dead. All had lost friends and compatriots to their spears or machetes.

The usual rumors sprang from one soldier to the next; they were ghosts, or shapeshifters, even demons. Those who fell in battle were revived within minutes without their wounds. Bor and Hendeff, weak and exhausted but already regaining their confidence, tried to reassure the others. Hendeff was full of genuine bluster but Bor's waned even as he spoke of courage. He remembered the terror of the night attack, the hopelessness he felt as one after the other, his squad fell around him.

Malskein gathered the men in the garrison yard before noon. Hot sun on their heads and backs, they listened as he outlined their situation.

"It's likely those plainsfolk dogs are already outside. Keep watchful, but they probably won't move until dusk or after dark. At that time, they'll enter the village and kill whoever they find alone, so stay together. They will wipe out this outpost, both in revenge for the dead, and to keep the myth that they are unstoppable, that these plains are theirs."

"Make no mistake—they are not men. They are vermin! But these rats are clever, cunning. They can smell your fear, and they will use it. They know the stories about them, and they love 'em. If we're going to survive, we've got to last out this night unharmed."

Malskein paused, surveying the faces around him. Many of the soldiers were resolute, hearing his matter-of-fact speech, but many still looked fearful. "Tomorrow," he said, "we'll show them that their terrorizing of people, people like your families, won't continue. We'll meet them on the plains, in the light of day, and show them who these lands really belong to."

—

"What should we do?"

Ahi'rea looked around at the other three. Haruu'na was once again about to speak when Ruun'gaphuu cut in.

"We shouldn't give them the chance to even think. I say we go in tonight in pairs and kill as many as we can. Prepared or not, if we catch them in pairs or alone, they won't stand a chance."

Haruu'na spoke, her voice old and dry like burning brush. "If what Ahi'rea has Seen comes to pass, they'll be waiting for just that. It's too easy for them to lay a trap for us."

"Then what do you suggest?" Ruun'daruun asked. "If we confront that many of them on the plains, in broad daylight as they plan, we'll be overwhelmed. I agree with Ruun'gaphuu. Our hope lies in stealth."

They fell silent. The sun beat down above them. Insects buzzed in the grasses and Ahi'rea could just make out the sounds of the outpost's activity to the south.

"Then we should do something they have not planned on," Ahi'rea said. "We will not go in, and we will not confront them— not in the way they expect." She explained her thoughts, and the others agreed, adding details of their own and questioning hers. A plan began to emerge as the three younger Huumphar spoke while Haruu'na looked on in silence.

—

Hendeff pushed the support into place and another soldier took to it with a sledge, hammering the post up against the over-turned cart. Others began to pile dirt at its base and Bor relaxed as the post took the weight of the cart. He stood back, inspecting their makeshift barricade. A shout reached his ears over the scrape of the spades and he turned. Behind him, Malskein was already waiting as the shouting soldier ran to meet him.

"Commander Malskein! A messenger just arrived, badly hurt by the plainsfolk—they're trying to cut off our communications. He says reinforcements are on their way. Revik Lasivar is leading them from the south. He says the king knew what was to come and has sent his aid."

—Six—

The night was long and tense, but the plainsfolk were neither seen nor heard. No attack came.

In the morning, messengers were sent to meet the reinforcements coming from the south. Though they waited for daylight and were given fast horses, they were not even out of sight of the makeshift barricades before they fell from their mounts, one by one. Others were about to be sent out to ascertain their fates, but Malskein intervened. He commanded that no more men be sent out until the plainsfolk were dealt with. The garrison captain was furious. He took Malskein aside and they spoke in low, heated tones. When they returned to the barricades, the captain was pale. No more messengers were sent.

The men were gathered and armed. All but a few defenders set out to confront the plainsfolk. "Do exactly as I say, when I say it. No questions," Malskein told them. "Don't hesitate. Don't think. Just act. You will live through this if you can do that."

Bor once again found himself amongst the waving blades of grass, almost as high as he was tall. Surrounded by soldiers, led by Malskein and his companions, he felt sure that they would find and kill the plainsfolk.

They marched, spread out but within sight of their fellows. A breeze blew from the south and the men could see dark clouds in the distance, though the sun was bright and hot above them. Though they tried to appear confident of success, the tension among the soldiers was palpable.

They circled the garrison, staying close together; at first they swept their weapons through the grasses or surrounded likely hiding spots, but after an hour of searching, there was no sign of their enemies. Without sight or sound of them, many of the men supposed the plainsfolk had run off. They began to joke and call out. Some mocked the plainsfolk and some mocked each other for their fear. Yet unease clung to Bor's mind and grew stronger with each passing moment.

They were beginning their second pass around the village when a pair of spears flew out of the grass, driving into two men and knocking them from their feet. As they fell, the others cried out in sudden panic, whirling about and raising shields. "Over there!" someone shouted, pointing, as two camouflaged forms rushed away through the grass. Several of the soldiers lunged, following them into the brush. Malskein called for them to stop but his orders were drowned out by panic and shouting. Some of the pursuers heard him and returned, but three men kept running.

"Damn fools!" Malskein called after them as they rushed away. "Let's go." He gestured for the remaining men to follow him. "Slow! Keep your shields up and your eyes sharp." He issued orders for some men to watch behind, others the front. They followed the three who had rushed away, with Malskein in the lead. Bor found himself just behind him. They had not gone a dozen steps before they heard screams, one after the other.

Some of the men began to push ahead, but Malskein stopped them with a wave. "Keep together. They're already dead, and you'll join them if you break ranks." He kept their pace slow and steady. A step at a time, the squad made their way through the waving blades of grass. Through their quiet rustling, they heard a call for help.

"They're alive." Bor kept his voice low as he scanned the grasses. "One is, anyway."

"Some kind of trick," Malskein muttered. "Go on ahead and find out if you like." Bor held ranks.

They found the wayward soldiers. They lay on the ground, moaning or crying out. There was no blood, no open wounds. All three had broken legs, their limbs gruesomely twisted.

"Look." Malskein pointed at the ground. There were holes all around, disguised by the grasses, just wide enough for a man's leg to slip inside.

One of the fallen soldiers grasped at Bor's trousers. Bor looked down, then looked back up at Malskein and moved his leg away, keeping his eyes to the plains. Several of the soldiers moved forward to help their fellows, but Malskein and his companions remained alert.

"Careful." Felsen broke his usual silence. "They haven't gone far."

Without warning, two more spears flashed out of the grasses and tore into fresh victims. Malskein called out to the men and tried to maintain their formation, but in the brief panic another soldier slipped into one of the holes. His leg snapped above the shouting and his screams drilled into their ears. The men were thus distracted, frightened, and reacted far too slowly when Ruun'daruun leapt into their midst.

Machete flashing, he cut down two soldiers and vanished, ripping a spear from a corpse as he went. "Stand down!" Malskein shouted as a few of the soldiers moved to give chase. "Shields!"

They saw no enemies. They hesitated. A spear shot back along the path of the fleeing plainsfolk, stopping halfway through the chest of one of the soldiers.

Malskein's orders rang out one after the other. "Don't think, just move!" They formed up defensively, shields making a wall. No more enemies appeared. Malskein made a quick count and found that nearly half of the force was dead or wounded. He ordered them to return to the village, dragging the wounded but leaving the dead against the protests of the other soldiers.

—

That night, the Huumphar sat some distance from the village, not far from the road, watchful for riders to or from the south.

Ruun'gaphuu's wound was worse, and while he agreed to sleep instead of take a watch he refused the others' insistence that he start back to the tribe. "The ones who killed our grandfather still live. I'm staying." Ahi'rea knew it didn't matter. The wound was too grave and Ruun'gaphuu had gone too long without rest or proper treatment. *The future is not set,* she told herself. Still, she knew he was going to die. There was nothing she could do but hope that, when the time came, he would have the chance to make his ancestors proud. She rested, sleeping while she could.

Ahi'rea awoke, her head on Ruun'daruun's chest. She knew by the moon that it was almost time for her watch. She gently moved Ruun'daruun's arm and stood, feeling the growing south wind on her skin. The clouds had almost caught the moon; by Ruun'daruun's watch, it would be hidden and the plains would be at their darkest.

Ahi'rea approached Haruu'na, sitting with her cloak wrapped around her. Haruu'na looked up at Ahi'rea's quiet steps behind her and smiled. Although the night was pleasant and cool to Ahi'rea, her mother looked as if she was cold.

Ahi'rea sat beside her, laying her spear to the side, close at hand. They were quiet for a while until she spoke.

"What is wrong, Mother?"

Haruu'na smiled. "It's impossible, even for me, to hide anything from you." She paused. "Nothing's wrong, exactly." She leaned into her daughter.

Ahi'rea was struck once again by how much her mother had shrunk in her age. She was still larger than Ahi'rea, but not as much as she remembered.

"I'm just thinking a lot these past days, Rea." Haruu'na fell quiet again.

Ahi'rea said nothing, but felt her breathing change and wondered if Haruu'na had noticed.

"This is a dangerous time. Things will change soon, and I'm not sure how." Haruu'na changed the subject. "The rest of the warband will be here soon. I hope it's before the southmen can send reinforcements."

"Please—do not leave me," Ahi'rea whispered.

"I'm not going anywhere." Haruu'na lay where she was and slept. Ahi'rea wondered if she had only pretended to misunderstand.

Ahi'rea's watch passed. Before she knew it, the moon had nearly crossed the night sky, vanishing behind the heavy clouds being borne up by the southern wind.

A voice, quiet and close, startled her. "Strange for the wind to blow so steadily from day to night." Ruun'daruun sat beside her—she had not noticed his approach. She would be angry with herself, but she also knew he was the stealthiest and fastest in the tribe. His hand felt good as it rested on hers. "It looks like a storm coming up from the south. I hope the Cheduna are dead by the time it arrives."

"The wind is unusual," Ahi'rea answered. "I would even say unnatural. I think Halkoriv is watching us, but I do not know why."

"Perhaps he's tired of us slaying his men each time they set foot in our home. When the warband comes and we wipe out this outpost and move on to the others, maybe he'll finally come here and face us. I've told your father and the other elders that this isn't enough. We can't just defend our own land, they'll just keep sending more—"

"I know," Ahi'rea said. "And I, and they, have told you that's all we can do. We cannot leave our lands. We are too few as it is."

"They'll just keep whittling us down." Ruun'daruun stared at his lap. "They lose a dozen or so to each of us, but Halkoriv doesn't care. We are too few, but we're going to die here unless we do something big. Taking these outposts… it's not enough."

They were both quiet for a few minutes until Ruun'daruun looked back to her. "Lasivar is coming this time, isn't he?" Ahi'rea nodded. "What could have happened to him? His family was fighting the southerners—and winning. My grandfather, your father and mother, they once fought under Lasivar's parents' banner. And now, Lasivar fights for Halkoriv. Ever since he came, it's been worse. Tribes have been driven out, whole swaths of the western plains burned, and more still aflame. Before him, Halkoriv was stalled at the borders. I heard that a whole tribe was just wiped out in the west."

"That's impossible." Tribes had died out before, but from disease or famine. Ahi'rea could not think of any time that southerners had killed a whole tribe since the great wars of the past.

"Still, it's what I've heard. And I heard that Lasivar was behind it."

"It feels wrong, every time I See him," Ahi'rea said. "Twisted somehow, by Halkoriv's sorcery maybe. There is a... a dark presence with him, as if it is not really him at all. Like it is only some evil riding him." *And it is coming here.*

"Maybe if we kill him, Halkoriv will finally come himself." Ruun'daruun sounded hopeful.

Ahi'rea nodded, thinking about the old stories of Lasivar's ancestors, the heroes who once fought alongside the Huumphar and the Gharven to the north. She thought of the warnings she had heard from those few who had survived the new Lasivar's fires, and the stories they had heard of his ancestors. *If the powers his family commands have not been exaggerated, it is we who will be dead by the time that storm arrives.*

—

They came before dawn: three dozen warriors from their tribe as well as two others, like ghosts over the whispering grasses. Ruun'daruun, his watch about halfway over, spotted them in the moonlight as they approached without word or sound.

Those of their own tribe were horrified to learn of Naph'oin's death; the others gave wishes for his spirit and their swift vengeance. In the early dawn hours they whispered and planned. It was assumed that those inside the garrison would not venture out again until reinforcements came, so the Huumphar decided to enter soon, without warning, before the southmen learned of their bolstered numbers.

Rain began to fall—the morning was dark with clouds and the south wind grew heavy, buffeting the Huumphar. With rainwater chilling her skin and running into her eyes, Ahi'rea checked her weapons as the Huumphar spread out into small groups, heading back toward the garrison. She ran beside Ruun'daruun, who spared her a grim smile and a squeeze of her hand before focusing once more on the coming fight. Haruu'na was behind them—she had said little since their conversation during the night. Ruun'gaphuu had been quiet as well—he avoided Ahi'rea, as if even the sight of her made him nervous.

The rain grew from a steady fall to a torrent. Dashing through the grass and rain, Ahi'rea and Ruun'daruun were joined by Khan'an, a warrior of their tribe. He was known for his sharp eyes and swift feet, even though he was nearly ten years Ruun'daruun's senior. There was a time when he had resented Ruun'daruun, as many had, but he had come to respect his skill in battle and tactics.

"Rider." Khan'an fell into step with them. "Alone, to the south. Be here in minutes."

"Just an advance scout. The rest must be on their way. Take him down," Ruun'daruun said.

Khan'an nodded once and disappeared back into the rain.

—

Bor stood, miserable, on the narrow walkway near the top of the garrison's sturdy wall. It had seemed safe and secure when he had first entered, but now even he could tell it was meant to deter attacks, not stop them. The rain pelted his helmet and the thin leather cape draped over his armor. The layers were stifling even in the chill wind. Rain dripped down his face and worked its way under his armor, mixing with the sweat on his neck and arms.

Crossbow in hand, he faced the south end of the village. One of the local garrison soldiers was standing a dozen feet away, equally weary and wretched. As Bor looked at him, a strange sense of foreboding overtook him. The rain made it nearly impossible to see the spears that, moments later, hurtled up through the downpour. Ripping into their target, they lifted the soldier off his feet before Bor's eyes. The spears drove him back off of the earthen embankment and sent him rolling and sliding through the mud and scree. Bor turned back to the wall and raised his crossbow. He saw a dark form rushing along the ground below. He fired but the figure was already moving in anticipation, twisting to one side even as a spear left its hand. Bor saw flashing green eyes, a demon's eyes, through the rain. The last thing he remembered was opening his mouth to cry for help.

—

Ahi'rea estimated that there were less than twenty soldiers remaining. The battle was short, quiet, and bloody. Seventeen southerners were accounted for in short order. When Ruun'gaphuu pointed out that two of those they had been hunting were not among the dead and wounded, the Huumphar left the silent garrison.

"There, on the road!" someone shouted. Two figures could be seen making haste to the south, discernable only to the keenest-eyed among the Huumphar. The southern sky was dark, but the first glimmers of sun shone in the east, glittering red through the heavy black raindrops driven on the wind.

Ruun'daruun, Ahi'rea, Ruun'gaphuu, and a dozen others ran after them, determined that the two soldiers not escape again. Despite his injury, Ruun'gaphuu stayed on the road and outdistanced those who chose the cover of the grass to either side. Ahi'rea hung back, a warning growing in her mind, but she stayed within sight of the others.

She saw Ruun'gaphuu raise his spear and hurl it, taking one of the fleeing men low in the leg. He hadn't even stopped rolling before Ruun'gaphuu's machete chopped into him as he raced past. Dark blood mixed with rain beside the still-shuddering body as Ahi'rea passed it a second later. She paused only to glance at its face, looking for that crooked-toothed grimace, but the dead man was not the commander.

Still pressing ahead, Ruun'gaphuu screamed a challenge in Cheduna, the southern tongue, but the fleeing man did not answer it nor slow his pace.

What Ahi'rea saw next, however, sent a chill straight through her. Far down the road, the single horseman Khan'an had seen and gone to dispatch came into view through the roiling clouds. It was no scout. He rode straight and tall in the saddle, unperturbed by the lashing rain and the wind blowing up behind him. *No—not un-*

perturbed, Ahi'rea realized, *but untouched.* At first he was barely a shade through the gray torrent, but his form was growing and darkening. Shadow clung to him, surrounded him, soon picking him out in stark relief, a towering lightless form against the dawn-lit rain. Tendrils of shadow lashed violently from him, reaching up and out, spreading all around him. The fleeing soldier ran on but Ruun'gaphuu slowed, gaping. *Lasivar*, Ahi'rea thought.

Ruun'daruun left the grasses by the roadside, followed by Haruu'na and the others. The soldier, now passed by the horse-man, was lost to view. Lasivar drew his sword, enveloped in shift-ing blackness, and made straight for the gathered Huumphar.

"He's attacking," Ruun'daruun breathed. "Alone."

Ahi'rea reached the others, spear and machete in hand. "Scatter!" She startled them from their awed inaction. "You, left," she gestured to some of the warriors. "And you, right. Spears first, then surround him! Wait for my signal."

Half of the Huumphar vanished into the grasses. Ruun'daru-un readied his spear along with Haruu'na and the others, squinting through the rain driving into his face. Lasivar was mere seconds away; Ahi'rea could see his shining black and gold armor, the sil-ver blade with the garnet pommel held over his head. She could see his pale face, filled with bloodlust. His eyes met hers and he raised the sword higher as he crossed the remaining distance.

Revulsion welled up in her as he drew closer. The lashing darkness around him sickened her—his very existence seemed wrong. "Now!" she cried, raising her spear.

Spears flew from all sides. Ruun'gaphuu sprang forward and Haruu'na drew her machete.

Ahi'rea watched as Revik Lasivar, alone against a force that would terrify an entire legion of Cheduna soldiers, rode into the midst of the Huumphar and smiled.

The spears splintered in mid-flight, crumbling like so much rotten timber. Revik dived from his saddle with unnatural speed as Ruun'gaphuu's machete passed through the space where he had sat. Whirling about, Ruun'gaphuu lunged to strike again. Revik's arm shot out and his hand clenched into a fist; though he was untouched, Ruun'gaphuu stumbled as blood erupted from his injured leg and from his face and throat. He took two more steps, then collapsed in the mud. Revik laughed as he turned to face the other Huumphar.

Ruun'daruun howled, a wordless scream of rage and anguish. He charged through the rain with Haruu'na at his side, her eyes alight. Those to the sides left their cover, converging on the lone warrior. Ahi'rea was still, but her eyes burned with a green flame as she forced herself not to attack. She wanted to shout to them, tell her people to defend themselves, just hold him off, but she needed all her concentration. Something was wrong—something in the corner of her Sight flickered and flashed around her enemy.

Revik lifted his sword. Huge bloody welts raised themselves on Ruun'daruun even as he charged. He fell face down in the road before he knew what was happening. He sputtered blood and muddy water and his agonized body refused to respond. A low, overpowering buzz filled the air before three Huumphar were shorn in half, one after the other, though Revik was still a spear's length away. Another let his machete fall only to find it buried in the back of one of his kin. Two more fell victim to Revik's sword as if they were stalks of wheat before the scythe. Haruu'na chopped down into empty space; as she turned her head to follow Revik's movement she saw him throw his hand out again and watched a tangle of skin and bloody bone ripped from another warrior by the inky tendrils lashing around them. She was thus distracted when Revik whirled back to face her and his blade took her in the stomach up to the hilt.

Ahi'rea's concentration almost broke, but she forced herself to remain still and cold. She pushed out her mother's scream and the cries of the dying, blinded herself to the blood and death. She allowed herself only one thought; *Find it, before we all die.*

She didn't even know what it was for which she searched—the flicker eluded her. *He is too fast… too perfect. No one can fight like that, son of heroes or not, not with Self, Sight, or Storm.*

Then she caught it. She held the knowledge of it in her mind.

Lasivar's eyes, joyful in his bloodlust, met hers. He approached, cutting down another of her friends, her family, and yet Ahi'rea did not move.

A pale glimmer, light and dark entwined, surrounded him. It flashed in her Sight, a flickering void, and it was that sight to which she held. She saw all its lines and connections, its facets and seams. Whatever it was, it supported him, bolstered him, lent him speed and strength and terrible power. She had the sensation of gnashing teeth, ravenous jaws. Whatever it was, it terrified her more than anything she had ever known.

Ahi'rea tensed her body, waiting as he drew within reach, as he raised his sword. *It expects me to hit him. If I try to strike him, it will save him and he will kill me.* When Lasivar was only paces away, she sprang. The battle grew silent around her; the rain lashed against her skin. She focused all the energy she knew, all she could, into her spear. One arm extended, she drove the spear forward, bringing it down with a focus she had never known before in battle.

She aimed not for Lasivar, but for the thing around him, the horrifying presence that hung over him like a shroud.

The spear's blade whistled through the air, then jolted as if stricken though it appeared to hit only air. Ahi'rea's arm felt as if it would shatter. Shadow screamed from Lasivar, and green light burst from Ahi'rea and surrounded them and burned the shadow away. The lines vanished, the facets cracked, the seams torn.

The spear drove into the mud, just beside and behind Revik. His sword continued its arc, and Ahi'rea saw the blade coming toward her. Just as it was about to reach her, Lasivar faltered, stumbling forward. The blow still caught her in the arm, sinking deep into her flesh. She fell back into the mud as Revik caught himself and came forward again, his steps less sure.

The shade hanging around him was gone. Two of the remaining Huumphar struck, driving their spears toward him. Revik swung to parry with one hand and thrust the other out at the second plainsfolk, who stumbled and doubled over. His parry, though skilled, was the slowest they had yet seen him move.

—

Revik had a moment to wonder how he had failed before the spear flashed past his sword and drove deep into his gut. He fell to his knees, sword dropping from his hand as he clutched at the weapon, gasping and gritting his teeth. He could not move. His power was gone. The woman, meanwhile, picked herself up, snarling through the pain of her wounded arm. *What has she done?*

—

Ahi'rea regarded the remaining Huumphar, now gathering around the fallen Southerner. He had killed so many. She tossed her spear, steaming and cracked, aside into the grass. Then she looked at Revik, still kneeling and pulling at the spear in his stomach.

"What did you do?" another Huumphar asked. "What happened?"

"I—I am not sure." Ahi'rea clutched her arm, trying to focus enough to heal it.

"Should we finish him?" the spearman asked, twisting the weapon lightly, causing Revik to cry out. "It's him, isn't it? Lasivar? This is the one who's been leading Halkoriv's armies, burning our lands the last few months. We should kill him now, before he uses his black magic to recover."

"No," Ahi'rea said. "I do not think he will recover. He is nothing now. Halkoriv laid a spell on him, was supporting him somehow. Still…" she said, kneeling to tend to the shuddering and choking spearman on the ground, "we may need him."

The remaining Huumphar searched the fallen for survivors. The spearman on the ground beside Ahi'rea began to recover. She stood again over Revik, waiting, while Ruun'daruun staggered first to Ruun'gaphuu, then Haruu'na. He knelt beside the old woman for a moment, then wept.

Ahi'rea stared at Revik, blood running in thick rivulets down her arm. Something told her he was more valuable alive than dead.

Logic told her to end him now—he was an enemy and would be a burden to guard. Instinct won out. If nothing else, he would answer fully for what he had done.

Drawing herself up, she lashed out with her foot, catching Revik full in the face and knocking him back. He did not rise.

"Take him. Take our wounded. We have to go." She tore a strip from Revik's cloak to bind her arm. The Huumphar complied and they headed east under the still-dark sky.

—Seven—

Too many of them had died, and too many were wounded. The Huumphar had planned to go on to harry more garrisons and kill or drive off more southern soldiers. They could not hope to face a massed force from the south, as they had in the past. They were too few to risk a large battle.

The previous attempt by Halkoriv to wipe them out in one blow had been decades ago, and had been disastrous for the Cheduna. For weeks the army had chased the Huumphar about the plains until the Cyclone, called by the elder Lasivar and his wife, Hera, descended on the southerners. It had been the greatest display of power Ahi'rea had ever heard of—a massive storm of lightning and tornadoes that came upon the soldiers from nowhere. The Huumphar fighters had swooped in on the scattered, tired, and injured troops like birds of prey, killing thousands before the army managed to escape and regroup.

After that, Halkoriv had grown more cunning and more powerful. Instead of soldiers, he plagued the Huumphar with magic; their children grew sick and weak; fewer and fewer babies were born each year. The Huumphar women were struck barren and the men impotent. The old fell to senility, the young to disease.

Now there were few tribes left. They gathered when they could, otherwise remaining hidden and on the move. They hit southern caravans, small guard posts and garrisons; they harried any troops that came to the plains, but they never attacked when the risks were too great. Things had only gotten worse in recent months. They had wondered what was different, and learned that the change occurred when the new commander, Revik, took control of the campaigns in the plains. He was ruthless. The plains burned. He had been untouchable.

Until now. Ahi'rea's mind raced along with her as she led the Huumphar away from the garrison.

The plan to gather and wipe out the Cheduna garrisons had been Ruun'daruun's. He was convinced that a group of Huumphar could go south, make their way in secret to Halkoriv's fortress, and kill him. The garrison attacks, he hoped, would divert Halkoriv's attention and draw the armies away. Most of the elders did not agree, but Ahi'rea's father had surprised her by convincing them to allow the series of attacks.

So many dead. Eleven Huumphar had been killed, and another was likely to die on the move. Others still were unable to fight, perhaps ever again; for a warrior of the Huumphar, it was a fate too terrible to bear.

Ahi'rea looked back at Ruun'daruun; he could barely walk, let alone run. Still he pushed on, grimacing in pain with every step, his welts cracking and running. Despite his pain, his eyes were stony and cold. He had lost a brother, a grandfather, and many friends. *So many dead.* Ahi'rea knew that the elders would never trust him again. It was over. They would sit and wait in the plains, be hunted down, grow old and weak and sick until they were nothing. It was over.

Ahi'rea ran at the head of the troupe of Huumphar. The sun was growing higher and warmer behind the clouds, making the air sticky and thick. The grasses were still wet with rain around them, drooping and sick-looking. Behind her, two others carried their prisoner, the man she knew was Revik, son of Lasivar.

She tried to push thoughts of what had happened from her mind. Her mother's face appeared before her eyes and she choked back a sob and banished the image. *You can't run and cry, not at the same time. Keep going. Cry later. Someone has to lead now.*

She organized her thoughts, trying to occupy her mind. The first priority was to find somewhere to hole up and tend the wounded. If the man being carried behind her was indeed Lasivar, the lost son of the great leader from the North, then he would be traveling with a larger group—a much larger group. They would be close behind, with trackers. The Huumphar needed somewhere to hide, or more would die. They would all die.

She found herself fighting against her own thoughts. She could not concentrate, could not even let her mind drift, let her Sight wander. Every time she tried, she saw Ruun'gaphuu, or Haruu'na, or the others. She struggled, but the more she tried, the more her tears welled, the more her breath grew ragged, her thoughts and emotions running rampant. Desperation began to take her. *We need a place to hide!*

Ahi'rea jumped as a hand touched her shoulder. She wiped her arm across her eyes as she turned and stifled a gasp. She had not yet had a close look at Ruun'daruun's face since the attack.

His eyes were dark, red with tears and anger. The welts and sores covering his skin were running with blood, joining like a network of tributaries into rivers running down his neck and chest.

"What do we do now?" He struggled to speak, his voice rasping and pained.

Ahi'rea's hopes that Ruun'daruun had an idea were dashed. She did not answer, concentrating on running for a moment and trying once more to pull herself together.

"I know a place we can hide," someone called up from behind them. Looking over her shoulder, Ahi'rea saw that the speaker was Tak'la, the one Lasivar had nearly killed even after Ahi'rea severed the spell binding him. He was a young warrior who had joined them from his own tribe, who were all lost to disease and war. A disturbingly-colored bruise covered his torso, but he seemed not to notice.

Tak'la was young, but tall and broad, among the biggest of the warriors. Despite his wound, he kept pace behind those carrying Lasivar, watchful for signs that he was waking. Increasing his pace, he caught up with Ruun'daruun and Ahi'rea. Ruun'daruun kept his distance from the youth; Tak'la was the death-touched, the last survivor of a dead tribe. He had been wounded, but lived on when the rest of his people had died; it was said death clung to such survivors like a sickness. He had been allowed to join their tribe, but few would dare speak to him or touch him.

"There's an old southern homestead, not far from here. It doesn't look like much, but there's an underground room which broke through to some caves. Anyone looking for us should just pass the old ruin by, or if they do try to get in they'll bottleneck at the cave."

"And trap us inside." Ruun'daruun glared at the youth. "We wouldn't survive."

Tak'la shook his head. "There's at least one other exit from the caves that comes up some distance away, in the Kan Manif Bur. We can lose them in the caves easily and escape through the canyons if we have to."

Ruun'daruun scowled and concentrated on the run again. "Kan Manif Bur is bordered by mountains and ocean. Those canyons would be a deathtrap if they followed us there."

Ahi'rea thought as she ran. It was the best chance they had to avoid pursuit and rest. "We need somewhere to rest. Tak'la, lead the way." Ruun'daruun looked at her, but said nothing.

Ahi'rea was grateful for Tak'la's suggestion. After the disastrous fight, she felt lost but would be expected to take charge by some and considered vulnerable by others. She might have to fend off others who would now seek to gain control of the warband. Now she at least felt that there was some sort of plan.

—

The Huumphar concealed the mouth of the cave with brush and debris from the abandoned structure above. Those with skill in healing tended the wounded while others guarded the entry. The only light came from a few thin rays streaming through nearly imperceptible holes in the earthen ceiling.

Mats of roots hung about the stony cave's ceiling like curtains, dividing it into many separate areas. The stone was yellow and red, and the floor was sandy. Somewhere, water trickled and the sound echoed through the cave in the silence.

Ahi'rea sat with Ken'hra and Ondoo'shaa, the two leaders of the tribes that had joined the warparty. Tak'la's tribe had spent much of their time in this area, so Ahi'rea had invited him to join her in meeting with Ken'hra and Ondoo'shaa. She inspected her companions; she had met them before, but not spent much time with them.

Ken'hra was more than a decade older than Ahi'rea, a respected warrior and tribal leader of the Whispered Thunder tribe. Her long, wavy hair was streaked by the sun and had only just begun to show any gray. She had suffered a grazing cut in the fighting and displayed a bright red line across the bridge of her nose and left cheek. She paced, frowning and inspecting the notched blade of her machete.

Ondoo'shaa was the only survivor of the warriors from the High Sun tribe. He had lost his daughter along with the rest of his warriors, but had avoided injury himself. He was large-framed and powerful-looking despite his advancing years. His eyes burned with his loss. Seated, he gripped his spear with white-knuckled fists. Following his gaze, Ahi'rea saw that he was staring not at a curtain of roots, but at who lay unconscious just behind it.

"We cannot stay long," Ahi'rea said, drawing Ken'hra's attention. Ondoo'shaa's eyes remained fixed on Lasivar. "Even if the Cheduna are not tracking us now, they will be soon if our prisoner is who I think he is."

Without turning his gaze, Ondoo'shaa spoke. "Before we left, I heard that this Lasivar wiped out two tribes in the west. Killed them all." He looked up at Ahi'rea. "If they are searching for him, we should just kill the murdering hellspawn now."

Ken'hra scoffed. "Don't speak nonsense. No Cheduna commander has managed something like that for decades."

"And still, it has happened. He wiped them out." Ondoo'shaa

looked back toward Lasivar. "I will do it, if none of you are willing."

Ahi'rea shook her head. "If he is Lasivar's son, we... we cannot kill him. Not yet."

Ondoo'shaa jumped up. "Why? Instead of disposing of him, you are healing him. This is idiocy. Our own people are wounded and we are being hunted, and you are wasting our time and supplies on this worthless beast from the south." His voice boomed through the caves.

Ahi'rea hesitated, unsure how to respond. She was once again spared by Tak'la's intervention. "Quiet, fool!" The youth rose to his full height and his head brushed the cavern's earthen ceiling. "You'll bring the Cheduna right to us. Do you want to kill us all?"

Ondoo'shaa pressed close to Tak'la. In the dark, their two silhouettes blocked out the light. "Know your place, boy," he hissed back. His eye level reached Tak'la's shoulders, but he was uninjured and just as muscular as the younger man. "If you do not learn to watch your tongue, I will see you trussed up beside your friend there. He is a dead man too—I am sure you will have much to discuss with him." Tak'la stepped back, embarrassed at his outburst.

"Stop this." The cave was bathed in green as Ahi'rea's eyes flared. Tak'la sat, but Ondoo'shaa was still until the cave grew dark again. He turned to Ahi'rea.

He chose his words, one by one, and employed them with a chill calm. "You seek to determine my course? Tell me what is wise? By what right, sorceress? I have seen over twenty battles and slain sixty men. I caught Ash'ne the Traitor. I took the head of the Viper of the Khuundoore Steppe, though he hid behind a thousand Cheduna soldiers. I have led warbands for twenty-five summers and been an elder of the High Sun for ten... and you see fit to command me?"

Ahi'rea stared back at Ondoo'shaa without blinking. "I see fit to command you because no one else will. We must approach this carefully. You think you are the only one who has lost? Calm yourself, elder. Give us your wisdom, but maintain your composure." Her eyes lit as she looked into his mind. She suppressed the urge to flinch; his anger and pain were overwhelming.

Ondoo'shaa stepped back involuntarily at the glitter in Ahi'rea's eyes. His face grew red. "Enough. I will not be intimidated by you, sorceress." He stepped away again and addressed Ken'hra, but spoke loudly enough that everyone else in the cave might hear. "I will take my chances outside. I advise you to do the same, if you value your remaining kinsmen." Still glaring, he snatched up his weapons and started for the cave's exit. He stopped and pointed at Revik. "That creature you are protecting will be the death of you all, and she," he turned his finger toward Ahi'rea, "will help him lead you to your end." With that, he ordered an opening made in the entry's covering and left.

"Selfish bastard!" Ken'hra spat. "We all lost someone today, but his loss blinds him. He talks of respect but offers none."

Ahi'rea said nothing, trying to calm her own emotions and regain her calm. She had to admit, she would like nothing better than to kill Lasivar herself.

Ken'hra continued, "They say Ondoo'shaa wants to withdraw further, pull all the tribes into one and hide out in the deepest part of the plains. Not only that, they even say he wants to make a deal with Halkoriv—"

"He wants to surrender?" Tak'la asked.

"That's not what he calls it, but that's what he wants," Ken'hra said. "Coward."

"Even if it were so," Ahi'rea said, "we need to move forward. I only hope he comes back to us when we need him, or that he returns to his people safely."

—

They spoke together for some time. Ruun'daruun soon joined the discussion. He seemed colder and more distant; he urged them to continue with the plan. He felt that, now that they had Lasivar, his plan could still work. The Cheduna would send their forces north and a small group of Huumphar could make their way south to Halkoriv. Tak'la pointed out that those left in the plains would surely die, weakened as they were. The statement was met with a chill stare, as if Ruun'daruun had already considered that.

Ahi'rea wanted to comfort him—the loss of her mother still seemed unreal in the urgency of their plight, and she saw that he suffered too with Ruun'gaphuu and Naph'oin dead. Their cause seemed hopeless to him. For the Huumphar warriors of this age, death in combat was the only worthy path, and many began to seek out that path when friends and family went before them. Ahi'rea feared that Ruun'daruun would welcome his end if he saw the chance.

Ken'hra agreed with Ruun'daruun. Her eyes were alight with fire, and her loss fed rage instead of hopelessness. "We can deal with whatever force is behind us—we could kill dozens each night before they knew we were there, more in traps each day to slow them down and drain their nerves. We have their leader! They'll already be ragged and scared."

Tak'la saw sense in their ideas, but still felt they should withdraw. He was younger, like many of the warriors, and knew that many of them felt the horror of Lasivar's attack more than the battle-hardened Ruun'daruun and Ken'hra, or the seeress Ahi'rea. "They're scared," he said of the other younger warriors. "One man has never attacked the Huumphar like that, in our home, and lived, let alone killed a dozen of us. Their nerves are weak. Their resolve is shaken. They're brave," he grinned, "but you have to admit, no one has seen anything like that before. If another dies, they may crack."

Ken'hra and Ruun'daruun had no answer.

Ahi'rea watched Tak'la. Although she felt no fear from him and he spoke as if referring only to the others, Ahi'rea heard in his voice that he was speaking from painful experience. "Tak'la is right," she said. The cavern was quiet but for the soft murmurs of the other warriors and the occasional groan of pain from the wounded. She listened for a moment to the sounds of the people— her people, people she meant to protect and guide.

By what right? Ondoo'shaa had asked. *Because others cannot. By the right of one who can see in the dark to direct the steps of another at night.* She closed her eyes, and Saw death waiting in the caves with them. "We must regroup. We will make for the tribe. My father will know what to do with him," she said, indicating Revik. "Ken'hra, you and your people are free to return to your tribe; they will need warning if there is a force from the South nearby. If Ondoo'shaa was right, and they have been wiping out whole tribes, then we are all in greater danger than ever before."

"We'll send a runner to warn them," Ken'hra answered. "The warriors of the Whispered Thunder won't abandon you."

Their course decided, they split up to get some rest. Despite their weariness, it was only early afternoon. It was cool and dark in the cavern, however, and in relative safety the Huumphar slept and waited.

—

Ruun'daruun sat near Revik. His turn to keep watch was done, but he was unable to sleep. Their captive's wounds were bound and cleaned, but he was still unconscious. Ruun'daruun stared at him; he was the savior of their cause if you believed Ahi'rea's father's visions. Ruun'daruun could see no way that it could be true now.

He did not understand the power this man and others like him wielded. Ahi'rea had said that she had severed his powers from him, but even after that, it seemed Lasivar had still been able to wound Tak'la. He wondered how. He wondered if they could hold him when he awoke.

Memory crept up on him as Ruun'daruun recalled with a mixture of scorn and longing a tale his grandfather had been fond of telling of the elder Lasivar, the man who had led them against Halkoriv for so long.

Ruun'daruun was a child again, sitting before the old man. Grandfather knew all the stories of Lasivar, and had even been there for some of them. He leaned in, meeting Ruun'daruun's eyes before meeting Ruun'gaphuu's. The boys had waited, nearly shaking. "Before the Cyclone, Lasivar had been the reason the southerners feared to leave their lands. Halkoriv's domain didn't even reach the plains, so beaten back had he been. When he mustered his greatest force and made to push his northern border and break the Huumphar and Gharven peoples, Lasivar had called his own army to meet them. But Halkoriv made a strange move and proposed a champion's battle, a proxy war between two fighters. 'Save your people,' Halkoriv had told Lasivar. 'Only fight with my champion in single combat. With your triumph comes my promise of freedom for the north. With mine, the end of your resistance.'"

Here, Naph'oin's eyes had always sparkled as he spoke. "Of course, Lasivar could not refuse. He was a courageous man, and to him the choice to risk his own life to save any other was no choice at all. He resolved to meet the champion and named a meeting place at the Cliffs of Shurguun, by the western sea. He chose his witnesses and waited at the Cliffs for Halkoriv's warrior.

"Sparkling blue waves crashed up about them. Storm winds blew from the north and met the hot wind of the south above; lightning and thunder crashed. It was as if the elements themselves were battling. Deceitful Halkoriv, however, laid a trap. Lasivar expected no less. When his champion and witnesses came, the champion was twisted with dark magic—his hide was rough and scaly, his jaws grown huge and jagged with sharp teeth. His muscles bunched and rippled unnaturally and his weapons were dark with a poisoning shadow.

"Lasivar met their champion. 'I'll eat your heart!' the dark warrior told him. 'I'll send you back to your master,' Lasivar replied. They clashed, and Lasivar's hauberk was shattered, but he slew the beast. Turning to the witnesses, he was about to declare victory when one of Halkoriv's legion of witnesses dropped dead. At the same moment, the dark warrior rose again, spitting black ichor and clearing his throat. He was somehow fouler than before. 'Hunger!' he cried, lunging once again at Lasivar. His spear pierced Lasivar's chest, but Lasivar sundered the haft and cut the beast down again. Staggering upright, he waited as another witness fell and the warrior climbed to his feet again.

"'Hunger…' the champion moaned. His voice was strange, echoing in the open air. He was more twisted and defiled each time he rose.

"Again and again, Lasivar fought the evil champion. He grew weaker as the creature, for human it was no more, grew stronger and more vile. But a power runs in Lasivar's line, and despite his wounds Lasivar's will kept him standing and fighting. The Wind gusted and turned aside his enemy's blows. The Sun blinded its many eyes. The Waves deafened it. Still, time after time it wounded Lasivar and brought him closer to death.

"His chest was pierced, an arm broken, a leg crushed by the monster's jaws. A dozen cuts pained him; blood obscured his sight. The roars of his foe deadened his senses and the jeers of Halkoriv's mindless, willing sacrifices, still a legion of lives against his one, assaulted his mind.

"He had a moment, then, when he again felled the warrior and awaited its arising; he saw his friends, those who came as witnesses. They wished to help him but at his command stayed their blades. He felt the wind of the North cooling his aches and wounds, the spray of the sea, biting and healing. He remembered his home and family—friends and comrades lost to war and strife, and he knew that nothing would stop the war save perhaps his victory and his death.

"When the dark warrior rose again, black tendrils now lashing about it, hunger on its breath and only death in its eyes, Lasivar cast down his notched sword and broken shield. He took hold of the beast, ignoring the gnashing jaws and rending talons. The Earth bolstered him and he pushed. The stone of the cliffs buckled before his will. 'Back!' he commanded, and the beast gave way. 'Fall!' he cried, and together they plunged over the edge.

"In the deadly, crashing waves and rocks they fought, Lasivar's resolve and the Storm in his blood sustaining him. Lasivar gained the upper hand as the creature floundered, the pure sea rejecting its vileness. He drowned the beast and held it below the waves. Upon the cliff Halkoriv's witnesses fell dead, one after the other. When the last one fell, the witnesses waited for Lasivar to climb the cliff, but he did not emerge from the sea.

"Of course, with his champion and all witnesses dead, Halkoriv could not dispute Lasivar's victory. His undisguised delight, however, when he heard the northern hero had also perished, pained Lasivar's witnesses. Their proposal of a truce was accepted and it seemed peace would finally be known."

Naph'oin had always paused here. The boys had struggled to keep still.

"Of course, the war went on again after a time. Halkoriv had no intention of giving up. But, unknown to him, Lasivar had lived—the woman who became his wife, one of his most powerful friends and allies, had dragged him from the sea and hidden him in the north. She was called Hera, and was a sorceress as well; Huumphar blood ran in her veins. Together they called the Cyclone that aided us when the Cheduna again invaded. Lasivar and

Hera remained hidden, and Elder Haaph'ahin's visions say they will bear a son. The great bloodlines of the plains and the North will be combined. When Hera and Lasivar's son returns, we will finally defeat Halkoriv and we shall have peace."

Ruun'daruun stared at the young man, filthy with mud, bloodied, clad in the trappings of their enemy. He realized he was fingering the blade of his knife. He put the weapon away, and forced himself to try to sleep.

—Eight—

The next morning, scouts were sent out to ascertain the dangers of moving on. Several large groups of Cheduna soldiers were indeed searching the plains, looking for evidence of their captured leader or those who had taken him. Still in their element and now well-rested, the Huumphar split up and evaded the soldiers, re-grouping several miles away along the crest of the Kan Manif Bur canyons. Revik still would not awaken, so he was carried.

Ahi'rea knew that the rest of the tribe was close by, but they were most likely on the move. She was sure they too had caught wind of the Southern soldiers. The warriors resolved to travel through the day and into the night, hoping to reunite with the tribe while they made camp. Ahi'rea took comfort in Ruun'daruun's presence, though he was even more quiet than usual. When she looked at him, she Saw a darkness around him, like shadows of circling vultures.

Tak'la was more reassuring, and seemed unperturbed by his injury. He would dash ahead, then return to the group to report anything he had seen only to sprint ahead once again.

The weather had turned and the clouds and rain had passed by in the night, but still a gloom hung over the Huumphar as they traveled. It was after dark when a distant, warm glow on the horizon, at first indistinguishable from the moonlight, alerted the weary travelers to the camp's location. Before Ahi'rea could suggest otherwise, Tak'la ran ahead to conduct the customary announcements as they approached. On the plains, especially at night, Huumphar sentries were always on the lookout for stalking animals, strangers, and spirits on the wind. The custom of greeting a tribe at night ensured that the warriors were not enemies or ghosts; only when attacking did the Huumphar approach a camp silently.

Ahead in the dark, the travelers heard Tak'la's chant and they slowed to give him time to announce them. The words were ancient—older than the Old Speech that only learned elders and the wisest travelers spoke. Their syllables were long and tonal, rising and falling with the wind. They were words passed down, used among the Huumphar since the gods' times, known only for their purpose, not their meaning. They heard the response from a night sentry, familiar, like a verse of song, then there was silence for a time. When Tak'la returned, the company proceeded.

They passed a pair of guards and quietly entered the camp. Many were asleep, the flaps of their small, round tents pulled shut. About a dozen Huumphar had awakened to greet them— concerned husbands, wives, parents, and children. There was no cheering; the worried silence was broken by whispers, gasps of relief, or sobs of anguish.

Ken'hra and the other Whispered Thunder Huumphar moved a polite distance from camp and began building their own tiny fires. They clustered around the flames to block the light and make the most of the heat. At Ahi'rea's direction, several warriors took them the few spare tents the nomads could afford to carry—mostly those whose owners no longer needed them. Their guests provided for, Ahi'rea gently pushed past the quiet reunions to the small, frail figure of her father.

He stood wrapped in a heavy buckskin cape, leaning heavily on his walking stick. No words were exchanged; he already knew, of course, what had happened. At the sight of his tears, Ahi'rea wept as well, rushing forward to feel her father's arms enclose her. Visions of Haruu'na passed between them; a loving mother and wife, lost to them both.

After a long embrace, Ahi'rea pulled away and dried her eyes. She was always a little surprised to see her father in person after being away for a time. His presence was overwhelming in the Dreaming, but in the flesh he had always been such a contrast to Haruu'na. He was prematurely shrunken and weak for his age. He had never been a great warrior. It was his presence that mattered, and when he spoke he could command the attention of all who heard him. His foresight was legendary amongst the Huumphar. Others came to consult with him from far away tribes and even from the North, and he had the Sight to thank for his survival on many occasions.

Now, however, he looked like nothing more than a grief-stricken old man who had seen too much loss. But there was something else, something in his eyes that she had only seen a few times before. Looking at his eyes, realization swept over Ahi'rea like a wind over the grasses.

"Why?" Her voice was strained. She squeezed her eyes shut against the tears. Her words came out in a whisper. "Why did you not tell us?"

He did not speak. He put his hand on her shoulder but she

pulled away, opening her eyes again to search his. Even without the Sight, she could tell. He had known.

"Rea... you know as well as I do—"

"What is the use, Father? Why See as we do if you refuse to change anything?" Her tears dried in sudden anger. Her father tried to speak but she cut him off. "You could have stopped it! And you—"

Just behind him, she noticed Revik being carried into a tent, still bound and unconscious. Her eyes widened and her stomach leapt to her throat. "Him? This was about capturing him?"

Her father bowed his head.

"You knew. You—you sacrificed them." Ahi'rea felt sick. She wanted to scream, to shout at him, but shock overwhelmed her. Instead she turned, her steps unsteady, and staggered away. She could not bear to face him. She could hear her father speaking to her, but she could not bring herself to concentrate on the words. The camp was a fog around her; she forced herself to stay upright as she stumbled, seeing nothing.

She felt a hand on her arm. She started and looked up into Ruun'daruun's face and discovered she had wandered out of the fire circle. Behind her, the group of warriors and their families was dwindling. The camp center was emptying as those who had returned and their families went off to their tents.

Ruun'daruun's head hung and his wounds looked as if they still pained him. His weary eyes sought hers. Her heart ached for him—he too had lost his family, and it could have been otherwise. She put her arms around him and leaned into him, holding him as tightly as she could.

"He knew," she whispered. "He did not tell us, but he knew.

If only my Sight were clearer—I could have stopped this."

"Don't, Rea." Ruun'daruun returned her embrace. The night was cool, and overhead the moon shone bright on the plains and the grasses rippled about them in the breeze. Ahi'rea felt his jaw rest against her head. "What's past is past. You can't feel like you could have stopped this. Everyone knows the danger—we don't fight so we can die of old age in peace."

You are wrong, she thought. *That is exactly why we fight.*

—

The nomads slept through the night and kept to their camp the next day to give the warriors time to rest. Wounds were bound and periods of mourning begun. Those who had lost family or loved ones began their fasting after a meager breakfast without meat. They made plans to perform the Sendings the following day, once the tribe could reach an appropriate location.

Loneliness and despair led Ahi'rea and Ruun'daruun to share a tent despite the implications. They were too distraught for some rumor mongering and disapproving glances to keep them apart. Both needed the other's closeness in the face of so much loss. Revik's capture, important as some believed him to be, was little solace to those who had seen the destruction he had wrought.

—

Revik had been confined to a small, uncomfortable tent usually used for smoking fish and meat. Upon being roughly dumped on the ground, he had been jarred into brief semi-consciousness.

He was force-fed a bitter infusion of some kind, then left alone. The unfamiliar smells of the smoking tent, damp animal hide, and the earth of the plains filled his nostrils. He was made more uneasy by an unsettling discovery: he could not see in the dark. He had grown so used to it in the recent months that he had forgotten what it was like to be blind without light.

Pain and a hot, throbbing burn below his ribs soon engulfed him. He probed at the wound with his bound hands, wincing, before his vision faded.

His unconsciousness was different now than it had been after the fight. His sleep was fretful and shallow, and between feverish bouts with wakefulness, he dreamed of a whispering voice. It was familiar, cold. He dreamed it was beyond a wall, or at a great distance, but that it was trying to grow closer to him. He was unsure if he wanted it to, and yet he yearned for it to reach him.

—

When they awoke, Ahi'rea and Ruun'daruun lay for a time, speaking little. Quiet voices outside indicated that most of the camp was awake and active. Ahi'rea wrapped a fur and hide blanket around her shoulders, then went out to retrieve water, medicinal herbs, and bandages. She saw her father seated by the fire; their eyes met but they did not exchange greetings.

When she had what she needed she returned to the tent and found Ruun'daruun waiting. He smiled through his pain and her heart melted; he smiled so seldom. She knelt in front of him. "Let me see to those wounds."

Ruun'daruun's chest, neck, and face were riddled with the

mysterious blackening welts Revik had given him. He sat, quiet and unflinching, as she tended to him, watching her while she worked. The rest and closeness soon had them both in better spirits.

"These will scar," Ahi'rea announced when she finished. Ruun'daruun nodded, pleased. "I have never seen anything like it. The skin just split, and they look almost like—" she paused, considering the wounds. "Like the time Ula'han had frostbite."

Ruun'daruun strapped on his machete scabbard, careful not to dislodge the new bandages. "It must really be him. Even the creatures Halkoriv makes out of men can't do such things. So much for Lasivar, the son of the hero."

"So much," Ahi'rea said, furrowing her brow. "It is strange though…" she trailed off, thinking back to the fight in the storm.

"What's strange?" Ruun'daruun turned to her when she did not go on.

She was quiet for a moment before responding. "Just…" she still saw it in her mind: the pale flicker around Revik, like a crack in the air, or the shadow of something vast and formless. "Nothing, probably. Let's get some food. We are leaving tomorrow for the Monument to perform the Sendings."

Outside, they ignored a few curious glances and mutterings as they exited the tent together. Ken'hra and her kinsmen had been invited to the fire circle and all those who had lost a friend or family member were partaking of their last meal before the fasting began. Ahi'rea's father stood as they approached. He hobbled toward them and stopped before Ahi'rea, eyes downcast.

"I am sorry I did not tell anyone. When you see that I was right, you will understand. Soon, I hope." The old man's eyes, when he looked up, were dry and hard. "I would have gone myself, if I could have. You know that." He set his jaw and locked eyes with Ahi'rea, then with Ruun'daruun. Even to his own daughter, the apology had been a major show of deference for an elder.

Ruun'daruun bowed, but perhaps a little less than he should have. Ahi'rea, however, was still. She stared right back at her father. "He is a murderer, Haaph'ahin, and a threat. After the Sendings are performed, we must decide what to do with him."

Her father's eyes widened at the use of his name. He opened his mouth, then seemed to think better of his words and turned and stomped away. "May the wind guide your thoughts," he said.

"And yours," Ahi'rea answered.

—

He heard the voice again. Revik could not make out its words, but he understood its meaning. It had been driven away, but it was coming back.

There was a light—Revik felt it more than saw it. When he opened his eyes, he saw a dim figure, rather small and hunched, with a walking stick. Little motes of dust flashed, hanging in the air, before vanishing as the tent flap fell shut. His vision was blurry and his head pounded. He tried to rise, but his limbs would not respond. The burning feeling around his wound felt duller. Revik was not sure if that was good or not. He tried to clear his muddled thoughts.

Captured. Captured, by plainsfolk. He remembered. He had been leading a force to exterminate them, eliminate them for good. *To make the plains safe for travel, to expand the border, to bring peace to the North. Duty.* He and his men had gotten word of an assault, and he had ridden ahead to stop it himself. It had almost worked. *Why do I feel so weak?*

Revik's head swam. The figure shuffled closer and sat stiffly, and he heard a gentle sloshing of water. His head was lifted and a water skin was placed against his lips. He tried to turn away but the rough hand tilted his head back and poured the water into his mouth. He could not bring himself to resist once the cool liquid reached his tongue.

The girl. He remembered cutting through the Huumphar until he reached her. He remembered her eyes, blazing light through the rain and shadow. She had beaten him, somehow shut him off from his power, and then they had taken him.

Revived by the water, Revik's eyes adjusted to the dark interior of the tent. The figure before him was an old, troubled-looking plainsfolk man with wild gray hair. His eyes bored right through Revik. He got the feeling the old man was looking for something.

The old man spoke words in a language Revik did not know. Then he said, in Cheduna, "How are you feeling?"

Revik clenched his teeth. "Go to hell," he spat. "You animals are not getting anything from me."

Haaph'ahin nodded. "We will heal you as best we can," he said. "We are moving tomorrow. You will have to walk again, or be carried."

"Running will not help you. Not this time," Revik said.

"Who are you?" Haaph'ahin asked. His voice was a mixture of hope and fear.

Revik smiled through his pain. "Your death," he said. "I was sent to end your people. Halkoriv sent me to exterminate you.

When I am healed, you will all die." He coughed through a weak laugh. "You had better kill me now, before I am well or my men find you. And if you do kill me, Halkoriv will come here himself."

The old man returned the smile. "We will not kill you, and we are aware of the force searching for you. They will not catch us—they never do. Not on the plains. Our plains."

Revik could see that the old man was trying to mask his fear. The army was the largest that had ventured into the plains for decades. The fires stormed the south like siege towers.

Haaph'ahin sat back, leaning against one of the tent's three support poles in feigned unconcern. "But what I want to know is, are you Revik Lasivar?"

Revik was amused. "You have heard of me then?"

"Halkoriv's chosen," Haaph'ahin muttered. "Yes, I have heard of you—and I knew your father."

"You know nothing," Revik snapped. He tried to sit up and winced, falling back. His side throbbed and his head pounded. He was still for a moment and the pain faded again. "I have no family. They were killed, and I do not remember them. Halkoriv gave me everything. He told me my father was a good man, a man who would not traffic with thieves and murderers like you."

"No family," Haaph'ahin repeated. He spoke more to himself than to Revik. "Of course. You were taken the night they died. You were hidden. Why do you not remember them?" He was looking past Revik, through him, and Revik saw the same green light in the old man's eyes as he had seen in the girl's. He continued to mutter to himself. The light faded and Haaph'ahin met Revik's eyes again. "Your mother and father hid with you in the North for a long time, and some of those with the Sight foresaw your death, or that you would flee," he said. "But not me. I saw something else. I saw that you would come to save us from Halkoriv."

Haaph'ahin closed his eyes and grasped Revik's hand. Revik tried to pull away but he was too weak. "Now that you are here," the old man said, eyes glimmering, growing unfocused, "I may finally discover what happened; so many questions, for so long…"

"What are you doing?" Revik said, still trying to free his hand. The old man's grip became a vice.

"Seeing…" Haaph'ahin whispered.

There was silence and Revik waited, unable to pull away. He felt nothing. The old man's eyes closed and a soft green glow emanated from behind his eyelids.

—

Halkoriv stormed through his palace, leaving his doctors and healers behind him. They stopped as he crossed the threshold to his sanctum and began to descend the stone stairs. There was no rich carpet here, no tapestries; the floor was featureless marble, cold as ice. The walls held no torches and no light reached those halls. To Halkoriv, it did not matter – he had ceased to need light to see decades ago. It was one of the first things the Ancestor taught him, one of the first things Revik had learned after he had ended Cunabrel.

Once Revik had done so, had proven himself, it had been a matter of hours to teach him to unleash the powers that had lain dormant in him. The Ancestor had awakened them. It was something that had never been done before. Halkoriv had been pleased to see it work. He wondered that Revik had not discovered them before, but brushed aside those concerns, just as Revik would brush aside the plainsfolk—or so he had hoped.

Halkoriv had been consulting with his healers when he had felt something was wrong with Revik. He rushed to his sanctum, to See. After over a hundred and twenty years of life, healers were of no use. They warned him that he must address his health, but Halkoriv knew that only the power of the Ancestor would save him. Only the power of Sitis. Revik was the key. Revik was life.

Halkoriv reached the bottom of the marble steps. In the dark, he heard only his footsteps and the trickle of water. His heart hammered with the exertion of walking. His breath rasped. He released his restraint, felt more power course through him, and his heart slowed. His breath grew steady. Halkoriv crossed the black hall, a cavern in marble, and ascended the dais at its center.

Atop the dais loomed a marble throne and a marble basin beside it. Water trickled from the basin, running over the top and down the sides. Halkoriv could see the water shimmer against the marble in the darkness. *I need him. We need him.* He sat, and felt the Ancestor with him, here in this seat that he had built hundreds of years ago. Halkoriv looked into the basin and released his restraint. He felt the Sprit, the Ancestor, stir in him and its icy, gossamer touch flowed through him and took hold of him. It had ceased to be unpleasant long ago. Halkoriv craved it.

He did not stir. The water's flow increased as Halkoriv stared into the basin. His eyes unfocused, and he Saw.

—NINE—

The plains grew hot. The light armor he wore was better in the heat than the plate Draden was used to, but not by much. From his mount, he looked over the waving golden grass and listened to the dull roar of the army encampment behind him.

The army was over five thousand strong, accompanied by hundreds of carters, smiths, and other support. They awaited only Draden's orders to move out. Before him was the north, once a vast blue sky over the limitless plains, now marred by columns of black smoke. Scouts approached, first seen only by the bending of the grasses and then coming into view one by one. Draden hoped that, this time, they would have something to report, but by the looks on their faces he feared that was not the case.

Draden wiped the sweat from his brow as the scouts came forward, and one after the other reported the same thing; that they had seen no sign of the plainsfolk nor of Revik. He did not relish making the report to Halkoriv's servant that his heir still had not been found.

"Damn you, Revik," he muttered to himself, not for the first time. "I told you to wait."

The first time Revik had gone out to face a group of plainsfolk alone, he had slain them all before the other cavalry even caught up. None survived to warn their kin about Revik. None survived to pass on the story. The plainsfolks' corpses had been strung up, paraded before the army, and the men saw that they could be killed. Even still, Draden had asked Revik to at least take a few men with him the next time, to stay under guard. Revik had laughed.

He had done the same thing on three other occasions. Now it had been nearly five days since Revik had ridden ahead to battle the plainsfolk. A storm had gathered over him as he rode away. By the time Draden and a squad of cavalry had reached the outpost, the rain had cleared. They had discovered the bodies of many fallen plainsfolk, but Revik was nowhere to be found. They had met Malskein fleeing along the road and found only one other, alive, but badly wounded, inside the garrison. Neither of them knew what had happened to Revik. The man from the garrison had been sent back to Halkoriv's fortress, at the servant's order, to be questioned. Draden wondered if he had survived the journey.

Draden's thoughts were interrupted by a voice. "We'd better move on with the mission without him, Count." It was Malskein, squinting up at him from the ground. "The best way to find lord Revik will be to force the plainsfolk into fighting. He'll turn up in one of their camps, or not at all."

"Thank you, commander. You're probably right." Draden sighed. He brushed his sweat-soaked hair off of his forehead and issued commands to move the army.

Revik had set out, after defeating Cunabrel, with one purpose: to destroy the plainsfolk and open the way to the north. Malskein and others with the most experience in fighting on the plains had been hand-picked to offer strategic advice and lead the men. The other lords had gone home, and Draden had been Revik's choice as second-in-command. They had fought side by side since the assault on Cunabrel's realm, when Revik had first taken his place as head of the army. Only a few months had passed, but much had happened. Draden owed it all to Revik, including lordship over Cunabrel's old county and his title.

Revik's plans were simple enough. The plainsfolk depended on hunting and gathering to survive and upon the frontier villages for a little trading. They hid in the plains and struck without warning, then retreated to their lands again. The villages had already been evacuated and traders were being turned away at the southern border of the plains. Groups of soldiers were hunting and killing game, poisoning the carcasses that they could not carry back.

Word came often from Halkoriv, guiding the army's movements, warning of plainsfolk raiding parties and traps. Most importantly, the men set fire to the plains around them. Winds came up from the south, guiding the flames away from the army. Revik and Halkoriv had said it would be so. The winds did not falter.

So much power, Draden often thought. *This is it. The war will end soon and we will finally see peace.* He did not pretend to understand his king's abilities. He had heard that Halkoriv now spent nearly all of his time in solitude, concentrating on expanding his power. They said he did not eat, nor sleep; some said that he could not die. A few whispered that he was not even truly alive.

On the sixth day since Revik disappeared, word came of a small plainsfolk warparty near the army's position. Draden gave Malskein command of a legion and rode out with him to confront the savages. Infantry pressed the plainsfolks' position while the men on horseback rode ahead to encircle them. Malskein commanded the soldiers to stay in groups, move slowly and carefully, never run blind, never fight on plainsfolk terms. "They're not ghosts, and they're not demons," he told them. "They're not even men. They are dangerous animals that need to be put down."

The fighting was fierce and bloody, and even against so few plainsfolk the costs were high. However, with their escape cut off and with Malskein's experienced oversight, they had little chance in the face of the soldier's overwhelming numbers and superior weapons and armor. Once they were defeated, however, it became apparent that the army's target was no warparty.

The soldiers killed thirty or more plainsfolk, but few of them were warriors. Most were too old or too young to fight effectively. When the last few remaining alive were rounded up, Draden was struck—all that remained were children, and they were sickly, as if afflicted by some disease that spared the adults. Some quaked before him and the other horsemen, but many glared at them through tears and blood.

Draden stared at them. He wondered if they were the last of a tribe. "Take them," he said to Malskein, turning his horse to leave.

"Count," Malskein said, "I thought you said our orders were to exterminate them."

"So I did," Draden answered. "These children are sick, and pose no threat. We will send them south to be cared for. Perhaps they can be brought to the light of civilization."

Malskein's gaze darkened. "They're animals, sir. You can't hope to make anything but feral murderers out of them. The order was no prisoners."

Draden turned back and rode up to Malskein, leaning in

close to him. Malskein did not budge. "Are you going to obey my orders, or not?"

"Are you going to obey our king's orders, sir?"

They locked eyes as the soldiers looked on. Draden silently cursed himself. Malskein seemed content to wait, his gaze unwavering. The barest hint of a smirk crossed his lips. Neither man moved or made a sound. What seemed like minutes passed.

Eyes still locked on Malskein's, Draden finally spoke. "Leave them. Let's go." Malskein stared a moment longer, then nodded and gestured for the men to move out. He knew as well as Draden did that the children would not survive alone.

"And commander," Draden said as Malskein turned to leave. "Never question my loyalty to our king again."

Malskein nodded, then gave a short wave to the terrified plainsfolk children before riding away.

—

Draden sat alone in his tent, exhausted. Parchment, pen, and ink waited before him, his letter unfinished. He was unsure what, if anything, to say about the day's events. Such topics were neither fitting nor pleasant, and Kara knew well enough what war entailed. He wished he could speak to her, hear her voice, feel her hand on his. The plainsfolk had killed and raided since before he was born, but for the first time he was unsure of himself in his duty.

He finished his note, saying little save that he longed to return home and that he loved her, and placed the note with the other messages and reports to be taken by couriers the next day.

He stared at the scroll case on his table; orders from Halkoriv, brought during the evening. He had not yet opened the case.

He had been ordered against taking prisoners before, but those had been other armies, not villages or whole tribes. Halkoriv wanted the plainsfolk destroyed, that much he understood. They were murderers who had been at war with the Cheduna for centuries. *But the children as well?*

He turned his mind to Revik and hoped that he would be found soon. While he had grown colder and more distant, Draden felt that something remained of their old friendship, at least as much of one as Revik was capable of having. He wondered, not for the first time, what in his past troubled Revik so. He had asked once, when they were still children, but Revik had seemed reluctant to speak of it. When pressed, he had answered, "I sometimes feel I am someone else. That I am watching... something else act as if it is me." He had not explained or spoken of the feeling again. Draden wondered if it was the sorcery, the power Revik commanded. *Such power must be a burden.*

Something also worried Draden about the plainsfolk that had taken Revik. They were men like any other—Draden knew that—but if that were true, then they could not have beaten Revik. He wondered if that was why Halkoriv feared them.

—

In the dark of the tent, Revik waited. His hand was going numb in Haaph'ahin's grip. He was too weak to do anything but watch the old Huumphar's eyelids twitch and flicker.

Haaph'ahin looked up, eyes opening wide as the glow faded from them. "You... you are not he..." he gasped, his voice weak, his breath short.

Revik started—the old man had not moved or spoken for an hour. "What? Not who?" he asked despite himself.

Haaph'ahin stared through him. "You are not Revik Lasivar. You are not Lasivar's son. I knew it. I could see none of him in you, nor of Hera." His eyes were wide. He babbled and stumbled to his feet, lurching one way, then the next. "You were stripped of your power—that could not happen, not if you were really him… it's not possible…"

Haaph'ahin looked at Revik again, and his eyes filled with tears. "For nothing… they died for nothing. You're no one." He looked broken, a feeble old man, lost and alone.

"What are you blubbering about?" Revik sneered. "I know who I am." He was not sure enough of what was going on to make any further response, nor did he care what the old man said. He knew his own power and his destiny. As soon as he was well, he would finish what he had started and, when Halkoriv died, take his rightful place as King of Feriven.

Haaph'ahin continued to mutter and cast about with his eyes, now ignoring Revik. "…not possible. I saw it, saw him take you—Halkoriv's chosen…" He whirled about and grabbed Revik's tunic, shaking him and shouting. "Who are you? Where is Lasivar's son? I let them die for him, not you!"

Taken aback by the sudden assault, Revik cried out as the old man shook and struck him. Fury roiled up inside him. Without thought, he released his restraint as he always did. He felt nothing, then the chill dark wended through his body. He shoved Haaph'ahin hard with one arm and felt the old man lift off the ground. He collided with a support pole on the opposite side of the small tent. It buckled and shook the tent and there was a sudden swell of shouting from outside.

Revik was unprepared for the exertion. His breath came short as a group of plainsfolk poured in to restrain him and retrieve Haaph'ahin. A warrior a few years Revik's elder, his skin marred by welts and scars, shouted incomprehensibly and held a bone-handled knife to Revik's throat. Others tended to the old man, who was still shouting, now in his own language and in a state of hysterics. He choked back tears and jabbed a finger at Revik. The others looked at him in horror and shock, and the shouting grew louder as the plainsfolk yelled to one another.

—

Ahi'rea rushed into the tent along with the others. "It's not him!" Haaph'ahin shouted. "He's just Halkoriv's pawn! A sorcerous monster sent to kill us! He's no one!" The Huumphar were flabbergasted. By now all of them had learned that their prisoner was their prophesied savior. Through the flurry of questions and shouts, Ahi'rea called for silence and soon quieted the group.

Haaph'ahin slumped to the ground and at Ahi'rea's urging, calmed himself and began to explain.

"Some twenty-five winters ago, I saw Lasivar for the last time. Many believed he had died when he fought Halkoriv's champion at the Cliffs of Shurguun, but I and a few others knew that he had gone into the North to hide. From there, he coordinated the war from afar, only venturing out himself in times of need. When my Sight showed me that he had been discovered, we met and I told him what I had Seen: that his family would be found and his son, Revik, would be taken by Halkoriv. The boy would be molded as Halkoriv's weapon. With Lasivar's powers of Storm and Hera's Self and Sight, combined with Halkoriv's dark magic, he would be a terrible force indeed. I urged Lasivar to hide his son. He agreed, and it was then that Hera prophesied that her child would come to lead us against Halkoriv.

"But Halkoriv took the child anyway. He sent his men into Gharven and they took him. Still I held out for hope that, one day, he would return to lead the Huumphar."

He sighed, continuing, "A few weeks ago, as Ruun'daruun planned the raids on the Southern garrisons, I had a vision. The storm gathering to the South would bring our destruction, unless we could meet it. I knew that Lasivar's son would finally come to us, to destroy us. If we captured him, I thought we could teach him, show him the truth, and he would fight against Halkoriv. That is why I let the plans go forward." He paused, tears tracing glimmering lines down his face. "I knew many would die. I knew many would lose someone they loved. But I thought that if we captured Lasivar, it would be a worthy loss.

"But something went wrong—this man is not Lasivar. He bears his name, he serves Halkoriv with dark sorcery, but he is not the true son of Lasivar and Hera." Haaph'ahin's voice broke and he choked, weeping. "I am a fool. My visions have brought only death. He is no one, and my Sight has failed!"

The Huumphar looked on in silence. Haaph'ahin always knew death approached before it arrived, and he was a pillar of strength and leadership for the Huumphar. None had ever seen him so. Some began to shake in silent sobs with him.

For a short time, the Huumphar had dared to believe that

they had a new chance of victory, that the son of great heroes would soon realize his true place and save them.

Now they saw in their prisoner their end; a foul warrior without lineage, the last of many threats, the one that would bury them all.

—Ten—

The day passed in fearful quiet. Ahi'rea felt each of the Huumphar, alone with his or her thoughts; some planned to leave after the Sendings, others to fight to the last, but all knew their end was near at hand.

Their warriors were dying; their children grew weaker and sicker, if they were born alive at all. Game had grown scarce and traders were not to be found in their lands any longer. Where before the Huumphar had dreamed of one day wandering the plains unhindered, as their ancestors had, it seemed now they would live out their days in hiding until their kind died out. Stories of Lasivar's son coming to lead them had embodied those dreams, even if they were only stories. Now, with those tales shattered by the truth, they had nothing.

Ahi'rea was sick with fury and anguish. Her father had let people die on the strength of a vision, a vision that proved false. He knew full well that the future was in motion, was never certain. He had often told her that her practicality and doubt were what kept her Sight from improving. Now, she was too bitter and broken to feel vindicated, and tradition would not allow her to chastise him.

Sorrow threatened to overwhelm her, but it would have to wait; the Sending ceremonies for the fallen could not. The prisoner's future would have to be decided, but he could wait, too. *If he dies during the move,* she thought, *so much the better.*

—

Revik was left alone, his solitude only interrupted when he was brought food and water. He thought about making an escape, but even the idea of standing sent waves of dizziness through him. His power would not answer his call again. He worried again that this time he had lost it forever.

That worry, and the old man's words, gnawed at him, and the darkness of the rank and filthy tent closed in around him once more.

One of Revik's earliest clear memories was being told by Halkoriv of his father, Koren Lasivar; he was told of his honor and valor, of his hope to see Feriven whole and at peace. Years in Cunabrel's prison had erased his parents' memory, but the idea of them was important. They had been heroes, martyrs even, killed by traitorous Cunabrel despite their loyalty and vision.

Another thing confused Revik. The old man had spoken of the Sight, of sorcery. Revik recalled the blazing eyes of the plainsfolk girl as she had severed him from his power. Surely Halkoriv would have known about sorcery amongst the plainsfolk, but he had said all other lines with the gift had been wiped out. So, either Halkoriv had not known, and his power had failed him, or he had been lying. Neither was a palatable thought. If Halkoriv had lied about that, what else had he withheld? What other lies had he crafted?

Revik tried not to think about it. He recalled from his lessons that a certain amount of deceit was expected from a good leader. The populace, and even trusted allies, need not know everything. Besides, not just anyone can learn of sorcery. Ancestry must provide the spark. He told himself that the idea that he was not Lasivar's son was ludicrous.

Revik was still not comforted and doubt robbed him of rest. He held up a palm, willing the inky tendrils to appear. They did not. What if he had merely been imbued with power, as Halkoriv had done before to some of his servants? The girl had somehow severed his power—could that be the explanation? He felt panic and fear for the first time in years—fear that the old plainsfolk man was right.

Revik was about to close his hand when he noticed a faint shimmer above his palm: a hole in the world, darker than the shadowy tent, darker than anything, darker than nothing. It was still there. He concentrated harder and the shimmer resolved itself into black, lashing shapes. They were faint and weak, but still they wound and writhed above his hand. Sweat beaded on his brow, but once more Revik felt calm and assured. His power was not gone, only suppressed.

He waited through the day and night, resting, and upon waking, calling up the icy, ephemeral tendrils over and over as if flexing an injured limb. Their touch comforted him, restoring their weight and pressure in his mind. They almost seemed to whisper to him: whispers of strength, whispers of power. It had found its way back.

—

The Huumphar broke camp after a long and quiet night. Their future was bleak; the one prophesied to save them was a fraud, their ranks were decimated, and the Southern army approached with a vanguard of fire. Tak'la was pleased to be moving again, regardless.

Ahi'rea and Ruun'daruun led the tribe, making haste for the Monument. They turned toward the rising sun, heading along invisible, age-old paths through the plains known only by memory and feeling. Tak'la knew that if they were slow, they might be ambushed during the important ceremony. Their prisoner was surrounded by warriors and was made to jog along himself. He exhibited surprising vigor for one who had been so injured. Tak'la made a note of it, but otherwise ignored him.

Haaph'ahin was slower than usual. He was quiet and made it clear that he would prefer to be left alone with his thoughts. He lingered at the back of the group, keeping pace despite his age. Those who could not run were unheard of among the Huumphar.

Though he had been present for most of the discussions the previous day, something troubled Tak'la. Most of the others were distraught and he had felt it would be improper to interrupt them in their mourning. However, he worried over the elder of his adopted tribe.

He approached Haaph'ahin, slowing his pace until the old man caught up with him. "Greetings, honored elder," Tak'la said, settling into pace beside Haaph'ahin. "I am Tak'la. It seems you are troubled." He smiled, hoping his deference would excuse his lack of a proper introduction by another tribesman.

The elder had not yet spoken to the youth from a lost tribe, though Tak'la had run with them for two years. The death-touched rarely spoke unless spoken to. Tak'la noticed Haaph'ahin scowling, looking at their feet. He took only one stride to cover two of the elder's. Haaph'ahin snorted. "Age is a terrible thing, Tak'la death-touched. The body and mind begin to fail just as you think you are beginning to master them." He huffed along for a few strides without speaking. Tak'la kept pace. "I would prefer not to be bothered," Haaph'ahin finally said.

Tak'la noticed Ken'hra just ahead, peering at him over her shoulder and giving him a look. Tak'la raised an eyebrow and smirked at her, then addressed Haaph'ahin again. "Of course, Elder. Elder, I have a question."

Ken'hra glared. Haaph'ahin almost laughed but he maintained his composure. He looked over, seeming to reevaluate the burly youth. His scowl seemed tempered by the edge of a smile. "What of mourning, boy? You do not feel the need to keep silence like the others?"

"No, Elder," Tak'la answered. "They call me death-touched—my tribe is gone, my people lost." The youth's eyes unfocused, past events fleeting behind them. "I died with them, they say. My Sending has been performed. I have more in common with those lost than those yet alive."

"You have no tears? No pain? Would your silence not honor them?" Haaph'ahin asked.

"Few will speak to me," Tak'la answered. "So I am often silent. And I will save my tears. Rather than tears, I offer the lost my resolve, as I am already dead."

Haaph'ahin ran in silence for a moment. "Many see a tragedy here, Tak'la the death-touched. We lost many warriors and friends to capture the wrong man. In addition, it is my fault. I could have stopped the raid, but the Sight failed me."

"That is my question, Elder. If he," Tak'la pointed his spear at Revik, "is not Lasivar, then who is he?"

Haaph'ahin sighed. "I do not know. I Saw a story like my vision of Lasivar. He came from the North and was imprisoned and corrupted by Halkoriv. He learned sorcery, but he doesn't have the spark. Lasivar would—Hera, his mother, had the Sight and the Self, and his father had skill in the Storm."

"So this spark—if he does not have it, how did he learn sorcery?"

"Halkoriv. And Sitis," Haaph'ahin answered, "the Ravenous Spirit. It rides him. Even still..." He lapsed into silence.

Sorcery was a mystery to Tak'la. He had only seen it from Ahi'rea, Haaph'ahin, and his own dead tribe's seer, Kiil'ana. He had heard of Sight and Self, and Lasivar's power of Storm was in all the old tales. He had never heard of Sitis. Tak'la decided to change his line of questioning, though he burned to know what Sitis was.

"Then... where is the real Lasivar?"

Haaph'ahin's eyes widened and he looked over at Tak'la in surprise. "A fine question... I had been too caught up in all the troubles to even wonder. He... he must be elsewhere, if he lives. Hidden. Well done, boy," he trailed off. Tak'la noticed the old man's pace quicken.

"Can't you use the Sight to find him?" Tak'la asked, moving a little faster to keep up.

Haaph'ahin shook his head. "It does not work like that. I

may dream it, or perhaps if I had something of his… or if I knew him. Or…" He looked up at Revik, eyes narrowing. "I am sorry, Tak'la," he looked down at the ground, brow furrowing. "I really must think. We will talk more later."

Tak'la almost asked another question, but thought better of it. He left the old man to run in silence, drawing ahead of him again. *Sitis,* he thought. The word felt dangerous and heavy and quiet in his mind, like the footstep of a predator in the dark.

—

The Monument rose out of the plains, a steep rocky hill in the midst of a flat and featureless land. The top was flat and paved with huge, flawless stones. The Huumphar did not know who had brought the stones there, or why. A dozen stony ridges, waist-high, jutted up and radiated from the center of the platform. Around the platform's edges, the remains of black marble arches, walls, and doorways stood like jagged teeth, reaching into the darkening sky. Toppled columns and broken bits of marble littered the hilltop. Hardy, gnarled bushes the color of ash had worked their way up through the stones and cracks; now, near the end of their bloom, their deep crimson flowers had begun to drop their petals. As the sun set behind the Huumphar, casting its last rays into the east, the hilltop lit blood-red as they approached.

They made camp on the northern side of the hill's base. The Huumphar marveled at Revik, who, though injured, had kept up with their pace throughout the day. Ahi'rea stared at him as he sat, arms bound, being given water by one of the warriors assigned to guard him.

Just two days ago he looked as if he would die. Father said he had no spark, but without command of the Self, he should barely be able to walk, let alone run like us. She noticed Haaph'ahin watching the prisoner as well. She shook her head and moved off through the camp, observing the others as they tended to their needs. A few older women were just returning with skins full of water from a small spring nearby. Others were gathering roots and wild plants to eat. Several of the warriors had gone for a short hunt since they had seen no game during the day. Few expected them to be successful.

Ahi'rea stopped near a young woman who was stooping over a basket, taking a moment's rest in the midst of setting up her tent.

"Rahi'sta," Ahi'rea said. The woman looked up through the sun-reddened hair across her face. The fiery tones gave her a wild and dangerous look, one that Ahi'rea knew was fitting. She was a fierce fighter, though she had not been involved in the disastrous raid.

"Greetings, Ahi'rea. How is your father?" Rahi'sta asked.

Ahi'rea glanced back at Haaph'ahin, who sat, stonelike, staring at Revik. She considered her answer. "I am not sure," she said. "He seems distracted, since yesterday. Perhaps less upset, though. How is your little one?" she asked, changing the subject. She stepped closer and knelt, gazing at the sleeping form of Rahi'sta's child nestled in his traveling basket.

Rahi'sta smiled. "Tired," she said. Her own exhaustion was evident in her voice. "Journeys are difficult for him still, but he grows stronger every day."

Ahi'rea smiled up at her. Rahi'sta's child had been the first born alive in the tribe in two years. They all felt great concern for the baby, especially now; his father had been one of those Revik had so recently killed. "And how are you?" Ahi'rea asked.

Rahi'sta looked down. "I almost wish I'd been there with him," she said. "But my place is here. We both knew that, and we both knew the risks. I'm sorry about Haruu'na, too." Ahi'rea nodded her thanks.

"Ahi'rea," Rahi'sta said, going back to work on raising her tent, "why are we keeping that hellspawn alive?" She nodded toward Revik across the camp.

"We will decide that tonight, after the Sending."

"We should have left him tied out in the plains today," Rahi'sta said as she set a tent stake.

Ahi'rea nodded. "We may yet," she said. "Despite who he says he is, my father is sure that he is not Lasivar's son. He is probably just another one of Halkoriv's spies or servants. He has sent soldiers cloaked with dark power against us before."

Rahi'sta looked up from the knots on which she was working. "You sound doubtful."

"No," Ahi'rea said. "There has just been a lot to think about. Be well, Rahi'sta. Take care of your little one, and yourself."

Rahi'sta wished her well and went back to work. Ahi'rea continued on her way, stopping from time to time to offer a word of encouragement or comfort. Thanks to her Sight, it was assumed Ahi'rea would be an elder soon—at a much younger age than was usual, due to the thinning of the Huumphar ranks. Her opinions were respected in the tribe and her guidance already sought by those who trusted her over her father.

As she neared Revik, Ahi'rea noticed him watching her approach. Hate welled up in her and the image of Revik running

Haruu'na through flashed before her eyes. She wanted to rush up and kill him right there. Bound and weakened, with a single spear thrust he would be repaid in kind for what he had done. She drew near, quieting such thoughts and turning her attention to Revik's guard.

"You," Revik said, addressing Ahi'rea in Cheduna. She looked at him, concealing her surprise at being spoken to. He had not said a word to anyone since the incident with Haaph'ahin. His eyes were wide, as if he had just realized who she was.

"What do you want?" she asked in Huumphar. She understood a few words of Cheduna, but not enough to speak to him without sounding foolish. When he did not respond, she tried again in her accented Gharven, the northern tongue.

He started and paused, looking down, and spoke in perfect Gharven as if each word were new to him. "You look different," Revik said, staring at the area on her arm where he had wounded her. The cut was gone, a thin, pale line all that remained of the deep slash. "If you can heal yourself, why not heal the others?" he asked.

He spoke without accent. Few southerners could speak the guttural northern language well. Ahi'rea narrowed her eyes, considering this new development.

"I cannot," she said. "I have no command of Storm. I can heal myself, but not others."

"I could," Revik replied, "before."

"You are from the North," Ahi'rea said.

He looked up sharply. "I am not." He recognized that there was no point in lying, however, and continued, "I may have been born there, but I am from Feriven. These lands are one."

"One land for you and the rest who will bow to your king," she answered, drawn in despite herself. "Peace for fearful slaves who live as your lord pleases, the sword for the rest."

"The powerful have earned what they have, and if it were not right, the rest would reject it," Revik answered, smiling. "It is only right. You, and your people, chose your own fate, chose war over peace."

Revik's calm only made Ahi'rea more furious. "Your lord and his ancestors attacked us! We wished only to be left alone! Your ways are not ours, your king not ours! Why should we follow commands we do not believe? Why should we bow to that filth?"

"King Halkoriv is a great man," Revik said, his voice rising. "And you should bow because he is stronger! If you had only submitted to his will you and the North and all the others would be at peace! Because of the stubborn foolishness of your ancestors, you will all die!" A small crowd had begun to gather to witness the exchange between the prisoner and the seeress. Revik's voice was a shout.

"You will be crushed and wiped from these plains! The flame of the South will burn you all away!" he said. The waning light of sunset grew darker around him as he went on. "Why do you continue to resist? You cannot stop us, and your actions bring only more death! You are beaten!" He rose to his feet. The darkness grew thicker, unnatural. "Unless you realize the error of your ways you will all be killed, as your fathers and mothers before you were!"

"Enough!" Ahi'rea's balled fist caught Revik full in the stomach. He doubled over and dropped to his knees, gasping. His wounds lanced pain through him in waves.

The shadow dissipated. Revik looked up in fury and pain, breathing through clenched teeth.

Ahi'rea's breathing was heavy with rage. "If you are so much our better," she said, leaning down, "why is it that you are now bowing to me?" Revik spat blood on the ground and met her eyes. He said nothing. Ahi'rea stood, smiling humorlessly, and strode away through the crowd.

—

That night, Haaph'ahin led the way to the hilltop. Ahi'rea carried a necklace she had made for her mother as a child, along with Haruu'na's doeskin cape. Others bore weapons, clothes, and other items which had belonged to those they had lost. The rest of the Huumphar carried bundles of grasses and wood. Revik was brought along, he assumed, for lack of a better way to keep watch over him. Small, ceremonial pyres were built for those lost and left behind in the disastrous raid. They, like the ridges built onto the hilltop, radiated in a circle around the platform of the Monument. Many a sorrowful or hateful eye watched Revik where he sat off to one side, bound and silent.

Each of the deceased had a Sender, one of their loved ones or friends who took on the responsibility of singing during the ritual. Ahi'rea stood at the head of Haruu'na's pyre, facing the center of a circle formed by the other pyres and their Senders. Haaph'ahin was behind her. Rahi'sta stood to her right, over the small pyre for her husband. She held their child, but otherwise she was alone. All was quiet but for the crackling of the spreading flames as the pyres were lit. The air was still, and the sparks flew high overhead, flickering and vanishing in the night sky. Revik didn't know who began, but one clear voice rang out, echoing through the ruins of the Monument. One by one the Senders lifted their voices, each beginning the chants in the same ancient words. Their chants diverged, many strands flowing apart and weaving back together as they sang. The other Huumphar, outside the circle, were silent but for a few sobs and moans of grief.

Revik tried to ignore them. The killings were justified. Not only had the plainsfolk chosen to resist all this time, they had massacred an entire garrison of soldiers by the time Revik attacked them. Looking down and studying the ground, he attempted to shut out the haunting voices and flickering firelight.

He was still in pain. Ahi'rea's blow had been stronger than he had expected. He would have to avoid underestimating her if he were to escape. He was annoyed that he had not gotten the chance to ask how she had blocked him from his powers, and was even angrier at himself for losing control and revealing that they were returning.

He had not expected to be beaten by anyone ever again after he defeated Cunabrel. Although he had torn through the other Huumphar with ease, Ahi'rea had stopped his rampage almost as effortlessly. How her eyes had blazed; though he could not recognize her power, she was a force to be respected. He saw her across the hilltop and watched for a time, trying to pick out her voice from the chanting. Even standing still, she was a thing of grace. The flames picked out the muscles in her legs and her sun-bleached hair reflected the fire's light.

He realized he was staring, admiring her even. He turned his gaze to the ground again, disgusted with himself. She was an animal, an enemy—possibly one of Feriven's greatest foes. Revik tried to clear his thoughts of her, but the chanting invaded his mind. Waves of sound crashed against him, sweeping him down, threatening to drown him; he fought against the tide, realized he was gasping as if for air. His sight faded as if he were consumed by dark water.

Flickers of memory arose, unbidden. Some were memories that had been mere fragments he had been unable to place, and others he did not recognize at all. A small, log house with earthen floors, covered by straw mats and sheepskins; a vast forest surrounding a cultivated orchard; two men and a woman, standing on the Monument, knives raised over bound and naked sacrifices, eyes blind and rolling in fear. High cliffs facing the warm north; his mother and father, their faces still lost to him. Feeling his skin and bones and guts and life fall away, burning and freezing, agony, casting barbs of darkness into waiting and open flesh; and finally, a night of flame and terror; a woman clutching a small boy close. Nearby, a man held a sword, his back to a door. Someone was slamming against it. An axe head drove through it. The boy looked at him. "Remember," he said.

The chanting rose in his ears. That night had been the last time his mother had held him, the last time before he was snatched away, before the long dark of Cunabrel's cell. The young plainsfolk woman sang for her mother that night. Revik had barely thought of his parents since Halkoriv had rescued him. Only the concept had seemed important. Not until now had he thought on what he had lost. The unfamiliar memories felt like those of another, but at the same time felt as if they belonged to him in a way that nothing else had in his entire life. Even his name had begun to sound foreign to him.

Revik did not weep for his parents or Ahi'rea's mother; he did not allow himself. However, for the first time he could remember, he knew remorse.

—

When the Sending ended, several of the Huumphar convened to discuss what was to be done with their prisoner. They needed to move early the next morning—the red glow to the southwest and the columns of smoke told them that the Cheduna were still coming, and the chances that they had seen the Sending fires were great. Ahi'rea, Ruun'daruun, Ken'hra, Haaph'ahin, and others remained atop the Monument, with Revik under guard not far away in case they felt the need to question him.

Ken'hra suggested they spear him and be done with him. This was seconded by Ruun'daruun and many of the elders. They looked at Ahi'rea and Haaph'ahin expectantly.

She paused, then shook her head in disagreement. Surprise was immediate among the others. "Rea," Ruun'daruun said, then corrected himself. "Ahi'rea, he's just one of Halkoriv's creatures. A weapon. He killed so many of us."

An elder nodded. "He is a danger. Why do you want to keep him alive?"

"I do not," Ahi'rea said. "I want him dead as much as the rest of you."

"Why, then? Why shouldn't we be rid of him now? He is not the real Lasivar, even if Halkoriv thinks he is..." Ruun'daruun trailed off, then he smiled.

"A bartering chip—Halkoriv thinks he's someone important," Ken'hra said.

"No," Haaph'ahin interjected. "He has surely realized by now. From what Ahi'rea has told me, Halkoriv may have had a direct link to this warrior somehow. Once the link was cut, he had to realize that it was only his own will driving this man, not true sorcery."

Ken'hra broke in, frustrated. "No, wait. This is ridiculous— are you telling us that all this time, Halkoriv thought he was raising Lasivar's son as his greatest weapon, and he was wrong? That he did not know, even when directly linked to him, that he had the wrong man? Halkoriv is many things, but he is no fool. It must be some trick."

Haaph'ahin smiled joylessly. "That is the nature of the power Halkoriv wields—his greatest strength and weakness are one." He took a deep breath, gathering his thoughts. "If the tales and my Sight hold true, then Halkoriv's ancestors forsook Sight, Self, and Storm—true sorcery—long ago. One of them, a man called Sitis, sought a means to become immortal. He succeeded, after a fashion, but all that survived, freed from its human shell, was his greed and rage, his lust for power and blood. The Ravenous Spirit.

"Since that time, all Sitis' descendants have sought immortality, but all have only been consumed by the power they wield. Instead of sorcery, they command the Ravenous Spirit, as long as it lets them. They can perform feats beyond the ability of most sorcerers, but their power betrays them to its own gain. It would seem that in this case, the Ravenous Spirit blinded Halkoriv to the true identity of his chosen heir."

"But why?" Ahi'rea asked. She was still angry at her father, but knew he was still wise and knowledgeable. She knew no more than the others about Sitis. "Why would it mislead him? What does it stand to gain?"

"I could not say," Haaph'ahin responded. "Sitis was mad even before shedding his life; I do not know if the Spirit even has motivations we can understand. It only speaks to those of the same line as Halkoriv, or those they have infected with it. I only know that it has grown stronger during the war; once, it was all Halkoriv could do to bring a storm against us or strengthen his warriors. Now, he controls the winds with ease and renders our women barren, our children sick. Perhaps it feeds on death and despair and saw only the chance to gorge itself by the deeds of this false Lasivar."

"In any case, he's useless to us now," Ruun'daruun said. "Halkoriv knows he had the wrong man."

Ahi'rea spoke up just as Haaph'ahin opened his mouth to respond. She stopped, yielding to the elder, but he motioned for her to go on. She grudgingly accepted the unspoken gesture of contrition. "I am not sure, but we may have a use for him still. He claims that he can heal others. At first I did not believe him—I thought no one could do that. However, it sounds as if with the command of this Spirit, it might be true. It would not matter, except—I think he is beginning to recover his power. Without it I do not think he could have traveled as he did, and I noticed something when I spoke to him earlier." She glanced over at Revik, still sitting quietly on the other side of the hilltop. "But if he is recovering, he is dangerous. And if what you say is true, then he must be one of Sitis' line. Otherwise he would remain cut off and Halkoriv would have to restore his power for him."

Haaph'ahin nodded. "I have noticed his recovery as well. I do not think he is of Sitis' line. It would be strange if there were more of them than Halkoriv and he did not know. That is what troubles me—it seems the Spirit has a hold on this false Lasivar, a hold he thinks he can control. Halkoriv did something in trying to combine true sorcery with Sitis' power. Indeed, I do not think the boy even remembers his own life before Halkoriv took him. His memory, what I could see of it, was... corrupted; hazy."

"As if Sitis is blocking it to keep him from changing—from realizing that he is not who he thinks he is," Ruun'daruun said, pleased that he could follow the conversation. Ahi'rea listened; she knew that sorcery was not something Ruun'daruun understood, but the mind of a warrior was. "If he learned the truth, it would shake his core—make him question his purpose, his training, everything. He's fighting for a person who has manipulated him and because he thinks he's the son of a hero. Take that away, and he's just another man, one who was lied to and used." Ruun'daruun stopped, looking across the hilltop at their prisoner. "Maybe he'll turn—hold a grudge against Halkoriv. He must have useful information."

"Not likely," Ahi'rea said. "He might hold such a grudge if he came to believe the truth, but how would you feel about the people who shattered your life?" No one answered. "No matter what we tell him, the only way he will believe us is if I or my father can heal his mind, if it can even be done. However, I think we may be able to convince him to help our sick and wounded."

"Why would he do that?" one of the others snorted.

"To save himself," Ahi'rea said. "If we convince him that we may let him go, he might cooperate."

"Let him go?" Ken'hra shouted. "He'll just come back again to kill us!"

"I said convince him—not that we need actually do it," Ahi'rea said. There was a murmur of approval, although some—Ruun'daruun among them—looked uncomfortable. It was not a crime to lie to outsiders, but some viewed such actions as a breach of honor.

Haaph'ahin's voice, gravelly, but strong and resonant, suddenly rose. "There is another matter with which he might help us; the true son of Lasivar is still alive, I am sure of it. I cannot See him clearly—I have never met him, have nothing of his. Without something to guide the connection, it is like searching the horizon at night. But," he said, his eyes fixed on the space before him, "he might. The power of Sitis does not have the same boundaries, and since his power is returning, we may get something of use from him before we are rid of him after all."

One by one, the others nodded. Ahi'rea was silent. She was not convinced that finding Lasivar's son was the answer they sought. "Do we really want him calling on this spirit? Could it control him? Bring Halkoriv down on us?"

Haaph'ahin was grave. "I do not know—but I think it is worth the risk if we can find the true Lasivar."

Ahi'rea's eyes turned southwest—to the dull orange glow on the horizon. She had little doubt death came for them on the smoke and flames, as it had not for many years. It seemed Halkoriv would obliterate the plains this time rather than even fight. She heard Ruun'daruun speak, but did not turn. The discussion went on—a slow excitement built among the Huumphar as a shade of hope returned to them. The return of Lasivar—scion of the family that had forestalled and fought Halkoriv and his line for generations—seemed a possibility once again. They spoke cautiously of him. Where had he been hiding? Why had he not yet revealed himself? Would he finally defeat Halkoriv, or would he only beat him back again as those before him had? Haaph'ahin spoke of visions of glory. Ruun'daruun, anxious for the chance to bring the fight to Halkoriv, was confident the real Lasivar could be found, and by his mere presence rally the Northerners and the Huumphar.

Ahi'rea's gaze remained steady on the fiery glow. The voices receded and she heard the sound of the fire crackling. Cool wind blew at her back, refreshing and biting at the same time. In her mind, a great white beast, serpentine, scales glistening with droplets of icy water, rose from the sea. It was borne by many hands up out of the water, and as it rose the hands sank beneath the waves. It clashed with a creature the color of fire. They ripped and tore at one another, sometimes one about to triumph, sometimes the other. With each wound, the red creature grew fouler—sprouting limbs and horns, scales growing slick and vile. The white creature grew brighter, glowing, and though it fought with unwaning strength, the beasts dragged each other down, drowning in their blood. They lay dead. The body of the red beast erupted and another, as foul as the first, dragged itself from the stinking, wet corpse.

She closed her eyes, the sounds of her surroundings returning. She heard the group's hushed discussion; they had noticed her eyes.

"Ahi'rea," Haaph'ahin whispered, "what did you see?"

She did not answer right away. Sometimes she hated the Sight—others thought it gave answers, but she knew what it really brought.

The words came, unbidden, in the Old Tongue, and she could not stop her voice. "He will come from the North. Like beasts of war, the clash of swords, the son dies like father. While flesh will burn, the Spirit endures."

—Eleven—

She hated it. She could not clarify, struggled to interpret. Words caught in her throat and her thoughts became jumbled and confused if she tried to explain the vision in simple terms. Some of those with the Sight claimed it was the gods' work, ensuring that no one knew too clearly his or her own destiny. Others thought seers mad because of it. Ahi'rea thought it was the worst of the curse—to see the pain and misery and mistakes of oneself and others and offer only poetry and doubt.

"What does it mean?" someone asked.

She knew what the vision meant—even if Halkoriv was beaten, another, just like him, would rise in his place. Unless something else happened, the course the Huumphar had chosen would lead to ruin. But to say all that, in the shadow of the vision, was impossible; the Sight itself stole her words away.

Ahi'rea concentrated, forcing the words. "We will fail," she managed.

The others debated the meaning of the dream. Haaph'ahin believed her, but others offered their own interpretations. Her father knew that asking her further questions about the vision would be useless. "Nothing is set," he said. "We must carry on, and be cautious. The future is not set until we reach it."

Ahi'rea felt sick. It means nothing, she told herself. Nothing is set. Nothing is sure. The beast lurked, rotting and vile, in the back of her mind.

The Huumphar decided to move north the following morning, to keep on the move and avoid the southerners. Lasivar would return yet; even Ahi'rea's dark vision prophesied that. Together they spoke the traditional words of parting to end the moot and began to follow the winding, rocky path down from the plateau to the camp.

Ahi'rea watched Haaph'ahin linger, falling behind the others. She knew he would not sleep until he met with the prisoner, who still called himself Revik Lasivar. She went on ahead while he intercepted Revik and his guards as they approached the pathway. Haaph'ahin sent the guards back a short distance. She knew he wanted to speak with the prisoner unheard, but she could not help but worry for him. She walked in front of them, but concentrated and felt her hearing strengthen. She heard the wind on the plains, the crackle of campfires. If she concentrated hard enough, she could hear her father's heart pounding.

—

The old man moved close to Revik, but he ignored him, not hesitating along his way. Revik wound between the ruined marble structures and started down the path, making Haaph'ahin work to keep up.

Haaph'ahin kept pace beside him in silence. Then he said, slowly, "I am told you are fluent in Gharven. That you are from the

North, as the true son of Lasivar would have been."

Revik snorted.

"I still do not believe you are who you say you are, regardless of where you are from. Halkoriv could have chosen any young fool from the North and corrupted him to his purposes."

Revik stopped and turned, his eyes daggers. "And why should I care what you think? I know who I am. You are a fool." He turned back to the path.

"Oh yes, you are far too clever for me," Haaph'ahin said, following him. "You could not even conceal for one day that your abilities are returning. Given a little more time, you might have had a chance to escape. Now you are not only useless to us, but a danger as well."

Revik felt a chill blossom in his mind and spread to his fingertips. He could kill this old man in an instant, bound or not. *Maybe. But not before those two behind you raise the alarm and spear you,* he told himself. The urge to lash out built in him, to release the power, to quell the cold in his mind. He resisted. He knew he was not strong enough yet.

"If I am so dangerous, then kill me," Revik said. "You will only destroy your most valuable bartering tool and bring the entire kingdom and Halkoriv himself down on your miserable dying tribe."

Revik could tell that the words stung. The old man spat, then pressed on. "Brave talk, if I believed it. You will not be the first over-stuffed hapless Cheduna lord we have set upon a spear, and you will not be the last. If you truly are as important, as wise, as powerful as you say, we would have seen as much by now. You are one of Halkoriv's pawns, nothing more. We will heed your advice and execute you in the morning. Halkoriv will not miss your loss."

Revik was drawn in despite himself. "My powers are return-ing," he protested. "What more do you want? What other proof could you need? You will be signing your own death warrants all the sooner if you kill me." Revik was beginning to worry that his time had run out. He stopped, but Haaph'ahin kept walking. Revik called after him, "Accept that you are wrong, that you and your people are at fault for this bloodshed. You may yet join Feriven in peace!"

At this Haaph'ahin stopped and turned to face Revik again.

After a long pause, as if thinking, he approached and allowed his shoulders to slump. "We are so weary of fighting," Haaph'ahin said. "Prove to me that there is no other son of Lasivar. Use your powers, if they are indeed returning, and search for him. I will be able to See what you see. As you may have noticed, you and your king are not the only ones with the gift after all." Revik narrowed his eyes. "If you are right," Haaph'ahin sighed, "we will surrender. If you are right, then there is no cause to go on fighting."

Revik saw Haaph'ahin's head droop and his eyes fall, defeat settling over him. *So, he knows it is over already.* Revik smiled. "Very well," he said. He had not doubted the old man's threat to kill him, but now it seemed he might even accomplish his mission after all, as a captive no less. When he failed to find another 'son of Lasivar' or saw only himself, the plainsfolk would end their resistance. With no hero, no one powerful enough to lead them, what choice would they have?

He closed his eyes and felt the familiar chill run through him. Doubt clutched at him—Halkoriv's lies about sorcery, and perhaps other things, nagged at him—but he concentrated and pushed those thoughts out, then relaxed his restraint.

The cold at the base of his skull spread. The warmth drained from him. He held the idea in his mind: 'son of Lasivar.' He waited for an image of himself or some other sense that he was the focus of his own search. Instead, he felt familiarity, as of discovering a possession he had not known was lost. Not for the first time that day, he saw in his mind a pale-haired boy, serene and brave even in youth.

Revik flinched; his mind became a mass of cold and dark, a hole to nothingness in the world. But he was not alone—he felt Haaph'ahin's mind in the darkness. *Call him,* Haaph'ahin pushed. *Call him to us. He must come!* Then he felt something else, something older and crueler lurking there with them.

Images bombarded Revik as the cold touch of his power grew stronger. The boy aged, passing through many strange and exotic locales. He became a man, and Revik saw him train and fight and learn; saw him hold men and women captive with his words; saw love and hope in their gazes.

Come to us, Revik thought. The words, the feelings, were not his. They came from outside, and were echoed from deep within. *Yes, come,* whispered the echo. *Help us,* came the first voice. *Come to die,* whispered the second. Revik shuddered at it.

Then, the man he knew to be Lasivar's son looked straight at him. Revik saw the people around the man follow him, take up arms and leave all they knew behind.

Revik saw the ocean—felt the cold spray, smelled salt and felt the wind out of the north. He had never seen it, but he knew it, could not remember it but felt it was home. The wind drove ships to a familiar coast; high cliffs fringed with tall autumn trees.

—

Revik dropped to his knees, eyes clenched shut, arms clutching his chest. Haaph'ahin stood by, watching. Cold sweat beading on his forehead as Revik shuddered and quaked. His guards looked on with fear in their eyes. Haaph'ahin started when Ahi'rea raised her voice behind him.

"What is happening to him?" She approached the fallen prisoner.

Haaph'ahin put out his arm to stop her and put a finger to his lips. "It is working," he whispered. "He has found Lasivar, I am sure of it!"

A shadow had gathered about them, noticeable even in the dark of night. The world felt closed, confining. It was too small a space. Standing beside her father, watching Revik writhe and convulse, Ahi'rea felt her breathing become labored. The dark was choking and thick. Her vision faded and sound receded. She could not see the stars overhead. Then, when she looked back at Revik, something invisible and cold caressed her neck.

She cried out in revulsion, recoiling from the touch. "Wake him up!" she shouted. "Something is wrong!"

"No!" Haaph'ahin said. "It is our only chance! We have to be certain he calls him."

Ignoring her father, Ahi'rea took a step toward Revik. Haaph'ahin reached out, grabbing her by the arm, but she pulled away roughly and grasped Revik by the shoulders. She shook him and called out in Gharven. He did not respond; his breath caught in his throat and he choked, his chest wracked with spasms.

Maintaining her grip, Ahi'rea calmed herself and concentrated. Her eyes flared green, driving back the shadows around them as if burning them. *Stop*, she said, her voice strange and echoing in her own ears. She felt resistance press back against her mind. She forgot what she was doing, struggled to recall. She felt gnashing teeth and deep-throated snarling, pain and madness and rage. She could see the Monument, stark and bright and burning around them, more real than the world fading around it. The Monument stood in relief, a void against the world. It was like nothing she had ever seen in the Dreaming, or with the Sight, or in life. It roared. Terror gripped her, but still she concentrated. *Stop. Now. NOW.* She pushed.

The pressure ended and her mind lurched. She was disoriented and spent and she was surprised to find she was sweating and gasping. Her vision was blurred and spotty; she repressed the urge to vomit. Her vision cleared and she found herself looking into a pair of fearful, reddened eyes.

Revik looked just as shocked as Ahi'rea that it was over. She felt the freezing skin of his bare arms. He had been imprisoned, hurt, stabbed, but never had he looked so close to death before. He stared at Ahi'rea, unable to move, his chest heaving. She was shocked to realize that he was terrified.

Ahi'rea shivered; inside she burned, but a chill clung to her skin and Revik's body was icy. He quaked, one hand moving up to grip her arm. Through the terror etched on his face, she saw something else that caught her off guard—gratitude.

"He nearly died," she said. She had felt the void grasping at him, terrible beyond imagining—no peace, no Journey, not even the quiet of nothingness. An ever consuming pit, eternal ravenous hunger incarnate, had nearly taken him. *Not that,* she thought.

Even he does not deserve that. And if it had taken him, she wondered what would have been left in his place. She looked up at Haaph'ahin. "Do you know what almost happened?" she shouted. All she could think of was the icy touch on her neck.

Haaph'ahin was unperturbed. "It was necessary. His life is nothing if it will end this war. Halkoriv must be stopped, at any cost," he said. "This man is our enemy! He killed your mother without a thought, and you would jeopardize our chances just to keep him alive!"

"You would condemn him to worse than death, looking for something that will make no difference!" she said, surprised that she could manage the words despite her vision. "I am tired of your manipulations; I am beginning to wonder where you will stop."

Glowering, Haaph'ahin ignored her and knelt, catching Revik by the jaw and searching his face. "You saw; you believe me now, do you not, boy? You have been misled by your lord and now you have seen the real Lasivar."

Ahi'rea started to speak, but Revik nodded. His eyes closed. He could not refute what he had seen. The son of Lasivar was another, the man in his vision. His life was a lie.

"Ha!" Haaph'ahin crowed gleefully. "Where is he? Did you call him?"

"North," Revik rasped. It seemed it was an act of will for him to speak at all. "He saw me. He is coming…" he said. Realization played across his features. "You… said you would see," he said, looking at Haaph'ahin.

"So I did," the old man cackled. "You have confirmed my hopes, and perhaps worn out your usefulness. That is, unless you can tell me where he will arrive."

Revik looked lost. He had seemed so sure of his place, and now he wept. "The cliffs," he stuttered. "On the north coast—a village between the forest and the sea. Please, don't kill me." All courage seemed to have left him. Ahi'rea reached out to his mind, and felt only fear and confusion. "I am not your savior and I... I am not your enemy," he said.

Haaph'ahin smiled triumphantly. "Some good came from you in the end. It seems we may not have to bring you along with us after all. You slaughtered too many to go free. Think on that till the morning."

With that, Haaph'ahin signaled the two guards forward and told them to take the prisoner back to camp. They complied, lifting Revik by his arms and dragging his unresisting form down the path. "Tomorrow we will move the tribe away from the Monument, then rest till nightfall to begin our journey north," Haaph'ahin called after them.

Ahi'rea stood. She stared at Haaph'ahin, her mind reeling.

"He is coming back! That boy's cursed power found him, and now he will return!" Haaph'ahin said happily.

Ahi'rea shook her head. "Did you not hear me?" she asked. "It will not matter." She looked after the prisoner. "That spirit almost took him—he did not deserve that."

"It would have been worth it," Haaph'ahin said. "You will see. This war is going to end." He looked at his daughter. "He deserves to die. I thought you wanted him dead."

She had, but not like that. She turned and walked weakly back to camp, Haaph'ahin's calls for messengers and runners echoing behind her. He bid them go out to the other tribes and the villages of Gharven with word of Lasivar's return.

All through that night, her arm remained cold where Revik had touched it, and her dreams were only of the fear and loss she had seen in his eyes. She tried to keep her gaze turned away from the Monument. She could not banish the feeling that it was watching her.

—

The next morning, Haaph'ahin awoke to find Ahi'rea was waiting, ready to leave, with Revik still bound but waiting nearby.

"He is coming with us," she said.

—Twelve—

Rahi'sta and Tak'la, among others gathering their things to leave, were a short distance outside the camp when the argument erupted.

"She has gone mad," Rahi'sta said, watching Ahi'rea. "Why would she protect him?"

At first, Tak'la did not realize she was talking to him. He watched the argument, sometimes scanning the boulder-strewn plains around them. The stones were the same black marble as made up the structures atop the Monument. They crouched, like penitents bowing beneath the aging structure towering above them. He noticed Rahi'sta looking at him expectantly. "I'm sorry." He looked back and forth between her and Ahi'rea and Haaph'ahin's shouting. "No one talks to me."

Rahi'sta smiled. "I know. And for that, I'm the one who should be sorry. But now..." she looked down at her child, cradled in her arms, "I think I understand you better." She looked back at Tak'la. "We're alone too."

Tak'la nodded his thanks. He looked back at Ahi'rea. "She's not mad. Something is different today." He clambered up a small boulder beside them and sat with his legs crossed.

Rahi'sta looked skeptically at Ahi'rea, then regarded Tak'la for a moment. He was reviled by the tribe as death-touched, but he fought as hard as any other warrior; he was tall and powerful, but sometimes so childlike; and though no one noticed him, he seemed to notice things no one else could see. "What's different?" Rahi'sta asked.

Tak'la pointed, and Rahi'sta looked back at Ahi'rea. Now Haaph'ahin was shouting, trying to shame her into listening to him. But Tak'la was pointing not at them, but at Revik, standing beside Ahi'rea.

Tak'la was right; he was different. He looked smaller, somehow. He no longer appeared as a proud prince held hostage. He looked like nothing more than a frightened young man, dirty, tired, and hurt. She might have felt sorry for him under different circumstances.

Rahi'sta knew no one would interfere between Ahi'rea and Haaph'ahin. They were both seers, one an elder, and many considered Ahi'rea an elder as well, despite her age. Siding with one or the other in the argument might lead to repercussions later.

Their voices quieted, and she did not hear how it ended. Ahi'rea walked away, proud and silent, with Revik in tow. His arms were bound, but no guards accompanied him. None of the Huumphar followed Ahi'rea too close, or gathered around Haaph'ahin.

Ken'hra had already left, leading the Whispered Thunder tribe north. They were not far away, still visible among the boulders littering the plains. The sun was rising, reflecting a vibrant red off the black stones, dragging long shadows like spires across the grasses. The Monument stood, darkening the plains for what seemed miles. Tak'la bounded off of his rock and began loping north. Rahi'sta secured her son's traveling basket on her back and set out after him. The tribe followed.

—

Over the next weeks, the knowledge that Revik had admitted he was not Lasivar spread among the Huumphar. They also learned that Haaph'ahin had now predicted the true Lasivar's return. Excitement and hope gradually made themselves felt once again during the long trip to the northern Gharven coast. Even as they marched, however, they began to find refugees; Huumphar whose tribes were lost, who spoke of fire and death coming from the south, of deadly raiding parties chasing down fleeing Huumphar.

They traveled by night, the wind at their backs, to avoid heat and detection. On the fifteenth night, Tak'la, as usual, had ranged far past the others in his zeal for scouting. He could hear them, far behind, but all around was the sound of the plains at night; grasses whispering in the wind, the chirping of insects. The cool, dry air chilled the sweat on his skin as he paused to gaze at the sky. The moon was but a dim, narrow sliver, and the stars overhead were bright crystals hanging in the dark. He smiled, relishing the purity of the moment—the night sounds, no light but the stars and pale moon; the war and bloodshed seemed for a moment like a bad dream.

The prisoner—now nameless and silent—had spoken with Tak'la a little when Tak'la had been assigned to watch over him. Tak'la knew a few words of badly accented Gharven—enough to ask him, "What is... yourself?" although he knew it was not the right phrasing.

The prisoner had looked at him—a look that made Tak'la flinch to recall.

"I have never known," he had said. "I am lost, only lies." Despite the intensity of the stare, Tak'la had steeled his resolve and stared back. Neither had looked away—though the prisoner appeared to be looking at something other than the burly Huumphar youth.

"Huumphar… give you, um, truth," Tak'la managed, smiling at himself. He furrowed his brow, moving on to a slightly simpler thought. "Help you. Ahi'rea save your life." It was frustrating, to try to express himself to one so thoroughly different.

"Ahi'rea," the prisoner had breathed, as if savoring the sound. After a long pause, he said, "No. It has all been taken from me. Understand? Huumphar gave truth, but took everything else." He had not spoken further after that.

Tak'la had shrugged it off—it was natural that the prisoner would be confused and angry. Standing on the plains beneath the stars, though, he wondered if he could feel the peace and purity he felt now if he had lost what the prisoner had. Tak'la's friends and family had died—but he could not imagine losing all of himself.

His reverie was interrupted when he heard a faint sound, almost indistinguishable above the whispering of the grasses. If he had been closer to the other Huumphar, he would surely have missed it. He turned to the west. It was dark, and nothing out of the ordinary was to be seen, but as he studied the landscape he saw something—far off, grasses being pushed and bent against the wind.

Tak'la hesitated—the next nearest scouts would be hundreds

of yards away. He wondered if he would have time to alert them without whatever was there noticing him. The next sound, however, told him all he needed to know; the distant clank of steel, the sound of a southern scout or raiding party.

He flew through the grass, head low, spear in one hand and machete unsheathed in the other. He paused, regaining his bearings as he neared the movement and sounds.

Tak'la came upon the first of them within moments—a small, frail body, slumped in a heap, blood still warm and oozing from fresh wounds. The grass around the old woman's corpse was trampled and hacked; a broken machete lay a few feet away, a testament to her futile attempt to defend herself.

It was something that they had heard of from the refugees—even without its leader, the southern army was decimating the tribes of the Huumphar. After the warriors were all dead, fleeing elders and children too young to fight were tracked down and slaughtered. Any who survived would be death-touched, like Tak'la. Fury rose in him. *Not tonight.*

The trail was easy to follow—a wide, trampled path headed northeast and the sound of voices speaking in Cheduna. Snarling, Tak'la charged along the trampled path, white-knuckled hands gripping spear and blade. He pushed through the brush and caught sight of a dozen soldiers, leather armor stained dark for camouflage, and clustered ahead of them was a small group of old and young refugees. They were Western Huumphar, wearing silvery rock-bird feathers in their hair and sheepskins instead of deer. They were near dead from fatigue—their home was hundreds of miles west. They must have been moving for days, or even weeks, as fast as they could.

Despite his speed, Tak'la's approach went unnoticed. His steps were silent and drowned out by the gloating of some of the soldiers as they menaced the refugees. He noticed that a few seemed less enthusiastic about their task; grim-faced, but determined to do their duty. As he chose his targets, he merely relegated them to the end of the list.

He lunged. A broad sweep with his spear to the backs of their legs brought two soldiers to their knees with yelps of shock and pain. A swift chop with his machete took one of them out of the fight before it began. With that, the others spun around, crying out their alarm at the surprise attack. The one who seemed to be in command put the others between himself and the hulking Huumphar, bellowing orders and pointing in turn at Tak'la and the refugees. His dirty, crooked teeth looked too small for his face, like an old wild dog's. Tak'la had hoped to kill the leader first, but he had positioned himself too well, too fast.

The other he had knocked down regained his feet and with four more of the soldiers surrounded Tak'la. The rest, under their commander's direction, approached the refugees. Some of the Huumphar held broken or makeshift weapons, but none of them were in any shape to fight.

Experience told Tak'la to dodge back out of reach into the grasses, to make the soldiers careless and angry, get them to chase him, to make mistakes. Logic told him that if he did, they would kill the refugees to draw him back. He told himself that he could kill every one of them on their own terms.

The commander shouted. As one, the soldiers lunged, axes and swords held high, spear points darting forward. Ducking to one side, Tak'la avoided some attacks and deflected another with his blade. A spear managed to find its target, biting into his leg. Gritting his teeth, Tak'la barreled into a soldier, slamming him to the ground. Swiping at another, he cut deep through armor and felt hot blood splash onto his sword-arm. He wasted no time, stomping on the throat of the fallen soldier as he turned, finishing the machete swing. He darted back amongst the soldiers, tripping one of them and in one movement driving his spear into the man's gut. A blade raked Tak'la's back; he roared and swept his machete around, then dived straight backwards. He crashed into his attacker and they both rolled to the ground. Tak'la swore as he lost his grip on his spear. He twisted, landing atop the soldier as they came to rest. Pulling the man up by a leather armor strap, Tak'la butted him full in the face with his forehead. The soldier jerked and fell back, but Tak'la was already moving again, rolling, pulling the dazed soldier on top of him. An axe blade crashed into the unconscious man's back instead of Tak'la. The Huumphar warrior shouted, whipping his machete into the nearest pair of legs. Their owner shrieked, falling hard to the ground, blood gushing from his ruined ankles. Tak'la pushed the body off and leapt to his feet, faltering on his own injured leg.

The other soldiers were beginning to withdraw, and the lone remaining man facing him was backing away. Tak'la did not see their commander. He spun around to look just as he felt a spear drive into his lower back.

Tak'la fell without a sound, dragging the spear out of the commander's hand. He saw the crooked-toothed man stand over him, saw the knife in his fist. The other soldiers were shouting. The commander looked up and to the east, then shouted as well. He looked down, smiled, and plunged the blade into Tak'la's chest.

—Thirteen—

"It is his time. He died back when the rest of his tribe was killed," Ken'hra said. "You have to let it happen."

Tak'la lay where he had fallen, blood pooling beneath him and seeping into the ground. They had found him amongst the trampled and crushed grasses by following the shouts and cries of battle. The knife in his chest rose and fell with his every shallow breath. Tak'la's eyes were wide, but he gave no indication that he saw or heard the Huumphar around him.

At first, they had not recognized him in the dark. There had been a group of western Huumphar standing around him, all children and old women, and five dead or dying southern soldiers. Ken'hra had been the first to discover him and had called for the others' aid before realizing who the fallen warrior was.

Ahi'rea, kneeling beside Tak'la, looked up at Ken'hra. "We have so few warriors, and he saved these people. We have to try to help him," she said.

Ken'hra shook her head. "Death follows him. Taking him with us would be a mistake—we don't want him with us when it finally claims him."

"She's right, Rea," Ruun'daruun said behind her. "Death has

come for him. There's nothing we can do without inviting it to follow us further." Ruun'daruun shrugged. "I am sorry. He was a powerful warrior, but we need to see to the living."

"He is yet alive, as long as he can draw breath," a grizzled voice called out. They looked up in surprise to see Haaph'ahin pushing his way through the gathered scouts and warriors. He stopped and stood over Tak'la, looking down at him with his eyes aflame. "This young one... his time may have come and gone, but we will do what we can. Send for healers. We will help him and keep moving, and if Death will claim him it will do so on its feet."

No one contradicted him. Haaph'ahin caught her gaze and Ahi'rea nodded her thanks. Tak'la was soon being carried back to the rest of the tribe. Few expected he would survive the journey, but all through the night he kept breathing.

—

He did not dream or feel the passage of time. When Tak'la awoke, he started in anticipation of the knife blow and felt his body wracked by the pain of his sudden movement. When his vision cleared it was not the face of the southern commander that greeted him, but that of Rahi'sta. Her fiery hair framed her face as she looked down at him.

"Try not to move. You were badly hurt." She put a hand on Tak'la's forehead. "They thought you wouldn't live." She was smiling. "You seem to have a knack for escaping death."

Tak'la blinked and turned his head from side to side. Even that movement was painful. "You have been watching me?" he asked. He looked around, trying to get his bearings. They were beneath a stand of thick brush, the only shade in sight. Rahi'sta's child lay sleeping in his traveling basket beside him. The sun was high; Tak'la saw the other Huumphar scattered about, using their woven grass capes like tiny one-person tents to shield them from the sun.

"Many were afraid," Rahi'sta said. She reached for a water-skin and held it to his lips. While he drank she continued. "They didn't want to be beside you when Death came for you. But you said you are already dead... so I knew there was nothing to fear." He finished drinking and she smiled again, putting her hand on his. He smiled his thanks.

"Rahi'sta," he said. "I'm hungry."

She laughed and ducked out from under the brush. "Well then I will find food for you. Don't run off."

Tak'la laughed, then groaned at the pain spreading through his chest. Rahi'sta bounded off through the camp and Tak'la found himself looking at her son, sleeping beside him. The child's nose twitched and he squinted, making faces. As Tak'la watched, the boy struggled against the basket holding him, gradually working one tiny arm free. He reached up, swiped at his nose, then lapsed back into comfortable stillness. Tak'la grinned and looked up through the brush into the clear sky beyond.

Throughout the rest of the journey, nearly a dozen more refugees were collected. Even more were found too late, killed and left for the vultures or dead of starvation or fatigue. Every time they were found alive, they told of a massive force of Cheduna who chased off the game, poisoned waters, and drove fire before them like a herd of maddened bulls. Tak'la's injuries were slow to heal, but the Huumphar's pace left little time for recovery. Though they sighted no more soldiers, the nightly red glow in the south grew ever brighter.

Tak'la had to be pulled on a litter behind a pair of Huumphar at first, bouncing along in a cloud of dust. After a few nights of choking and crashing, he forced himself to run on his own. It was not easy, but he bore the pain of his wounds in silence. He was forced to stay with the main group rather than scout ahead. If anything the other Huumphar avoided him more than usual, although Rahi'sta spoke with him often and Haaph'ahin even sought him out once to ask about the Cheduna. Desperate to contribute, Tak'la volunteered to guard the prisoner, allowing others to take on more important duties.

They were unsure what to call him, now that it was clear their prisoner was not Lasivar. The change in the prisoner's demeanor intrigued Tak'la. He resisted most attempts at conversation at first. Tak'la had many questions he wanted to ask him, but most of his queries were met with one word answers at best. Tak'la noticed, however, that he spoke more freely whenever Ahi'rea was nearby.

They were on the move for weeks. The peak of summer had gone and the nights began to lengthen. By the time they reached the northern edge of the plains and passed into the unfamiliar forests of Gharven, Tak'la's wounds were still not healed.

—

The prisoner ran without thought, following the Huumphar and scarcely noticing the passage of weeks on the move. He was more lost than he had ever felt. He had been so sure of his place, but Halkoriv had used him. He did not even know his own name—

had never known it. More lies. Moreover, he did not even know his allies from his enemies; Ahi'rea, the person he had felt was most likely to kill him, had risked her life to save his. She had not spoken to him since that day. He wished she would.

As the sun was rising and the tribe settled in to camp amongst the tall, dark trees, his guard wordlessly placed a portion of dried meat with the more meager rations meant for him. The prisoner stared at the gift for a moment, as if contemplating the gesture, then nodded his thanks to Tak'la. The big warrior smiled, nodded back, and leaned up against a tree trunk and proceeded to concentrate on his meal.

The prisoner ate slowly, savoring the dried meat. He was reminded of his time in Cunabrel's cell and Halkoriv's arrival. *Strange*, he thought. *I was given the finest food in Feriven in Halkoriv's palace; I forgot that a tough little piece of venison could taste so good.*

He stared at his Huumphar guard in the dim forest light. *He nearly died fighting me, and then again saving those others from soldiers I once led, and here he is sharing food with me.* He had been led to believe the plainsfolk were cruel savages, more like beasts than men. His guard displayed more compassion than he would have shown were their situations reversed.

The prisoner suddenly broke his silence. "Thank you." Tak'la, as he had heard his keeper named, looked up in surprise. His youthful face slipped into a grin, and he nodded. As if taking the words as a cue, Tak'la spoke, summoning up his halting Gharven.

"Why Cheduna hates Huumphar?" he asked.

The prisoner answered without hesitation. "You attack us,"

he said. "We want one land, and peace. The Huumphar fight, so we fight them." As Tak'la considered this, the prisoner asked, "Why do the Huumphar hate the Cheduna?"

"You attack us," Tak'la echoed. "Cheduna leave, we... forget hate."

"The Cheduna bring knowledge, safety, and peace. We want to make one land for everyone."

"Cheduna bring war and fire and pain," Tak'la answered, his face souring. "Land is... always one. Cheduna gods not Huumphar gods, Cheduna ways not Huumphar ways. Cheduna want land and power. Cheduna do not rule Huumphar." The prisoner was about to protest when Tak'la added, "And Huumphar do not want fight Cheduna."

The prisoner stopped and closed his mouth. Tak'la sat for a moment, then opened a leather pouch beside him. He looked down and probed his leg wound, then began changing the dressing on his chest. The wound was healing poorly—the flesh surrounding it was discolored and pus ran from the deep puncture. As Tak'la gingerly set about his task, gritting his teeth, the prisoner felt a strange sensation—a grim whisper in his mind. He saw for a moment the wound worsen, grow darker and fouler; he saw Tak'la in great pain, unable to run or even to breathe. He closed his eyes tight, breathed deeply, and said, "I can help you."

Tak'la hesitated, then sat back, resting his weight on his hands. He nodded and the prisoner approached, kneeling beside him. He leaned over the wound, eyes still closed, and lessened his restraint and let his power rise in him. This time, however, he concentrated, pressing back against the familiar cold sensation. He held his hands a hairs-breadth from the wound.

The prisoner saw Tak'la's face fill with horror as a shadow fell over him, then surrounded them both. He seemed about to shout for help, but something stopped him. The discoloration around the wound faded, then vanished. The wound knitted shut. The prisoner flinched, grimacing, struggling against the pressure in his mind. His arms shuddered and he jerked once, then again, and then he lurched away. He fell back onto forearms, breathing hard, and turned his face up to the sunlight creeping through the leaves overhead. Tak'la gaped at his mended chest, then at the prisoner.

"Thank you, Revik." All that remained of the wound was an ugly scar.

The prisoner shook his head. "That is not my name," he gasped. He looked like he was ill.

Tak'la reached out a hand and patted his shoulder. "Thank you," he repeated.

The prisoner nodded, but said nothing for the rest of that day.

—

A sound, both familiar and utterly new, crept into the prisoner's mind throughout the next night's march. Like a faraway roar, it grew in strength and fell quiet, over and over. Dim recognition fluttered in his mind like a moth around a candle flame. *What is it? Another of the things I have lost to Halkoriv's lies?*

He had heard about the Northern Sea during his upbringing in Ferihold, though it was not until he heard the far-off crashing waves that he truly thought about it. At first, he could not distinguish it from the sound of the wind in the trees overhead. The sound grew, but nothing could have prepared him for the sight of the sea as the plainsfolk moved through the final stand of trees and out onto the rocky and windswept cliffs.

Ahead, the land simply ended; there was no beach, no long gentle slope, just sheer black rock stretching down hundreds of feet. At their base, the north wind drove the waves hard against the cliffs, so hard that the prisoner could feel the water below as well as hear it. From the base, the ocean stretched away, vast and unending, glittering with the reflection of the moon and stars.

They made camp at the cliffs. The prisoner was entranced by the waves and positioned himself as best he could to look out at the sea. Tak'la sat by him seeming to have lost his remaining fear of him. As the others bedded down and retired to their tents, together they watched the sun begin to send forth its rays from the east, stretching and dancing across the waters.

The plainsfolk elders were meeting some distance along the cliff. The prisoner and Tak'la were too far away to hear their conversation, but the discussion was short and they were soon off to their tents with the rest of the plainsfolk. The prisoner watched Ahi'rea pulling shut her tent flap, but did not realize that he was staring until he noticed Tak'la watching him. The prisoner's gaze returned to the ocean and did not leave it until the sun was high in the sky.

It was only a short hike the next evening to finish their journey. The few hours walk, with the sea always in view to their right, ended at a place the prisoner felt he should remember, but could not. He knew it from his vision of Lasivar, the true Lasivar, but the cliff landscape was more familiar than that. Memory, deep and buried and almost dead, stirred. His inability to recall pained him, but he knew the memory was not only from his vision. He felt alone and frustrated, feeble, like a man who had been healthy all his life and one day awoke unable to walk.

The edge of the Gharven forest stood just to their south. Beyond them, he could make out a few twinkling lights and thin wisps of smoke rising into the nighttime sky. Haaph'ahin and several of the others headed in that direction—to announce their presence to the local village, Tak'la explained. They returned a short time later, pleased, and ordered the tribe to make camp.

There was a new energy among the plainsfolk that night. They laughed and spoke freely to one another around their fires.

"What is all the excitement about?" the prisoner asked. He was not sure how to think of himself anymore. Revik, son of Lasivar, was the only name for himself he could remember, and he could no longer think of himself as that. Still, he wondered what the plainsfolk had been told about his vision.

"They have heard that the true son of Lasivar will return to us here," Tak'la answered. His Gharven was improving by the day, now that he had someone with which to practice it. "Elder Haaph'ahin says he can See it now—that you…" he stopped. To the prisoner, he looked almost embarrassed. "He says that you stopped his visions with your dark magic."

The prisoner nodded. Tak'la seemed at a loss, as he often was when he spoke with his charge. "They will not kill you," he said. "You healed me. Ahi'rea want you alive."

"Wants," the prisoner corrected him absently, his face a mask in the light of their campfire.

"You would return to the South?" Tak'la asked.

"No," the prisoner responded. That was one thing he had decided during the journey. Tak'la waited, so he went on. "He lied to me. Everything Halkoriv gave me was in exchange for something that I never agreed to give. He took me for his own uses, not to help me. He said it was to help me. He told me I was the son of a hero who wanted to unite Feriven—but I am not that man's son." He laughed, not a shred of humor in his voice, and added, "I do not even know what the hero really wanted. Besides, I failed. My powers are not half what they once were, and now you all know that I can be beaten. I doubt Halkoriv would welcome my return."

Tak'la was silent. He touched at the scar on his chest, then looked out at the dark northern landscape. "Stay with us," he suggested. "Repay him. Teach Halkoriv that he should not use you. You are still powerful—as much as Ahi'rea. Turn your power against Halkoriv. He hurt you." He stared at the prisoner, as if searching for a reaction.

The prisoner turned, looking first at the distant village, then the other direction, over the endless expanse of the Northern Sea. There was a lull in the crashing of waves around them, and for a moment all they heard was the crackle of their small fire. "No," he said. "Your cause is hopeless. Your hero will come, sure enough, and lead you all to very noble deaths."

Tak'la stared. His mouth twisted into a scowl. "What will you do, then?" The prisoner didn't answer. He lifted an arm and pointed north. On the horizon was a tall ship, invisible in the dark but for the moonlight reflecting off of its high white and gold sails.

—

The ship approached as the gathered Huumphar and Gharven villagers celebrated and cheered. In the short time since their sighting, other groups of Northerners and plainsfolk had arrived. Haaph'ahin's runners had alerted all they could find.

The prisoner watched from afar as the ship neared the coast with dawn's first light. There was a winding path leading up the rocky cliff face, made years ago by the local fishermen. Smaller boats were launched from the ship and carried a landing party to the path. The party disembarked, and the prisoner saw tall banners in white and gold and a group of soldiers in glittering armor. They crested the cliffs and the prisoner saw, for the first time that he could remember, the true Revik Lasivar.

He was tall and broad shouldered. Long, dark hair fluttered behind him and his bright blue eyes seemed to take in every detail. The last, lingering hope that it had all been a bad dream fled the prisoner; the air of majesty about Lasivar was almost tangible. The prisoner was no one—a mistake wrapped up in lies.

He ignored the new arrivals as they were greeted in the distance. He was at a loss. Throughout all his life, he had felt so sure of his place, his purpose. He had been destined for greatness—or so he had thought. Everyone had told him he would be powerful and wealthy, respected, strong; a man of significance; heir to the kingdom of Feriven, a kingdom he would unite. Now, all of that was gone. He was nothing, just like the rest of them; just another small, meaningless life, a single drop of rain falling into the ocean.

The prisoner wanted to die. He looked at the cliff and imagined stepping over the edge. The weightless fall, seeing the water and rocks rush up to him; he wondered if he would even feel the impact, the frigid water pulling him under, filling his lungs and freezing his body. No one would mourn his loss.

At the thought, a chill ran through him. He shuddered as something gnawed at his gut and his skin grew clammy. Cold washed over him from the base of his skull and the feeling intensified—like jagged teeth, devouring him from the inside. His vision blurred, all sound faded, and time slowed around him as something clawed its way into his mind.

—

Ahi'rea could not help but be excited as she watched the foreign warriors process up the cliffside path. The gathered crowd, hundreds of Huumphar and Gharven villagers and warriors, met Lasivar as he reached the top of the cliff. When she saw him, there was no doubt in her mind that she stood before the son of heroes. He was one destined to lead. His eyes bored into her with just a glance, as if he was looking at her with Sight. When he spoke, she wanted to agree, wanted to follow.

He was a head taller than most of the crowd, Huumphar and Gharven alike. His eyes flashed as he spoke and Ahi'rea felt a shock run through her, a percussive blast without sound. *Storm*, she thought, even though she had never seen it used before. *He did that effortlessly.* His voice rolled out and pervaded the air as if he spoke directly to her. She glanced around at the others, who stood as if transfixed. *The power of a leader.* She found herself listening just as raptly as the others if she did not concentrate. The words almost did not matter—the man did. What he said was like every speech from the old tales, every general's rally. It was the power in the words that held them all spellbound; a surety that here was the one to lead them to victory. By the time he finished speaking, she and the other Huumphar and Northerners felt ready to march on Ferihold itself. Through the cheering, a small voice inside reminded her of the seriousness of their plight. The plains were burning. Her people were dying. Halkoriv was stronger than ever—and yet, a man she had never met, newly arrived, somehow seemed like the best hope they had ever known.

Lasivar moved through the crowd, his face a picture of strength as smiling, cheering men, women, and children reached out to touch his armor, clasp his hand, or shout their thanks. Perhaps it was her own power, but Ahi'rea felt withdrawn from it all while the others remained enthralled. For a moment, as she watched, the hero seemed to diminish. He was tired—exhausted. What she had at first taken as resolve was in fact hard concentration. Whatever power he was using, it must have been difficult to maintain. She saw no sweat on his brow, but could tell that he was struggling.

Soon he reached the Huumphar elders and Northern leaders who had traveled there at the news of his approach. He focused, as if instinctively, on the most important of them. He greeted Haaph'ahin and the others, leaders of tribes and Gharven villages. They welcomed him as they would have welcomed family or a longtime friend.

As they spoke, Lasivar's eyes took in everyone nearby; Ahi'rea herself, Ruun'daruun, Ken'hra, and others. Something in his gaze gave Ahi'rea the feeling of being counted—noticed, but not remembered, the way one might take stock of supplies.

The soldiers who had come with him seemed just as stony as Lasivar. The rumor circulating was that he had been of great service to them in their own land. They wore heavy, thick armor like the southerners, and their tongue, when it was heard, was unfamiliar. They looked hardy, with rugged, pale complexions and features.

Tak'la appeared behind Ahi'rea. She was still surprised that one so big could move so quietly. "What will happen, now that he is here?" he asked.

"A war council," she said. "They will waste no time in deciding how to proceed. The Southerners approach, our people have been waiting, and he... he was born for this."

She wondered—when was he told what was expected of him? How young had he been when others started placing that weight on his shoulders? Did he even want it? She shook herself from her reverie. "There is something he must know, first." She pushed forward to Lasivar with Tak'la falling into step behind her.

—

The prisoner was sitting, arms bound, staring out to sea as Ahi'rea led Lasivar and the rest toward him. "You left him without guard?" Haaph'ahin cried.

Tak'la was about to apologize but Ahi'rea spoke first. "Tak'la had the situation in hand, Father. As you can see, he is right where he was left."

"Mind your tongue," Haaph'ahin said. "It was careless and foolish. He could have done anything." He turned to Tak'la. "Just because I brought you with us when you lay dying, does not mean I will tolerate failure. You must work harder than any to keep your place amongst us."

They stopped a short distance from the prisoner. He still had not moved. Lasivar stepped forward, and Ahi'rea saw his façade crack. He ceased, for a moment, to be a hero and became a man, sorrowful, remorseful. Something about what he saw deeply affected him. He extended a hand toward the prisoner.

There was a wordless shriek, primal and hate-filled. The prisoner arose, the rope on his wrists rotting away in an instant. Blackness fell around him and ephemeral, oily tendrils burst and snaked from his body. One of his hands shot, clawlike, toward Lasivar's face. The prisoner, a head shorter than Lasivar, somehow dwarfed them all. Before Ahi'rea or the others could react, Tak'la was lunging forward, his machete already halfway out of its sheath.

There was a burst of light and silence, a drowning of senses—she could not see, heard nothing. Blinded, Ahi'rea stumbled back a pace. She felt Ruun'daruun catch her and move in front of her. When her vision returned, Lasivar was holding back Tak'la's machete—by the blade—with one hand. The other, outstretched, was planted on the prisoner's chest. The prisoner's eye sockets looked empty—black holes in his face—and his hand hovered just shy of Lasivar's face.

Lasivar's eyes flickered, a brief white flash. Ahi'rea thought she heard him say, "Azra." The prisoner's eyes closed and he collapsed without a sound. The phantasms vanished and the light returned to normal. The prisoner began to sputter and choke on the ground as he bent double. Lasivar released Tak'la's machete. Tak'la stepped back, gaping at the bloodless weapon in his hand. Ahi'rea saw that the blade was curled and warped as if by heat. Lasivar knelt and rolled the prisoner onto his back and held one hand over his chest, the other on his forehead.

Ahi'rea rushed up to them, pushing past the others. "What did you do to him?" she asked.

"I healed him," Lasivar said.

"Healed him? He attacked you." Ahi'rea could see the concentration etched on his face, along with something else. Fear? No—worry.

Lasivar shook his head. "That was not him. The spirit had nearly taken him. Its hold on him is very strong. His mind was almost gone, but I have brought him back, for now."

Ahi'rea stared. Tak'la came forward too, followed by Ruun'daruun, although the rest hung back. She watched as the prisoner choked and gasped and wondered if it might have been better if he had died—if Tak'la had been a little swifter.

"What is 'Azra?'" she asked quietly.

"He is. It is his name."

"You Saw his true name?" She had never heard of anyone who could do that, read a mind so easily.

"No." Lasivar sighed, shaking his head. "I remember him. He was my best friend."

—Fourteen—

"We grew up together—on this coast, in the village just south of here. My parents, who you call Lasivar and Hera, came here to hide when Halkoriv thought my father dead. They secretly continued to lead from this humble place. I knew nothing of this as a child, until I followed them one morning as they left home. They left me with Azra and his family every time they went south. Even then, the true nature of what they were escaped me. Eventually Halkoriv discovered us. When he came, my father and his allies decided they had to protect me. I only found out years later what they did."

Here Lasivar paused for a long time. The prisoner Azra had calmed and now lay, sweating and cold, but recovering. Lasivar's hand remained on his brow.

"When Halkoriv's men came, Azra's parents and he were with us. My father's men, his fastest and most trusted riders, snatched me away." He sighed. "My parents were killed that night, along with most of the village. When they found Azra there—" he paused. "They planned it that way. So they would not think to look for me. Azra was offered up in my place." Lasivar was still, calm, collected, but his voice had grown edged and dangerous.

"Until recently, all I knew was that another had been taken instead of me. When you told me that there was one with you who thought he was me, I had no idea. Not until I saw him." His jaw clenched. "He was twisted by Halkoriv and saddled with this darkness; he was corrupted, and he was used. This should never have happened." The next words rang clear in Ahi'rea's trained mind, even though he did not voice them: *They should have taken me, but then Halkoriv would already have won.*

"How could Halkoriv have been fooled for so long?" Ruun'daruun asked.

"Sitis guides him. It may even control him now," Lasivar said. "It is a spirit of hunger and immediacy. A child to consume may have proved too much to pass up. I am not sure." Lasivar stared into Azra's unconscious face. "It has invaded him in a way I did not think possible."

No one spoke. Lasivar stayed for a long time with his hand on Azra's forehead, concentrating. After some time, Azra passed into an untroubled slumber and was still—the darkness that had threatened to consume him had passed.

Ahi'rea peered at Azra. "Have you removed the spirit from him?"

"No," Lasivar said. "Merely pressed it back. The barbs of Sitis are too deep in him. He was channeling extraordinary amounts of power." He looked at Haaph'ahin, who stood several feet away muttering with some of the others. "This spirit will kill him."

"Good," Ahi'rea snapped despite herself. "He is a foul murderer. He deserves to die." Tak'la opened his mouth, but did not speak. Lasivar looked at her—his eyes once again appraising, measuring.

"You told me you were the one who kept him from death, before," he said. "Why, if you hate him so much?"

Ahi'rea glowered. "My father used him just as Halkoriv did," she answered. "That was unjust. He should die for his own crimes, not while being used for another."

Lasivar held her gaze. Ahi'rea found herself unable to look into those clear blue eyes for long. "If he believed he was someone else, perhaps he was," Lasivar said, getting to his feet. He faced the coast. "He needs rest. Tell me when he wakes."

—

Azra dreamed, and remembered. The life he had once had, that had been taken from him, returned in a scattered torrent as he slept. The familiar coast, the sound and smell of the ocean and the trees. The face of his friend: a tall, dark-haired youth with piercing eyes and a strange charisma. The boy had been called Revik Naghan then—a name Azra, even dreaming, now understood to be assumed, false, to hide him and his parents.

He relived portions of his happy early years and the days leading up to his capture. He remembered how despondent his parents had become, and now understood that they had known what would happen. He remembered them fighting. He remembered huddling in a house of logs, with an earthen floor. It was autumn. He remembered fire, and crying, and screams. Men had come. There had been blood. His mother had held him, then took up a sword herself. He still could not see her face, but he remembered now seeing her run through, seeing the red-stained sword suddenly protrude from her back.

How could they? How could they have given up their son like that? To protect another child, one somehow of greater worth than he? Perhaps they meant to deliver him into imprisonment instead of death. He felt that he should hate them along with Lasivar and his parents, the heroes, but somehow he did not. Only a few weeks ago, he would have been enraged. Still, anger clawed at his heart, seeking another hold on him. But somehow, he felt he could understand why they made their choice.

His had been, for many years, a good life with Halkoriv. He had food and shelter, an existence of luxury. Images of the Huumphar came to his mind, of their slaughter and loss and tears, images of pains inflicted by him and those like him. His parents had died when he was taken, along with many others. Even in his sleep he found he could not blame anyone for their choices, except Halkoriv—and later, himself.

—

Ahi'rea stirred, and cried out. She pulled away in horror at an icy touch on the back of her neck. When she opened her eyes, however, all she saw was the inside of her tent. A comforting voice murmured, "It is only me. I came in when I heard you shout. You were dreaming." She rolled onto her back and could just make out Ruun'daruun's form beside her, dark against the pale glimmer of moonlight through the tent flap. He lay down next to her, his dark eyes betrayed his concern.

Shivering, she pressed against him, thankful for his warmth. He wrapped his arms around her and held her close. Ahi'rea pulled herself tight to him, savoring the touch of his skin to hers, tracing her fingertips amongst the scars on his back and chest.

"Our first night of easy rest in a month, and you're having trouble sleeping?" Ruun'daruun said. It was more observation than question.

She nodded.

"What's wrong?"

She stared, her eyes looking beyond the tent as she tried to organize her thoughts. "It is the prisoner—the false Lasivar."

Ruun'daruun nodded, frowning. His hatred of him had not abated.

"Revik Lasivar called him 'Azra.' I suppose... hearing his real name... I never thought of him as a person, until then. He was a story, a prophecy, and then a monster. Now..."

"He is still a monster," Ruun'daruun said. "You saw him today. You saw what he will still try to do. He can't be trusted, can't be allowed to live."

She shook her head. "That is something else. He may be a wicked man, but that power, that evil that comes on him, was placed there by another. It is as if Halkoriv nurtured the anger and rage in him until it became something else, something alive." She shivered against Ruun'daruun, the memory of that incorporeal touch on her skin, weeks ago at the Monument, forcing its way back to the surface. "His spirit to fight us is broken." Her words surprised even herself. "It is the power he thought he commanded that is dangerous. It will kill him. It is more of a danger to him now than to us."

Ruun'daruun grunted. "I still do not see why you saved him. He may not wish to fight us any longer, but he has done unforgiveable things. All the scattered tribes, the slaughter of our people—

he was behind it, whether he was deceived or not."

Ahi'rea felt her hands become fists. "You are right." She sighed. She relived, as she had so many times, the moment Azra had killed her mother; watched his blade rip through her, watched him toss her aside like refuse. She shook as anger and hate overwhelmed her—and yet, somehow, she still no longer wished Azra's death.

—

Lasivar waited, and listened. Haaph'ahin, livid, was protesting his earlier actions with Azra. Though he knew how to conceal his rage well, he knew that Lasivar could see it, could feel it radiate from him. It irritated him that he could not hide his feelings from him.

"He is useless to our cause, and he is dangerous," Haaph'ahin said. "He knows about you! He is riddled with the Sitis spirit! It could seize control of him at any time. If we let him live, he will just return to his master and come back to fight against us."

Haaph'ahin had restated his arguments in as many ways as he could think, doing everything he could to appeal to Lasivar's reason. He was determined that he not go through with his plan to let Azra go free when he awoke.

He had felt such glee at Lasivar's arrival. He had cheered his own visions, the final vindication of his actions and the deaths of so many. He had finally felt they had been justified. That glee and pride had been soured by Lasivar himself. Haaph'ahin had expected Lasivar to heed him and take his counsel. Instead, the young man and he had disagreed over almost everything.

Haaph'ahin had hoped to gather a great army, as they had in his youth. It would take time, but the rest of the Huumphar could be found and many able warriors raised in the North as well as rebels from the South. With Lasivar, he had said, such a force would be gathered to challenge Halkoriv again. Lasivar had disagreed, declining to explain, and forbade the sending of search parties and messengers to find other tribes and raise the Gharven.

Haaph'ahin had hoped to finally kill the false Lasivar. On this too, they disagreed.

Lasivar stared at him. "Killing Azra will solve nothing. He will pose no danger to us, and he will not return to Halkoriv." Haaph'ahin, glaring back, began to falter as he tried to hold Lasivar's gaze. Something in the younger man's eyes upset him; he was not used to being looked at so steadily. To being chided. "Be careful, Elder, lest war and desperation make you into the very thing you seek to defeat."

Haaph'ahin looked away and scowled. "I am nothing like Halkoriv," he said. "Son of Lasivar or no, mind what you say."

"I always choose my words carefully, Elder. Now I must rest; we set out tomorrow."

—Fifteen—

The prisoner awoke the next morning as the first rays of sun broke over the cliffs and ocean in the east and shone down on the camp. He found himself beneath a makeshift shelter, a few hides stretched over poles stuck in the earth. His bonds were gone, and he had been left where he was on the cliffs. A Huumphar guard stood nearby while another hustled away, presumably to report that he had awoken.

He had vague recollections of what had happened; he remembered attacking Lasivar, but could not think of why he had done it. Lasivar had stopped him—but not the same way that Ahi'rea had, back in the plains. Instead, it had felt as if Lasivar had helped a dam to break in the prisoner's mind, and the sudden flood of memory had overwhelmed him. He had heard a name—but did not dare to hope that it was his. Now, in the morning's light, the dreams and images that had come back to him were fading again—fading, but not vanishing. The landscape was familiar, the sound of waves and the smell of the sea somehow comforting. Had Revik Lasivar been his friend when they were children? He could not tell if the memories were his own or not. What if they were more illusions, crafted and molded and cast into his mind by Lasivar for his own ends? The prisoner tried to focus on other thoughts, though the visions and dreams flitted through his mind. They were not his. They could not be his.

There was water and food waiting for him—small fish on skewers, roasting by the campfire, and some berries from the woods. He ate, hoping to distract himself from thoughts of the previous day.

The food reached his tongue. The salty, smoky fish and the sudden familiarity of its taste assaulted him. He had eaten such food before—when he was a boy.

The memories were his. He choked back sobs.

This land had been his home. He knew his name, a name he could not recall and had never heard until Lasivar had said it. He struggled to bring himself to accept it.

Autumn, the harvest season, was approaching—something he had not recognized until that moment. Long ago, his parents would have been together with the rest of the village, collecting and preserving grain and fruit. He dried his eyes and gazed down toward his old village. He remembered then, that it was just beyond the trees—and he wondered if he could just go back. Could he forget all that had happened, as he had once forgotten his life before, and become a simple farmer or fisherman? Images crashed through his mind—Cunabrel telling him that Halkoriv had ordered his capture; his enemy's brutalized face as he had raised a sword over him. He thought of the old Huumphar woman, Ahi'rea's mother; he had gutted her just before he had been captured. He thought of Halkoriv, his eyes emotionless and his smile kindly, sincerity arranged and settled upon his face like a mask.

"Azra," a voice said, an echo of the last word he remembered hearing—his name. He hated it, did not want it. He looked up from his seated position to see Revik Lasivar approaching, towering over him. Ahi'rea, Tak'la, and several others stood a short distance away. The prisoner stood and faced Lasivar's piercing gaze. The other man's eyes went through him, but the prisoner felt a chill grow behind his own eyes and Lasivar seemed to diminish before him.

Lasivar blinked. "It's all right, Azra. Calm yourself—I am here to tell you that you are free to go."

The chill vanished. The prisoner felt a familiar satisfaction at having unnerved Lasivar, but tried to ignore it. *I am not that man. That man was a lie,* he thought. *Then what am I?* Still, he held Lasivar's gaze. "You are not going to question me? Try to press me into helping you?" the prisoner asked.

"No." Lasivar shook his head.

"I remember you, Revik," the prisoner said. "You are here to stop him. To kill Halkoriv."

Lasivar nodded.

"He is strong. The power I had was nothing compared to his."

"I know," Lasivar said. "I am sorry for what has happened to you."

The prisoner glowered and said nothing.

"The power he planted in you will kill you, Azra. I cannot stop it."

"What are you talking about?" the prisoner asked. "I am not Azra. Azra was a boy, taken away in the night to save you." *He is trying to use me, just like the others.* "And I am not going back—you do not have to worry about me or what I can do. You do not need to lie to me or trick me."

"I am not trying to trick you," Lasivar said. He had started to say 'Azra,' but stopped himself. "The power you use, that is in you, is not sorcery. It is a spirit, riding you, and as soon as you outlive your usefulness to it, it will consume you. It will do the same to Halkoriv. It may already have. It is old, and stronger than both of you. It is too ancient to know anything but hunger. Each time you use it, its hold grows stronger in you and it is easier for it to control you, to take everything from you and keep you. That is the immortality Sitis found, and it is the lie Halkoriv's line has pursued for generations. It will betray him to its own hunger, just as it will devour you."

A snarl formed in the prisoner's throat. "You are lying!" he shouted. "I remember how you always had to be the best! You never wanted anyone to be able to match you."

"I am trying to warn you," Lasivar said, his voice rising. "We are friends! Why would I lie to you?"

"We were friends, a long time ago, but much has changed, Revik. I know what you are; I know that you are lying to me because I would have done the same. They think you are a great hero, a leader—but I know what you really want, because it is what I wanted. You want more power, you want the fear of these people, and you want control. You may say you are here for peace or freedom or whatever will please them and you, but I know what it is like, and what you are truly after. Even if you do not mean to simply replace Halkoriv, even if you do not just want his throne, it is power you want—but you do not want any rivals for it."

Lasivar sighed and lowered his gaze. When he spoke again, his voice was quiet and collected. "Remember, Azra," he said, "try not to use it. I am sorry for what happened—truly I am. I hope you can forgive the choices that were made on my behalf. It is not how I would have had events unfold." His tone was cool again and his manner unruffled.

The prisoner turned away. "I hate this place."

"You are free to go where you wish," Lasivar said. "What will you do now?"

The prisoner looked out over the sea. He could leave—leave Feriven behind, his past, the people and conflict. He imagined forgetting about all of them as he had forgotten everything else. His memories were a jumbled mass of half-truths and misinformation. He thought of making a new life for himself, a new name. He could forget Lasivar and Halkoriv and all the others—and then his thoughts turned to Ahi'rea.

He glanced over his shoulder and saw her, still waiting a short distance away. Their eyes met. Desire stole over him, but the look of hatred she returned made him look away. "I want my sword," the prisoner said. "I may leave Feriven some day, but for now… I just want quiet. I will go west along the coast." He did not know what he hoped would happen if he stayed, but he knew he could not imagine forgetting about her.

Lasivar turned and said something in Huumphar. Tak'la disappeared, returning a short time later with the prisoner's sword, scabbard, and armor. The tall warrior handed the prisoner his things, keeping his eyes to the ground. The prisoner turned away the armor, but took the garnet-pommeled sword. "What about you?" he asked Lasivar, wondering why he bothered to ask. "How will you go about your purpose?"

"We leave at dawn," Lasivar said. "We will go south. I have

work to do, old friend. I hope you can find peace on your journey."
He extended a hand.

The prisoner ignored the gesture, adjusting his sword belt.
He turned to the west, looking along the coast. The sun was high
and the wind blew cool off of the ocean. Green waves peaked and
crashed, and to the south they were echoed by the treetops rustling
and waving in the breeze. The tallest branches were turning; hues
of red and gold were beginning to tinge the forest leaves.

He turned back, addressing Tak'la. "Thank you for speaking
with me," he said. Tak'la nodded but did not answer or meet his
eyes. The prisoner reached out and put a hand on his shoulder, then
approached the group of Huumphar waiting nearby. He stopped
before Ahi'rea.

She was beautiful—he allowed himself to notice, to admit it
to himself. He wondered, for a moment, if she might accept him
if he agreed to stay and help them. He looked into her eyes and
spoke. "Ahi'rea," he said, "you saved me. Thank you."

She glared at him and said, "Thank Lasivar. I did not want
to see you taken by the spirit, but do not mistake my choice for
mercy. If not for Lasivar, you would not leave these cliffs alive."

Her words stung, but he had expected them. He knew she
hated him. His foolish hope now seemed even more ridiculous. He
waited for anger to rise in him, but it did not. The prisoner stood
for a moment. "I understand why you would want that," he said.
"I... I am not sorry for what I have done. I was led to this. It was
not my choice." He kept her gaze as she glared in silence. "Do not
do what he says just because of who he is," the prisoner cautioned,
eyes flicking to Lasivar and back. "He will only be able to rule you
if you let him. If you want to kill me, do it."

Ahi'rea's hand, already on the hilt of her machete, tightened around it.

"Do not tempt me," she said. "You are no match for me. You had better take our charity while it is offered and go." Behind her, Ruun'daruun's hand went to his machete as well.

The prisoner resisted the urge to step back. "As I said… what happened was not my fault. I will not say I am sorry, but…" he paused, unable to go on. Ahi'rea looked on, and something crossed his face that she had never seen before. The prisoner breathed deep. "But I hope someday, you will forgive me."

He turned and began to walk away. Ahi'rea called out after him, despite herself. "You always had a choice, Azra. When you realize that, maybe I will."

—

The prisoner could not bring himself to leave the area while Ahi'rea was still nearby. He stopped atop a small rise within sight of the camp and decided to wait there until she left with the others. Gazing down, he watched as the Gharven, Huumphar, and Lasivar's escorts prepared to march, as he had watched his own armies gather before. Their force seemed so small—they had no chance. He caught occasional glimpses of people he had come to know— the closest things he had to friends, he realized, were his jailers.

The prisoner made a makeshift camp—Lasivar's men had given him a bedroll and a few supplies as he left. He set out the bedroll and gathered some kindling for a fire. His clothes were ragged, having gone over a month without repair. The foreigners accompanying Lasivar had also given him new breeches and a heavy gray shirt, along with a long, dark gray oilskin coat of the kind worn by sailors. He set his old clothes aside and dressed in the rough foreign garb.

He went through some old sword drills to clear his head. Everything felt different without the force of Halkoriv's will behind him. It was strange, he mused, that he had never realized how much Halkoriv had been helping him until he was on his own, and help far away.

The blade was heavy and his movements were slow and clumsy. He found that if he concentrated, thinking about every step, every twist of an arm or movement of a wrist, he could still perform the maneuvers and strikes as he remembered—although he could not remember it ever requiring so much effort.

His mind wandered. Lasivar's words came back to him: *The power he planted in you will kill you, Azra.* Why had Lasivar let it go when he argued? If Lasivar were trying to trick him, use him, why had he not pursued the matter?

The power was still there, a dull pressure in his mind, water at a floodgate.

Breathing heavily, he thrust the sword into the earth and sat. He held a hand out, palm up, and ever so slightly relaxed his restraint. Thin dark tendrils rose from his palm, lashing, insubstantial and somehow more real than the grass around him or the hard earth beneath him.

He felt no danger—the sensation was familiar, almost comforting. What did Lasivar know of it? He was just trying to scare him away from his potential.

Still, something in his old friend's voice worried him. He knew of only one way to find out the truth. The prisoner had divined answers before—Revik Lasivar's true identity; the attack on the garrison where he had been captured. Would he be able to tell if his power was a danger to him? If it really were some sort of spirit?

The prisoner allowed himself more power, focusing on the feeling of the energy itself. He opened his mind to it, probing, sensing for an intelligence or presence.

He felt nothing. He exhaled and shook his head. *Foolish.* There was nothing wrong, no spirit. Still, he was not comforted. Lasivar had seemed so earnest.

Why would Lasivar set him free, then lie to him? He had demanded nothing—not even information. The prisoner tried again, releasing his restraint, allowing the power to wash through him. This time, he felt for the source of the energy. He felt a familiar chill core in his mind, something he had felt many times. He looked deeper, pressing through the cold and silent mass. It was like forcing his way through loose, clammy earth. The prisoner felt as if many small, damp forms were crawling up from the ground and into his skin. He winced as innumerable tiny barbs hooked into his flesh, but maintained his concentration; Halkoriv's help or no, he had endured pain before. He focused, releasing yet more energy as he pressed closer to the source of his own power.

He reached it—and it was like pushing against a force only to have it suddenly removed. He felt as if he stood before a vast emptiness, unknowable and dark. He was reminded of his cell, long ago in Cunabrel's dungeon, except he could sense no walls, no boundaries—just blackness. His consciousness teetered on the edge of the chasm and Azra struggled to pull himself back lest he lose himself in the vast well of shadow. As he regained his mental balance and cast about him, he realized that this emptiness was the source; the wellspring of the dark power he commanded.

As if in response to him, however, the void began to change, warping and coalescing, focusing itself.

The prisoner became aware of another mind. The other was silent, a part of the void yet circling him like a predator.

Terror rushed through him—Lasivar was right. He tried to pull away, to withdraw from himself and shut away the power, but it was as if the path behind him had vanished into the shadow. He panicked as the predatory mind inspected him; he could feel its hunger, an overwhelming voracity that eclipsed every other aspect of it. He felt himself being drawn into it, felt his own mind being stripped away and dissolved. Azra struggled, unable to free himself. His shouts were swallowed up. The more power he released in trying to force the spirit way, the stronger its hold became. More pieces of his mind were torn from him. He was becoming as empty as the spirit. He had nothing to cling to but the power, and it was useless. He could no longer tell where it ended and he began.

He needed a border, something to hold onto; something to separate him from the spirit. *A name,* he thought. *My border. My self.* The prisoner knew only one name to use. *Azra*, he thought. *I am Azra.*

Still it assaulted him. Images and memories were pulled, squirming, to the surface of his consciousness only to be ripped away and devoured. Azra saw them torn apart—a lesson in swordsmanship, a moonlit night on the plains, the sound of wind, the scent of the kitchens in the palace in Ferihold—one after another they vanished in flashes of pain. His name was not enough; he needed something else.

Ahi'rea—the time she had called him back when Haaph'ahin had goaded him into searching out Lasivar. He remembered opening his eyes to see her face, tired and fearful, beautiful and full of anger. The memory was tearing, splitting apart as it was pulled away.

Azra rebelled—he would not lose it. If she had ever cared for him, it had been then. With every ounce of will he possessed, he resisted. He needed that memory. *That is mine.* He realized then what it was he wanted, how he hoped she might, somehow, come to feel about him—and that she never would.

He found himself staring into the beast, the ravenous spirit that now dwelt inside him, perhaps always had. He held tight to the memory of Ahi'rea and unflinchingly he forced the spirit away—and found himself back on the clifftop under the sun.

He concentrated on regaining his breath for a long time. Hours may have passed—Azra was unsure of how long he had sat, unmoving, and how long he had fought before that. He could feel the strange gaps in himself, memories like dreams he remembered having but could not recall. He remembered Ahi'rea, and her face as she had pulled him away from the spirit once before. Through his fear, he smiled. He had beaten it. The spirit had tried to take him, just as Lasivar had warned, but he had fought it off.

His pride was short-lived. He realized that, if Lasivar was right, he had merely escaped for a time. Every time he used his powers he gave the spirit a new hold. Azra stood and picked up his sword, wiping the tip against his pants to remove the bits of soil that clung to it. He replaced the sword in its scabbard at his side, recalling the hatred he had felt for Cunabrel when he had taken it from him years ago.

Azra resolved to use his powers no more. *I have been handed back the life that was taken from me. I will not lose it again.*

Ahi'rea's voice called his name close by. He started, hand dropping to his sword as he turned. She stood only a few strides away, pale hair flowing like gilded waves over her shoulders. A spear was in her hand and her eyes smoldered with sudden light at the sight of Azra gripping his sword.

"I only came to talk," she said. A light breeze picked up behind her, blowing past them both and out over the cliffs.

Azra felt his power strain against his control. Desire to loose it was strong upon him, but he knew it was not his. He shut it out and released the sword, nodding. Ahi'rea lowered the spear. The breeze died away and the air was still once again.

Ahi'rea took a few steps forward and Azra turned away to avoid staring at her. He pushed his dark hair out of his face; it had grown unkempt during his captivity. "What do you want to talk about?" he asked. He could feel her scrutinizing him.

"I do not understand you," she said.

Azra looked at her over his shoulder. "Nor do I," he said. "I am afraid I will be no help with that." He tried to smile at her, but his smile was not returned.

"You came here to kill us all," she said, "then you help us find the man who will end your empire, and you heal our wounded, and then you ask for forgiveness and leave." She shook her head. "Who are you?"

Azra closed his eyes, then looked up at the sky. "I suppose I am no one," he said. "The man I thought I was—that was a lie, a mistake. Without that... I am just Azra." The words comforted him even as he said them. He smiled, genuinely, for the first time in what seemed like his whole life.

Ahi'rea shook her head again. "You cannot just strip away your past. You may feel like a new person, but to me you are just… you are like the same path from the opposite direction. At first it looks different, but if you look closely you see that you have gone this way before."

"I am not Halkoriv's pet anymore," Azra snapped. Ahi'rea raised an eyebrow. "And I am not Revik Lasivar, he is," he said, gesturing at the camp. He turned his back again, squeezing his eyes shut. "If you have already decided who I am, then why are you asking?" She gave no answer. "Perhaps you did come up here to kill me, but you were hoping that I would attack you first," Azra said.

"I think," she finally said, "it is you who wishes that I came here to kill you." He did not respond. "I came here to say you were right before," Ahi'rea said. Azra turned to look at her. The sun was beginning to set and he saw goosebumps on her skin as cool air rushed in from the ocean. "I did choose to spare you before," she said softly. "I do not know why, but I hope I made the right choice." Her eyes met his before she cast them to the ground.

"Ahi'rea," he said, "you… you should come with me." The words surprised even him, but he continued. "I am leaving, leaving this war. You will die if you stay and fight. Lasivar cannot beat Halkoriv." His heart ached. "Come with me," he pleaded.

Ahi'rea looked up, eyes wide. Realization crept over her and her confusion turned to revulsion. She tried to mask it and immediately wondered why she bothered to try to hide it. "No," she said. "I would never do that. It… I have said what I came to say. It is getting dark." She turned to walk back toward the camp.

Azra cursed himself and felt tears well in his eyes. He could not stop himself. "Will you at least forgive me?" he called desperately.

Ahi'rea stopped, then looked back. "No," she said. "I will not."

She turned and continued away. Azra sat, his head in his hands, as she walked off the rise and vanished in the failing light.

—

A red glow interrupted Azra's dreamless sleep and he opened his eyes. The morning was cold, but the sun breaking over the eastern ridge promised a clear and warm day. He stretched his limbs, stiff from the cold night, and stood. He watched the sun rise for a few moments, watched the camp below him begin to awaken and move. The foreigners, Gharven, and Huumphar were packing their tents and goods, making ready to march.

He was about to turn away when he saw a form, tall and broad, break from the camp below and lope swiftly up the hill. He realized it was Tak'la, wearing loose Gharven-style pants and his grass cape, carrying a spear and a sack made of animal hide, sprinting up to meet him.

The Huumphar stopped before Azra, hoisting the sack over his shoulder.

"Tak'la?" Azra said. "What are you doing?"

The big Huumphar looked back at the camp, then at Azra. "I will go with you," he said.

—

Ahi'rea stood beside Ruun'daruun, leaning against his solid frame as they watched Tak'la and Azra begin to descend the hill, headed south toward the forest.

"Why is he going? Did he say?" asked Ruun'daruun.

"When I asked him," Ahi'rea said, "Tak'la only told me that since death followed him, he felt he should lead it away from the rest of us."

Ruun'daruun nodded. "A noble act," he said. "He will lead death away from us and our allies then. It has stalked him for so long—he was surely a danger to all of us here."

"He was a strong warrior, and brave to the point of reckless-ness," Ahi'rea said. "We could have used his help in the times to come. I feel we may all be death-touched."

Ruun'daruun shook his head. "We will win, now. The son of Lasivar leads us to Halkoriv. Tak'la the death-touched leads death away from us." He looked down as Ahi'rea tightened her grip on his arm. Her eyes were unfocused, flickering, seeing something else. "What do you See?" he asked.

"I See two beasts," Ahi'rea said, her voice distant and halt-ing. She struggled to describe the vision, the words writhing and changing on her tongue, becoming more obtuse and disconnected than she meant them to be. "They clash in stone and flame, and a darkness swallows the dead." She persevered, sweating despite the morning chill, her voice weak. "The hand presses into barbs; they grow as thorns. Thorns grow deep-strong. They spear through the red beast, and let loose the darkness' captive. Hunted pursues hunter; thorns burn to ash; all burns in fire."

She gasped as the vision fled, her eyes returning to their nat-ural hue. Ruun'daruun studied her. "What does it mean?" he asked when she finally looked up at him.

She shook her head. "Time will tell," she said. "I feel we can do little to change the outcome of this fight. It may depend on Lasivar's son... but I do not think that it does." She found herself straining for a final glimpse of Azra, but he had passed into the trees and was lost to sight.

—Sixteen—

They left within hours. Lasivar's people were prepared ahead of time and the Huumphar were always ready and able to pack up and leave within a moment's notice.

Ahi'rea bounded through the myriad assortment of assembled warriors. Her own people milled and paced, a few wearing light armor of hide and bone, with spears and machetes their only weapons. The foreign soldiers were imposing in their shells of shining metal, but Ahi'rea estimated there were no more than two hundred of them. The few hundred Gharven people who had managed to gather with them were by far the most numerous and the most eclectic; occasional raids by Cheduna forces from the local garrisons made it difficult for them to keep armor and weapons. Despite this, they had learned from long years of rebellion, and blades and bows that had lain hidden beneath floorboards or in remote caves saw the light of day for the first time in years. They wore dull rust-colored cloaks and no armor; the elder Lasivar had taught them a quiet but deadly warfare. When the host entered the forest heading south, the Gharven nearly disappeared amongst the ruddy tree trunks, silently taking positions around the louder, more visible foreign troops. The Huumphar, out of their element but determined, warily led the way through the woods.

Ahi'rea spotted Ruun'daruun, Ken'hra, and Lasivar walking together, speaking quietly at the head of a column of armored foreigners. As she approached the group, Ruun'daruun was briefing Lasivar. "Our scouts haven't returned yet with their numbers, but the refugees we've met report that there are several thousand Cheduna soldiers. Our warriors fight well and have driven them from the plains before, but that's because they can't catch us when we break away. With a force like this they'll have a target, and we're outnumbered. We'll lose too many if we meet them head on."

"I have Seen them, and there are over ten thousand of them," Lasivar said. "And Halkoriv's will is driving them from afar. No, I do not plan to engage them head-on. Even if more Gharven and Huumphar join us, our few hundred could not withstand something so direct." Lasivar gestured. "We will go around, toward Ferihold."

Ken'hra spoke, her brow furrowed. "If we lay siege to Ferihold, they will surround us—it won't be head-on, it'll be on all sides. We're too few to attack the city. We fight best in the plains and the Gharven are woodsmen and hunters. We'll be crushed if we don't address the army."

"I hope not to engage in a siege," Lasivar said. "You must trust me. My plans depend on speed and flexibility."

"Speed and flexibility we have," Ken'hra snorted. "But them…" she glanced at the heavily-armored soldiers behind them.

"Do not worry about them," Lasivar said. "The Vanadae can move quickly when they must."

"Will you drive them to greater speed yourself?" Ahi'rea asked, joining the group. *Can you?* she wondered.

Lasivar raised an eyebrow. "For now we must move as fast as is possible."

"Where are they from? The Vanadae?" Ahi'rea asked.

"A beautiful place." Lasivar smiled and seemed to look beyond the trees around them. "It is called Vanador, and it is where I was taken to train and learn. It is a warm land of rolling golden hills; their city shines in the sunlight, and the grand sea beneath it glitters and dances in the warm winds."

"You sound as if you miss your home." Ahi'rea studied his face, watching his reaction.

"This is my home." Lasivar turned his smile on her and caught her gaze. "But yes, I miss that place."

They walked on in silence for a few moments. "Why did they come with you?" Ruun'daruun asked. "This isn't their fight."

Lasivar's eyes were steady on the path ahead. "They come because I ask it." His voice took on a faraway quality, as if he were now looking on something distasteful and almost forgotten. "Their home is beautiful, but not always peaceful." Ahi'rea thought she saw, just for a moment, that he was troubled. The look vanished as soon as she noticed it. "I have much to do," Lasivar said. "We will talk more in time. Alert me when your scouts return."

—

Deep in his sanctum, Halkoriv sat unmoving on his dais, eyes unblinking and dark as he stared into the black marble basin beside him. The sound of the water trickling from the basin was interrupted as soft footsteps began to echo through the chamber. Halkoriv did not notice. The footsteps stopped; a pair of robed figures stepped into the dim circle of light around the dais. They waited in silence.

Minutes passed. Halkoriv's eyes flickered, then closed and he turned away from the basin. The water's trickling slowed.

The figures made no sound or movement as Halkoriv sat with his eyes shut, utterly still. When he opened his eyes again, they were dull and sunken even as they darted about his dark hall. They settled on the two figures.

"We have Seen... he... for us..." Halkoriv muttered, then stopped. He began again and his tone grew controlled, calm. "I... have Seen him... our enemy has come. The true son of our enemy. My enemy. How were we so blind? Why did we not See?" He looked at his hands, turning them over, inspecting them as if he had never seen their like. He directed his attention back to the waiting figures. "He is here. They landed on the coast of the Gharven north. He is leading many to the plains."

"My lord," one of the figures whispered, its voice cold and wet, "calm your mind. The Ancestor is still on you. What are your orders?"

Halkoriv closed his eyes again and waited. His lips moved and he flinched. He grew hunched and his shoulders shook. His eyes clenched and his brow furrowed. A shudder rushed through him. Then he straightened, becoming tall and powerful and serene. His eyelids parted and he turned black, featureless eyes on the waiting servants.

"Send word to Draden. He is to move east, immediately. Speed is the priority. They will find a force of plainsfolk and foreigners from Vanador, and Gharven warriors with them. Draden is to stay ahead of them, to make for the eastern sea and seek a place to gain advantage over them."

"And Lord Lasivar, majesty? The rumors of his disappearance grow more prominent. Lord Draden has inquired after him. His messenger reports that they have not found him, nor his remains."

"Spread word that he is dead." Halkoriv's voice echoed and warped in the marble chamber. "A commander from Vanador slew him, and took his name to fool the northerners. They have been deceived."

The figures nodded.

"Send our newest servant to us—to me."

The figures bowed, then left. Moments later, another, taller and broader than the others, entered the hall. Wrapped in a dark cloak, the figure approached the dais and let his hood fall back. Halkoriv's featureless eyes drove into him.

"You were dead, but I have given you new life," Halkoriv said. "Your life was bereft of purpose, but now I have given that to you as well. Go to the North with all speed. Take whatever forces you see fit. Find Lord Lasivar—he is travelling the northlands. He must come to me, alive, at the place you now call Ancestor's Stone. Tell no one what you know of him."

The figure bowed, then turned to leave. Halkoriv's gaze returned to the basin. The flow of water increased. The footsteps of the figure faded, leaving behind only the sound of the water's flow.

—

Azra, as if for the first time, strode through the village he once knew. Memories came to him in slow waves and, like waves, broke and receded around him even as he tried to grasp them. Images and feelings drifted past him with every corner turned.

He remembered Lasivar—or Revik, as he had known him. All their parents had told them they were special, but even in their youth the children could see it in Revik. Azra remembered looking up to the boy almost as much as he had his own father. Though Azra still could not recall his own parents, Revik now stood out in his mind, even as a child, like a beacon in the shadowy reaches that were his memories.

Tak'la followed a few paces behind as Azra continued through the village. The small homes were deserted. Some of the residents had gone to join Lasivar; the rest had left, seeking safety in other settlements or in hiding.

Azra wandered, circling and crisscrossing the empty village. He leaned against a tree, pressing his back to it and hanging his head.

"What is it?" Tak'la asked.

Azra felt tears in his eyes. "This was... my home. I can barely remember it. I cannot remember my parents, not really. I... I cannot even remember which house we lived in, or if it is even still standing." He stopped as the words caught in his throat. He sank to the ground, his head in his hands.

Tak'la shifted from one foot to the other, then sat beside Azra. He reached out a hand to clasp Azra's shoulder.

"I do not know what I am supposed to do, Tak'la. Everything I can remember... I was supposed to be someone with a purpose, someone special. Now I find that it was a lie, and even the life I thought had only been stolen is truly gone."

Tak'la stared at the ground, then looked up and said, "Your

life is now all yours then. No one can tell you what it should be."

They sat in silence, listening to the trees, feeling the cool sea air from the north. Autumn was coming but somehow Azra felt warmer, comforted.

"You are right, though discovering what that is on my own may be more difficult than it sounds," Azra said. He stood up. "I am finished with the past, Tak'la. The war, Halkoriv, my old life— none of it matters. I can..." he searched for the words. "I can leave it, cast it away—but not here." He beckoned Tak'la to his feet. The Huumphar stood, confused. "I am going west. I want to find a place to get away from the past, to just... live."

"You cannot forget what is happening out there," Tak'la said, his eyes growing stony. "The war will come to you, wherever you go."

"There has been war for generations," Azra said. "I cannot change it." He started west with new life in his stride. Tak'la hefted his pack to follow when Azra stopped and turned north. "Cast it away," he murmured.

Azra broke into a run and Tak'la raced to catch up. "Where are you going? I thought you said west?" he shouted.

"There is something I have to do!" Azra dashed through the village and the orchard to the north, and then reached the cliffs. The sun was high and bright, and the wind gusted from the sea. The waves crashed below as Azra, standing on the brink, took the garnet-pommeled sword from its sheath at his waist.

"I took this sword from a man who I hated my entire life," he said softly. Tak'la came closer to hear him. "It was the most important thing I owned, because it reminded me of how I overpowered him." He looked at Tak'la. "This was my life. Power.

Prestige. I lived every day to take revenge on that man, and after I did I only wanted more. I am through with it."

Azra spun and hurled the sword into the wind over the cliff. It flashed and whirled in the sunlight, the garnet in its hilt glittering and blazing before it vanished amongst the waves and rocks below.

Azra turned back to Tak'la. "I know you want to help your people. Go. I am grateful that you offered to come with me, and you have helped me more than I could ever have helped myself."

Tak'la shook his head and scowled. "I will go with you. Perhaps I must forget as well." His scowl became a smirk. "Besides, you may need protection, now that you threw away your weapon. The Huumphar were right. Outlanders are stupid folk."

Azra smiled broadly. Without the sword he felt lighter, as if he had loosed a chain from his neck that he had not known was there. Still, something nagged at him. He strove to ignore it. He felt free.

Together Azra and Tak'la faced the west and started walking. Only when the other was not looking did either of them turn and look to the south.

—Seventeen—

After a week's travel, the army left the forest and entered the plains. With each day's march the red glow in the southern sky grew more vivid and the air smelled more and more of smoke. There was no way to hide such a large group in the open, so Lasivar relied on his Sight and the Huumphar scouts to watch the horizons and steer clear of the Cheduna. The army met no survivors or refugees—all had fled the conflagrations set by the southerners. The scouts reported to Lasivar daily, sometimes twice a day. After each report, the direction and speed of the march was adjusted.

The smoke grew omnipresent. It hung so thick in the air that the army lit small fires at night without fear of being seen.

Lasivar spoke little of his plans, which did not seem to bother his Vanadae soldiers. Few of them spoke any languages of Feriven and so they kept to their own groups. Some of those with Lasivar turned out to be from Gharven. They had been his bodyguards from the time he was a child. They had fled with him over the sea and were now old, grizzled men. At least one of them always within sight of Lasivar, and they were present for the discussions of planning or strategy, offering words of advice or experience. Ahi'rea had never seen their like before, but her father appeared to know some of them from many years past.

It had grown unnaturally cool for the beginning of autumn. By midday it was still warm, but the nights were already cold. The wind swirled around them, sometimes blustering from the south and other times rushing from the north.

Ahi'rea strode amongst the massed warriors and soldiers as they made camp. Despite their heavy armor and packs, the Vanadae seemed well-rested and strong. The Gharven woodsmen set up their tents and bedrolls; they carried their own dried rations and relied on what little remained of the local game and flora for their food. They gave Ahi'rea wary nods as she passed. Despite the old friendships between their peoples, the northerners still regarded the seeress with awe and a little fear.

She spotted Ruun'daruun setting up his tent and noted that he had chosen a spot closer to the center of the camp than he used to. She joined him in placing the last of the hide coverings. She shot him an encouraging smile, but said nothing. Ruun'daruun met her gaze then glanced over one shoulder at Haaph'ahin, who was watching them from across the camp.

As they worked, each enjoying the other's presence, a rust-cloaked figure materialized out of the gathering darkness—one of Lasivar's bodyguards.

"Lasivar would speak with you," the old man said. His voice creaked; in the dimness Ahi'rea could just make out the line of an old, deep scar on the right side of his throat. "And after that, he will need your help as well," he said, addressing Ruun'daruun. "Also the one called Ken'hra. Where can I find her?"

"I'll be here," came Ken'hra's husky voice from behind the old warrior. He started and turned, nodding to her and smiling. "I should have known better than to try and impress the Huumphar in their own plains. After Lasivar sees Ahi'rea, he will come to meet you."

"What does he need me for?" Ahi'rea asked.

The old man shook his head. "I did not ask. He's camped by those small trees just over there." He indicated the direction to Lasivar's tent and disappeared into the camp.

"He did not call for my father," Ahi'rea said.

"Nor any other elders," Ken'hra said. "Lasivar plays a dangerous game. He risks angering them."

"I trust him," Ruun'daruun said, tying the final knots to secure the tent. "Maybe it's foolish, but I would follow him on the Last Journey if he wished it. Some, though, who once spoke of him as a god now treat him as a child." He unconsciously ran his fingertips over the scars Azra had left on his face. "He knows what he's doing; fate has led him to us."

Ahi'rea allowed herself to do something she rarely did; as Ruun'daruun turned back to his tent to finish securing its ties, she focused a flash of power on him, catching a glimpse of his mind. The old stories and legends lingering in his thoughts told her all she needed to know. She caught his hand for a second and he met her eyes.

Ruun'daruun nodded toward Lasivar's tent. "He is waiting for you," he said. She thought she detected both envy and jealousy in his voice.

Ahi'rea squeezed his hand, then nodded at Ken'hra before starting toward the tent.

When she reached it, Lasivar was outside, speaking with a pair of his foreign soldiers. Their language was staccato and filled with rapid changes in tone. She contemplated an attempt to See their thoughts but knew that Lasivar would notice. She hoped she could trust him to translate if it were important.

As she waited, she caught a glimpse of the inside of Lasivar's tent through its open flap. She noticed the rich furs and rugs laid out upon the ground; it was finer than some Gharven homes she had seen.

After a brief exchange, the Vanadae bowed low to Lasivar and left, passing out of the ring of light from his campfire. Ahi'rea had a moment to wonder why he isolated his campsite from the safety of the group, and then he spoke and she found herself absorbed in what he had to say.

She forgot what she had been thinking about, forgot her curiosity, her concerns about Lasivar, even the nagging wonder about Azra and Tak'la. Lasivar outlined his plans to her, leaving out details of the larger picture. His words filled her with hope and surety, invigorating her mind even as he directed it.

With an act of will, she shook off his influence. A tiny corner of her mind had remained her own, and, free of the effect of his words, she could see his eyes glimmering. *Storm*, Ahi'rea thought. *No wonder our ancestors followed his father, and his father before that.* She held back her indignation at being dominated by this strange man's will, but would not let him think he had overcome her so easily.

"Lasivar," she interrupted. "Do not think me weak-minded. You are not the only one here who can See."

Lasivar blinked and the light faded from his blue eyes. He smiled and nodded. "Of course," he said. "I am unused to speaking to others with the understanding you and I have. Even in Vanador,

227

those like us are few."

Ahi'rea nodded, but noticed he did not apologize.

"Halkoriv is stronger than I thought," Lasivar said. "He seems to have been ready for my arrival. I think he discovered that I was coming at the same time as you did. His army is close, and approaching too quickly."

"Will they be able to catch up to us?" Ahi'rea asked.

"Yes," Lasivar said. "He anticipated we would go this way. His men will cut off our path to the South. Unless something is done, and soon, we will never make it out of the plains."

—

"When will we be through this blasted smoke?" Ken'hra asked. "My eyes feel dry enough to roll out of my skull."

Ruun'daruun chuckled. "That smoke has been all that's protected us and our scouts for days now," he said. His smile faded. "You haven't been as far south as I have. The grasses are gone. They've burned everything and the fires still won't stop. If the winds change, I fear we would be completely exposed."

"Is it true the Cheduna are only two days' march away? And they still don't know how close we are?"

"It is, but I think they'll begin to figure it out when their scouts don't return to them. I heard that some of ours killed two of them today," Ruun'daruun said.

"Yes," Haaph'ahin's voice creaked. He approached them from his place by the fire. "You overhear much, Ruun'daruun. That information was given only to elders and the Gharven and foreign commanders." Haaph'ahin stopped before Ruun'daruun, carrying his staff at his side. "You disrespect me, eavesdropping on private meetings."

"No, elder," Ruun'daruun said, taking a step back and locking eyes with Haaph'ahin. "They spoke to me as well."

"You would spread rumors and undermine my authority," Haaph'ahin snapped. "Halkoriv is canny. He may be listening. He may have spies among the outlanders."

"Elder," Ruun'daruun said, "I lead many of our scouting parties, as does Ken'hra. I trust her with my life. I have led several warbands and so has she—with respect, I know what I'm doing."

Haaph'ahin fumed. "You think yourself as capable and wise as I, then?" The light flashing from his eyes illuminated the campsite.

Ruun'daruun's eyes narrowed. They stared at one another, neither of them willing to blink. "No, elder," Ruun'daruun finally said, casting his eyes down.

"You could lead the Huumphar as well as I?" Haaph'ahin asked.

"No, elder."

"But still you eavesdrop, you distribute information that is not yours. You confer with Lasivar as if you were an elder, when a loyal tribesman would defer to those wiser than he."

"Elder Haaph'ahin." The three of them turned to see Lasivar approaching with his guards, Ahi'rea, and the Gharven and Vanadae leaders. "I had hoped to find you," Lasivar said. "You must gather your people. Our survival depends upon the next several hours, and the Huumphar have an important part to play."

Haaph'ahin ignored Ruun'daruun and addressed Lasivar as he might an overexcited child. "Such haste, Lasivar. Let us discuss your plans and I will be your voice of experience. Perhaps with our Sight combined…"

Lasivar held up a hand. "There is no time, Elder. My plans require two things; that we move quickly and that those who have pledged their forces to our cause trust me." Haaph'ahin scowled. "Besides," Lasivar continued, "I am afraid you would See as little as I. The future is in motion and is veiled to all of us."

Haaph'ahin took a deep breath. "Lasivar, the Huumphar are not yours, they are m—they follow their elders. And while I am elder, I demand to be treated with respect. I will know what you plan for my people, or they will not join you."

Ahi'rea watched the exchange in silence. She did not expect what happened next.

Lasivar stepped forward and spoke in a voice of Storm; only she and Haaph'ahin heard his warning while the rest looked on. *Do not obstruct me, old man. Your power-hoarding may have been tolerated by others, those who feared you or thought you wise by virtue of age or power; not I. I will free the Huumphar, the Gharven, and all Feriven—only you and others who are allies of opportunity can stop me. You must trust me—or we all die. Hope is in our cooperation and trust. Choose your words carefully.*

The message was instantaneous. Ahi'rea could not even blink before Haaph'ahin responded. With eyes downcast, he nodded, his nostrils flaring. "Very well, Lasivar. They will be ready."

The others looked at the two men in confusion. Haaph'ahin addressed Ken'hra and Ruun'daruun, gritting his teeth. "Go, alert the tribes and gather them. Lasivar would have us ready to act." They paused, but shook off their hesitation and dashed away when the elder looked up. He said nothing more, but glanced at Ahi'rea before he shuffled away.

"I must speak with the Vanadae and Gharven," Lasivar said. He put a hand on Ahi'rea's shoulder. "Thank you for your trust. We will need the Huumphar's speed and knowledge of the plains if we are to have any chance. Go to your people." He strode off toward the other camps, followed by his bodyguards.

Ahi'rea found herself alone. She rubbed her eyes, starting toward the Huumphar tents, giving herself a moment to reflect. Lasivar seemed to have Feriven's interests at heart—but his secrecy and force of will and personality worried her. Should one man command so much power? Perhaps others followed Halkoriv just as Ruun'daruun followed Lasivar.

Haaph'ahin offered no comfort through his actions. He had always cared for his people, but he resisted everything Lasivar said and offered no alternatives but to wait. Something was different about him. He was like one who wandered without sun or stars to guide him. His own secrecy and the things he had done angered her, but she knew she could not say anything. Any question of his actions would be a challenge to his leadership.

She wished Haruu'na were still alive. She may not have known what to do, but would have given comfort and wise words without effort. Ahi'rea clenched her eyes shut, forcing away her tears. Azra had taken her away. Why had she not let him die? Why had she not killed him herself? She knew why—he had been collateral, at first. As time had gone on, however, she had realized that he had been deceived. Like so many others, Halkoriv had taken Azra's life and twisted it to his own ends. If there was ever to be peace, she thought, all those like Azra had to be able to be saved.

He had changed—become quiet, sad even. He had seemed to have accepted the truth. But it must have been through him that Halkoriv learned that Lasivar had come.

Ahi'rea wondered again if it might not have been better for all if Azra had died.

—

"They are planning something, Draden. I would not have returned myself if I were not sure of it."

Draden sat in his tent, head bowed, massaging his temples with one hand. He raised his head with a deep breath and regarded Malskein. "I sent you to watch them because you are a strong warrior and you know how to fight and evade the plainsfolk," he said. "I sent messengers to collect your reports, yet, two nights since you left, here you are. Why is that, commander?"

"We observed movements in their structure. They broke camp and the force divided. It appeared that the northerners and foreigners were headed south and the plainslanders were headed more inland, closer to us. There are not enough of them to pose a threat, so I anticipate—"

"I don't need your analysis, commander," Draden snapped. "I said, why are you here instead of in the field where I sent you?"

The corner of Malskein's mouth turned up. "Probably because you don't like being corrected… sir. No one else will tell you when you're being a fool."

Draden lunged, cuffing Malskein across the jaw. His left hand came up and he caught Malskein's arm as he swung to return the blow.

"I'm going to overlook that, soldier," Draden said, nodding at Malskein's balled fist. "I gave you orders, and I expect them to be followed. You were in the field because that is where you are most valuable. Your scouting party is surely dead without your guidance."

Malskein jerked his arm away, but said nothing. He licked the blood trickling from his lip.

"Make yourself useful; ready a double watch to the north and east. Send in my squires when you leave. Don't fail, commander. I have bare use for insubordinate men, and none for inept ones."

Malskein saluted. He turned his back and left, nearly tearing the flap from the tent as he did so. Draden began to ready his armor, and when his squires arrived, buckled it on with their assistance. While they worked, a dark-robed figure entered the tent and stood, silent. Draden met the servant's milky eyes and suppressed a shudder. Halkoriv was with it; he could always tell.

It spoke in a whispering, wet voice, a voice that seemed to come from everywhere but its throat. "Your orders stand, Draden. Make for the eastern coast with all speed." The squires ignored the creature, doing their best to avoid looking at it.

"Lord Halkoriv," Draden addressed the servant, "their forces have split…"

"We know this. The plainsfolk cannot harm us. East, with all speed."

"Of course, Lord. But I fear they will strike us, soon. They may have followed our scouts back. They are planning an attack to slow us, I am sure of it."

The servant said nothing. It did not move, or breathe. Draden started when it spoke again. "We will bring the Rider." The figure turned and left.

Light seemed to return to the tent. Draden was thankful for the ease of communication with Halkoriv, but less so for the presence of his servants. They never spoke, save in Halkoriv's voice. They did not eat, sleep, or fight. They simply followed, and waited.

Draden left his tent, stepping out into the night. The air was growing cool, unseasonably so. The sun had just sunk behind the horizon of the western plains. He could smell the smoke of the army's brush fires, see its red glow behind them. To the east, the sky was dark and starless. There was still some distance between the army and the sea, and somewhere within it was the gathered force of all Feriven's enemies.

He issued the orders to break camp and begin marching, despite the onset of night. He shivered and awaited the Rider.

He arrived within moments. He was young, blond, still with a boy's face. Draden might have thought him a raw recruit if he did not know him to be one of the finest cavalrymen in the army. He had once been called Surgund, but his skills had caught Halkoriv's attention. He was more alive than the servants—but something was frightening about him. He was too calm. He approached and waited, staring at Draden with dark, empty eyes.

"Plainslanders are on the move, Surgund." Draden said.

"I know this," the Rider answered. His voice was soft, restrained. "Halkoriv has been with me. The army must continue east, but the plainsfolk must be stopped. They are cunning foes."

Draden nodded. "I understand that you have been studying their tactics?"

The Rider smiled. "Yes, sir. I have."

—Eighteen—

Ahi'rea crouched beside Ruun'daruun on the scorched, ashen ground. Together they peered over the low rise behind which they hid, surveying the arrayed Cheduna forces. The camp was busy and seemed to stretch for miles; Ahi'rea had never seen such a large number of people in one place before. The sound of it was deafening. *And this is only part of their armies,* she thought. *How can we fight so many?* The ash hanging in the air blurred her vision and made her eyes water.

"It looks like they're getting ready to move out," Ruun'daruun whispered. "It's the middle of the night. They don't march at night."

"Lasivar was right," Ahi'rea said. "They know they are close, and they know Lasivar is hoping to escape. Halkoriv must be watching him. They duel through Sight, until one outmaneuvers the other."

"Do you see any scouts?" Ruun'daruun asked.

"No," Ahi'rea said. "Lasivar said that the Cheduna change their scouts for rested ones just before moving." She scanned the mass of people. They had little time. "The cavalry are our priority. If we do not find and slow them, Lasivar and the army will have no chance of outrunning them."

As they watched and waited, one of their kin arrived in a silent run, dropping to the scorched grass beside them. "Nuun'ran. Did you see their horses?" Ahi'rea asked.

Nuun'ran nodded, his shaggy hair made gray by the ash floating in the air. His barrel chest heaved as he recovered his breath. He leaned close to be heard over the camp without shouting. "Further west," he said, pointing. "I couldn't make a count. I can't get close enough with the grasses all burned. The smoke and darkness is all that will keep us hidden."

"It's enough," Ruun'daruun said. "We just have to get in and out." He started heading west, keeping low. "Go gather the rest of us and tell them to come this way."

Nuun'ran nodded, and with a last deep breath, crept away as fast as he dared.

Ahi'rea and Ruun'daruun soon met with others who pointed out the horses. As they prepared, Ruun'daruun turned to Ahi'rea and took her hand. "Can you See anything?" he asked. Ahi'rea turned toward the camp and reached out with her Sight, her eyes casting a glow about the gathered Huumphar.

Almost immediately she looked back at Ruun'daruun. "We can't! They are waiting for us!"

Ruun'daruun drew close and hissed, "Are you sure?"

"We must leave, now!" Ahi'rea answered. She stood, but Ruun'daruun gripped her shoulder and pulled her back down.

"Lasivar said we must not fail. The army will be caught if we do. Lasivar will never reach Halkoriv." Ruun'daruun looked Ahi'rea in the eyes. "Are you sure?" His words fell like hammer blows.

She held Ruun'daruun's gaze. "If we go into that camp, we will be slaughtered," she said. "We cannot do this."

Ruun'daruun sat back, placing a hand over his eyes. Ahi'rea scanned the camp and surroundings, her every nerve on edge. "We must leave, Ruun'daruun. Please," she said.

"Every time before this you have discounted your own visions," he said.

Ahi'rea stared.

"You called them a curse and said we cannot depend on them." Ruun'daruun looked at her, waiting for her response.

Ahi'rea was speechless. She shook her head, could not speak.

"Lasivar would not send us to die," Ruun'daruun said. "He would have foreseen this. We must do what we can, even if you are right." He stood, jaw set, eyes straight ahead. He gestured to the waiting Huumphar, then readied his spear and blade.

Ahi'rea grabbed Ruun'daruun by the upper arm. "He cannot See everything. No one can! Please, Daruun," she said. "We will not survive this."

Gently, Ruun'daruun pulled his arm from her grasp. He looked first at her, then at the other Huumphar gathered around them. "We must do this, for the future of our people," he said, addressing them all. "We are all warriors. We do not fear death, only the cage that awaits us should we fail. Tonight, we have our purpose; it is vital that we succeed. We will go on. We must go on. And if death should come for us, we will meet it with spear, and blade, and the will of the Huumphar!" He turned toward the Cheduna camp and gave throat to a roar. The cry was lost against the sound of the Cheduna camp. Ruun'daruun charged, and the others followed, crying out their frustration, their rage at home and loved ones lost; crying out their vengeance.

Ahi'rea watched her people dash toward the camp, other Huumphar joining them all along the perimeter of the enemy force. She stood, stricken. She could not will herself to follow them, but they were heading into an ambush, of that she was sure. Fear and doubt threatened to overwhelm her.

The grasses were gone; she felt only ashes beneath her feet. Nothing but the dark of night and a few hundred feet of open ground hid her kin from the Cheduna. They would have a few moments of confusion when they reached the edge of the camp, if that—if their ambushers had not already seen them.

She thought of Haruu'na, Ruun'gaphuu, Naph'oin, and all those others that had been lost. Their faces came before her in flashes. She watched Ruun'daruun running at the fore and realized she would lose him too—him and all the rest. What could she do? In her mind hoofbeats and the smell of death crushed out all thought and she felt despair dragging her down. She felt her spear slip from her hand.

A thought forced its way past the darkness in her mind. It seemed so long ago, but it had been only a month.

Why See as we do if you refuse to change anything? she had asked Haaph'ahin. He had given no good answer.

She bent and grasped the spear. Black ash darkened her hand as she lifted it. She set her gaze, willing her Sight to reveal what the night had hidden, what intent lay buried in the minds of the Cheduna. Green light flooded the air, a corona in the hanging ash.

It took only a moment to See them—horsemen, on the move, still hidden within the ranks of the otherwise unaware army. In seconds they would emerge from the camp and run down the attacking Huumphar before they even reached their targets. She could feel the horses' hooves pounding the earth, hear the rumble of their approach. Through her Sight, she could tell something rode at their head, something like a man but lightless, a shadow in her mind. She could not focus on it. It looked back at her, and she had the impression of dripping jaws.

She ran. She remembered the sight of Azra charging against the Huumphar before his capture; one against many. He had been confident, sure of victory. Ahi'rea knew her limits.

The night was clear around her as she covered the distance to the camp, her eyes alight with inner fire. Smoke and darkness seemed to part before her. She ran without any attempt at stealth. She risked one look at Ruun'daruun, now ahead and to her left, rapidly approaching the camp. *They believe in him. I must save as many as I can. Lasivar will have his chance to escape, to lead the army onward, and at least some of us will survive.*

She turned her eyes forward again and pushed the Self through her limbs, pushed herself to run even harder. She knew she risked overexertion, but it did not matter. She did not expect to last long. She did not need to.

The Cheduna ranks seemed to burst ahead of her. Startled soldiers scattered and mounted warriors rode out of the camp and made straight for the nearest Huumphar, a group of warriors who had outdistanced the rest. Without the cover of the grasses, they were easy targets. The Huumphar, taken by surprise, hurled their spears but the soldiers were ready. "Shields!" their leader shouted, and the spears were battered aside. The Huumphar drew machetes; the Cheduna leader called out orders and the soldiers drew their mounts into small groups and charged their targets. The Huumphar were unable to dodge or parry all the lethal lance points at once.

The cries and screams of her people bombarded Ahi'rea. She used them, discarding horror for rage as she covered the final steps to the cavalrymen.

With a scream of fury, her eyes blazing, she leapt amongst the horsemen with her machete in one hand and spear in the other. The blade sliced one of the surprised Cheduna and the force of her attack drove another from his saddle on the point of the spear. Before they realized what was happening, she was dashing past the legs of the spooked horses. Her machete flashed one way, her spear the other. Cheduna soldiers shrieked and cried as tendons were cut and sides pierced. She passed among them like a revengeful ghost, eyes blazing. The Sight was a roar in her mind. She dodged and rolled, whirling out of the way of blades and lances. Horses bucked and reared but their hooves struck only air.

"Run!" she called. "They were waiting for us! Get away!" Their leader barked orders and Ahi'rea found herself at the center of an expanding circle of horsemen. Dozens of them immediately made for the other Huumphar. Her way was blocked by readied lances, but Ahi'rea charged after the horsemen. Three soldiers barred her path, their weapons stained red and gleaming in the camp's firelight. Others tried to join them, to head her off, but their armored mounts maneuvered too slowly.

The first of them thrust out with his weapon, but Ahi'rea was already moving to avoid it. She spun and felt the lance pass through her hair. The other two drove their lances at her, but Ahi'rea was ready with her spear. She knocked the points of their weapons aside even as she planted the spear blade in the burnt earth and jumped, vaulting herself into the air. She cleared the horses' height and slipped between two of the soldiers. Her machete slashed through one of them in passing. She landed behind them, rolled to her feet, and sprinted after the ones who were headed for her kin.

The Sight flashed urgency in her mind and she threw herself flat on the ground. A charging horseman, as if from nowhere, passed over her prone form. She rolled and regained her feet in time to see the Cheduna cavalry commander wheeling his mount back to face her. In her Sight he was a rider's shadow, the shade of a man overtaken by something else. Faster than she thought possible he lunged forward, lance ripping through the air with a shriek. Somewhere nearby, she heard Huumphar cries of fear and pain. The horsemen were on them, and she could not get to them. "Run!" she yelled again. She hoped they could hear her.

Her Sight blurred, so quick was the Rider. Ahi'rea struggled to avoid his lightning fast lance-strikes. She dodged and rolled and swung her machete to parry the attacks. She heard the Huumphar crying out, screaming; she only hoped some of them would escape. She tried to charge past the Rider to draw in more of the horsemen, but he was impossible to evade. In her zeal to escape, she lost her focus. The lance found her leg and dealt her a bloody gash across the calf.

Ahi'rea stumbled to face her attacker even as the other horsemen kept their distance. The voices of the Huumphar were growing distant, but she knew they were being pursued by the cavalrymen. Their numbers seemed endless, and yet she could not evade even this one of them.

She kept low to the ground, coiled and ready to spring. The Rider atop his circling mount was only a dozen paces away. His horse snorted hot steam into the night air, bucking and pacing. All the while, the Rider's gaze was fixed on Ahi'rea from behind his helmet, and his lance point was steady and poised. Ahi'rea's eyes lit him in green, but she saw more than what the light revealed. *One of Halkoriv's servants,* she thought. *He must be.* She remembered the feeling of danger when she had first Seen him.

"The Ghost Witch of the Plainsfolk," he said in Gharven and laughed when she snarled. "My king knows of you. I have heard tales of you."

"Good," Ahi'rea growled. "Then you will be one of the few who know that it was I who killed them."

He laughed again. "Indeed. I know of only two who have escaped you before, and they have taught me much. My master will be pleased to see you dead, and I will be honored to make it so. Your powers are nothing like my king's, nothing like the power he has given me."

Ahi'rea circled, clenching her teeth and trying not to limp or show her pain. She could feel hot blood running down her ankle. She concentrated her Sight, aware that the Rider's banter would not last. *Keep him here,* she thought, the fading cries of fleeing Huumphar still in her ears. "And you are a fool to think I am only as dangerous as my Sight," she said, eyes flaring. "You pretend to be so sure of victory, and yet you keep your men at hand to pull my blade from your throat."

The Rider removed his helmet with one hand, circling close on his steed. Ahi'rea gasped at his boyish features and his dead eyes. His voice echoed strangely. The spirit Sitis was devouring him before her eyes. "I would be a fool to give up my advantage and face you alone. I know your people's tactics and strengths.

Burning the grasses should have been our first move against you, not one of our last. But we must end this now. We must get to rounding up the rest of your warriors before they get too far away." He readied his shield and set his lance. "It has been an honor to face you, and you shall be among the many who know that it was the Rider that killed them."

He reached up to replace his helmet; Ahi'rea saw her chance and sprang. With one hand in use, distracted, and with impaired vision, the Rider would be helpless before her. She willed her charge faster and moved in a blur, sprinting, leaping, one arm flung wide to bring her machete around in a powerful arc. Her eyes, blazing as with green fire, fixed on the narrow, unprotected space between his helmet and shoulder. She could not miss.

He moved. Ahi'rea felt crushing pain in her ribs. At the last moment, the Rider had turned his arm just enough to rotate the rim of his shield into her path. At the same time, he shifted his shoulders. Ahi'rea's machete clanged harmlessly against his armor and she crashed into the shield's steel rim and dropped to the ashen ground, choking, curling into a ball and clutching at her ruined ribs. The horse did not even have time to react until the assault was over, but the Rider easily reigned in his mount. He grunted in what sounded like disappointment and dismounted.

Through tears of agony, Ahi'rea could see his boots directly before her, surrounded by puffs of dust and ash. She labored to breathe. Her ribs shot fire through her with each attempt. Blood welled up in her throat and she spat, which hurt just as badly as breathing. She could not concentrate, could not mend her wounds. The pain was too great. She was unable to catch a breath for the blood in her throat. *At least some of us escaped,* she thought. She hoped she was not lying to herself.

"Your people's fighting style is, in fact, very predictable," the Rider said, tossing aside his helmet. "Strong, but predictable. Training will always win out." Ahi'rea looked up as she heard the cold, sliding ring of a sword leaving its scabbard.

"I do not mean to sound dismissive," the Rider continued. "You were a fine warrior—among the best of your people, no doubt."

Ahi'rea choked and groaned. *As long as he is talking, more of us are escaping.*

"Your time has come. There is no place for you or your kind in Halkoriv's world."

Ahi'rea felt a mailed fist grab her by the hair. She cried out as she was yanked to her knees. She was bent backward and through her pain she could see the Rider looking down on her. Her ribs felt as if they would tear from her body. The Rider held her by the hair so her throat was exposed. Ahi'rea was unable to summon the strength to fight.

"I would rather die," she choked, "than live in a world ruled by someone like you."

The Rider smiled; she had the impression of dripping jaws. "We will enjoy this," his voice echoed. He lifted his sword over Ahi'rea's throat, drawing back his arm for a killing stroke. He swung, and Ahi'rea shut her eyes.

There was a sharp whistle, and an impact.

Ahi'rea felt her hair released and found herself on the ground. She was not dead. Her ribs were in agony, but she forced her eyes open and her head up. The Rider lay a few paces away, gaping at his sword arm. His blade was just inches from his fingers, but his hand grasped reflexively at the air. A Huumphar spear, slick with blood, had impaled his bicep.

Ruun'daruun charged into view and seized the Rider's sword. The surrounding cavalrymen dashed in to attack, but Ruun'daruun was faster. He roared, striking like lightning, lunging from one soldier to the next with his machete flashing in one hand and the Rider's sword in the other. Before his ferocity, several of the horses bolted and many of the soldiers were cut down.

Ahi'rea summoned every ounce of her concentration. She tried to block out the pain, struggled to draw breath. Her power evaded her grasp; it was like catching at smoke. The pain overwhelmed her and she felt unconsciousness fall over her like a shroud.

As the cloying darkness began to block out sight and sound, she thought of Ruun'daruun. She forced her eyes open to see him fending off half a dozen Cheduna horsemen. The darkness fell away and Ahi'rea drew breath despite the pain. *If I die, so will he. He will die fighting for me, as I would have for him.* She exhaled and her eyes blazed as she channeled her Self. The Rider was close, struggling to his feet. His sword arm dangled, useless, dragged down by the spear. Ahi'rea breathed again and felt her bones shifting, her wounds knitting shut. The Rider drew a dagger from his boot and lurched toward her, eyes empty, mouth twisted in a snarl.

Ahi'rea lunged forward and to her feet. One arm shot out and she caught the Rider by the throat, and with the other she snatched the dagger from his startled grasp. In one motion, she rammed the dagger into his neck.

The Rider sucked at the air like a fish out of water, producing only a wet gurgle. He reached for the blade but Ahi'rea held him steady. She drew close to him so that he could hear her over the sound of men shouting and dying. "I was wrong," she said. "It's your blade your men will be pulling from your throat." She twisted the hilt, then let him fall and snatched up her machete. She pulled Ruun'daruun's heavy spear from her fallen foe's arm, then sprang to join her rescuer.

Five lay dead around Ruun'daruun, whose breath came in hard bursts of steam. He held his machete and the unfamiliar Cheduna sword at the ready as more of the cavalrymen circled just out of reach. Ahi'rea stopped beside Ruun'daruun and noted the cut on his forehead and the blood running from his nose and mouth. A deeper wound in the middle of his back flowed with blood. "Can you run?" she asked. The horsemen gaped at the bruise receding from her ribs and the disappearing wound on her calf. The bleeding slowed, then stopped, but the green fire in her eyes did not wane.

"I can," Ruun'daruun said. "But I would rather stay and kill every one of them." His voice was a tortured rasp.

"Another time," Ahi'rea said. "Our people will need you more than ever after this." She could see more soldiers running toward them from the Cheduna camp. She faced away from the camp and advanced on the nearest horseman, forcing him to give ground or fight her. The soldier, quaking under her gaze, backed away. "Quickly, before more of them can come."

Ruun'daruun followed, turning to keep himself between them and Ahi'rea. Meanwhile, she maneuvered to gain a clear path of flight through the surrounding cavalrymen, and found it. "Now!" she said, and Ruun'daruun bolted alongside her as fast as they could past the startled horsemen.

Their pursuit was disorganized and in the dark, smoky landscape Ahi'rea and Ruun'daruun soon lost sight of their pursuers.

She did not know how long they ran; they had to escape, no matter how long it took. Once her Sight quieted and she felt they were alone, Ahi'rea slowed to a walk. Exhaustion soon caught up with her as the adrenaline faded. She staggered and dropped to her knees in the ash and dust. Her ribs ached and her leg still burned, though the cut was gone. She struggled to keep her eyes open, let alone summon the power to finish healing.

Ruun'daruun stopped behind her and placed a hand on the back of her neck. He swayed, fighting to remain upright. Ahi'rea heard dripping. She looked behind her and saw heavy drops of blood collecting in a pool on the ground, mixing with the ash and dirt, as they fell from Ruun'daruun's back. "We have to keep going," he murmured. "We won't stand a chance if they find us again in the open."

Ahi'rea forced herself to her feet. She tried to get beneath Ruun'daruun's arm to support him but he took her hand instead. Side by side they made their way through the dark plains, speaking little. They stopped only when they sighted bodies sprawled across the ashen ground. Most were Huumphar, not Cheduna, and each was marred by many lance wounds. Their killers were nowhere to be seen. Ahi'rea hoped they had gone back to rejoin the main force.

After they passed the eighteenth body, Ahi'rea asked, "How many were killed when they attacked?"

Ruun'daruun set his jaw. "Perhaps forty were with me when we started," he said after a few more steps. "Of those, half were cut down when the Cheduna riders first hit us. The rest scattered."

"Then the other groups probably fared just as poorly," Ahi'rea said. She felt tears build in her eyes. In the hazy moonlight, she saw that Ruun'daruun's eyes were wet as well.

"It's because of you that any of us survived," he said. "There were at least thirty Cheduna horsemen around you, thirty who could not stop you. Your distraction saved many. They escaped, I'm sure. We will find them and we will see Halkoriv's end yet."

—Nineteen—

Azra and Tak'la traveled west, staying near the cliffs. Tak'la had seldom gone as far as the coast; Azra could barely remember seeing it before. Both were entranced by the crashing waves and the reflections of the sun and stars. At Tak'la's insistence, Azra armed himself with a piece of driftwood that he fashioned into a staff, but he intended to use it for nothing more than walking.

"How else will you defend yourself in danger?" Tak'la asked. "You fear to fight." They were picking their way over a rockslide which blocked their path. Small plants had begun to grow amongst the rubble, woody stems with small leaves and tiny yellow blossoms.

Azra scowled. "I do not." The familiar pressure was building in his mind, goading him. He forced it away. "Yes," he admitted. "You are right, I do." The anger receded further with the realization. Azra continued clambering over the rocks and did not look back at his companion.

Tak'la paused atop a boulder and regarded Azra. "Is it because of your magic? Because of the spirit that rides you?" Azra stopped. The pressure came back in a rush and he heard a buzzing, droning sound. Again he forced the feeling away. He started again without a word, making his way over the last few rocks before hopping down onto the grassy cliff. Ahead of them the path descended, leading to a wide gravel beach. "This spirit. What is it like?" Tak'la asked, following.

Azra turned and waited, fighting back the darkness that pressed him with Tak'la's every mention of it. He thought about telling his friend to leave the subject, that he would not discuss it. But despite the pressure, the struggle, Azra felt better for fighting it.

"At first," he said, "I thought I commanded it. Now I know it is there, always pushing me." He considered how to describe it; he had never tried before. "I want to be rid of sound and light. Movement. People. Everything angers me. It is like never sleeping." He paused. "At the same time, it is a stone on my back. I know that if I just release it, I will be strong and fast, that I can do almost anything—except put it away. Pick up the stone again." Tak'la reached the edge of the rockslide and hopped down. "If I fight, if I release control—" Azra hesitated.

"You will lose yourself," Tak'la said.

Azra nodded.

Tak'la looked west and pointed. "Village," he said. Azra could see thin wisps of smoke rising at the horizon. They started walking. "A stone is heavy," Tak'la said. "But if you carry it far, you will grow strong."

Azra thought of how Tak'la must miss his people; how Ahi'rea had to lead them against a foe of superior numbers and strength; how Lasivar must bear his father's legacy, the legacy Azra had thought was his, had thought he knew. "I hope you are right," he said.

—

They passed through the village, stopping only for a few hours. Azra wanted to get farther away from the half-remembered place of his childhood so they moved on after Tak'la traded for some supplies.

They spent the next several days along the rocky beach, heading farther westward. Tak'la would hunt and fish as needed, sharing his food with Azra without comment or reservation. Azra felt useless and asked if Tak'la could teach him, to which the Huumphar agreed.

Early in the mornings they would fish in the ocean, situating themselves on bluffs or rocks over the deep pools. Looking north over the endless water, Azra felt at peace with only the water and waves and sky before him. More than once, he would turn to address his teacher and catch Tak'la staring at the black columns of smoke in the south, dyed orange and fiery crimson with the rising sun. *Tak'la is with me of his own volition,* he told himself. *The Huumphar used him for his strength and skill in battle, but they did not respect him.* He wondered at the younger man's desire to rejoin them, but said nothing of his thoughts.

Over the following days the weather alternated between summer's heat and the chill of autumn. As they moved west the smoke in the plains seemed to move east. It began to dissipate, turning from smoke to a thick, dirty haze. Tak'la did not mention it and Azra ignored it. Those concerns were no longer his. When his mind wandered, though, he thought that the Cheduna army must

OURS IS THE STORM

be on the move and he wondered if they and Ahi'rea's force would soon meet. During the day he shrugged off such thoughts, only to dream of her at night and awaken in fear that she would die and he would never know. He did not mention his thoughts or dreams to Tak'la; he spoke only of his desire to leave behind the war and everything else from his past.

Azra and Tak'la met few travelers save the occasional hunter or fisherman. Small villages were not uncommon on the Gharven coast, but most seemed at least half vacant. While Azra avoided conversation with the few other people they saw, Tak'la was eager to exercise the Gharven he had learned or converse with anyone who understood Huumphar. He would enter villages with fish or game to trade, then emerge with news or descriptions of the surrounding countryside.

On one such occasion, Azra waited by the water, letting the lapping of the waves drown out the ever-present pressure in his mind. He heard Tak'la's approach and turned to face his friend. "We may as well camp here. The sun will be down soon."

Tak'la stopped and leaned on his spear. "They say some of their people have vanished. Never returned from a hunt."

Azra looked at him, raising an eyebrow.

"We should find them." Tak'la kept his eyes on the waves.

Azra shook his head. "I think we should camp here and keep moving in the morning."

Tak'la met Azra's gaze with a scowl. "Where? You have a place to go, or will you just wander further?"

Azra felt a snarl twist his face but he forced himself to take a breath before answering. "I do not think we should get involved. If you want to go, then go." Tak'la paused and then started setting up camp, but did not answer. Azra joined him.

They left the village behind the following morning. Azra's mood brightened as the village passed from sight, but he could tell Tak'la was still troubled. He told his friend yet again that no bond held him there, but Tak'la expressed no desire to go back.

They kept going and the smoke in the southeast soon vanished from sight. Tak'la's energetic and optimistic spirit soon returned and he did not speak again of the war or even the missing villagers, much to Azra's approval. Azra reveled in the pleasant early autumn weather and the gentle, ever-present roll of the waves. They conversed only seldom, Azra desiring quiet and Tak'la complying. The Huumphar noticed that Azra became less irritable and touchy the less they spoke. When a rare autumn storm blew in from the sea, Azra insisted on standing on a bluff in the rain while Tak'la took shelter beneath a rocky outcropping. Tak'la did not ask why.

After another week, they spotted another village situated along the coast. The weather had cooled and rain was rare. It was the height of harvest season. Images insinuated themselves in Azra's mind, but they were unfamiliar: men with sickles reaping the fields, apples plucked from high branches, the smell of hay drying in the sun. They were memories that he couldn't believe were his own, but lived in him nonetheless, buried and lost.

As he and Tak'la passed near an outer field, Azra saw tools but no workers. Half-cut rows and partially-filled baskets had been abandoned and forgotten.

"No farmers." Tak'la scanned the field and outlying buildings. "Why would they leave their work?"

They would not, Azra thought, looking up at the clear sky.

The sun was hot and bright and a cool breeze blew. "Perhaps they saw us coming and thought we were Cheduna scouts." Tak'la grunted, as confident in the guess as Azra.

They entered the field and paused in the middle of a half-harvested row. The sea could still be seen some distance to their right. More fields were to their left, and the forest was beyond those. Ahead they could just make out the outline of the village, built amongst the trees. Azra knew that it would be the work of a moment to allow his eyes to see farther, to let his ears catch any sound from the village. The urge to do so was weaker than it had ever been, but still it pressed him—as it always did. He knew that as soon as he was away from the village the encouraging whispers, the pressure, would lessen—a little.

"You wish to move on." Tak'la's gaze, when Azra looked at him, was accusing and resigned.

"We should not—"

"Get involved," Tak'la interrupted. "No, you are wrong. We should see. Maybe we can help."

"Tak'la," Azra said, "we do not know what is there. They may have left in hopes of avoiding us, or there may be a hundred Cheduna soldiers waiting. Either way, I think it is better to mind our own business."

"But why are we here, to do nothing?" Tak'la asked. "No one else will help them, if that is what they need—and if they are hiding, then we will see no one and move on. I know you fear to fight, but even without the spirit you are a warrior. You have grown strong, carrying your stone!"

"It will lead Halkoriv straight to me," Azra snapped. "It will give the spirit control. It will take me!" He felt the whispers grow agitated, excited. His anger was bolstered even as he fought to suppress it.

"It has already taken you!" Tak'la's voice grew harsh. "You fear it, and your fear commands you. What will you do but survive, chained, if you do not fight fear? If you do not try?"

Azra closed his eyes, pressing back against the power straining in him. "I only want to be left alone. Others can look out for themselves," Azra said. "It is not my concern."

Tak'la nodded. His face became blank, impassive. "Very well," he said. "I was happy to travel with you. I hope our paths will cross again. Goodbye, Azra." He clasped Azra's arm once, then shouldered his spear and set off toward the village, towering over the waving stalks of the wheat fields.

Azra watched his friend—his only friend—grow farther and farther away until he vanished amongst the trees and houses. He was only a little surprised. He had expected Tak'la to leave someday, but he had thought it would be out of loyalty to his people or to pursue Halkoriv's defeat. The anger he had felt at Tak'la lingered. It pressed him, urged him to follow the Huumphar. He wanted to show him that he was wrong and perhaps even to punish him for his foolishness. Azra took a step after Tak'la before stopping and forcing away the rage. He turned back toward the ocean, determined to follow the coast and skirt the village unseen by its inhabitants, or anyone else who might be watching.

Tak'la could do as he wished, Azra told himself as he picked his way through the rows and fields. He left them and traversed the final distance to the rocky beach. *He is capable, can make his own decisions. He knew I would not go with him.* Still, Azra was troubled and his anger continued to smolder just below the surface of his conscious. He knocked a chunk of driftwood aside with his staff.

He is going to get himself captured or killed, Azra thought. *If not now, then later.*

He remembered Tak'la's question—it came unbidden to his thoughts, small and quiet, creeping past his anger and pride. *What will I do, besides survive?* He shook his head, pressing on over the stony shores. *What else is there?*

—

Azra sat before a small fire, situated amongst a stand of rocks by the shore. He was sure he was too far away from the village to be seen now, but he felt the rocks would shield the firelight from any watchers. The night was the coldest yet and Azra had been unwilling to rest without a fire's warmth. Usually Tak'la had made the fires, but Azra congratulated himself for thinking to learn when he had the chance. Tak'la had been a good teacher—Azra did not think he would have any trouble getting along without him.

The anger had waned, though it threatened to return if he dwelt on it. He allayed his own fears, telling himself once again that Tak'la's well-being was his own affair, and no one else's.

He stared into the small flame, at times reaching out to drop another small stick into the glowing coals and watch the flames consume it. His mind wandered without someone with which to speak. It occurred to Azra that, only months ago, Cunabrel had said things would turn out this way.

He had been Revik Lasivar then, warrior, leader, and heir; not Azra. He would never have imagined then that Cunabrel would be right, that Halkoriv could have lied, used him, and cast him aside. He could have imagined even less that he would be glad of it. The times since then seemed just as hazy now as his vague memories from before. Azra's life was a wash of the lives of others, of a man he could not be and a child he did not remember. Only the last few months seemed real—traveling with Tak'la, meeting the true Revik Lasivar, and before that being a captive of the Huumphar... and her. A ghost with green, blazing eyes who had killed him, a woman who had saved him.

Ahi'rea. Why was he thinking of her now?

She had kept him alive when others would not, even after wishing to see him dead. She captivated him with her strength, her confidence, even as she refused to forgive him for his misdeeds.

Azra had never admitted, even to himself, how much he desired her forgiveness, a kind look from her eyes, a gentle touch from her hand.

Now, alone—truly alone—for the first time that he could recall since his imprisonment, Azra wept. He wanted her presence, her forgiveness, even her love—and he knew he would never have it.

His small campfire grew weak and cold. Azra did not notice. He shook with silent sobs, his head in his hands. He realized why he was keeping as far to the north as possible—it was because she was going south. He realized why he wanted silence and solitude—because he wished to be with no one but her. *Why did she let me live?*

He raised his head from his hands, gazing into the graying embers of the fire but not seeing them. His tears slowed, then stopped. They dried on his face in the ocean's nighttime breeze.

Azra did not sleep, nor did he move until the sun cast its first rays into the eastern sky. The smoky columns in the south glowed against the still-dark canopy with a pale light; they were dissipating, spreading across the sky in great streaks of silver.

He stood, ignoring his hunger and the stiffness of his cold muscles. He picked up his staff and turned east, looking toward the village. *Ahi'rea saved me when she did not have to. As soon as I know Tak'la is safe, I can go on.* With a deep breath, he strode across the rocky shore, heading back the way he had come.

A single wisp of smoke rose from the village where Tak'la had left him. As he drew close Azra could make out the glow of a fire among the small, dark houses. He was still a few dozen paces away when a voice shouted out to him from a hidden vantage point. "Stop right there! Drop your weapon!"

Azra scanned the nearest structures and cover, but could not find the source of the voice. "Show yourself," he shouted back. He hesitated. "I, Revik Lasivar, command it."

There was a pause, and then a Cheduna soldier with bow in hand emerged from behind one of the houses. "Lord Lasivar," he breathed, lowering the bow. He knelt, clapping a fist to his mailed chest. He kept his eyes to the ground. "Forgive me, lord. I didn't recognize you without your armor. And we didn't really expect to meet you alive. They said you were killed, that an imposter was in your place." The soldier looked up, eyes bright, a grin spread across his broad jaw. "I'm glad to see it's not so, my lord."

Azra motioned for the soldier to stand. "How many are with you? And what are you doing so far to the north?" He swept his hair back as best he could, realizing how long and unruly it had grown.

"Looking for you, my lord. We heard you died, but me and the others were sent here to find you. King Halkoriv himself sent one of his servants to lead us—Lord Bor."

Azra had never heard of Bor, but said nothing as they made for the center of the village. The sentry followed him, continuing, "Good thing, too. There were twenty of us, but now there are fourteen. It would've been worse, but Lord Bor stopped the plainsfolk warrior that happened on us yesterday before he could kill any more."

"Plainsfolk?" Azra stopped, turning to face the sentry. His stomach twisted into a knot.

"Yes, lord. Like a nightmare, it was. Got two of the men on watch almost before they raised the alarm, three more before the rest of us could get to them. The last, Olak, didn't die till he bled out this morning." The soldier's face twisted in anger. "Bor put an end to it, though. Me and the boys wanted to pay the brute back proper, but he wouldn't let us—made us leave him alive. He's bound up in one of the houses. Let's get you to camp sir. Bor said it was urgent that we find you." The soldier motioned for Azra to continue.

The soldiers had just begun to rise. When they saw Azra their haggard faces displayed first confusion, then joy as they realized who the scruffy stranger was. Many were wounded and all looked travel worn, but their lord's arrival did wonders for their spirits. They were soon clustered around, shaking Azra's hand and telling him how glad they were to find him, that now the war could finally end, that they could get back to the main force and wipe out the plainsfolk and the imposter Lasivar. Azra shared their happiness, clapping shoulders and distributing praise. *Could it really be this easy,* he wondered, *to just go back to the way things were?*

His escort was trying to guide Azra from the pack of excited soldiers when Azra spotted a man who could only be Lord Bor. He stood just outside the group, a cold smile etched across his features. He looked young and strong, with sandy lank hair and a stubbly jaw, but something ancient hung over his countenance—something Azra recognized. There was a lurch in his mind and Azra realized that the pressure had been gone all morning—until now. Azra suddenly wondered if his plans had been wise after all.

Bor, already armed and armored, stepped silently up to the group and the soldiers quieted and parted to let him pass. He approached with an unusual grace for a man of his size and stature; he was a full head taller than Azra.

"All right, boys," the sentry murmured. "Let's get back to it so we can get moving soon." The others nodded and muttered agreement and returned to their duties, giving Bor a wide berth.

Bor stared into Azra's eyes, and Azra returned the gaze. Neither man spoke. Azra felt something prying, searching, digging, like cold fingertips in his mind. The power in him stirred and he knew he could force Bor out with a thought, cripple him with pain, pry into his own mind—but he resisted. *Never again,* he thought. He gritted his teeth and focused on keeping the darkness at bay. He knew Bor would find whatever he was looking for. It would be impossible to fend off both Bor and the spirit. They were almost one and the same.

Still the pressure, the yearning to fight back built in him. Azra's hands balled into fists as he gave all he had to restrain the rage in him that was not his own. Bor's search went deeper. Azra's eyes lost focus, but not before he saw Bor's cruel smile widen. His mind began to slip. He felt creeping cold in his shoulders, on the back of his skull. The power was forcing its way to the surface—Azra was going to tire, then lose, and the spirit in him would rip its way out and consume him.

That is what they want, Azra realized. *Halkoriv. Sitis. They are the same, and Halkoriv will not live forever. Sitis needs me, and it needs me alive so that it can live on. Bor and those like him are only servants—I was something else.*

Azra's leg buckled and he stumbled, falling to his knees. He felt mud under his fingertips as he pitched forward. He cast about for strength and found nothing in him to hold to, no support, no hope. It occurred to him that even if he did not die, was not lost to Sitis right now, he still had nothing. Even if he rescued Tak'la, which was all he had set out to do, he was still going to be alone—and his death would mean nothing. Halkoriv would send others to fetch him or Sitis would consume him eventually, and he would become again what others had set out to make him.

I hope I made the right choice, he thought. The words were an echo—someone had said it before. *Who?*

Ahi'rea. She had been speaking of her decision to spare him. *If I do nothing after she saved me, then how could her choice have been right? If the spirit takes me now, how could mine?*

Suddenly, Azra knew what he had to do. He knew why he had to live, and what her choice would mean. He knew what he would do, besides survive. But he would not be able to do it alone, and would not be able to do it now. He had to hide the thought. He could not let Bor find it. Could not let Sitis find it. Azra fought them away. He held the thought like a lifeline and the cold pressing him receded as if from a fire. The power remained at the fore of his mind, but he resisted it, anchoring himself to his decision. The prying stopped. His vision returned and Azra was once again before Bor in the midst of the camp in the center of the abandoned village.

Bor was still smiling, but his smile held a trace of true amusement, as of one staring at a strange but harmless-looking insect. He folded his arms, looking down at Azra while he regained his feet and caught his breath.

"Come speak with me... Lord Lasivar," Bor said. He turned toward the south side of the camp and strolled away. Azra followed.

Out of earshot of the soldiers, Azra spoke. "I am here for the Huumphar you captured."

Bor nodded, the dark cloak across his shoulders rippling with the movement. "Yes, I know," he said. "I know everything."

Do you? "Let him go, and I will come with you," Azra said.

Bor chuckled. "You will, but we will not be releasing your friend. You will both accompany us to the Ancestor's Stone."

The Ancestor's Stone. The name was one Azra had never heard, but he knew it. He remembered what he had felt, what he had seen at the Monument with the Huumphar. In his mind, he had seen two men and a woman on the Monument, felt his skin and bones burn away; the memories had not been his—they had been far too old.

Sitis. Sitis, the Ancestor of Halkoriv, the spirit that lived in him. Azra grabbed Bor's shoulder to turn him, to meet his eyes, and felt cold, freezing pain shoot up his arm. The larger man caught Azra's wrist, easily forcing his grasp away. Azra almost cried out with the agony. Bor half-turned to Azra, looking down at him with the same detached amusement he had shown before. "You hold no power now," he intoned. "I have your friend, and now I have you. And I am every bit as powerful as you used to be. I am Halkoriv's chosen now, not you. I will do as he pleases, and he orders you to the Ancestor's Stone. You may have turned your back on our cause, but you still have some uses." Bor released Azra's wrist. It felt as if all the heat had been drained from it. Azra clutched at his arm, trying to warm away the numbness.

"And what use is that?" Azra asked through gritted teeth. "I will not fight for him again."

"How could you?" Bor asked. "You have made yourself weak, sworn off the abilities you had mastered. You willfully chose weakness. You could have been great. The others still think you are, as I once did."

How much did he see? Azra wondered. *Does he know what I must do?* The idea was developing, taking form. The Ancestor's Stone. He released his wrist, which had regained a modicum of feeling. "As if I care what they or you believe. What does Halkoriv want from me?" *How much do you know? Are you really like me, or are you just another slave?*

"I do not question our Lord," Bor answered. He was looking away to the south, out past the abandoned homes of the village and through the deep green forest, the tips of its leaves beginning to tinge with red and gold. "For my part, I do not understand why he does not give the power of sorcery to other loyal followers, like me—but it is not my place to know his mind. He wants you alive, and so he shall have you."

—

Within the hour the Cheduna soldiers had packed their gear. Azra rode in front with Bor, as befitted his station. Only he and Bor knew that he was as much a captive as Tak'la, who was led bound and gagged behind them, guarded by four of the soldiers at a time.

They traveled light and fast, heading southeast through the forest and toward the plains. Azra knew that without his powers he would be little match for even the soldiers, let alone Bor. The creeping cold presence was still there, a constant reminder that he could fight them, destroy them—but that in so doing he would seal his own fate, lose himself to the Ravenous Spirit, lose his identity again and toss away many lives for nothing. And so, he waited.

—TWENTY—

The hours after the ill-fated assault on the Cheduna passed Ahi'rea in a featureless blur. After they evaded the remaining riders she and Ruun'daruun had somehow found a place to rest. She awoke, bruised, stiff, and still exhausted, amongst a stand of tall yellow stones. Beside her, Ruun'daruun was sprawled on the ground with a crude, blood-soaked grass poultice bound to his back. He breathed in shallow, but steady, bursts.

She was hesitant to leave him, but Ahi'rea forced herself to her feet. She was able to summon enough concentration to channel a weak effort to heal herself and felt some of her soreness and pain subside. After surveying their surroundings from the cover of the stones, she set out to gather some food from the flame-scoured landscape. It was not pleasant fare—insects, a few dry roots, one or two hardy edible plants—but it would provide a bit of much-needed nourishment.

She returned and woke Ruun'daruun with some effort. He was weak from fighting, running, and blood loss, but between her coaxing and his own will he rose and rested up against a rock. She presented the meager rations she had gathered, and as they ate she felt more energy return to her. Ruun'daruun seemed to regain some strength as well. As she watched, he crunched and swallowed the food and muttered. "It is good you have the Sight. You would never survive if you had to rely on your cooking."

Ahi'rea looked up in surprise to see him wink at her. Smiling back, she tossed another insect at him in mock anger. "Stop whining and eat your beetles."

They drank most of what remained of their water; Ahi'rea advised that they save more, but Ruun'daruun disagreed. "We'll get nowhere if we don't drink," he said. "Our minds will wander and our steps will be unsteady. For today, let's drink now and find more as we go, while our lives are still in our own hands."

Ahi'rea nodded. Despite the solitude, the loss of their fellow warriors, the failure of their goal—despite all of these, she and Ruun'daruun were still the masters of their own path. "It is midday already," Ahi'rea said. "If we hurry, we may still outpace the Cheduna in time to warn Lasivar. If he has not Seen them still coming, they will be cut off."

In the daylight the two Huumphar were in renewed danger—unless they could reach the cover of the unburned grasses. Then, they could relax a little and Ahi'rea could expend the time and energy needed to See any of their remaining companions and Lasivar's army. Both would have preferred to wait for cover of night, but both knew that they could not afford the time to wait.

They scanned the horizon from dawn to dusk, on the lookout for enemy scouts and soldiers. Ahi'rea and Ruun'daruun were not sure where the nearest cover was, but the Cheduna army had been moving southeast at speed. Traveling southeast would lead them into the Cheduna forces. That left only east, toward the coast. They were only a few days' travel from the ocean, and Halkoriv's fires had not yet burned that far. Fearful of being sighted, they ran as fast as they could over the flame-swept plains. By sundown that day, Ahi'rea spotted the inviting shelter and concealment of the tall grasses and she and Ruun'daruun were among them by the time the moon rose.

Though they were back in their element, Ahi'rea and Ruun'daruun kept their guards up. They were able to find better food and fresh water, and soon were looking for a place to bed down for the night.

"I'll stand guard," Ruun'daruun announced once they found a suitable spot.

Ahi'rea frowned. "You need to rest. You cannot heal yourself like I can."

Ruun'daruun shook his head. "You must See who is left—who escaped. I'll stand watch so you can See."

Ahi'rea could not help but smile, warmth flooding through her. He was badly wounded, had walked all day, and was now refusing rest to protect her. Even bruised and exhausted, he was beautiful.

"Daruun," she said, sitting, "rest." She patted the soft ground beside her. "Even if our people are nearby, we cannot travel any farther tonight. I will look for them in the morning, after we have both slept."

Ruun'daruun took one last look around the horizon, taking the moment to consider what she had said. He then gingerly lowered himself to the ground and lay down; he made no sounds of discomfort, but his expression belied the pain he was in.

Ahi'rea pressed up against Ruun'daruun, placing one arm and leg across him. He wrapped his arm around her shoulders, holding tight to her. Overhead the moon was a bright crescent; smoke still marred the sky, but in the dark of night she imagined it was only cloud, drifting on the cool, pleasant breeze of the plains. The stars stood out, glittering above them like blue fires in the distance.

"Do you realize," Ruun'daruun asked, "that this is probably the only time we can be this close without any nosy elders clucking about us?" Ruun'daruun pulled Ahi'rea closer.

"You are right," Ahi'rea said. "Even if we were elders ourselves, they would have something to say about it."

"Can you imagine if they had followed us to battle?" Ruun'daruun asked. "'Why are you fighting that way? That's not how our ancestors held their spears.'"

Ahi'rea giggled and lifted herself up on her elbow to gape in surprise at Ruun'daruun. "Another joke! Do you have a fever?" She reached a hand up toward his forehead, but withdrew it to protect herself when he started tickling her side.

The tickle ended in an embrace. Ruun'daruun and Ahi'rea locked eyes, staring into one another, and then Ahi'rea leaned forward and kissed him. They held each other as if in desperation, neither wanting nor willing to pull away.

Ahi'rea was the first to do so. She lifted herself on her elbow again, gazing down at Ruun'daruun. In their tussling, she had gotten almost on top of him. Their eyes remained locked for what seemed like a long time.

Ruun'daruun's eyes flicked away, looking past Ahi'rea's shoulder. She turned and saw a glow to the south—light from Halkoriv's army. They remembered where they were and why.

"We should sleep," Ahi'rea finally breathed. "We have a

long way to go still." Ruun'daruun nodded. She rolled back to his side, placing her head and arm on his chest. He wrapped his arm around her shoulders again. Together, they soon slept.

—

Once Bor allowed the soldiers to make camp, Azra was able to speak with Tak'la. He dismissed the Huumphar's guard, then removed Tak'la's gag and loosened his bonds. Tak'la nodded his thanks, ignoring the raw, rubbed wounds from the ropes and the injuries he had sustained in being captured. He was tied to a tree and the ropes held his wrists close together behind him. He was tied in such a way that he had to remain sitting or kneeling.

Tak'la's prison was a stand of trees and brush not far from the main campsite. The forest was cold and damp and moss grew on the many gray stones protruding from the black earth. The trees were ancient, tall and twisted things hung with moss. Their colors had changed much more here, and despite the damp and cold, the deep forest was bright with leaves the colors of fire, red and yellow hanging from the branches and carpeting the woodland floor. The black trunks stood in stark relief to the colorful branches like the bars of a cage. Only a few dozen feet away, the Cheduna soldiers chopped wood and heaped logs to build a fire.

Azra was worried that Tak'la would still be angry or misunderstand his intentions, but those fears were dashed when a slow, tired smile spread across Tak'la's face. Azra was reminded of just how young Tak'la was—even younger than Azra himself.

"I had hoped our paths would cross again." Tak'la grinned.

"It is just like you to joke around when we could be killed

at any moment," Azra grumbled. Tak'la's smile remained. "I am glad to see you, too." Azra smiled despite his efforts to be serious. "Next time I tell you to mind your own business…"

"Yes," Tak'la interrupted. "We shall go fishing instead."

Azra sat down beside his friend. "If I let you go now, I fear we will both be killed," he said. "When I see an opportunity…"

Tak'la nodded. "It wouldn't be any use right now."

"And I am almost as much a captive as you," Azra lamented. Tak'la gave him a sidelong look. "Almost," Azra said again. "The soldiers do not know, but their leader, Bor…"

"Ah." Tak'la nodded once. "He is strong."

"And he knows about me," Azra said. "He says you will die if I leave and that there is no way for you to escape alive."

Tak'la raised his chin. "They could not find me if I left their sight."

Azra shook his head. "He might not have to. Did Bor cut you? Touch your blood?"

Tak'la nodded as his eyes grew wide. "He took my blood on his hands."

Azra swore.

"That can kill me?" Tak'la asked in disbelief.

"It could. He is like I used to be, Tak'la. Like me but… not quite," Azra said.

"What do you mean?"

"Sitis only lives in those of its bloodline, but Halkoriv has many servants. He rides them, controls them. He gives them power, but they do not realize the power owns them. Bor is like that. He thinks he wields power, but he is the sword, and the spirit in him is the hand. Not even Halkoriv's hand, but the hand of something older, something worse. The power can but cut away, and he would be just a man—it might even kill him—but it will never be a true part of him." Azra felt the pressure in his skull. "But that's not what Halkoriv did to me. Because Halkoriv thought I was special, he did something different."

"Did what?" Tak'la asked. "What was different?"

Azra paused. Something Lasivar had said came to him. *It is growing in you.* Slow realization crept through him, but still he struggled to put all the pieces together. "He hollowed me—removed from me everything of who I was—to make room for the spirit." Everything rushed back to him in flashes—his imprisonment; his lack of memories; the human sacrifice Halkoriv had made in Cunabrel, a sacrifice Azra had made to himself; they had all been planned and executed to do one thing—let Sitis the Ravenous Spirit take root in him fully. "That's it…" he breathed, getting to his feet.

"What?" asked Tak'la.

"That is why my power came back," Azra said. "That is why he wants me alive. I am not of his blood, and Halkoriv did not know it, but he gave Sitis a way out of the bloodline. It is not Halkoriv at all—it is Sitis. Sitis wants me back because if Halkoriv dies, if Lasivar kills him, it needs me to live on. That is why Halkoriv never figured it out—never knew he had the wrong man."

Tak'la struggled to keep up—he had not understood Azra's powers to begin with. "So… what does this mean?"

"It means Halkoriv will not kill me, and neither will Bor. The Spirit will not let them. It rides Bor and owns Halkoriv, just like I fear it could own me—but for now, that means it will do whatever it must to keep me alive."

"Then you can kill Bor," Tak'la grinned.

"Maybe," Azra answered. "He is powerful, and has nothing to stop him from using his power. The Spirit wants me to open myself, to use it, but I cannot. If I do, then it may take me. There are dozens of ways Bor could stop me without killing me." Azra sat again, unsure how to use his newfound knowledge.

Tak'la said nothing. He recognized Azra's look and knew it was best not to disturb him.

After some time, Azra looked up. "I should not linger. Even though they trust me now, the other soldiers may become suspicious—best not to have any of them looking over our shoulders." He got up and clasped Tak'la's arm. "Do not worry, my friend. I am going to get you out of this."

Tak'la smiled. It was the most hopeful thing he had ever heard Azra say.

—

Azra could spend little time with Tak'la if he wanted to avoid suspicion. Bor would surely have his limits. He was confident and it seemed to amuse him to allow Azra his autonomy, but if he became at all worried he was sure to keep them from speaking—or just kill Tak'la. Many days they were not able to speak, instead giving each other a look or nod of reassurance in passing.

Azra wished he could ride alone, but wanted more than anything to avoid Bor. That was best accomplished by speaking with the soldiers, who exhibited a restrained excitement to be in his presence. They rode alongside Azra, speaking about the army's progress in the plains, their clandestine journey into the North, and more mundane topics like their families and homes in the South. Azra was reminded of how he had been told the plainsfolk were little more than animals. He wondered if their warriors would be surprised to hear Cheduna soldiers speak of farms and fishing, of sons and daughters and wives. *They fight for the same reason I did,* he thought as a man called Holden described the barn he had built after the previous campaign. *They are told to fight, and they gain from it. They are turned toward the one called 'enemy,' and they charge. The difference is that they do not all enjoy the killing as I did.* He looked ahead at Bor, leading the group along the forest path. Tak'la estimated that they would reach the plains within a week. Bor would ride ceaselessly if the others had not needed the rest, and Azra almost wished they could. The days were interminable, the hours crawling by without end.

He grunted agreement to whatever Holden had just asked him. The soldier looked pleased and went on, changing the subject to his daughter's approaching marriage.

Azra's head pounded as his thoughts wound about him in great, circuitous paths; thoughts of Halkoriv, Ahi'rea, Tak'la's safety, the constant pressure in his skull—they all led back upon themselves and to the same reality. There was little Azra could do but ride and wait.

"As long as I'm back home before winter, I don't much care," Holden was concluding. Azra glanced up to see that the soldier was looking away to the south. "They said this push would only take two months. Turned out a stretch longer, eh, sir?"

What would he think if I told him the Huumphar have only as much desire to fight as he does? Azra wondered. Holden turned his grizzled face back to Azra, waiting for a response.

"You are an honorable man," Azra said, and meant it. "To stay and fight when your heart tells you not to."

Holden looked confused. "My job, sir. My duty."

Azra nodded. "Would that your leaders discharged theirs so faithfully."

Holden's mouth opened, then closed. His gaze went from Azra to Bor and back.

"A family must be a precious thing," Azra said. "You have a duty to them as well. You will be home for your daughter's marriage." Azra smiled at Holden, then set his jaw and rode ahead and called out to Bor.

—

"Lasivar passed through here," Ruun'daruun said. He waved at the trampled grass and earth—there was no need to look too hard when one was tracking an army.

"Yesterday, probably," Ahi'rea agreed. "We are getting close now, but so are the Cheduna. I Saw them closing in, and they have a head start on us." She cast her eyes over the horizon, scanning the south. She could just make out the faint, far off sound of the eastern sea.

"Their scouts stand out like stars in the night sky," Ruun'daruun said. "If they were near, we would see them—or you would, in any case."

"Daruun, the Sight does not show me everything," Ahi'rea said. "We should be careful. I know you are feeling better but it has still only been a few days."

"My wounds are healing. Even if their scouts were nearby,

it should be no trouble to sneak past them—and only little more to put a spear to them." He beckoned her and started south. "Let's go—we might be able to catch up to Lasivar by nightfall if we hurry."

Ahi'rea cast her eyes to the west, but then turned and followed Ruun'daruun. It felt good to move; the motion of her legs began to work off the night's chill; the weight of her spear felt good in her hand. She looked up to see Ruun'daruun looking over his shoulder at her, slowing his pace to watch her run. He smiled.

"You have the most graceful stride," he said.

She caught up to him, giving him a playful shove. "And you will fall headfirst in a ditch if you watch me instead of your path."

Ruun'daruun spun, jumping just in time to avoid a rut dug in the earth by runoff. Ahi'rea marveled at him—he had been running for days, injured, without complaint. He flashed her one last smile and caught her hand for a moment before turning his attention to the task before them. She squeezed his hand, just to feel his reassuring squeeze in response. No matter what happened, no matter how badly he was hurt, how numerous their foes, how great their troubles—she knew he would never leave her, never rest as long as he drew breath.

The smoke from the plains fires lingered. The sun's glow was red and the clouds above were a brilliant orange in the dawn. Autumn's approach hinted that the air would remain cool throughout the day, for which Ahi'rea was thankful. A gentle breeze blew from the south, and the grass around them rolled like waves on a sea of gold.

The beauty of the plains struck Ahi'rea, as it always did, and only the memory that others were trying to take them away recalled her attention to her surroundings.

On they ran, conserving their breath and only speaking when necessary. Mile after mile passed beneath their feet. Urgency pressed itself on them when Ahi'rea noticed a telltale dust cloud to the southwest. The Cheduna army was not far—but they had finally caught up. They ran faster.

Hours later, they saw signs of Lasivar's army's camp. They had lit no fires, but Ruun'daruun estimated they were now only a few hours behind. Excitement was clear in his voice. "We'll reach them by tonight; I'm sure of it."

They stopped seldom and but for a rest beneath the boughs of one of the few hardy plainsland trees. Ahi'rea lay on her back, gazing up while droplet-shaped red leaves the size of her fingertip floated down and alighted on her skin. Ruun'daruun kept watch until she insisted that they switch, but he fidgeted and remained vigilant during his turn to rest. After too little time, she extended a hand to help him to his feet. He grasped her wrist and rose, pulling her close into an embrace. He lifted up his hand to her chin and she turned her face up to kiss him.

They forgot the world for a moment, locked together, and felt only each other's touch—then the moment passed and they remembered their fallen kin and the enemies just over the horizon. They ran on.

The sun left its peak and began to sink into the west. They were not far; the grasses were freshly trampled around them. The army's path had turned further east and now Ahi'rea and Ruun'daruun could see the ocean in the distance, growing dark as the sun grew low.

Ahi'rea was uneasy. They had seen none of their own scouts,

nor any other Huumphar since the failed assault. She was anxious to catch up to Lasivar and find out if any of the others had returned.

Lasivar—had he foreseen this? Had he known what would happen? She pushed the thought away, but did not disregard it. *Plenty of time to worry about that when we reach him.*

On and on they ran. Ahi'rea ignored her protesting muscles and willed her lungs to greater effort. She took a swig from her waterskin, keeping her pace. She thought of landmarks, mapping mental routes around the plains to keep her mind occupied while she ran. It was a meaningless exercise; the routes looped and doubled back, leading nowhere, but while she did it she forgot her weariness and ran without effort.

There was still enough sun peeking up over the plains to last them another hour or so. She hoped they would not have to wait out another night before catching up to the army.

Ruun'daruun snatched her wrist, pulling her from her thoughts. Together they slowed, dropping low to the ground. Ruun'daruun pointed and Ahi'rea glimpsed a Cheduna soldier in light leather armor just as he passed behind a low rise before them.

"Scouts," Ruun'daruun whispered. "We must be close." He slid his machete from its scabbard.

Ahi'rea put her hand on his. "Better if they do not know we have returned."

Ruun'daruun looked over at her and hesitated. He replaced the weapon in its sheath. "You're right," he said. "Even if all they find is a body, they will know the Huumphar were not all killed."

They crept forward, eyes and ears alert for the southern scouts. The sun was low and the shadows deep. Despite the Huumphar disdain for Cheduna attempts at stealth, Ahi'rea and

Ruun'daruun knew better than to underestimate their foes now, so close to their goal. Together they stalked through the grasses, each footfall silent, each motion matched to a breeze.

They spotted the scout. He faced north, watching the area in which they had waited moments before. His armor blended well with the plains and he was motionless—which was how they had seen him. Around him, the grasses waved and shifted with each gentle breath of wind.

They were about to move on when Ahi'rea caught sight of another scout, on the other side of them. He too was still and silent, bow at the ready. He was looking right at them.

She tensed, grip tightening on her spear. She could not lift and throw it in the time it would take the scout to fire—but perhaps she could draw the attack so that Ruun'daruun would have time.

Her eyes flickered once and she stayed her hand—she felt no imminent danger. She realized as the scout looked away that he had not seen them, though he had seemed to be focused on their position. She exhaled, relieved she had not attacked. She caught Ruun'daruun's attention, indicated the second scout, and slunk away from the southerners, continuing south. Ruun'daruun followed, watching behind to ensure they were not noticed and followed.

They were soon out of earshot, but they remained low and quiet. Ruun'daruun jerked his head west. Ahi'rea followed his motion with her gaze and noted thin smoky columns; campfires. The Cheduna army was indeed close. She thought she could hear their voices in the distance.

To the south they saw no smoke, no fires giving away Lasivar's position. As Ahi'rea took stock of the landscape, however, her heart sank.

The land was rising away from the sea, and she could hear the crash of waves on bare rock away to the east. Far ahead, in the darkening sky, she could just make out the Calshae mountains, the border of Halkoriv's realm. More importantly, however, was that Ahi'rea knew that between here and the mountains lay the Kan Manif Bur; the Canyon of Red Water. The canyon was impassable for miles inland. Lasivar's army was trapped, boxed in between the ocean, the canyon, and the Cheduna army.

Why Lasivar would lead them here she could not fathom. As they pressed onward, she reminded herself that he was not infallible; everyone merely thought he was. She still could not See their victory, nor anything of their end. By what visions Lasivar guided his actions, he had not said.

Perhaps he had reason to come here—and perhaps, she thought, he had simply made a mistake. With so many of the Huumphar gone on their raid, he might not have had the guidance to avoid the area. A more costly mistake, she could not imagine. That his raid had nearly sent the Huumphar to their doom was not comforting, but she had not spoken of that concern with Ruun'daruun. She would not, until she had spoken of it with Lasivar.

They passed another rise, leaving the Cheduna scouts behind them and now well out of sight. No sooner had they descended the hill but Ahi'rea spotted something hidden in the grass and darkness ahead of them. She was about to warn Ruun'daruun when the figure moved and she saw its rust-colored cloak. "Gharven," she whispered, pointing. Ruun'daruun nodded and they stood, making no secret of their presence. They approached the scout, who gave no indication of having seen them. As they neared her, she made eye contact and crossed a hand over her lips in a gesture of silence. The Huumphar nodded, and came close enough to whisper.

"Southern scouts," the scout muttered. Her heavy hood obscured most of her face in the twilight. Ahi'rea could just make out the curve of her jaw. "Good to see some of you coming back."

Ruun'daruun's voice was flat. "We are the first?" The northerner nodded, and Ruun'daruun clenched his teeth.

"More will come," Ahi'rea said, putting a hand on his shoulder. "Where is the camp?" The sentry gestured. Ahi'rea followed her gaze to another rise in the plains, beyond which she knew the earth dropped toward the canyon. *So close?* Ahi'rea wondered.

As if she had heard her thoughts, the sentry spoke. "Lasivar. He—I don't know. He's done something. The sound doesn't carry. It just—stops." Her voice held an edge of awed fear.

Ruun'daruun seemed about to speak, but Ahi'rea took his hand and made for the camp, nodding her thanks to the sentry. "He can do that?" Ruun'daruun asked. "Such power."

Ahi'rea said nothing. Storm was a mystery to her, but what she had seen of it thus far inspired other feelings in her than Ruun'daruun's admiration.

They crested the hill and she could not restrain a gasp. There they were—hundreds of people, tents, and fires, but no sound, no smoke. She heard the grasses whisper in the breeze, the far off waves of the sea—but no speech, no movement—nothing from the army encamped before them.

They descended, gaping. Ahead of them, a horse reared and stomped. A group of men shook with laughter, slapping each other's shoulders while one tossed scraps of wood on a fire. A cart bounced over a rut in the camp as it moved between tents, delivering food and fuel; all without a sound.

The sunlight was gone and fires illuminated the camp. Their light seemed to stop at the camp border—even it could not escape Lasivar's power. Overhead the sky was clear, and beyond the encampment the mountains blotted out the starlight, visible only by the silhouette they cast. To the west, Ahi'rea could see the glow of the Cheduna camp.

She and Ruun'daruun started when they were but a few yards from the outermost tents—the sound of a far-off crowd slashed through the silence as they crossed some invisible border. With each step the sounds rose in volume until they passed into the camp and it reached its peak.

It was almost deafening after the quiet of the plains, and it took them some time to become accustomed to the noise as they wound through the camp. Ahi'rea could not believe her ears. Ruun'daruun wore a broad smile. He caught her gaze and put an arm around her waist. He leaned toward her. "After the last few days, I was losing hope. But now—he is so powerful. Lasivar will lead us to victory." Ahi'rea only smiled, putting her hand on his. She did not wish to dampen his mood.

They reached the center of the camp and saw the tents of the few Huumphar who had remained behind. Ruun'daruun withdrew his arm, reluctantly, letting his fingers trace across Ahi'rea's lower back. She took his hand for only a second and wished she could hold tight to it. The elder Huumphar looked up from their seats around the fire, eyes widening in excitement. They began to call to each other that the warriors had finally returned.

Haaph'ahin was sitting amongst the others. He stood and rushed toward them, eyes locked on Ruun'daruun.

"Massacred! You led our people to their deaths!" he shouted. He stopped just short of Ruun'daruun, stretching to his full height and seething. "They may as well have died by your hand!"

Ruun'daruun was about to respond, but something stopped him. Ahi'rea opened her mouth to speak, to defend him, but realized why he had stopped when she saw tears rolling down her father's cheeks.

"I Saw! I Saw what happened," he cried, voice rising in pitch. "You have doomed our people. I should never have given such responsibility to you!"

Ruun'daruun could restrain himself no longer. Towering over Haaph'ahin, he thundered down at the older man. "Our people fought with honor and courage. We were ambushed. And you, who claim to have such vision, would cheapen their sacrifice to some error or madness, when you yourself sent us all to die once before!" He shook with rage. The other elders jumped to their feet, shocked at Ruun'daruun's disrespect. Haaph'ahin's eyes lit and blazed green.

"How dare you speak so to me?" he replied. "You have—"

"No, father," Ahi'rea broke in. Haaph'ahin turned his flaring eyes on his daughter. "Ruun'daruun is right," she said. "And if you had truly Seen what happened, you would know that! Your vision is clouded, and you put such stock in what you See that you ignore what you experience yourself, what others see and feel and do. You trust an invisible power more than your own eyes. Does Ruun'daruun look well? Do I? Do you think we do not grieve, do not feel every one lost, every friend slain?"

Haaph'ahin diminished, the light in his eyes fading. He let her speak. Firelight reflections glimmered on his wet cheeks.

"You are a good man, Father," Ahi'rea said, lowering her voice. "You have led our people well and taught all of us much. But of late, your fear has made you blind." She stepped forward and put her arms around him. Haaph'ahin did not move. "I love you," Ahi'rea said. "It is urgent that we speak with Lasivar. We will return later, and speak together." She felt her father bow his head. She stepped away, looking at him and at the others gathered around them. She took Ruun'daruun's hand in hers. If they reacted, they did not show it.

"What is happening affects more than just our people," Ahi'rea said. "Things are changing. We must speak to Lasivar, then we will return to discuss the Huumphar's part in it."

One by one, the elders met her eyes. One by one, they returned to their tents and fires. Haaph'ahin was still, his eyes downcast. Hand in hand, Ahi'rea and Ruun'daruun turned and went in search of Lasivar.

—Twenty-One—

"He was supposed to save us."

The tone of Ruun'daruun's voice made Ahi'rea's heart ache, but could not quiet the anger she felt. She stood, despite her exhaustion, while he sat nearby. They were both inside Ruun'daruun's tent—neither cared anymore what was being said about that. It seemed that the chiding words of elders and gossips soon would no longer matter.

He was right. Azra's warning ran through Ahi'rea's mind. *He has been using us to get to Halkoriv—nothing more. He had no interest in liberating us.* She held her tongue, rather than speak such thoughts aloud. Ruun'daruun was already crushed.

She knelt behind him, wrapping her arms around him. He touched her arm and leaned his forehead against hers as she leaned over his shoulder.

"We will just have to save ourselves," she said. Ruun'daruun smiled but said nothing.

—

When they had reached Lasivar's encampment and been

stopped by his bodyguards, they had been turned away at first. The bodyguards insisted that Ahi'rea and Ruun'daruun leave, but Ahi'rea had managed enough Gharven to convince them of the visit's importance. The guards had acquiesced and they had entered Lasivar's tent. It had been dark and it had taken their eyes a moment to adjust.

Lasivar had been sitting on the hides and blankets strewn over the ground. His eyes had been closed, and he had said nothing when they entered. Ahi'rea had noticed beads of sweat rolling down his face.

She had realized that he was projecting the power to mask the camp's sound and light—hiding them from the enemy. She could not fathom the concentration such a feat would take. Ruun'daruun had been unsure of what to do, so Ahi'rea had taken the initiative and spoken.

Lasivar's clear blue eyes had opened, but it took a long time for him to focus on them. When he did, he had spoken little.

"I cannot devote much time to you. I am sorry," he had said. "The raid?"

Ahi'rea had yelled. She did not remember everything she had said—only that tears had streamed from her as freely as her curses. She had asked if he had known what would happen.

"You have the Sight," Lasivar had said. "Did you know what would happen?"

She had asked what his plan was to deal with the approaching Cheduna army. He had said he did not know. Ruun'daruun had not believed him. Ahi'rea had asked, "Did you come here to lead us all to our deaths?"

"I came to destroy Halkoriv," he had answered. Then he told

them he needed to concentrate and that they had to leave. He had closed his eyes and spoken no more, and to their surprise, Ruun'daruun and Ahi'rea had turned and left. They did not make the decision themselves, nor could they bring themselves to reenter the tent.

—

"You're right," Ruun'daruun's voice cut through the fog in Ahi'rea's mind. "We can't give up like him—we can't let go of the others, let go of our goal, just so the hero can achieve his," he said with scorn. He turned his body to face her. His eyes were dry and sharp, his jaw set.

Ahi'rea nodded. A smile grew across her face—*he understands.*

"I'm finished with these visions of his, of your father's," he said. "Ken'hra was right…"

—

"Enough of this vision pit-waste!" Ahi'rea and Ruun'daruun had just returned from their meeting with Lasivar when Ken'hra had arrived, hurt, furious, and cursing, at the Huumphar encampment. Her arrival, with two other Huumphar, had cheered Ahi'rea and Ruun'daruun and the others, but her news did not. She had seen no more Huumphar, and her raiding party had fared even worse than Ruun'daruun's.

"I don't care what you see—I'm not going to just roll over," Ken'hra had said. Haaph'ahin, who had begun to speak of a vision, lapsed into silence. To the surprise of the other Huumphar, he did so without protest.

Ken'hra had stormed off to a healer. Ahi'rea and Ruun'daruun told the others more of what had happened—that the Cheduna had anticipated the attack, that they were aware of the army's position, and they told them of the horror and lives lost during the raid. Ahi'rea shuddered to recall the Rider and the evil leaching through him. Haaph'ahin had not spoken and the others seemed lost without his voice. Some thought the Huumphar should withdraw, while others said there was no escape—that the Huumphar were finished. They made no decisions that night—no voice united them, no leader stepped forward. Ahi'rea and Ruun'daruun had been as unsure of how to proceed as the rest. Soon the group broke up and they all returned to their tents.

—

Ruun'daruun's arms were tight around Ahi'rea and he looked into her eyes. It was not over. It was never over.

"We may not be heroes and we may not be destined, or powerful, or prophesied—but we will not give up," he said.

In their tent, holding to one another, Ahi'rea and Ruun'daruun felt not despair, nor hope—but resolve.

—Twenty-Two—

Tak'la stumbled over a root, caught hold of a tree trunk to break his fall, and kept running. His breath was ragged, such was his haste, even though he had only covered a few miles; it turned to steam, visible in the shafts of moonlight slipping through the boughs overhead, before dissipating around him.

Still he heard nothing behind him. His heart pounded, his blood rushed, the night sounds in the forest surrounded him—but he heard no hoofbeats, no shouts. Perhaps they had told Azra the truth; perhaps he would not be pursued. Tak'la took no chances, changing direction yet again. He heard water running—another stream to cross, another chance to throw off trackers.

His leg ached and his ribs were still bruised and dark. His capture had not been gentle and even though over a week had passed, his captors had ensured that his wounds persisted. He had been fed little and kept on the move—the road was no place to recover.

For each branch he ducked, a bramble tore at Tak'la's legs. For each root he avoided, another seemed to spring up from the earth. His unfamiliarity with the forest frustrated him; he would never struggle so on the plains. He knew that somewhere to the south he would find Lasivar's army, so on he went, hour after hour, despite pain and hunger and exhaustion.

He thought of nothing but reaching the plains—though the forest hid him, in the grasses he would vanish. His lungs burned, but it was his wounded leg which gave out first. He tripped, stumbled, and finally fell to the ground, unable to catch himself.

Tak'la sat up and dragged himself to a tree. He leaned against it, gasping and closing his eyes. He told himself to keep them open, to remain watchful, but felt as if it was all he could do to keep breathing. After he had caught his breath, he forced his eyes open and inspected his surroundings.

The Gharven forest was thick with stout trees and dense undergrowth. The trunk against which he leaned would have taken three people, arms outstretched, to encircle. The ground was soft, at least, padded by fallen leaves. In the moonlight, Tak'la could not make out their colors.

He heard yet another of the tiny streams that crisscrossed the forest. Thankful that he had not fallen in it, he braced himself against the tree and stood, pushing with his left leg and holding the right still. A grunt of pain came to his throat. Once he was upright he extended the injured limb and found that it would bear weight, if only just.

He listened, keeping still. No hoofbeats. No shouts. Tak'la crept from his tree toward the sound of the water.

The stream was a short distance away, running along a shallow depression. The water shimmered in the moonlight as it rolled over mossy stones and around black, fallen branches. Tak'la crouched beside it, lifting the cold, clear water to his mouth with his hands.

His thirst sated, he rose again and sought about for a fallen branch. He had been given none of his supplies when he left.

While he searched, he considered his release. Whatever Azra had told Bor, it had worked. The guard had approached him, cut his bonds, and gestured with his dagger. The message had been clear—go.

He had made for the edge of camp without wasting time trying to speak to the guard. He had just passed out of sight of the camp when he noticed Azra, waiting amongst the trees. He had rushed up to him and Azra spoke in Gharven, almost too fast for Tak'la to understand.

"I convinced Bor to let you go," he had said. "You must reach Lasivar and the others. He must know what Halkoriv is planning." He told Tak'la what he had learned—what Halkoriv was doing, and why. Then he gave Tak'la a message for Ahi'rea, but it had made little sense to Tak'la. "You must remember to tell her," Azra pleaded. "I have to go—Bor will be suspicious."

Tak'la had nodded, then embraced Azra. "You have been a good friend."

Azra at first recoiled, but then returned the embrace. "I have been no such thing—but I hope to change that."

Tak'la had stepped back, but kept a hand on his friend's shoulder. "You will," he had said. "You have changed much. You are a new person—choose well how to live the next moment." He laughed. "I'm sorry. I speak to you as an elder would to a child."

"You have taught me more than anyone else," Azra laughed. "But you are right. I am your elder, so do as I say, young one." Azra pointed south. "Run."

So he had. Tak'la had run for hours, hearing no pursuit, with only a glimpse of the stars and Azra's last farewell to guide him.

Tak'la soon found a branch, as tall as he, for a makeshift staff. He broke one end, leaving it a jagged point. He planted the end in the ground and found it was much easier to walk with even the small amount of support the staff provided.

His breath was steady again, his heartbeat slower. He started walking, hoping to take it easy, recover his strength. He worried that if he overexerted his leg he would lose the use of it.

He hobbled on for perhaps an hour, watching the moon drop lower when he caught sight of it through the branches overhead. The forest felt alien—close and heavy, claustrophobic. He wondered how far it was to the edge.

Tak'la reached a clearing and paused at the center of it. Moonlight bathed the small meadow and he stood still, eyes closed, and imagined he was on the plains after a long, difficult hunt. The sound of the wind in the trees was not unlike when it was in the grasses. The rustling rose and fell in time with his breathing. The cold air soothed his aches, filled his lungs. The earth under his feet felt like home.

A sound reached his ears, out of the rhythm of his breath and the air; hoofbeats. Shouting. Azra's voice echoed in Tak'la's mind. Run. So he did.

—

"You told me he would go free!" Azra yelled. His hand reflexively grasped at his sword, but found nothing. He clenched his fist.

"He has gone free," Bor intoned, riding a few paces ahead.

He did not look back.

"You sent those soldiers to kill him. You said they would go home!"

"And so they shall, as soon as they have dealt with the plainsfolk." Bor's voice was infuriating in its calmness.

Azra wanted to shout, to rage. His frustration boiled, urged and pressed by the darkness in him. It would be so simple, he knew, to loose the rage he felt; to relax his hold, let free all the anger, the potential. He was not sure if he heard his own thoughts, or the spirit's. He could slay Bor, ride to the Monument, the Ancestor's Stone, kill Halkoriv himself—but he knew that the Ravenous Spirit would never let him win. Whatever he might do, if he used the power in him, it would be for nothing. It would not allow its own demise, just as it had not allowed Bor to call his bluff.

When Azra had told Bor that Tak'la must be released and the soldiers sent home, Bor had laughed—until Azra had said what he would do otherwise.

"I will kill you, Bor. You can't stop me, and neither can your master. He will let you die before he lets me, and I will escape. Lasivar will kill Halkoriv, and you will fail."

Bor had stared at him for what had seemed like hours. Azra knew that Bor could search his mind, but was not sure how well. When, at last, Bor had conceded, he knew.

He also knew that Sitis would protect itself, at any cost. It would do all it had to in order to endure—even if it meant taking risks.

He should have realized that it would also lie. Bor belonged to the spirit. It had him, completely.

Azra rode in silence, regaining his composure. Bor—Sitis—wanted him to lose himself in his power. He needed to stay his own. He told himself that Tak'la was strong, courageous, and would soon be back on the plains—his home. Azra tried not to remember that Tak'la's pursuers were among the finest soldiers in Feriven, that Tak'la was injured, that he had days of unfamiliar forest to cross, let alone the plains themselves.

He will make it, Azra thought. *He must.*

Azra and Bor rode for days without speaking. The air was cool even during daylight now. Azra estimated that they were still about a week's travel from the Monument when they finally crossed out of the forest and into the plains. They turned east, each morning riding with the sun before them and ending the day's travel when it set at their backs.

They sat apart after making camp—neither made any attempt at conversation. Each intended only to keep an eye on the other. Bor was usually still, eyes hooded. Azra had yet to see him sleep. Part of him remembered that before that day on the plains, before he had ridden out to meet the Huumphar, he also had seen little purpose in sleep. Azra wondered if Bor missed it. He had not.

He was startled one night when Bor spoke. It was not so much the breaking of their silence as it was the quality of his voice. There was a tremulous note that he had not heard before, a lack of surety. It occurred to Azra that for the first time, he was hearing Bor speak instead of Sitis.

"Why, with all that was before you, all the power you could have had, did you give up?" Bor asked. "Why turn your back on it?"

Azra studied Bor's face. He saw no guile, only confusion. He was youthful, around Tak'la's age. He almost looked like a new recruit, uncomfortable in his armor, frightened of the foreign plains. In the light of their tiny campfire, Bor's eyes flickered with life—a dwindling life that Azra could tell was almost all gone, or perhaps already was.

"You can see my mind," Azra said. "It was a lie—everything I had been told, everything I believed about myself." He was unsure why he was even answering, even entertaining Bor's questions. He would not allow himself to hear the small voice inside which wondered if he could save Bor the way he had been saved.

Bor shook his head. "I don't understand. Even if it was—our Lord would have kept you. You were the strongest. You could have been great. But now, you've ended up with this," he said, gesturing around them. A little of the dangerous, familiar edge crept into Bor's voice. "No allies, no hope—nothing. Our Lord will still win. Your plainsfolk will be exterminated, this land will be finally tamed and united—and you'll serve your purpose to Lord Halkoriv, dead or alive."

"Then what is the use of it either way, Bor?" Azra asked.

"You could be with us, and alive, and regain your true potential," Bor answered.

"What potential is that?" Azra asked, bolting to his feet. "For what? Power over others? Wealth? Prestige? I have found I can live without them." He gestured around, mimicking Bor's mocking wave. "This is the world. What you have is nothing. You have these things, given to you, not earned, and as easily taken away—and they mean nothing. What do you really have? What did he give you? What does your life mean?"

Bor watched and listened in silence. Azra could not help but continue; his mind strayed to Ahi'rea, to her resolve and beauty and strength. "Only when I was beaten, did I find what I was. And only when I lost—no, not lost—only when I gave up what you have, did I begin to decide what I am. What it is to live, and what I want to be…" he trailed off. He saw in his mind how she had looked at Ruun'daruun, "…to be remembered for."

Azra felt cold pinpoints sting his mind. Bor was searching, prying. The flicker was gone, the life swallowed up again. The young man was gone, and the spirit had returned.

"The woman," Bor murmured, drawing out each syllable. "Is she what this is about?"

Azra looked up, eyes narrow, rage rising in his mind. He recoiled from his anger, until he realized that it was different. This time, it did not begin with the pressure, the whispers, the icy touch of the spirit. This time it burned from his gut and spread through his arms and legs—his own rage. Still, the familiar cold of the spirit followed it in a chill, gleeful wave, pressing him to act. He held back. *That is what it wants.*

"She," Bor hissed, "will remember you." His teeth gleamed in the firelight, and his dead eyes glittered. "And I will see to it that she remembers much more."

Azra lunged. His arm moved with a speed he had forgotten as his hand caught Bor's throat. Strength both alien and familiar pulled Bor to his feet, then off of them. Dark tendrils coalesced and lashed around them. Whispers filled Azra's mind and cold power pressed him. All he could see was Bor's mad smile, and all he desired was to crush the smugness out of him.

Not yet, something said, a voice coming as if from deep inside him. The thought cut through the cold pressure, hot and powerful and just as dangerous, and Azra recognized his own fury, his own mind, as if hearing it from afar. The feeling was unfamiliar; the spirit's whispers were drowned by it and he wondered when the spirit had first begun to push him, for he had never felt this before, not even all those years ago in Cunabrel's cell.

Not yet, he told himself again. His fury smoldered, not yet a blaze, but a threat of one instead. The blackness faded in his vision. His arm weakened under Bor's weight. *This is what it wants.*

He thought of his decision—what he had resolved to do. He held tight to it, thinking of Ahi'rea and Tak'la and the resolve they had shown. If he gave in now, they would lose and Bor—Sitis—would be right. *Not yet.*

He released Bor. The larger man's mad smile faded. "You are nothing," he said.

Azra forced back the cold, insidious pressure. He turned his back on Bor and sat again.

"Perhaps you will be remembered by no one," Bor said. "We will live forever. You may as well have never existed."

Azra smiled to himself. He did not answer. He did not have to.

—Twenty-Three—

He could hear them. Sometimes it seemed they were within moments of sighting him, and other times the sound of them faded from Tak'la's ears. Always the hoofbeats would return, or a distant voice would ring across the plains. Tak'la ran on, sacrificing his own silence to speed and to the pain in his leg. Sometimes the sound of hooves pounded the dirt all around him.

The night was at its darkest. All glimmers of twilight had disappeared hours before and there was yet no sign of the sun's return. The smoke from the fires that had ravaged the plains had all but dissipated in the days since Tak'la had left the forest behind, and the moon hung, a dim crescent, in the autumn sky. The lands west of him were burned; he had seen them some days before. Here, frost cloaked the tall grasses in silver and steam formed with Tak'la's every breath. He had lost track of the days he had run, and now knew only that he must be nearing the coast. He would find Lasivar there. He had to go on. His pursuers were shouting to each other, looking for him.

Tak'la was numb. But for his leg, he had stopped feeling his body's protests; the cuts, the aches, and the bruises seemed as if they had always been there. All he felt was fatigue. He had never wanted to stop and rest so badly, just as he had never known so urgently that he could not. His last true rest had been after leaving the forest. Since then, he had done all he could, used every trick, every tactic, to lose his pursuers but always they returned. The sound of their horses always came back. When he could not hear them, he stopped—but he dared not sleep. He feared he would not wake before they were upon him.

Sleep. Tak'la tried not to think about sleep. *You can't stop,* he thought. *Azra stayed behind so I could run.* He kept moving, though exhaustion hounded him. Thoughts came to his mind unbidden, fleeting, flashing in of their own accord each time his concentration waned, each time his bodiless, tireless foe sought to fell him. *They will catch me. I'll never find the Huumphar. There's no stopping Halkoriv. I can't go on. What I'm doing doesn't matter. I'll fail. I can't go on.* Each time, he despaired. The hoofbeats seemed louder, the shouts closer. Each time, he felt like giving in.

Each time, Tak'la asked himself aloud, "Why do I live, if not to run?"

He ran on.

A new sound came to him, invading his thoughts; waves crashing. In the next moment, the sound was gone—along with the sound of his pursuers. Tak'la wondered if exhaustion was playing tricks on him again, or if he had been running the wrong way all this time. Only the sound of the wind remained, growing stronger, gusting up about him from the south. He could not think. It could not be the coast, not yet. He imagined standing in the shallows despite the cool air, feeling the waves rush about his feet. He imagined the icy water, the stinging salt. He stopped, forcing himself to think, to remain standing.

Waves. The coast. Not real, he decided. It was then that the faint, part sweet, part acrid smell of smoke reached him on the southern wind. Campfires. As he took in the smell, looking toward the south for telltale firelight, the sound of waves returned. He was close! Tak'la felt as if he might collapse as relief washed over him. He expected the smell to vanish, a phantom on the breeze, and put his hands to his face, pressing his eyes. He wavered, holding his breath. The smell did not vanish. He fought away the exhaustion, the relief, and spoke aloud. "I'm not there yet." The disappearance of his pursuers worried him. That he had evaded them, or that they had given up, was too much to hope for.

He started off again, retrieving his stick from the ground. His muscles cried out and his cracked skin burned. Tak'la focused on the pain, using it to keep himself alert while he walked. Ahead of him, the land rose to a crest. He knew that on the plains, even this small hill was a landmark, something he should remember, but he could not. Halfway to the top of it, he paused, against his better judgment, and stared.

He forgot how long he stood there; it did not seem to matter. He would soon rejoin his people and deliver Azra's message, or die. For a moment, however, he wanted to remember why he lived.

The moonlight was enough to see by. Ice crystals from the dew sparkled all around him on the grasses and again he heard the far-off rush of waves. In the south, he could see the shadows of the mountains. His breath slowed, given fleeting form in a burst of curling steam. Silver light seemed to emanate from the earth itself. Tak'la could not imagine a finer sight.

He blinked, breaking his reverie. He would rejoin the Huum-phar before dawn, or not at all. He leaned on the stick and climbed to the top of the crest before him.

The grass grew shorter as he advanced until it only reached his waist. He heard the trickle of water close by—a stream. When he reached the top, he saw it: the hill upon which he stood swept down a dozen paces toward a creek bed. The water glittered beneath the moon and Tak'la could make out the distant ocean in the east. The grasses obscured much of the creek—but it did not obscure the mounted soldiers awaiting him.

He had seen three of them earlier in their pursuit. Three more were with them. They were spread out along the creek, swords in hand, eyes fixed on him.

Tak'la could not run. They were too close, too many, and on horseback; they would ride him down. Not far beyond them, he suspected, he would find the Huumphar camp and Lasivar's army.

The soldiers waited, watching. They did not speak or move.

Tak'la's leg throbbed. His lungs burned. He was exhausted, starving. He looked past them again, at the moon-bathed plains and the dark mountains beyond. He thought he could make out a glimmer of what might be firelight. But still in his way were the soldiers, intent on ensuring he never took another step.

One of them shouted, breaking the silence in the southern tongue. "Surrender," he cried again, this time in Gharven. "We will spare you if you surrender."

Tak'la stood still, looking down on them, contemplating the soldier's words. He could not beat them. Not in his state.

He sighed. "I'm coming down," he shouted. Even his throat hurt. He raised his hands, holding his staff aloft, and limped down the slope, approaching the speaker. The others remained vigilant, drawing closer along with him. Tak'la stepped into the cold water of the stream and shivered.

He reached the horseman's side, looking into the man's face. He had been Tak'la's guard, as they all had, on a few occasions. The soldier grinned as he reached out to take Tak'la's walking stick.

Tak'la struck with a roar, his cry echoing through the night. He snatched the soldier's extended arm, pulling him down as he drove the sharpened stick into his neck. The soldier's sword fell from his hands as he tried to defend himself. His companions cried out in alarm and moved in to attack, but Tak'la grabbed the sword and dived into the tall grass before they could reach him. Amongst the swaying blades and darkness, he all but disappeared.

The soldiers did not hesitate, urging their mounts into a circle around where Tak'la had vanished. His leg trembled and burned even from the few sudden movements he had made. Five left.

The horsemen shouted to one another, searching the grasses. They held their swords at the ready. One step at a time, they tightened their circle, swiping their blades through the grass.

When a rider was almost upon him, Tak'la lunged again. He shouted and the soldier parried his sudden thrust, crying out as well. Tak'la struck again and as the soldier again parried, Tak'la snatched his wrist and pulled him headfirst from his mount. He heard the others closing in and spun, battering aside another soldier's attack. A third swung, and again Tak'la avoided the blow.

The sword was heavy in his hand. His head swam, and his leg felt ready to fail him. Still he fought, barreling into the unhorsed soldier in hopes that the others would hold their attacks. The soldier was strong and better rested than Tak'la, however, and the Huumphar found his wrists caught and held in his foe's iron grip. He felt his good leg kicked from under him. The other leg gave, and Tak'la's breath was knocked from him as he fell hard on his back with the soldier on top of him.

His wrist was still in the soldier's grip. The soldier slammed it against the ground again and again, knocking the sword away. A fist smashed into Tak'la's face and his vision blurred and fluttered with dark blotches. He tasted blood. He could not breathe. Tak'la was struck again, then he felt cold steel press against his throat. Through the haze of his vision, he could just make out the soldier's face looking down on him.

"You should have given up," the soldier said in accented Gharven. He pressed the blade harder against Tak'la's neck. "Anything to say before I take your head?"

Tak'la turned his head, spitting blood onto the ground. He looked back up at his captor, and then opened his mouth in a hoarse roar. "Aim here!"

There was an answering cry from the south. The soldier looked up just before an arrow whistled into his body, catching him with such force that he was rolled off of Tak'la's chest.

More arrows followed, accompanied by the shouts of the approaching scouts. Tak'la lifted himself on his forearm, wincing, and watched as rust-cloaked northerners dashed past him and scattered the Cheduna soldiers. Through his pain and exhaustion, Tak'la was impressed—they fought like Huumphar. He was unsure how many of his pursuers were killed but within moments they had all fled or fallen. He saw the concerned, bearded face of one of the northerners lean over him.

"Hold on, boy," the northerner said. "You're almost there."

—

Ahi'rea pressed through the camp alongside Ruun'daruun. The word that the Gharven scouts had rescued a plainsfolk from a Cheduna squad had been welcome, but the Huumphar's description, who it might be, filled her with a strange dread.

They wound between the tents and fire circles, pushing through crowds of Lasivar's foreign troops and Gharven warriors. As they neared the edge of the camp they could hear a growing commotion. They saw other Huumphar, following a pair of rust-cloaked scouts dragging a litter. Ruun'daruun broke into a sprint to catch up to them, with Ahi'rea on his heels.

When they reached the group, Rahi'sta was already there, walking beside the litter with her child in one arm. Tears were on her face. It was difficult to tell who it was, so beaten and bloodied the body on the litter was. Rahi'sta looked up as they arrived. "Tak'la," she said. Ruun'daruun nodded, falling into step with her. The small group of Huumphar following did not wail or cry; Tak'la's time had been long ago. Ahi'rea knew she should not be surprised—but the dread she felt did not dissipate. Had Azra turned on him? Or had he been killed as well?

"How did he die?" Ahi'rea asked.

"He's alive, barely," Rahi'sta said. "He is badly wounded."

Ruun'daruun looked at them in turn. "You know that's not true," he said. "His body may yet hang on, but that may not last this time." He spoke as of one long dead—and Tak'la was, Ahi'rea reminded herself.

"No," Rahi'sta said. "He is alive. He came back for a reason." She turned away, keeping pace with the litter and ignoring

Ruun'daruun.

Ruun'daruun fell back to walk beside Ahi'rea and placed a hand on her shoulder. He leaned close to whisper, "It's for the best. Death followed him, but it met him far from others who could have been harmed."

They brought Tak'la to the Huumphar camp where Rahi'sta stood watch over him while the remaining elders were summoned and healers gathered. Ken'hra arrived and she and Ruun'daruun discussed what the scouts had reported when they found Tak'la.

"They tried to leave one of his pursuers alive, but most of them fled on horseback," she said. "The soldiers the Gharven wounded died quickly—they said it was as if they couldn't breathe."

"What do you mean?" Ruun'daruun asked. "Couldn't breathe?"

"That is what the scouts told me," Ken'hra said. "They sucked in air but died while the scouts watched. Like someone was stealing the breath from them."

"Halkoriv," Ruun'daruun spat. "He is watching. He'd kill his own servants before letting us have them."

"If he were so concerned about Tak'la—if Halkoriv himself was watching those men—then we had better hope we can find out why," Ahi'rea interjected. She moved closer to Tak'la and knelt beside where they had laid his litter on the ground.

A pair of healers was beside him, pouches of herbs and pots of tinctures open beside them. One waved a smoking bundle of acrid-smelling branches over Tak'la's chest and face, fanning the smoke toward him. The other shook his head at Ahi'rea. "His spirit fades. Its grip was tenuous to begin with," he said. "He yearns to join his tribe on the Journey."

"Ahi'rea," Rahi'sta said, kneeling beside her, "can you help him?" She held her baby close to her. He cried, tired and upset by the noise and activity. "Please, you must help him."

"There is little I can do," Ahi'rea said. The healer began a chant for those passing to the Journey and Rahi'sta wept, her hand on Tak'la's battered cheek.

Ahi'rea looked up at Ruun'daruun. "Get Lasivar. He can use the Storm to save him," she said.

"His life hasn't been his own for years," Ruun'daruun said. "Even Lasivar can't call him back from the Journey."

Ken'hra nodded. "If he can't survive this himself, nothing can save him. Death has caught him."

"Go get him," Ahi'rea said. "Tak'la came back to us for a reason, and Halkoriv has gone to great lengths to make sure he did not live. I will not allow him another victory." Ruun'daruun hesitated, then nodded and dashed away.

Ahi'rea put one hand on Rahi'sta's shaking shoulder. "He will not die in vain," she said. "And we may save him yet." Rahi'sta looked up, tears staining her face. She nodded her thanks.

Ahi'rea's eyes pulsed once, flaring green in the fire lit camp. Sweat and blood, mingled on Tak'la's brow, reflected the light onto her as she settled her hand on his forehead. *At least,* she thought, *we will know why you ran.*

Fear, stark and sharp. Pain. They flooded her. Tak'la's pain flowed into her and became her own. Her leg ached, her face, her ribs. She was more exhausted than she had ever felt. Through all of it, though, was the fear. Not fear of death, or fear of hurt, but fear that she—that Tak'la—would not reach Lasivar and Ahi'rea before being killed.

She could feel the message he carried. It was like a locked door, protected, secure. What she could not find, not feel, was any fear for himself.

She had heard that those like Tak'la, death-touched, lost all the fear everyone else carried. Now she felt it. Now she knew. She realized how it was that one so young fought with such power, such abandon. It was not courage—courage was the facing of fear. Fear was the only thing that had died in Tak'la along with his tribe.

Something took hold of her and she flinched. She was forced out of his mind without warning. As her eyes refocused she found she was looking into Tak'la's face, one eye swollen shut but the other open. He was smiling. His hand held Rahi'sta's and still she cried, but now was smiling.

"It's all right," he murmured. "I'm not leaving yet."

—

The healers wanted to take Tak'la away for rest, but he protested. Even barely able to speak, he insisted on seeing Lasivar. He told Ahi'rea he had an urgent message, but as he spoke his speech slurred and his eyes closed. He awoke every time they tried to move him and tried to arise from the litter. He was in no condition to relay messages, but it was only when Ruun'daruun returned with Lasivar's promise to come soon that Tak'la allowed the healers to take him away to see to his injuries.

Dawn came and went. Ahi'rea and Ruun'daruun waited with the others. Only around twenty Huumphar warriors remained, along with a few families. It felt strange to Ahi'rea, looking around the fire circle in the autumn morning's light, thinking that this was possibly all that remained of her people.

Those fortunate enough to be alive sat with their families and those of their fallen comrades. She saw many grandparents, wounded, a few children—but few of fighting age remained. Many mothers and fathers had not come back. Older siblings had been lost forever. Most of those that remained were the old, the young, and the infirm. Rahi'sta, her infant beside her, was repairing the bindings on her machete's grip. The Huumphar spoke little, in low voices. All around them, the sounds of the war camp rose and fell, but within their small circle it was quiet and still.

Ruun'daruun and Ken'hra whispered together of gathering a search party to seek other Huumphar. Ahi'rea half-listened; her mind wandered as she looked about at their people, wondering if it would even matter. *We must try,* she reminded herself. She jumped at the sudden touch of a hand on her arm.

Ahi'rea looked up into the concerned face of her father. "You are troubled," he said, seating himself on the ground beside her. Even close to the fire it was cool, and he was wrapped in skins and furs.

She hesitated, then leaned against his small frame. He put a bony arm around her shoulders. "Of course," she answered, looking into the fire. Her father said nothing, merely holding her close. The quiet murmur of conversation drifted around them, and the sounds of the camp around that.

"I miss your mother," Haaph'ahin said. Ahi'rea was surprised to hear such a blunt and vulnerable statement from him. She felt tears in her eyes.

"So do I," she said.

"She was my… I trusted her more than anyone, more than myself. I loved her." His voice had never sounded so old to Ahi'rea before. "Before the two of you left, that raid—I told her that the journey might lead to Lasivar. That it might lead to something terrible, but that we might find Lasivar's son. The man who could kill Halkoriv. But I told her that I feared she might not return. That I feared many of you might not return."

Ahi'rea heard his tears in his voice. She looked at her father. "What did she say?" she asked.

Haaph'ahin took a few deep breaths. "She asked if I were sure. I said yes. She asked if you would live, and I said you would. It was then she decided to go. She said we had to find Lasivar's son, whatever the cost." He closed his eyes and put his head in his hands. "I wish I had said no."

His body shook, but he made no sound. Ahi'rea returned his embrace.

"What I have done," Haaph'ahin said, "has brought about the death of our people, of my own love, instead of saving them."

They looked up at the sound of loud voices. They saw the two healers, imploring Tak'la to return to his rest. He had been washed of blood and grime; cuts and bruises were clear on his face and bandages wrapped his ribs. He wore thick furs around his shoulders but his chest was bare. He leaned heavily on a stick as he made his way through the gathered Huumphar, breath visible in the chill, heedless of his caretakers.

He smiled and waved to Rahi'sta but walked straight to Ahi'rea and Haaph'ahin. He paused, about to speak, then stopped and bowed with difficulty to the older Huumphar. The healers fell silent behind him, waiting for a sign from Haaph'ahin.

The old man regarded Tak'la, then the healers. "You have forgone the Journey yet again," he said, his tears gone, his voice once again rough and strong. "Tak'la death-touched. We might call you death-dodging now."

Tak'la addressed Ahi'rea as much as the elder, looking back and forth between them. "I have come back to speak to Lasivar. And you. Azra freed me—we were captured. He sent a message, two messages—"

"Slow down, young one," Haaph'ahin said. Ahi'rea marveled at him. Only she knew how pained, how guilty, he was. She wondered how he would have spoken to Tak'la a few days ago. "We will hear, but recall what Azra did; what he was. We can hardly trust one such as him," Haaph'ahin said.

"Tell us what happened," Ahi'rea said.

Tak'la sat, holding back grunts of pain. The act seemed to be almost more than he could bear. Several deep breaths later, he began to speak. He told them of the days he had spent with Azra—how he had cast away his sword and foresworn his powers, the fear he carried with him. He described how and why they had separated, his capture by Bor, and how Azra had come back for him and later gained his freedom.

"But you were pursued," Ahi'rea said. "Those soldiers would have killed you, and we believe Halkoriv himself was watching and directing them."

"Yes," Ken'hra said. "You were foolish to trust him. A man like him can't change. He was probably happy to go back to the Cheduna."

Tak'la pushed himself up, a protest on his lips.

He was interrupted by Haaph'ahin's cool and stern voice.

There was a murmur of surprise from the gathered Huumphar. Haaph'ahin had been quiet all through Tak'la's story, but now he spoke with surety. "Azra had nothing to gain by betraying Tak'la so. To release him, even injured, risked that he would reach us. If it were he that wished Tak'la dead, and it were in his power, it would be so already. No—since Tak'la was released, then pursued, we must conclude that it was Azra who was deceived. He secured your release from this other, Bor, who wished you dead." Tak'la nodded with a breath of relief.

"Then it would seem your messages were important enough to you both to risk your death," Ahi'rea said.

—

A short time later, Lasivar joined them. He was accompanied, as always, by a group of Gharven and Vanadae protectors. Satisfied that his message would reach its intended recipients, Tak'la spoke.

"Azra told me that he is being taken to something called the Ancestor's Stone. Halkoriv will be there. He's hoping that we will concentrate on the army long enough that he can get past without notice. Azra said," he paused, trying to remember the exact words. "He said, 'Halkoriv is afraid. He will go to the place his power was born to gather strength. They call it the Ancestor's Stone.'"

Lasivar nodded, saying nothing. His clear blue eyes searched Tak'la's face.

"If it is true," Ruun'daruun said, "then we should find out where that is and go immediately. We could bypass the army and ambush Halkoriv."

"No," Lasivar said. "If the whole army goes, he will See it. He would escape. I can find him. I will go, but the army must remain here."

Ruun'daruun looked down, his jaw set. Ken'hra, however, felt no compunction to restrain her tongue. "You'd leave us here to face half the Cheduna kingdom alone while you go off to settle your family score," she snapped. "You care as much for us as you do the dirt you stand on."

"He is right, Ken'hra," Haaph'ahin said, standing. "There is more to this battle than Halkoriv. He and the army are linked, but not inseparable. We must stay and fight. Even without their lord, his vision will linger. His men will fight on. And if our army goes, Halkoriv will know we are ready for him." He looked over at Ahi'rea, then out at the other Huumphar. "Lasivar has his part to play, and we have ours. Only our resolve will save us, even after Halkoriv is dead. We must stay, and we must hold our lands. If we do not, the Cheduna will hunt us and destroy us."

Ruun'daruun nodded. Ken'hra looked away, scowling. Others murmured agreement while Lasivar called Haaph'ahin and Ruun'daruun to him. Ahi'rea was about to join them when she felt a hand on hers. Tak'la looked into her eyes and glanced outside the fire circle. "He said only you would understand," Tak'la whispered. Ahi'rea looked over at Lasivar, her father, and Ruun'daruun, then nodded at Tak'la. They walked together, just outside the group.

They stopped between a pair of tents, sheltered from the cold morning wind but far from any fires. The excited buzz of planning and conversation seemed far away. Beyond the tents and smoke, Ahi'rea could see the wind-swept plains to the north, smell the salt sea to the east. Beyond her sight was the Cheduna army; though smoke no longer darkened the western sky, she knew they were close.

She pulled her deerskins tighter across her shoulders and faced Tak'la. He stood tall, stone-faced, heedless of the cold and his wounds. She had to remind herself how close to death he had come not hours before.

Tak'la's face broke into a smile. "He said you would not want to hear his message," he laughed. "I told him you would listen."

Ahi'rea smiled back. "He was right—but still, I do not think he would have sent you without good reason." She reached up and placed a hand on Tak'la's shoulder. "You faced much danger to come to us. It would be wrong to ignore the sacrifices you have made." Tak'la nodded his thanks, regaining his serious demeanor. "When this is over, I mean to see you are made one of us—and are called death-touched no longer," Ahi'rea said.

Tak'la nodded again. When he looked up, she saw his eyes were wet. "It has been long since anyone was as kind to me as you are—you, and Rahi'sta, and Azra. Thank you," he said.

Ahi'rea nodded, but could not help but scowl at the name. "What does he want?" she asked. "He said he would not help us before."

"Truly, I didn't understand his message," Tak'la said. He breathed deep, as if summoning up the words. "Azra said to tell you that you made the right decision—and that when he meets Si-tis, he hopes you will be there to accept his apology." Tak'la's curiosity was palpable. "What does he mean? What decision? What does he mean to do? And where is the Ancestor's Stone?"

Ahi'rea stared, then took hold of Tak'la's arm, her eyes widening. "Thank you, Tak'la. You must promise to say nothing of this to anyone—even Lasivar, and especially Ruun'daruun."

—

Ahi'rea found Ruun'daruun speaking to the remaining warriors; Haaph'ahin looked on, making no move to interrupt. She watched Ruun'daruun for a moment and felt her sense of urgency overcome as her heart swelled with pride. He was confident; he spoke without arrogance or distortion. Watching him, she knew he would one day make a fine elder. Her heart sank, however, as he detailed Lasivar's plans.

When he was done and the warriors began to disperse, she approached him. "Does he really mean for us to lead an attack against the Cheduna?" she asked.

Ruun'daruun nodded. "Tomorrow at sundown. But not just him. We decided together," he said. "We will surprise them, fight as we know best. The Gharven and Vanadae will follow us—and if we are to have any chance, together we must shake their army to its core. We must take the initiative, or they will crush us here between the canyon and the sea."

Ahi'rea put her hands on his arms and looked Ruun'daruun in the eye. "We cannot survive—there are so many of them—"

"It's what we must do," Ruun'daruun said, pulling her into an embrace. He put his chin on the top of her head. "Lasivar has already left to meet Halkoriv, and we must take back our lands. We have to show his men that our resolve will never fail. If we wait, and fight on their terms, we have no chance." He held her close;

she could feel him trying to keep his breath steady. "Tomorrow is the beginning. Our home will be ours again."

She wanted to tell him that she could not be there—that she had to leave, had to follow Lasivar to the Monument. She remembered her vision, the one she had the night of the Sendings. She knew that if she told Ruun'daruun, he would follow her—and that he was needed here.

Ahi'rea took his hand. She led Ruun'daruun back amongst the tents, past the campfires and people and carts. They reached his tent and, once inside, she turned and pressed herself against him. She sought his lips in the dark as if she were drowning and sought air. She felt his hands on her arms, then her waist. He returned the kiss, drinking her in. He pulled the deerskin from her shoulders while she loosened his cloak.

She guided Ruun'daruun down with her to their bedrolls. Ruun'daruun kissed her again as she felt his hands caress her. The chill air raised goosebumps on her naked breasts and she pulled him close to her for warmth as she lay back.

"Rea," he whispered, a reluctant protest.

"I know," she said. "I do not care."

"Neither do I." He brushed her hair from her face, trailing his hand down her face, then her neck and shoulder. "I'm only glad we'll be together to face—"

She kissed him, not wanting to hear the rest of it. She only wanted to feel him close. Tears welled in her eyes and she clutched him tight. He held her, running his hands across her skin as they removed each other's remaining clothes. His touch was like fire in the cold night air. She wrapped her legs around him, wanting to feel that touch everywhere.

She felt his heart in his chest, beating faster. Her own seemed ready to break free from her. She fought for air and for a while, they forgot where they were, what was soon to happen; they forgot fear and pain and knew only one another's touch.

—

As the feeling ebbed, Ahi'rea pulled Ruun'daruun's lips to hers once again. They lay together, still holding tight; she almost feared to let him go.

Ruun'daruun rolled onto his back and Ahi'rea clung to him, rolling over with him to lay her head on his chest. He wrapped his arm around her and pulled his discarded cloak over them. The world came back to her—but something was different; a hope she had not felt before, like the glimmer of a lone star in a storm-ridden sky.

"I love you," she said. She felt Ruun'daruun shift to look at her. She raised her eyes to his. "Whatever happens, remember that."

A shadow crossed his features; *Does he know?* she wondered. *Does he know what I'm going to do?*

"I could never forget," he answered. He held her tight and kissed her again. Warm in his arms, Ahi'rea slept.

—

Ruun'daruun awoke alone. The first light of a cold dawn peered past the tent flap. He knew he would not find her in the camp. He clenched his eyes shut against the tears and thought of her last words to him. He sat up and felt something fall from his chest to his lap. He looked down at a lock of sun-bleached hair, gleaming in the dark of the tent. He found a cord and wrapped it about the hair, then placed the cord around his neck, closed his eyes, and took a deep breath. When he opened his eyes, they were dry.

I will see her again. It is not over.

—Twenty-Four—

Azra turned his face and pulled his collar across his cheek in an attempt to gain some respite from the biting wind. It had grown cold and hard and blew unceasingly, changing only in its direction. It had begun from the south, and now came from the east, ahead of them—the direction of the Monument, the Ancestor's Stone.

Bor rode just ahead, heedless of the cold and wind. The flesh on his face was red and raw. He had quickened their pace in the last two days. They were close.

Sundown came, and still the wind blew. As the sun sank in the west, stretching their shadows before them, Azra glimpsed a sudden glow; a mirror of the sun, a blaze of burning orange, towering on the horizon before them. The sun's last rays lit upon the looming rock of the Monument, illuminating it where before it had been invisible in the gathering twilight. The black marble ruins glimmered and shone like fire.

"We will ride until we arrive." Bor did not look back. "Our master has waited for us long enough." Azra did not see the point in arguing. He only hoped Tak'la had made it in time.

The Monument faded to deep red and then grew dark again

as the sun completed its descent. Azra thought he lost sight of it amongst the stars, but then realized the ruin was decked in torches, flickering in the dark. As they drew nearer he saw many Cheduna soldiers standing guard. They called out, reporting the arrival of the two travelers, and Bor and Azra were greeted at the base of the towering rock by a trio of figures in dark cloaks.

"We knew of your coming," one whispered. Its voice was emotionless, flat, cold. Azra saw their glazed, dead eyes beneath their hoods—Halkoriv's servants. Their skin was white and their faces blank; there was even less of them left than there was of Bor. Something more bothered Azra though, something worse still; even before the creature had spoken, he had felt its words forming in his own mind. He felt Bor beside him, felt Halkoriv above on the Monument—and something else, something older and stronger and fouler. Something that dwelt in the stone and in all of them. Something that hungered.

Bor dismounted, gesturing for Azra to do the same. A pair of soldiers took charge of their tired horses and then Azra, Bor, and the three servants headed for the great sloping path toward the peak of the ruin.

Azra felt Halkoriv in his mind. He made no effort to resist— opening his mind to his power so close to Halkoriv, at this place, frightened him more than he could fathom. He knew that Halkoriv was hoping he would try. He had foresworn its use, and knew that to break that vow would bring only his doom. Bor had almost got the better of him at their camp; Azra would not be goaded again.

They reached the peak, where a group of soldiers stood at the head of the path. Azra recognized one of them—a man with small crooked teeth and a wicked smile. He had been one of Draden's commanders. Azra wondered if his old friend were here, but saw no sign of Draden. He was glad, for he did not know what he would do if he had to face him.

One figure, lit only by moonlight, stood at the center of the ruin, ringed by the crumbling columns and stony ridges. The figure turned and moved among the ancient stones until it reached the edge nearest Azra and Bor. Halkoriv's face, now bathed in torchlight, looked down on them. His eyes were pits, featureless and void, reflecting nothing. *No,* Azra thought. *It's not Halkoriv, not anymore. The spirit has taken him. They are the same, now. Lasivar was right. He's dead.*

Halkoriv turned toward Bor. "You have failed us." The voice came from Halkoriv's lips, but it was not his. "Lasivar is coming. The plainsfolk you released was not slain."

So he did live, Azra thought. He shuddered at the voice, but could not disguise his joy at the news of Tak'la.

"Impossible," Bor stuttered. His smug smile had vanished. Looking at him, Azra again saw the man, not the slave. "He could not have escaped—our finest soldiers—"

"You gambled on ordinary men, weak creatures without purpose. You have failed us," Halkoriv said again. "We have little time, and we have need of every modicum of our power." He raised a hand, palm toward Bor. "Would that there were time enough for a fitting punishment."

He turned to face Azra, seeming to forget about Bor. Shadow gathered around them and Bor's form receded, growing dark and small. He began to scream.

"Go to the center of the platform, boy. You shall still serve us, vow or not. Your wall is nothing to us—whatever thoughts that you guard shall be known to us soon enough."

Bor's screams almost drowned out the voice, but Azra still heard Halkoriv in his mind. Flickers of emptiness ripped through Bor, through the shadow he had become; dark tendrils lashed and whipped between Halkoriv's form and Bor's, as if dragging something toward the king. Bor's voice became detached, as if it no longer came from his body. Azra covered his ears and saw that the nearby soldiers did the same. The screams went on, growing shriller, animal-like. With a final choking cry, it was over. The shadow vanished, leaving only a crumpled, bloody heap where Bor had stood. Azra almost vomited, catching himself against one of the stone ridges. It was warm and he would have sworn that he felt it pulse under his hands.

"Go to the center, now," Halkoriv said. Azra felt his limbs move and realized he could not fight the king's command. The cold pit within him, the feeling of his power in his mind, was what was driving him. Puppet-like, he stumbled past the ridges toward the center of the platform. He was helpless; he could not resist it to buy time. He had failed. He had not even gotten the chance to make things right. He focused on Ahi'rea as he had before, but it was futile. He gritted his teeth and felt tears in his eyes. Inexorably, his body approached the hub of the Ancestor's Stone.

Something Halkoriv—Sitis—had said came to him. "What wall?" he shouted, trying to turn his head. He could just see Halkoriv's form, following behind him. "What do you mean?"

"The wall in your mind, and in your heart," said Sitis's voice. "The secret you guard. How you are managing to protect it is a mystery to us, but one we will solve when you are part of us. Perhaps your method will even be of use." Halkoriv stepped before him, his empty eyes peering into Azra's. They had stopped at the center of the platform. "If you think Lasivar will come for you, he cannot save you," the voice of Sitis said. "In fact, we should thank you. When he comes, we will wear him down, fight him, and weaken him. We shall let him strike, and when this body falls you will join with us. Your body will become ours. Yours shall be a new line, and the gateway to others. We will be free. We shall consume all. We shall let Lasivar taste victory, and he will think us dead. Then, when he is spent and thinks himself safe, your hand will be that which ends him, and thus his defeat will be sweeter when we rip his life away."

A cruel, mad smile twisted Halkoriv's face as he licked his lips. "We had planned to face him later, the last son of our enemies. That you have brought Lasivar here, while unexpected, will play into our plans. Whatever secret you think to keep from us is of far less consequence than the manner in which you have hidden it. We will know both soon enough, when you are part of us." Halkoriv turned and called to some of the soldiers. "We must be undistracted. Chain him here." He indicated the center of the platform. "Here is where we were born. Here is where we must be born again. The rest of you, prepare. The Son of Lasivar approaches. He comes on the storm."

Overhead, a roll of thunder rang out over the plains and a great wind gusted from the south, clashing with the wind pouring out from around the Monument. "He is near!" Sitis's voice declared. Clouds rushed up from the south, crashing into those above the Monument, churning and roiling. Light flickered deep inside the thunderheads and another rumbling growl echoed over the grasses. Azra could feel Lasivar growing close. The spirit was like an animal in a cage, pacing back and forth in Halkoriv's body. Its hunger was palpable.

Two burly soldiers approached and took hold of Azra. He struggled but they held him in mailed grips. Panic crept up on him—what if Ahi'rea could not find him here? Would she make it in time? Would she even come? He felt the cold pit in his mind, pressing for release. Even in its plan, Sitis was fractured, ravenous in its lust to dominate, to consume. Azra knew he could not unleash it, not now, not after what he had sworn. He would be lost; he would become Sitis's servant, a part of it, a willing sacrifice to it. His hopes would amount to nothing and Sitis would win even as Halkoriv died. As he fought the spirit in him he wrestled against the two soldiers, but their hold was like the iron shackles in which he soon found himself. *There might still be time,* he told himself. *She will come.* He pulled at his chains, now linked to a rusted iron ring set in the stones of the Monument. *She must come.*

The soldiers left without laughing or jeering; they seemed not to even notice him. They were focused on Halkoriv and on the hero of prophecy who approached. Azra remembered a time when he could have corroded and ruined the iron with a thought—but knew that now he must wait if he was to have any chance. Sitis needled and whispered in his mind, ever pressing and goading even as it demanded his stillness and subservience. He fought the ceaseless whispers, the driving presence, and once again felt the hot edge of his own fury burn at the cold pressure of his unwanted power. The pressure dissipated as he felt the first cold drops of rain strike his face. Lightning cracked and Azra, looking south, saw a dozen figures on horseback racing toward the Monument. Revik Lasivar had come.

—

When the sun set, they started walking. Ruun'daruun led them through the gathering dark, a mere handful of Huumphar warriors. Ken'hra was with him, and Rahi'sta, and Nuun'ran, and all the rest who could fight. Behind them the fires and lights of the camp winked out, extinguished by the Vanadae and Gharven soldiers and woodsmen. Before them, Ruun'daruun could see the fires of the Cheduna camp come into view. The sun, low in the sky, was hidden by roiling black clouds. It sank while they walked, making the darkness complete. They would not be seen.

He felt rain on his skin and saw lightning to the north. Peals of thunder rolled out from the direction of the Monument. Ruun'daruun did not know what was happening there, and knew that he could not think about it; his fight was here, and the Huumphar's cause in his hands.

Haaph'ahin had come to him just before they left, while the sun was setting. "May the wind guide you tonight, Ruun'daruun." He had looked east, his eyes glowing and pulsing. "War was never my domain. I suppose, because of that, I have never truly understood it. But I think that you do." Ruun'daruun had said nothing. "I had never thought to dream your destiny before now."

Ruun'daruun had waited, but Haaph'ahin had seemed deep in thought. "And what did you dream?" He had feared to ask more than he feared the coming fight.

Haaph'ahin had turned back to him. "Would it change your course if I told you? Would you go to hide in the plains, or wait here for death?" He smiled and looked back to the east, toward the Cheduna. "I think you would still go to them, no matter what

I said."

Ruun'daruun had nodded. "I would."

"And that is why I will not say. Though the dark of night comes, and we are closed in by enemies, and the storm bears down on us, you would go on. Come hell to you, you would meet it. I will not say—until you and my daughter come back." He had grinned.

Ruun'daruun now stood in the dark and rain, waiting on a ridge overlooking the Cheduna camp. He saw the lights of their fires, guttering in the storm; he heard only the wind and rain. Even so close, he knew the Huumphar would not be seen; the storm was on them, the sun's light lost. He wondered if he would live until the dawn.

He felt the warriors around him, arrayed along the ridge. He felt their fear, but even more strongly, he felt their resolve. Ruun'daruun stepped forward and turned to face them. They stood, dark shades looking over the camp; they were so few.

"The Cheduna king sent his armies to enslave us. We have resisted them for all our lives, and the lives of our mothers and fathers, and theirs before them."

"This time they came with a demon. They came with fire. They have come with hell to our home, but we have met it. They could not destroy us."

"Though the dark of night comes, and we are closed in by enemies, and the storm bears down on us, we will go on. Come hell to us, we will meet it.

"Theirs was the demon and the fire—but ours is the storm, and even its fury cannot match ours! We will drive the Cheduna from our lands! And they will ride back through hell sooner than face us again!"

Ruun'daruun shook his spear at the sky. The Huumphar roared, and the storm bore away their cries. Ruun'daruun turned back toward the camp and charged.

—Twenty-Five—

Halkoriv grew still and his soldiers and servants gathered on the southern slope of the Monument. Lasivar and his riders disappeared from view, blocked by the crest of the platform, but Azra could hear their hoofbeats grow near, then come to a stop. Between thunderclaps, flashes of lightning lit the hilltop and over the driving rain he heard Halkoriv call out to Lasivar.

"You have traveled far to die, last son of Lasivar; you should have stayed in Vanador and left Feriven to its master."

"Would you have stopped there, Halkoriv? Would you truly have stayed here in this land, or would you have come for the others next?" Lasivar asked.

"No," Halkoriv chuckled, "but you might have lived longer. Now you will be destroyed here, and still we will rule Feriven and other shores as well." His voice was almost his own—but Azra still heard Sitis behind it.

"This is my home," Lasivar said. Azra could picture him, flanked by silver-armored warriors, dismounting and slowly climbing the path. "And I would never leave it and its people to be conquered and enslaved by you." Their banners would wave and snap in the wind as they strode forward, heedless of the rain and wind. Halkoriv and his men stood like statues, armor dark and glistening in the rain.

"I will destroy you this night, Halkoriv," Lasivar finished. He came into view, flanked by his men, sword in hand. His eyes shone with silver light, too bright to look upon. "For my home; for my mother and father; for Feriven!"

Halkoriv drew his sword, the harsh scrape of steel cutting through the night. Shadows rose about him, a towering column of lashing, writhing darkness. "The line of Lasivar will end here, at the place of our birth," Halkoriv gloated. His voice changed and echoed despite the storm, a dead voice in the wind. It came not from Halkoriv, but the shadows around him. It became a roar. "We have hungered for this day!"

Their swords clashed; steel rang on armor and shield and the shouts of men and gods drowned out the roaring wind.

—

Azra could only watch as they fought. He called out to Lasivar's men but they could not hear him; he shouted, trying to warn Lasivar, but knew his voice would not carry over the sound of the gale and the battle. When Lasivar struck, Azra would become part of Sitis. Lasivar would win the fight, but in doing so he would doom Feriven to yet more war and death.

Lightning cracked, and in the sudden light Azra saw a figure rise, pulling itself atop the hill from the sheer rock face of the Monument. It went unnoticed by Sitis or the Cheduna. Its eyes blazed even brighter than the lightning as it caught sight of Azra and rushed toward him.

"Ahi'rea," Azra breathed. "You came!"

She reached Azra and took hold of his shackles. "We have to help Lasivar," she said. "This has to end here, or Halkoriv will hunt down what is left of my people and yours. They have little chance as it is." She pulled at the shackles, eyes ablaze.

"Halkoriv—Sitis—is going to trick him," Azra shouted over the wind and sound of battle. "It's me—Sitis is going to use me to—"

Ahi'rea stopped, looking past Azra. She dropped the chain and drew her machete, and Azra turned his head. Behind him stood Draden's commander, Malskein. His rotten teeth gleamed like bloody fangs in the lightning.

"Thought someone might come for him. Some thing, anyway," he said in crude Huumphar. He spat, drawing his blade. "Never thought I'd be so lucky as for it to be you, plains-witch. I've heard of you."

"You—I saw you—the man from the raid," Ahi'rea said. Rain ran down her face and soaked her hair. "You killed Naph'oin—"

"I've killed many," Malskein said. "I don't remember each of you I've killed any more than the insects I've stepped on."

"Ahi'rea," Azra said, but she stepped away, raising her blade. Malskein circled her. "Ahi'rea, wait!"

The Cheduna soldier rushed forward and as his blade met Ahi'rea's, Azra's words were lost in the thunder and the clash of steel on bronze.

Malskein rained down blows on Ahi'rea, hammering at her blade with his sword and his shield. She spun and parried, dodging or deflecting each strike. Her eyes were aglow but Azra could see that she was struggling to match Malskein's ferocity. He kept her on the defensive; she could not risk an attack without leaving herself open. Atop the platform, so close to her foe, and with no cover, she fought on Malskein's terms and he battered her toward the edge of the Monument.

Azra felt his shackles move and turned in shock to see the pained, rain-soaked face of Tak'la at his side. His eye was swollen shut and fresh bruises shone on his face and ribs. The Huumphar spoke, but his voice was drowned in lightning and thunder.

"You're hurt," Azra shouted. "You should not be here."

Tak'la smiled and motioned for Azra to lower the chains and hold them taut against the stone platform. "Your message seemed very important to Ahi'rea."

"You were not supposed to understand it." Azra complied, stretching the chain over the stone.

"I followed her. You came back for me," Tak'la said. "And I wanted to know what you planned." He hefted a rock, grunting under its weight. Azra pulled the chains tight and Tak'la hammered at them with the stone.

Behind them, Malskein looked up at the sound. "Stop them!" he shouted.

Lasivar and Halkoriv struggled alone, almost all their followers slain. Halkoriv's servants stood motionless amongst the bodies of the dead soldiers, swords in hand, decked in shadow. They looked up at Malskein's cry and surged toward Tak'la and Azra.

Tak'la hammered at the chain once more, but still it held. With a snarl, he turned and hurled the rock, striking one of the creatures in the face and crushing its skull in a spray of blood. As it fell, the others reached them but Tak'la was already diving, rolling beneath their blades. He snatched the sword from the fallen servant and was stumbling to his feet again by the time they spun to face him. His face betrayed his pain, but he raised the blade and roared.

The creatures attacked him together, their strikes in perfect unison. Tak'la fought them off as best he could but fell back beneath their combined attacks. Azra struggled with the shackles, aware that, even were he free, he would be worthless against them. *Halkoriv will know if I die,* he thought, *and he will either kill Lasivar himself, or flee if he cannot win. And all this will be for nothing.*

Cold pressure grew in Azra's mind. The knowledge that he could snap the chains and kill the servants in seconds tormented him.

The servants assaulted Tak'la, blades flashing white in the lightning. Tak'la cried out as one of the weapons met his flesh and stained red. He stumbled to his knees, holding out his sword to ward away the servants' attacks. Ahi'rea leapt in front of Tak'la, and the two servants and Malskein closed in on them. Azra fought the desire to release the power in him. Halkoriv was still alive; Sitis was too strong. The spirit screamed to be released, that he could save them if he would only give in. He doubled over, squeezing his eyes shut and clenching his teeth with the effort of resisting.

Ahi'rea cried out in pain. Azra battled the spirit while he futilely pulled at his chains. *I cannot give in.* The whispers and pressure grew louder and stronger. He struggled and felt rage—his rage—filling him, hot and dangerous. He let it come, let the feeling surge through him; he took hold of it, and with it he forced down the pressure. He hauled on the chains and roared. His cry drowned the whispers. He strained against the iron holding him with all his might. Behind him he heard Tak'la and Ahi'rea shout in terror and agony. Azra looked over his shoulder in time to see Halkoriv's servant lunge; in time to see Tak'la, exhausted and bloodied and beaten, parry too slowly; in time to see the servant drive its sword into Tak'la's gut up to the hilt.

Azra screamed. Inside him, something snapped. He threw his head back and pulled. His arms felt as if they would rip from their sockets. The chain rasped and shrieked. The pressure in his mind fell away before the fire that coursed through him.

Azra gave the shackles one more jerk, and they gave way.

He fell to the ground, but felt flame burn through him as he got to his feet and turned. This power was not Sitis—not fully. It was something else, something *with* the spirit but not *of* it, a feeling older and stronger. The rain vanished in puffs of steam as it reached Azra's skin.

His arms were still chained together, but he was free. Azra saw Ahi'rea standing over Tak'la's fallen form, her broken machete in one hand. Malskein and one of Halkoriv's servants still stood before her. Blood-reddened rain dripped from Ahi'rea's face. Over her foes' shoulders, her blazing eyes met Azra's, and he charged.

He saw them turn, heard Malskein's warning shout. He saw their blades arc around to him and with his hands outstretched, Azra felt the new fury in him surge. He felt his eyes flare, felt fire beneath his skin, and saw his enemies' blades turn to ash. The chains on his arms burned away.

From the corner of his eye, he caught sight of Halkoriv and Lasivar. Their strikes shook the Ancestor's Stone. Lasivar's eyes lit the corpses strewn over the hilltop, and Halkoriv's shadows drew away their last sparks of life. Lasivar pummeled Halkoriv with a sword-blow that knocked the king's blade from his hands. Azra felt Sitis' glee and Halkoriv's sudden terror.

Halkoriv's servant leapt at Azra, but he caught the cloaked horror by the throat and held it aloft as if it were weightless. He felt life, or something like life, leave it, flowing back to the spirit. Sitis struggled against him now, and seemed to grow stronger.

Malskein tried to grab Ahi'rea but she dodged his grip and swung, slashing the broken machete across his throat. Malskein's hand went to his neck as he fell to his knees, his eyes wide in shock. Blood spurted and ran through his fingers in a torrent.

Azra looked back at Lasivar, who held his sword high as Halkoriv knelt before him. "Revik, stop!" Azra shouted. Lasivar did not seem to hear him.

"Here your line is ended, Halkoriv. My family is avenged, and Feriven is free." Lasivar brought the sword down with all his might, his eyes twin silver suns. All but lost in lashing shadows, Halkoriv's visage twisted into a smile as the blade sank into him.

A blast of black shadow threw Lasivar against the ruin wall. Halkoriv fell, and Azra fell with him, wracked in agony, and felt all that Sitis was, hunger and pain and despair and greed, rush into him like a dagger's blade. He could not think. *Hunger.* He felt himself diminish, crushed beneath Sitis' ancient weight. He could not breathe. His limbs were not his; they clenched and shook with spasms, and then grew numb. The torment closed him in, blocking out all else.

He felt himself drawn to his feet and a roar took his mind; he could not see, could barely hear. He had never felt so strong and so helpless. He felt hunger. The spirit froze him and tore at him; hunger was everything, cold and vast and endless. He was taken.

But somehow, some part of Azra persisted, hidden and protected. He had not recognized it until that moment, but now he felt the wall Sitis had spoken of. Somehow, he was still aware, even though his body was no longer his own and Sitis was in control. As the spirit looked around, seeking Lasivar, Azra saw nothing but red and shadow until two points of green fire, blazing in the dark, came into view.

"Azra," Ahi'rea's voice echoed. "What is happening?"

The gaze focused on her. He felt Sitis' cold hunger, and Azra fought and raged and felt hot anger boil in him, burning the cold away. He felt himself draw nearer to her and heard his voice, reassuring her that it was over, that they had won, that Halkoriv was no more.

No—you will not take her!

Azra's vision returned. The world flooded back to him and he backed away from her. "No!" he shouted. "Ahi'rea—it has me. Sitis is in me, it will live on in me. You must cut it off from this world. You can't let it—" his eyes grew wide as he realized that these might be his last words to her. "I am sorry for what I have done."

He saw her step away and felt his voice leave his control. As his limbs grew numb he saw his hand rise toward her and felt the cold, gathering shadows come through him and stretch out to her. Ahi'rea did not run—in fact, she stepped forward, her hand raised to him. He saw his hand grip her throat. He felt her life leaving her. In desperation, he fought to force the shadows away.

—

Ruun'daruun kept low and sprinted toward another target. He was invisible in the pouring rain and his spear felled the Cheduna soldier while his back was turned, then he dashed back into the grasses.

The battle was heavy with losses, and they would be worse still; there seemed to be no end to the Cheduna army. Screams and shouts rose and fell between blasts of thunder. Steel clashed on steel. The stink of blood hung in the air even through the downpour.

The Huumphar had struck, and had killed many. After that they had been routed, as planned, when the Cheduna counter-attacked, and had fled back toward the sea. When the Cheduna followed, they were ambushed by the waiting Vanadae, then flanked by the hidden Gharven.

The battle had begun as Ruun'daruun and Lasivar had hoped, but now the numbers of the Cheduna had come into play. They poured from the west like a flood, and slowly, they were washing the army to the sea and cliffs.

The Huumphar attacked from hiding, then vanished into the lashing rain and darkness. The Gharven and Vanadae fought the bulk of the southern army, but already too many of them had fallen, and too many Huumphar had been caught and struck down.

Ruun'daruun found Ken'hra and Rahi'sta, crouching in the darkness, catching their breath. "It's no use," Ken'hra said. "They are too many." Blood soaked her side.

Rahi'sta looked down at Ruun'daruun as she stood and hefted her machete. "We can't stop," she said. "There is nowhere to run."

Ruun'daruun nodded. "We have to trust that Lasivar and Ahi'rea will do their parts." The storm in the north, over the Monument, had grown only more violent.

Rahi'sta smiled and reached down to pull Ken'hra to her feet. "Why did Ahi'rea go? What is she doing?"

Ruun'daruun looked out at the field. There were so many enemies, and they fought without regard for their own lives, as if something was driving them. They would fight forever—unless Lasivar beat Halkoriv. And even then, they might fight on.

He looked back at Rahi'sta and Ken'hra and smiled. "Lasivar may be the one to kill Halkoriv, but Ahi'rea will be the one to end this."

—

The Cheduna pressed them back; they were simply too many. Ruun'daruun's wounds were mere days old, and he felt as if he had been fighting forever. The wind and rain only compounded his exhaustion, and his hands were slick with other men's blood. Still the Cheduna came in waves, and Ruun'daruun found himself alone, with only the cliffs of the Kan Manif Bur behind him. He could see none of his allies, only the faces of his enemies all around. He swung his spear and they dodged back, only to press in closer. He had nowhere to go. He waited for them to come for him, but they shouted and called to each other and held their ground, as if waiting for something.

They parted ranks, and a tall man in fine silver armor strode out of the mass of soldiers. He removed his helmet, revealing sable hair, and Ruun'daruun saw blood on his face.

"I've been ordered to kill all of you." The man's Huumphar was slow and careful, but he spoke without hesitation. "Every last one of your people. I have almost succeeded. But if you stop now, and lay down your weapons, you will live."

Ruun'daruun stood tall, and looked at the canyon cliffs behind him. The water below echoed up, audible even over the storm. He felt the mud and stone of the cliff beneath him. Rainwater rushed past, swirling around his feet, digging ruts and gouges in the cliff top in its race to the edge. "Who are you?" he asked. He heard the men fighting and dying around them.

"I am called Draden, Count of the Northmarch," the soldier answered. "I lead this army. If I say you will live, you will."

Ruun'daruun nodded. He took another step back toward the edge, careful not to disturb the mud and loose stone. He searched Draden's eyes. "Were our places reversed—would you stop?"

Draden stared back at Ruun'daruun. He sighed, and motioned his men forward.

They closed in around him, a legion of lives against his one, and Ruun'daruun heard his grandfather's voice: *The stone of the cliffs buckled beneath his will.*

They came closer. Ruun'daruun lunged, slamming his feet in the mud. He parried one attack, then another. "Fall!" he shouted.

Too late, Draden called for them to get back.

Under the combined weight of armored soldiers, the rain-soaked mud of the cliffs gave way.

Ruun'daruun was ready, but there was little he could do. He slid and tumbled and tasted mud; he crashed against rocks and the cliff side, and lost hold of his spear. The world spun and shook and weightlessness met hard stone. Then he felt water swallow him, and heard nothing but its roar, and he struggled to breathe.

When he pulled himself from the river, he saw the red stone of the canyon walls around him. The sound of the battle was far away. He saw some Cheduna soldiers lying nearby, others being carried away in the waters. Others still lay buried beneath the crush of mud and rock.

Sputtering and coughing, Ruun'daruun struggled to his feet and then was sent crashing back to the ground as pain blossomed between his shoulders. He rolled and looked up at the armored form of Draden; red water streamed from him as he loomed over Ruun'daruun, drawing his sword.

Ruun'daruun rolled as the sword came down, then lashed out with a kick. His bare shin struck Draden's armored wrist, but through the pain he saw the sword fly from the soldier's grasp. Draden snarled and caught hold of him, landing blow after blow with a mailed fist. Ruun'daruun felt sharp pain in his nose, then his jaw, but he caught Draden's fist and held him, battering him with kicks. The knight stumbled back into the river, and Ruun'daruun regained his feet.

The two men crouched, blinking against the downpour, wiping mud and water and blood from their eyes. They circled, looking for openings and weaknesses, then charged. Draden was fast, but weighed down by his armor and waterlogged clothes. Ruun'daruun dodged his bearlike swipes and fell to one side, then the other, but the knight's armor kept him from striking. Draden swung again; Ruun'daruun dodged, then leapt on his back, snaking an arm around his neck. He squeezed.

—

Draden knew before he fell that it was over. His vision grew narrow and clouded with dark flashes. The water's roar became a muffled whisper.

Before unconsciousness drew over him, he thought he felt the downpour stop. The drive to fight dissolved and suddenly seemed unnatural and false. The clouds overhead rolled away far too quickly and he saw the stars wink down on him.

He wondered if he could stop now and go home. He wondered if the plainsfolk warrior crushing his neck would drown him in the red waters. He wondered if Kara would ever know what happened to him.

—Twenty-Six—

The rain ceased when Lasivar's sword struck. The wind fell, and overhead the stars began to creep from behind the clouds. No more torches lit the hilltop—only starlight illuminated the bodies and blood. Lasivar lay still where he had been thrown. Halkoriv was dead. Tak'la's body was where he had fallen. The roar of the rain was replaced by screams of pain.

Ahi'rea watched as Azra collapsed, crying out, and as he then rose and spoke to her. She knew something was not right, but then his voice changed, and his eyes grew wide. "I am sorry for what I have done." Then the void took his eyes and he raised his hand.

She was finally sure why he had come back; why he had called her here. *When he meets Sitis, he hopes you will be there...* As Azra's body raised its arm toward her, her eyes blazed and she let her Sight flow.

A pale glimmer, light and dark entwined, surrounded him, bound him, held him. She caught hold of it, held the sight with her mind. It was larger and greater than Azra, and her eyes watered to try to focus on it. She had the impression of gnashing teeth, of hunger. The power pulsing around him was ancient and foul and wrong, and it had taken him. His eyes, empty and void of all but the hunger, met hers. He approached, hand outstretched, but Ahi'rea did not move.

The glimmering shades flashed in her Sight. She saw all its lines and connections, the facets and seams. She saw the spirit binding Azra, consuming him. She tensed her body, waiting as he drew within reach. When he was only paces away, Ahi'rea stepped forward and extended her arm and found the point she sought, the same as the one she had found before, months ago, in the plains. It was stronger this time, reinforced, a ley line to the void. This time, it was a part of him.

She put her hand on Azra's chest and focused her power as his hand closed around her throat.

"Hunger!" Sitis roared.

Ahi'rea felt death in its grip. Her concentration faltered; her strength waned. Her heart grew slow and the breath was sucked from her chest. Shadow invaded her Sight. She knew, then, that she was about to die.

Without warning, it stopped. The feeling vanished, and her will returned. She did not question the spirit's hesitation; all she was, every ounce of her power and hope and desperation flowed through her and she gathered it all into her palm.

"Ahi'rea." Azra's voice was once again his own.

She opened her eyes, and saw that he was holding a small knife. The hilt was decorated with the symbol of the eagle, and the blade was dark. He held the knife out to her with a white-knuckled hand. It was a blade that might have been made for a child. She wondered why he had it.

"I'm sorry. For everything," Azra said. "I love you. Please—

end this."

Ahi'rea took the knife and felt the weight of it as she closed her fist around it. She looked back to the man standing over her. He was in pain, struggling to fight back the darkness that had almost taken him. Ahi'rea put the point of the knife to Azra's chest. He nodded, and clasped her hand in his.

"I forgive you," Ahi'rea said. "Azra—be free."

He smiled, and then his eyes clouded with the void. His mouth twisted into a snarl.

"You," she said. "Fall."

She pushed, and let everything go in a torrent.

Azra was thrown back and shadow screamed from him, and green light surrounded it and burned the shadow away. Ahi'rea felt her arm shatter. All sound was lost in a wordless roar that seemed to arise from the stone itself, and she felt her breath stolen away and her eyes burn in the emerald fire.

—TWENTY-SEVEN—

A hi'rea shivered; the wind that swept in from the ocean was cold, and she pulled her doeskins tighter around her with one arm.

She felt Ruun'daruun's touch and leaned into him. He put his arm around her and together they looked on as Haaph'ahin himself set flame to Tak'la's pyre. It was an honor they had seldom seen given to the death-touched; a Sending of his own, on his own death, and an elder as his Sender. Ahi'rea had insisted on it, and Haaph'ahin had readily agreed once he had heard all that had happened.

They watched the flames consume his body and send his spirit on the Journey. In the east, the sun rose over the ocean, and the salt breeze carried the smoke away into the sky. Rahi'sta sang the chant for him, her child in her arms.

When it was over, the few remaining Huumphar began to drift away; Lasivar was leading the rest of the army south, to Ferihold, and there were others to mourn before they left the coast. Though Halkoriv's army had scattered mid-battle, around the time the rain had stopped, they had killed many. Other Sendings had yet to be held.

Soon Ahi'rea and Ruun'daruun were alone on the beach, watching the pyre smolder. Beside it stood a small cairn, a dozen gray stones in a pile. No one had asked Ahi'rea why she built it, and she was not sure how she would have explained it to those who had not been at the Monument.

How Lasivar had lived, Ahi'rea was not sure; she had never understood all his power. He had not seemed surprised to learn that she and Azra had been the ones to destroy Sitis, nor had he seemed surprised when they did not find Azra's body. Lasivar could not, or perhaps would not, explain it.

Ahi'rea's vision was still weak, and she doubted she would ever regain the use of her arm. Lasivar had tried, unsuccessfully, to heal it. Her Sight, however, was stronger than it had ever been.

She and Ruun'daruun looked at the little cairn. She mused that this was all that remained of Azra, who had changed the course of so much—yet so few knew it. It was too much to explain to any but perhaps Lasivar and Haaph'ahin.

Ruun'daruun pulled Ahi'rea closer. "The other Sendings will be soon." Ahi'rea nodded. "I must go—Ken'hra has no one to Send her—nor do many of the others."

"I will be along soon." Ahi'rea put her hand on Ruun'daruun's arm and met his eyes. "Go. They need you."

Ruun'daruun nodded, then looked again at the small cairn. "We'll have to move as soon as it's done. Lasivar says they will come for us again." He smiled. "We still have much to do—and I am glad we are together to face it."

Ahi'rea smiled back, then kissed him. "So am I." Her eyes flickered.

"What do you See?" Ruun'daruun asked.

Her vision became unfocused, and her words were not all her own. She did not fight it this time, did not hate the feeling; she let it come. "Conflict. Halkoriv is gone, and Sitis's spirit is cut off from this world. One storm has passed, but there is always another on the horizon." Her vision came back to her, and Ruun'daruun looked at her, then toward the south.

"I'll get our rain-capes." He gave her hand a final squeeze.

As Ruun'daruun walked away, leaving her alone on the shore, Ahi'rea stepped toward the small cairn and the embers of Tak'la's pyre. She reached down and picked up another stone from the rocky beach. It was heavy in her hand, and she was tired.

She reached out to place it atop the cairn she had built for Azra, but something stopped her. Instead, she drew her arm back, and then threw the stone out over the ocean. It whirled and flashed in the sun, and then it fell and vanished beneath the waves.

About
D. Thourson Palmer

David Thourson Palmer
sheared sheep in rural
Ohio, studied in the
Appalachian foothills,
explored Japan by train
and pack, and wandered
the Central Valley of
California. He currently
lives in Columbus, Ohio.